Praise for Tri

'Trisha Ashley writes with remarkable wit and originality
– one of the best writers around!'
Katie Fforde

'Trisha Ashley's romp makes for enjoyable reading'
The Times

'Full of down-to-earth humour'
Sophie Kinsella

'A warm-hearted and comforting read'
Carole Matthews

'Fast-paced and seriously witty'
The Lady

'Packed with romance, chocolate and fun, this indulgent
read is simply too delicious to put down'
Closer

'A lovely, cosy read'
My Weekly

'Fresh and funny'
Woman's Own

www.**penguin**.co.uk

Also by Trisha Ashley

Sowing Secrets
A Winter's Tale
Wedding Tiers
Chocolate Wishes
Twelve Days of Christmas
The Magic of Christmas
Chocolate Shoes and Wedding Blues
Good Husband Material
Wish Upon a Star
Finding Mr Rochester
Every Woman for Herself
Creature Comforts
A Christmas Cracker

Trisha Ashley was born in St Helens, West Lancashire, and believes that her typically dark Lancashire sense of humour in adversity, crossed with a good dose of Celtic creativity from her Welsh grandmother, have made her what she is today . . . whatever that is. Nowadays she lives in North Wales, together with the neurotic Border Collie foisted on to her by her son, and a very chancy Muse.

A Christmas Cracker was her eighth consecutive *Sunday Times* Top Ten bestseller. Her novels have twice been short-listed for the Melissa Nathan Award for Romantic Comedy and *Every Woman for Herself* was nominated by readers as one of the top three romantic novels of the last fifty years.

For more information about Trisha please visit her Facebook fan page (Trisha Ashley books) or follow her on Twitter @trishaashley.

A LEAP OF FAITH

Trisha Ashley

BLACK SWAN

TRANSWORLD PUBLISHERS
61–63 Uxbridge Road, London W5 5SA
www.penguin.co.uk

Transworld is part of the Penguin Random House group of companies
whose addresses can be found at global.penguinrandomhouse.com

Penguin
Random House
UK

First published in Great Britain in 2001 as THE URGE TO JUMP
by Judy Piatkus (Publishers) Ltd

Published as A LEAP OF FAITH in 2016 by Black Swan
an imprint of Transworld Publishers

A CIP catalogue record for this book
is available from the British Library.

ISBN
9781784160869

Typeset in 11/14pt Adobe Garamond by Falcon Oast Graphic Art Ltd.
Printed and bound by Clays Ltd, Bungay, Suffolk.

Penguin Random House is committed to a sustainable
future for our business, our readers and our planet. This book is made from
Forest Stewardship Council® certified paper.

MIX
Paper from
responsible sources
FSC® C018179
FSC
www.fsc.org

1 3 5 7 9 10 8 6 4 2

Author's Note

The beautiful Gower peninsula in South Wales certainly exists, but the village of Bedd and all the characters portrayed within this book are the product of the author's fevered imagination alone.

For Carol Weatherill, with love.

Foreword

Originally published by Piatkus in 2001 under the title *The Urge to Jump*, this is the second of my romantic comedies. It's been long out of print and difficult to get hold of, so I'm delighted that Transworld have released this new edition.

It features Sappho, possibly my favourite heroine, who is tall, bossy, opinionated and outspoken – but also the kind of best friend we wish we all had.

I haven't rewritten it, merely tweaked and polished a little here and there, so since it was created on the cusp of the new century it's obviously very much of its time, especially with regard to mobile phones and computers. It's amazing how things have changed in such a short space of time, but back then they were a luxury, rather than the norm.

Happy reading, everyone!

Trisha Ashley

Chapter 1

It's All Greek to Me

Another glorious Grecian Two Thousand day was dawning over Bob's Creative Break Centre on the island of Lefkada, and outside the air was like warm milk, tinged with the scent of burning charcoal . . .

Thank goodness I'm a woman of strong resolution. I needed to be, for not only did the island try to seduce me away from my morning's work, so too that day did the stack of birthday mail on my bedside table.

But I'm like a jogger: I need my daily buzz and I'm programmed either to write every morning or self-destruct. It doesn't matter which far-flung corner of the globe I'm in, whether I'm boarding a ferry, sitting in an aeroplane or paddling a canoe – between the hours of five and seven in the morning I'm either muttering into a tape recorder or scribbling in a notebook. *Spiral Bound*.

When I got a car of my own, I vowed I'd have a 'Writers Do It Anywhere' sticker on the bumper.

Still, there were ten more minutes and the current chapter of *Vengeane: Dark Hours, Dark Deeds* to wind up.

Nala, the heroine, shares with me (and Margaret Thatcher,

too, apparently), the traits of needing very little sleep and having great self-control.

Come to that, she's a bit like a nubile Margaret Thatcher in leathers, for while she doesn't exactly roam around the forest with a row of wizened willies dangling from her belt, she does have a nifty line in verbal emasculation.

Wish I did.

'*The realm of Mirrign was now rightfully Nala's . . . but was she fated to rule it entirely alone? During her years of outcast wandering she'd dreamed of finding a true mate, her equal in skill, knowledge and strength.*

'*Once, she'd thought Raarg was the man, until the scales had been torn from her dazzled eyes, and she'd seen the shallow, vain, self-seeking reality behind the beautiful façade.*

'*In the bitterness of his rejection he'd followed her like a malignant shadow, stirring his followers to vile deeds fuelled by the evil, lichen-brewed Laag.*

'*And now the mysterious and alien Dragonslayer, tall and wraith-pale against the dark forest, had come to haunt her life. His eyes, like clear crystal, seemed to pierce her very soul . . .*

'*Dragonslayer? What sort of place could the Darkside be, if dragons were enemies who needed to be slain? And what did he want from her?*'

'I don't know, blossom,' I told her, clicking off the tape recorder. 'You'll just have to work it out for yourself.'

And I needed to find another name for the evil-inducing drink: I couldn't have Laag Louts in my fantasy novel, it was just too much. I'd think of something else that afternoon, while the current crop of Creative Breakers were utilizing their free time by writing, sleeping, or fornicating, according to their tastes (and luck).

I might be writing, but I certainly wouldn't be fornicating.

It's such a meaningless quick fix without love that I hadn't been really tempted for years, though lately for some reason I seemed to have been thinking about sex almost as much as about my novel. (That's about every thirty seconds.)

Perhaps it was something to do with my birthday approaching, heralding yet another upward step on the spiral stair to forty, with no vestige of a Significant Other in my life, and a decreasing chance of ever finding one.

Let's face it, by this stage the only available men left on the shelf were the last few date-expired ones, for whom genetic modification could only be a good idea.

In a lesser person desperation might have set in, but I was not about to grab the nearest male flotsam like the Incredible Sinking Woman. I had a rash and ill-considered fling in my youth, so I know that the game is definitely not worth the candle.

Raarg, my novel's gorgeous but evil anti-hero, is loosely based on my ex-lover, Dave (so he's pretty loose), although Dave isn't really evil, just a bit vicious round the edges like a marginally untrustworthy dog.

He turned a little odd after I realized I'd made a big mistake and ditched him, and he took to stalking me down dark streets, making peculiar phone calls, and stuff like that. Then one night I mistook him for a mugger and laid him out cold.

Had he known about the kick-boxing classes I was taking he might have been a little more circumspect in his approach, but the hospital let him out next day, so there was no real harm done.

He still kept track of me, though, sending little keepsakes in the mail to let me know he was still crazy after all these years, like the postcard I'd got the other day.

I know where you are, Sappho.
Dave

Well, that hardly put him in the running for the Christopher Columbus Discovery of the Year Award, since I've been teaching here every August and September since Bob set the place up.

And Dave is quite a well-known freelance photographer, with contacts everywhere, so even though he's sitting darkly brooding in the middle of his web, he can always feel me twitching on the edges, no matter which remote corner of the globe I've got to.

I usually only responded to his little sallies by doing something particularly horrible to Raarg, but this time I sent him a postcard back.

Dave,
I know where I am, too.
Sappho

Then I did something horrible to Raarg.

This was the third book in the *Vengeane* series, and I wasn't too sure how the fourth and (possibly) final one would go, but I didn't hold out much hope for Raarg.

And where the hell did this mysterious Dragonslayer suddenly pop into my subconscious from? I *mean* – Dragonslayer!

Last time I was in London I met two other fantasy writers for lunch – Tom Mac and Rana-Raye Faye – and we agreed we really ought to start a breakaway Fantasists' Society, with rules like: 1) No More Bleeding Dragons, 2) Less of the Big Fiery Swords, and 3) Definitely No Wizards.

Vengeane may be a wizard-free zone, but boy, has Dragonslayer got a big fiery sword! I didn't know why he was coming across as so strangely sexy, since I didn't go for blond men.

Nor did I go for handsome men, since Dave 'call-me-Narcissus' Devlyn, nor stupid men, nor men shorter than I am.

The pool of tall, single, dark-haired, intelligent, attractive-but-not-handsome men had shrunk away to a small muddy puddle, so while I may have given up fornication originally from conviction, by now it was more necessity.

I was getting older and pickier: the world was filling with married men, married men whose wives didn't understand them, divorced men, weird divorced men, gay men and seriously mother-fixated men. Oh, and adolescents, like the only single man among the current crop of Creative Breakers: the dew's still on him.

Just to depress myself further, lately I'd been reading some of the women's magazines that the Breakers had left behind, and they were all about sex, with lots and lots of ways to sexual gratification, though frankly the traditional way had seemed OK to me at the time, and if you had to do all this other stuff nowadays, well, count me out.

The only oral gratification I was interested in came in a Cadbury's wrapper.

It seemed that some strange sexual tide had raced past me, and not only had it *not* swept me along with it, it hadn't even left me damp around the edges: beached on the shores of love like a bit of faded flotsam.

These were dismal thoughts for a birthday, so I reached for the stack of mail and chose a fat cream envelope inscribed in the unmistakable scrawl of my best friend, Mu.

With what innocently happy anticipation I pulled out the

13

beautiful, hand-made card, the numbers picked out in pearly buttons – and with what horror I found that something dark, fully fledged and monstrous had slithered out with it: my age.

Thirty-nine? I mean – thirty-*nine*?

Mu just had to have got it wrong, for although I stopped counting when I turned thirty, I was sure that was only a couple of years ago . . . wasn't it?

Maths is my one weakness. It took me ten minutes of furious calculation to accept that it was true, all too true! I was blind-fold on the brink of forty and the abyss loomed at my feet.

One year, one little year away from the big Four-O. It was so unfair: I wasn't ever expecting to be forty. You don't; it always happens to someone else.

Why didn't someone warn me it was coming, before it jumped out of an envelope, smote me with the Bladder of Mortality, and capered off giggling insanely?

And there was another thing – not only did I suddenly have to cope with the realization that I'm not immortal, it meant that the next year I'd be a forty-year-old female living alone in a country cottage in Wales.

Do you know what that would make me? A Single Eccentric Female, that's what – I'd need only the cat. And maybe the broomstick.

The only upside was that I'd be unlikely to be burned as a witch these days, unless the Greeks do it too: Stathis, the local café owner, made the sign of the evil eye when I told him I just didn't believe he regularly used the flea spray I gave him for his cat. While I don't have any particular affinity with cats, I don't like to see them with great bunches of fleas dangling over each eye like grapes, so I seemed to be waging some sort of one-woman campaign here. My friend Mu sent the flea stuff out: she has Cat Mania.

And cats may just turn out to be the Immortals in feline form, and put in a good word for me, for they always looked at me as if they've seen everything since the Dawn of Creation and found it – ho hum! – boring.

Almost anything seemed possible bathed in the magical early morning sunshine of a Greek island – except my being thirty-nine.

But I supposed I'd have to learn to accept it gracefully, along with middle age, because the only alternative was to cling to the crumbling ledge of thirty-nine for ever like the very last lemming. I'd so much rather jump off voluntarily, as did the famous, high-diving, ancient Greek poetess my parents named me for.

To Boldly Go where neither of my closest friends, Mu and Miranda, have travelled before, since I'm the eldest.

Dave, of course, must be well into the foothills of the forties since he was a mature student when we were an item. And anyway, he's not a friend – more an old poltergeist who pops up unexpectedly from time to time and throws things about in a fit of pique.

Even *Bob* is younger than me, which is not fair, because being a man he will become distinguished, not old, and even if he gets puckers round his mouth like a chicken's bottom he can grow a moustache to hide it. (I suppose I could too, come to that, but it's a little frowned on by women outside Mediterranean countries.)

Shell-shocked, I opened the rest of my cards and letters, all confirming the unwelcome truth, then went up to the cliffs to digest the implications of my future: rebirthed as a wrinkly.

I felt much better about things once I was standing on the edge of the nearest cliff – I always do, though so far, unlike the original Sappho, I've managed to resist the urge to jump off.

It might have been rash of my parents to give me the name, but according to Aunt Pops, Mother took one look at me when I was born and said: 'Sappho!' I thought this romantic until I read Plato's description of the poetess as small, swarthy and having a big head on a little body. Pops, who brought me up after my parents abandoned me for the Great Archaeological Excavation in the sky, said I was never swarthy, just red and cross.

Sappho Mark One was supposed to have jumped off to purge her anguish when her lover deserted her, but maybe they got it wrong and it was the trauma of turning forty that really tipped her over the edge.

And lots of people did it at the time without ending up dead – it was a sort of early bungee jump, without the sixty metres of knicker elastic. Sappho was just unlucky.

Perhaps I ought to try it on my next birthday, since I think I'll need some form of extreme catharsis.

Turning forty is definitely a rite of passage needing to be marked in some way. For most people it would be a time to jump off the rails and do something totally different, but unfortunately I've never quite managed to be *on* the rails in the first place.

It might *have* to be the cliff jump.

I seemed to be getting the urge to jump in more ways than one lately . . .

But now I came to think of it, my life *was* going to change this next year anyway, because the tenant in my Welsh cottage had died, leaving me with no excuse not to go and settle there . . . for part of the year, at least.

I'd never had a home of my own before. In between travels I'd stayed at Pops and Jaynie's in Portugal, or Mu's house in Pembrokeshire, or here on Lefkada, with Bob and Vivi.

When I bought the cottage, plus tenants, it was with the intention of settling down there when I was much older – forty, maybe. Some great age like that. But suddenly it was upon me, and I was to move there in the spring – before I lost my own spring altogether.

I also vaguely envisioned living there with a soulmate – maybe a writer or an artist of some kind – though when you see what comes of that sort of marriage of equals, like Plath and Hughes, I thought maybe getting a dog would be a better bet.

But I was still not entirely without my dreams. For instance, were Daniel Day-Lewis to jump out of my birthday cake in half-naked *The Last of the Mohicans* mode with the words: 'Take me, Sappho, I'm yours' on his lips, I would be prepared to give it a go, though I expect his novelty value would soon wear off.

While I stood there ruminating, with the sun warming my impervious complexion (brown hair, brown eyes, sallow skin – like a six-foot sparrow), time had already marched past me and I wanted to grab it with both hands and haul it back.

I opened my eyes and came back down to earth – the crumbling bit of cliff edge I was standing on, for some reason with my arms outstretched in classic *Titanic* pose, Medusa locks swirling.

Waves creamed on the rocks way, way below, and I let myself sway slightly towards them, savouring that heady feeling that down is up, and up is down, and everything is one . . .

'Sa-phooo!' shrilled a horribly familiar voice, nearly sending me into a fast Icarus down the cliff face. 'Sa-phooo, dooon't jump . . .'

17

Stout, perspiring, panting, gesticulating, Ken Smollett thundered towards me like a mad sea urchin.

'Don't be silly,' I told him repressively when he was close enough to spray-grease me. 'What do you mean by startling me like that?'

'I was looking for you,' he said reproachfully, caught a glimpse of my bare feet and reddened as if they were indecent. 'And don't mind me mentioning it, but shouldn't you have shoes on? There are scorpions, snakes . . .'

'While I'd be sorry to tread on any creature, they'll just have to take their chance,' I said patiently. 'I'm not a Buddhist so at least I won't think they'll be a defunct relative.'

And my soles are so leathery, due to my unfortunate habit of walking about in my bare feet like a superannuated hippie, that I don't suppose I'd even notice unless it was something *really* squidgy.

Ken eyed me strangely. 'Are you on something?'

'Borrowed time: isn't everyone? Why were you looking for me?'

'Well, because it's the last day of the course, and I didn't want to waste a minute of it. So when I looked out early and saw you—'

'It's *your* last day, not mine,' I cut in ruthlessly. 'My sessions run at clearly stated times and none of them before breakfast. In any case, you aren't on my course, you're supposed to be doing poetry with Nigel.'

His face fell, but he stood his ground and took a determined grip on the sheaf of papers clutched in one sweaty paw. 'I've written a villanelle – for you!'

He wouldn't recognize a villanelle if it snuggled up and licked his ear. And one more of Ken's appalling poems and I might be jumping off the edge voluntarily.

(Another theory – maybe Sappho *Numero Uno* was hounded into the leap by awful poets following her around trying to read her their work.)

'You are so much more sensitive and sympathetic than Nigel,' he pleaded, edging too close considering I couldn't step back. 'In fact, I hoped we might be able to meet in London from time to time to discuss – work.'

By now he was leeringly eye to eye with my bosom, and I was just contemplating the bloodless infliction of a little agony upon his portly person, when His Master's (or Mistress's) voice yelled: 'KEN!'

Barbara Smollett's voice is a rare gift: deep, powerful, strong, commanding – you could use it as a foghorn in emergencies.

Ken gave a galvanic jerk as if a rod had been strategically inserted by an invisible hand and hissed: 'It's Barbara – act casually. Later we can arrange—'

'KEN!'

His little fat legs turned about of their own volition and marched him jerkily off, while with turned head he was still mouthing at me.

Interesting . . .

I moved away from the cliff edge and, taking out my notebook, scribbled: *The power of her voice was irresistible – even Dragonslayer, though not of her race, felt its resonance jerk his limbs commandingly . . .*

Chapter 2

Birthday Letters

There were three letters among my cards, though one was not strictly speaking a *birthday* letter, but an indignant epistle from one Dorinda Ace, who was writing on behalf of her husband '. . . Gilbert Ifor Ace, last direct male descendant of the Gower Aces, and as such the rightful inheritor of Aces Acre.'

Then she went on to accuse me of exerting undue influence on the two elderly Ace brothers in order to buy the property, and ended by demanding that I instantly restore it to her husband, for: 'I am not without influence in the Gower: before my marriage I was a Penryn.'

I dashed off an immediate reply.

Dear Mrs Ace,

I will not begin by thanking you for your letter, since it was offensive in tone and slanderous in content.

Reading between the lines I take it that your solicitor has already informed you that you don't have a leg to stand on. When I bought the cottage more than twelve years ago Dafydd and Gethyn Ace were fully aware of what they were doing, and more than happy with the price I paid and the

agreement that they could continue to live there, rent-free
and without interference, for the rest of their lives.

I understand that your husband has inherited all the
contents of the house, including family documents, which
I'm sure will be a consolation to him.

I was most interested to learn your maiden name. Tell
me: are you any relation of Chinless Charlie Penryn, who
was arrested last year for posing as a nude Greek statue at the
Acropolis and frightening a party of female tourists nearly to
death? I believe the police have agreed to let him go back to
Britain, providing he undergoes medical treatment. I expect
you will be glad to have him home . . .

Of the other two letters, one was from Aunt Pops and Jaynie
in Portugal, saying they thought they'd made a pretty good job
of bringing me up for an Odd Couple, and now I was about
to move to my Welsh hovel they were having fun collecting
old pieces of Portuguese china and furniture for it, including
a door.

I only hoped they didn't try to gift-wrap it.

Miranda's note gave me the welcome though surprising
news that she had moved down to what had been her parents'
house on the Gower:

. . . which Dad left to me provided I lived there: otherwise
it would have passed to the Pondfish Preservation Society.
We're going to make it our main home, although we will
have to keep the London house on too, since Chris needs to
be there so much.

I'm sure he's quite pleased to have me down here, because
I'm an embarrassment now I've put on all this weight, but
actually I prefer it in the country and so does Spike. He's

21

pretty old for a Labrador, but the fresh air has given him a new lease of life.

The Gower peninsula has changed a lot since you and Mu spent that summer here when we were students. There was a magazine article recently that called it the New Cornwall, since lots of writers and artists are moving here, or buying weekend cottages. Even the ruined house at Penryn Castle is now a craft centre.

I meet most of the newcomers, since when Chris is down for the weekend it always develops into a sort of open house on a Saturday night, but there are some old friends here, too. I bumped into Lili Ford Jakes recently, who said she'd just bought a weekend cottage in the next village, and she wrote down the recipe for the Cabbage Soup Diet and gave it to me.

It was well meant, but when I read it I realized that being fat with permanent wind would be even worse than just being fat.

Also, I'm terribly busy working out biscuit recipes for Chris's next TV series, *Chris Goes Crackers*, so there are thousands of tempting biscuits around all the time . . .

It was great news that Miranda would be living in Bedd too, so what with Mu being only in Pembrokeshire, we would be practically all together again for the first time since we were students. Also, since Miranda was on the spot, she could keep an eye on the workmen who were supposedly fixing the roof of Aces Acre, and installing an indoor toilet.

When shall we three meet again?

Mu and I hadn't actually seen very much of Miranda since she married Chris Cotter, and the Iron – or maybe Slab Cake – curtain came down.

He really doesn't like me. Maybe it was the time I told him that since he'd built his career on Miranda's creative cookery skills, he should at least credit her contribution in the series and in the books. I thought he was going to spontaneously combust, which would have been the most interesting thing I'd ever seen him do, on or off screen, but unfortunately he didn't.

What sort of a man can't take a little criticism? Especially when it's clear to anyone who knows them that Miranda is the real creative cookery genius. She even produced her own cookery book, *The Stuffed Student*, while we were still at college. Mu did the illustrations, we persuaded Miranda to send it off to a publisher, and it's been in print ever since. But then she married Chris the Succubus, who has the culinary skills of a dead donkey, and that was the end of her personal career. I don't know what she saw in him, though apparently some women do find him sexy in a foxy kind of way, but he *was* persistent and she is very persuadable.

I wrote a note back to her, since there was no point in ringing to tell her the glad tidings about the cottage: she has the mother of all stammers, and it's worse on the phone.

After my last class with that week's budding Fantasists I went into the hall and phoned Mu, who sounded wraith-like, which she isn't, her slenderness stopping just this side of skinny.

'Happy birthday, Sappho,' she said cheerily.

'Yes, but I'm thirty-nine, you heartless hag! What's there to be happy about?'

'It could be worse – you could be forty *now*.'

'Thanks for that Thought for the Day – and there's only a year to go. How can I possibly be nearly forty, Mu? I mean, isn't forty wearing your hair in a bun, twinsets, Mantovani, and changing your library book twice a week? Middle age?'

'I am old, I am old, I will wear my Levis rolled,' she intoned sepulchrally. 'Come on, Sappho: that might have been what it was like once, but not now. Forty today means changing your hair colour twice a week, not your library books, twin-sets aren't compulsory, and even if you could get all that hair into a bun the weight would squish your face up like a rubber mask.'

'But then no one could see the wrinkles,' I pointed out. 'And what about the Mantovani to Manilow?'

'I think Motörhead's the Mantovani of our generation,' she suggested.

'Forward into forty on a wave of "The Ace of Spades" and hennaed hair? You know, I think I'm beginning to feel better.'

'Good. And don't forget it will be my turn next, then Miranda's, even though it doesn't seem five minutes since we were all dewy little innocents sharing digs.'

'I was never a *little* anything, dewy or otherwise, but no, it doesn't, though I do feel much more mature inside – I've gone from seventeen to about twenty-five.'

'That's probably going to be the hell of it,' Mu said thought-fully. 'Inside our heads we'll still be young, but our bodies won't cooperate. Pity we can't slough them off from time to time like a snake.'

'That would be lovely. I'd like to hand my folded papery self to one of the Creative Breakers and walk off fresh and uncreased . . . But – well, it's not going to happen, is it? The only coil I shuffle off will be a mortal one.'

I shivered, goosed by Time. 'You know, Mu, I never actually realized until this morning that I'm not going to live for ever!'

There was a surprised silence. 'How odd!' she said at last.

'I've never thought of it like that either. I mean, you know you're going to pop your clogs one day, but you don't accept it. The bullet's always got someone else's name on it.'

'There can't be many that say Sappho or Mu. We just have to keep dodging.'

She sighed. 'It's funny, I've been watching my biological clock ticking away, but not my life.'

I cursed myself for my tactlessness, but she added more cheerfully: 'At least your books will be immortal: O Immortal Sappho!'

'But they're not the Great Literature I thought I was going to write.'

'Great fantasy, though – brilliant. Everyone reads them. Even teenage boys read them,' she pointed out.

'I know, I have to answer their letters.'

'Well, have little cards made. Or get computerized – so much easier than compiling all those tapes and scribbles together into a book, too.'

'Oh, yeah, and I ought to get a degree in computing while I'm at it.'

'It's not that difficult – I type up all Ambler's adventures on to a computer now to send to the publisher, though my illustrations have to go separately.'

Ambler, Mu's husband, goes on Boy's Own 'Cycling up the Limpopo on my pedalo with a llama'-type adventures, having much more money than sense. He's big, blond, friendly, enthusiastic and not terribly bright.

'My agent thinks I've nearly finished *Dark Hours, Dark Deeds*, but I haven't. There's the most pestilential little man among this intake of Creative Breakers who keeps following me – he thinks I'm on tap twenty-four hours a day. Hot and cold running Sappho. Mostly running.'

'There always is one – attracted helplessly like a moth to a flame. Why do you do it? You don't need the money any more.'

'Bob's been such a good friend to me over the years, and there's always the hope that one or two will go on and become good writers. Anyway, I've only one more group to teach before I can settle down and finish the book – and meet you in Rhodes.'

'You could be a personality at home. You're a cult figure.'

'A what?'

'Cult.'

'Oh, *cult*. The original Sappho's already one of those, though I don't know what she'd make of all the lesbians flocking to her island on an *Olives Are Not the Only Fruit* pilgrimage. But all I want is a bit of peace to finish this novel and the next *Spiral Bound* guidebook.'

'You could do that over here, and help me with the Fantasy Flowers business,' she offered. 'It's been fun, but I'm getting bored with it now. Speaking of which, you'd never guess who phoned up and ordered a very special little bouquet to be sent to you?'

'Yes I would,' I groaned. 'You didn't, did you?'

'He didn't recognize my voice, and *I* didn't see why I shouldn't have his money, so expect a parcel in the post if it hasn't arrived already. I've done you proud.'

'Thanks a lot. Look, I'd better go – see you in Rhodes.'

'Oh-oh,' she said in a muted voice. 'Ambler's waving something at me.'

'You should be so lucky.'

'Not that sort of thing – a piece of paper. Looks like the bill for importing and quarantining that Egyptian cat – the one I told you about, that attached itself to me when I was out there helping Ambler make arrangements for the canoeing-down-the-Nile thing he's doing this winter. I couldn't leave her behind, could I? I think I'd better go . . . Bye-ee!'

There was just time to hear Ambler roar: 'Aren't there enough bloody cats in Britain without—' before the line went dead. But I wasn't worried – Mu can, except for one important thing, twist him round her little finger.

As I stood smiling, the crunch of gravel alerted me to danger: the portly shape of Ken Smollett was trudging hotly up the path, the inevitable sweaty handful of papers clutched to his bosom.

I tiptoed to the rear of the gloomy hall and backed through the kitchen doors, almost colliding with Bob's wife, Vivi.

'What—'

'Shh! Listen, Vivi, you haven't seen me all afternoon, so you think I must be out until dinner.'

Her brown eyes sparkled with laughter. 'Is it that Ken? Always it is the little men who chase you. But he has a wife – he should behave himself.'

'At least he's going home tomorrow, and Lili's arriving tonight, isn't she? That'll distract him – he might even stay another week and take "Putting the Spice into Your Fiction".'

'That Lili,' she sniffed disdainfully. 'Married three times, and can she pass anything in trousers? I said to Bob: "What does she know about romance?" She thinks love, romance and sex are the same thing.'

'It doesn't seem to affect her book sales.'

'Then other people, they cannot tell the difference either.'

'That's a very sad thought, Vivi.'

'You need a husband before it is too late – a Greek, perhaps, romantic and cultured? You are thirty-nine, I know, for Bob tells me, so it must be true – but I know a very nice widower, in Athens, teaching at the university, and—'

'No, thanks,' I said hastily. 'I need a husband like a fish needs a bicycle.'

She wrinkled her broad, smooth forehead. 'It is a joke? But you must be serious, Sappho – already it may be too late for the babies, and when you are forty you'll need—'

'Shh!' I whispered. 'He's coming down the hall. I'm off!'

'I will head him off at the pass, as they say,' she nobly volunteered. 'He is not allowed in the kitchen under Eleni's feet while she's preparing the special birthday dinner, the lovely cake, all white icing with candles – many, many candles . . .'

'Oh my God!' I exclaimed ungratefully, and bolted.

'Later I will tell you of the handsome widower,' she hissed after me, and then I heard her voice raised, clear and cool: 'Ah, Mr Smollett, can I help you? Coffee for all will be served on the terrace in one little half-hour and—'

She's worth her weight in birthday candles. But what did she mean, it might be too late for babies? Had someone cancelled my option without telling me?

Not that I wouldn't rather be sacrificed as a Born-Again Vestal Virgin than give birth, of course, but it was *my* choice.

Wasn't it?

Was that another buffet from the Bladder of Mortality?

Chapter 3

Say It with Flowers

Dinner was served outside on the terrace that night, the long trestle tables lit only by the soft flickering light of candles.

This proved a blessing when Lili Ford Jakes made her appearance in a slinky green garment whose top half consisted of a narrow, horizontal strap. She's the type of diminutive brunette sometimes described as a Pocket Venus, though I really wouldn't recommend it unless your clothing is fire retardant.

'Oh, am I late?' she drawled huskily, posing her assets artistically in the doorway.

'That dress!' whispered Vivi, scandalized. 'Surely she has it on the wrong way round?'

'For goodness' sake don't suggest it – I don't think it's got a back at all. As Aunt Poppy would say: "She's all fur coat and no knickers."'

'All fur coat and no knickers?' Vivi echoed doubtfully.

Bob took a mouthful of wine down the wrong way and choked, and when I resumed my seat after patting him on the back (fortunately the Heimlich manoeuvre was not necessary on this occasion) Vivi was in fits of helpless giggles at something or other.

Perhaps it was Ken Smollett's face – his mouth had been hanging open for so long while he goggled at Lili that his tongue had dried to something you could sole shoes with.

He was even oblivious to the evil eye his wife was casting on him from her seat further along, but at least for once she wasn't glaring at *me*. So restful after a week of it – and did she really believe that I had been trying to wrest her little tub of lard away from her?

Lili glided up to the empty chair next to Ken with the sort of oiled motion you only see in vampire films, and passed a tissue-wrapped parcel across to me.

'Happy birthday, sweetie. Frankly, I don't even want to be reminded such things exist, but Vivi did say this was a birthday dinner, so . . .' She shrugged, and the strap of her dress shifted to Indecency Point and hung there.

Ken went puce and missed his mouth entirely with his glass, without noticing the stream of wine trickling down his chin.

'Thanks, Lili,' I said, unwrapping the parcel to find one of her historical novels, the cover featuring a big, blond man entwined with a swooning redhead. The title was *Some Day My Prince Will Come*.

How does she get away with these things?

Inside, under the usual birthday greetings, she'd written: 'Get a piece of the action before it's too late.'

'I've already had a piece of the action, thanks, Lili,' I assured her, wrenching my eyes away from the lurid cover with some difficulty, for there was something tantalizingly familiar about the man . . .

'Yes, but not in living memory, darling. Blow the dust off it and have another,' she suggested.

She means well, but she's addicted to love.

I had more presents to open, the first an excellent reproduction of an antique vase depicting the poetess Sappho made by Vivi, who is a very talented potter, and the second a joint present from the Creative Breakers of a jingling little bracelet of fake coins. It chimed every time I breathed.

I now know how the belled cat feels.

I knew what was in the last parcel because Mu had warned me about it, but in any case I helped design the packaging for Fantasy Flowers when she set the business up two years ago, so it was instantly recognizable.

She'd really gone to town: the long, shiny black box contained a lot of purple tissue paper, adding a sepulchral effect to the bouquet inside, which was constructed of very artistic and lifelike silk flowers and leaves. We tried dried, at first, but finding sources for, say, dried hemlock, is difficult.

'Oh, urgh!' Vivi said, leaning over for a closer look. 'The yellow roses are all right – but against that purple! And what are these things that look like weeds? And those spiky things? And look, here is a little book.'

I handed *Meanings of Flowers and Foliage* to her, and pointed out the message in my bouquet: yellow roses for jealousy, rosemary for remembrance, rue for obvious reasons, wormwood for absence, begonia for dark thoughts and hemp for fate.

Isn't it ironic that the nasty little objects Dave dispatched to me from time to time over the years should have inspired Fantasy Flowers? (We literally *did* say it with flowers.) And the wheel had now come full circle, with Dave using our service to send something to me!

Lili was frankly envious: 'You must have made quite an impact on someone to get that kind of message!'

I shrugged. 'Just an old boyfriend who likes to remind me of what I loved and left behind me.'

'Was he so awful he put you off men for ever?' she asked.

'He was dark, tall, handsome, and the "I'm-totally-incapable-of-faithfulness-but-forgive-me-because-I-love-you" type.'

His main asset was his undiluted and rampant sexual magnetism. He had the power. The force was with him. And he wasn't selfish with it, either – he would sleep with anyone youngish and female who was up for it.

'He sounds *so* Heathcliff,' sighed Lili. 'And he must still be mad about you if he keeps sending you these things.'

'I think he's mad *at* me, not *about* me – or even just plain mad, going by the nature of his little offerings.'

She should have seen one or two of his early gifts, like the sealed plastic package containing a rotting pig's heart that had followed me out here the year I was helping Bob to set up the place. He got more subtle later, but not much.

'Beware Englishmen bearing gifts,' Vivi said merrily, her eyes taking on a new, assessing look. I hoped she wasn't going to bring up the eligible bachelor from Athens again. 'Sappho, always you stride through life as though you were a goddess above such things, when all the time you have a Past.'

'The Greek goddesses don't seem to have been above earthly pleasures,' I pointed out. Still, at least I didn't have to explain myself to Bob, who went to the same university – so restful.

He gave me a lazy smile now and said, 'I suppose it's Dave again?'

Vivi stared at him open-mouthed: 'You knew? And you never told me? Bob!'

He shrugged. 'I'd forgotten, or thought he'd given it up, or something.'

'This is all so intriguing,' Lili exclaimed, eyes shining. 'You must tell me more about this – what was his name? Dave?'

'There isn't really anything much to tell. His name's Dave Devlyn, and—' I began.

'Not Dave Devlyn the portrait photographer?' she gasped, with unflattering amazement.

I nodded.

'My God – he's gorgeous! You have to be really famous to be photographed by him . . . and wasn't there some scandal recently about him and a foreign princess? He was photographing her, and he—'

'Very, very likely,' I broke in before she could recall the more sordid details. 'Have you met him?'

'No, but I've seen him. Darkly sexy,' she added hungrily.

'Yes, he's all of that – or was. I haven't actually clapped eyes on him for quite a while.' He was also, despite his intuitive way behind a camera lens, vain and shallow, and permanently unbalanced by yours truly. He hadn't seen me for quite a while, though, so maybe if he did, horror at my time-worn carcass would send him recoiling upon something younger and more nubile.

Lili's heart-shaped, slightly raffish face wore quite a tinge of the child-at-the-sweetshop-window. 'Why you?' she asked, puzzled. 'Not that you aren't attractive,' she added hastily, 'but Helen of Troy you're not.'

'I don't really know, unless it's an extreme form of pique at my being the only woman to chuck him and walk away – even after he'd proposed to me. I keep expecting it to wear off. I suppose if I'd been around all these years instead of globe-trotting, it would have done.'

She sighed again, wistfully. 'If I hadn't just fallen in love with an angel I'd ask for his address.'

'You've married again? I hadn't heard.'

She always married them – for love. Then divorced them once she'd worn the bloom off. (Except the first, I give her that, who died on her: literally, the way she tells it.)

'Not yet, but I met this amazing man in London at a big craft exhibition, where I got all this lovely barbaric jewellery. Look.'

She swung a heavy pendant from between her Twin Peaks and dangled it like a pendulum.

'Rose quartz is so good for my love chakra. I sent you a letter, with his photograph – didn't you get it?'

'Of course – I'd forgotten.'

'If you'd seen him in the flesh you wouldn't forget him! Fortunately he was having a huge argument with this dreary girl in hand knitting and big boots, who he's had something going with for years – since art college! But he hates London and she loves it, so they've split up. The only snag is, he lives in South Wales, so I've had to buy a holiday cottage down there to be in with a chance.'

'Oh, yes – Miranda Cotter mentioned that. And he really must be something else if you're prepared to buy a cottage in the country just to get to know him!'

'Well, softly softly catchee hunky – and I don't mind too much, the Gower is terribly trendy: all the mags say so, and everyone's buying cottages down there. We all get together at Miranda Cotter's house on a Saturday night when her husband's down for the weekend – they throw good parties.'

Lili turned to Vivi, who was following all this with wide-eyed interest, and explained: 'The Gower's this sticky-out bit near Swansea, in South Wales. My cottage is at Rhyss, near Bedd.'

'I think it's pronounced "Beth", Lili,' I said.

'Not by me, it isn't. People would think I had a lisp. Anyway, how do you know? You're not Welsh, are you?'

'No, but as it happens *I've* owned a cottage in Bedd for years and my tenant's just died, so I'm going to be spending a lot of my time there from next spring.'

'Really?' She looked genuinely pleased. 'Oh, do come, darling. The place is littered with arty-farty types, so the more civilized company the better. Only you mustn't steal my Potter.'

'Is that his name?'

'No, it's what he *does*. He has a workshop in this sort of big craft centre made out of part of an old castle. Terribly romantic.'

A potter seemed an unlikely choice for Lili, but if she'd spotted him at a major London exhibition I expected he had many talents.

'If he's a handsome blond he's definitely not my type, so I can promise not to steal him even if I could. He's all yours.'

'He looks like the hero on the book cover I just gave you,' she said, slightly piqued.

'Oh?' I looked at it doubtfully, and that same sense of familiarity nagged at me again.

'He's very big,' offered Lili.

'I can see that.'

'No, I mean *tall*,' she giggled.

'Right. Not my type, though I do feel I've seen him somewhere before.'

'You have: I told you – that photo I sent you.'

'Of course, *that* must be it,' I said slowly. Big, broad-shouldered, blond . . . it was Dragonslayer! Clearly my subconscious had taken one glance at the photo from Lili and filed him away for future reference! *Wonder where I put the photo . . .*

Lili went on about the Gower to the others for a bit, while I pondered whether the magic place I remembered would all be totally spoiled. I hoped not. As to her potter . . . well, by next spring she'd probably have sucked him dry and be ready to sink her fangs into fresh meat, so if Dave came around bothering me I might be able to set her on to him. She's sort of a female version of Dave, only intelligent, and you really *don't* want to see her in a feeding frenzy.

'There are two things in life I'm serious about,' she confided to me later when we'd both drunk too much wine, though not as much as Ken, who had subsided under the table and was snoring.

'Sex, of course, and my writing, which released me from the sheer hell of teaching. Or maybe they're the same thing?'

She upended the bottle into her glass and watched the last glistening viscous drops trickle down in the candlelight.

'The sex is research for the novels – impure research.' She grinned. 'And wouldn't that be a Chair everyone would want to occupy if I endowed it at Oxford or Cambridge? The Lili Ford Jakes Chair of Impure Science. You could lecher in it.'

'Oh, Lili!' I groaned, but I knew she was serious about her writing, at least. Professional and meticulous. I wouldn't know about the sex, but that was probably well researched, too.

Now she poked the supine figure of Ken with the toe of her Manolo Blahnik and said: 'I just hate snoring men, don't you, Sappho? Too pig-like for words. Shall we stick an orange in his mouth and ask Eleni to prepare him for dinner tomorrow?'

'I think he'd be a bit fatty.'

She plucked an orange out of the bowl and looked at it thoughtfully.

'Better not, it might stop him breathing,' I warned.

'Don't tempt me, darling,' she said with a grin, turned, and threw it with surprising force at the only young, unattached man among the Breakers, who caught it from sheer nervous reaction.

'Well, does anyone want to bowl a maiden over?' she asked brightly.

Back in my room I searched out Lili's letter with the grainy black-and-white photo of her potter, which she'd had copied from the exhibition brochure.

He *did* look a bit like Dragonslayer, but it was only a general likeness. He couldn't possibly have Dragonslayer's strange, crystal-clear eyes, or white-blond hair . . . or any other of the interesting attributes I've given him, so no one would be able to recognize him from the novel.

Chapter 4

Dipped Wicks

Mu and I were booked into a small hotel on Rhodes which, while comfortable and inexpensive, was not really luxurious enough for Mu's tastes.

Since she married Ambler (he saw, he was smitten: he didn't hang about) she's never roughed it anywhere, having had more than enough of that in a childhood spent being shuffled from one foster home to another.

This lack of parents made an instant bond between us when we met as students, for even though mine didn't die until I was twelve, they were so wrapped up in themselves and their delvings into ancient Greece that I already looked on Jaynie and Pops' home in Portugal as my own during the school holidays.

I'm not complaining – Pops and Jaynie always made me feel loved and secure, and also managed to instil a sense of tolerance for others that has stood me in good stead during my travels. Now I feel at home wherever I am, with the possible exception of Japan, where I stood out like the lead in *Attack of the 50 Ft. Woman*.

And at least I know who my parents were. Once, when

we were watching a performance of *The Importance of Being Earnest*, Mu said she always envied him having been found in something as classy as a handbag, for she'd been dumped on some convent steps in a mere Woolworth's carrier bag.

'And a paper one, at that. I'd peed in it by the time a nun found me, and when she picked up the bag the bottom fell out and me with it.'

Mu hadn't been to Rhodes before, although I know it very well, and we strolled about companionably on the first evening looking for somewhere to eat.

We tended to attract attention even before I stopped a man leading a heavily laden donkey and applied a salve I always carry with me to a small open sore on its neck, amid much good-natured banter from the onlookers as to where I should apply it next.

'Why is everyone staring at us?' Mu asked plaintively when we'd moved on, and I was busy rejecting the first restaurant we came to as smelling of drains, even though the proprietor assured me he hadn't got any. There was clearly no point in inspecting *his* kitchen.

'Why are they staring? Could it be because *I'm* six feet tall, with hair down to my ankles and breasts the size of the Great Pyramid, and you look like a small Albino Goth Mushroom in that outfit?'

She adjusted her black, vintage-straw coolie hat with much fluttering of gauzy dark draperies. 'I'd burn up without it, my skin's so pale. Anyway, it would ruin my look.'

'Which is?'

'Small Albino Goth Mushroom.' She gave my arm a squeeze and added: 'This is fun, isn't it? Just you and me for a few days. I mean, I'm not really expecting the pilgrimage to work, but once I've done it tomorrow we can relax and have a holiday.'

'You've just been to Egypt,' I pointed out.

'Yes, but that was work. Ambler needs me to hold his hand while he sets up his little adventures, and I like to do some sketches for the book on the spot.'

'This one could be tricky, though – aren't there still crocodiles on the Nile? A canoe isn't much protection.'

'He can beat them off with a paddle or something, and there has to be an element of danger or the books wouldn't be interesting,' she pointed out callously. 'Anyway, he always comes out safely – then thinks up the next one. And goodness knows what that will be: "Hang-Gliding Down Everest with My Yak" probably.'

'It would have to be a big hang-glider to carry a yak, Mu.'

'I was joking – but for God's sake don't mention it to Ambler, or it might give him ideas.'

Eventually we found a pleasant café where I chose lobster while Mu had stuffed vine leaves. She said she'd no intention of eating something that had been happily swimming round a tank only moments before. If she'd lived in some of the places I have, where they kill your dinner in front of you and you have to look pleased about it, I think she wouldn't be so picky.

Once we were eating and well oiled with local wine, I prepared the ground to Confess All about my cottage.

'Mu, you remember when we were students, and we spent that holiday in Miranda's house on the Gower while her parents were away?'

'Of course – it was wonderful, wasn't it?' She sighed. 'Before I met Ambler, or you became involved with Dave, and Miranda was going through boys faster than she thought up new recipes.'

'Yes, life seemed so uncomplicated, then,' I agreed.

'Absence of any feeling of responsibility, I suspect, though we all had our plans for the future.' She unrolled a vine leaf, inspected the contents, then rolled it up again and began to eat it.

'We've pretty well done what we wanted to, haven't we?'

'*You* have – you wanted to travel the world and write, and even Dave couldn't deflect you from that,' she said. 'And I suppose Miranda started out OK, with *The Stuffed Student* published before she even left college, but she hasn't done anything else, what with Chris leeching all the talent out of her. As for me – well – I get regular illustrating work, especially anything feline, but I expect I could have got out there and done more if I hadn't had Ambler's security and money to fall back on. Cushioned.'

'He's a very nice cushion.'

'Yes, he is,' she said rather restlessly. 'He doesn't change, either: Forever Ambler.'

'Groan.'

'How did we get on to men, anyway?'

'I don't know; we digressed. I was asking you if you remembered the Gower, and Bedd, where Miranda lived.'

'Why?' She examined me with green-eyed suspicion. 'What are you up to?'

I shifted guiltily. 'I bought a house there.'

She stared at me. 'A house? What do you mean? When? Where?'

'In the same village – Bedd. Actually, I bought it years ago when I was twenty-five and came into my inheritance, such as it was.'

'You mean you've owned a cottage not much more than an hour's drive away from me for all this time, and never said a word?'

'I knew you'd think I was mad – and it's not like I could use

41

it, because it had sitting tenants. Do you remember one day Miranda took us round to visit two elderly brothers who lived right at the edge of the village? She was taking them some of her marmalade.'

Mu wrinkled her brow. 'Vaguely.'

'It looked just like a tumbledown barn at the front, but then you went round it into a cobbled yard and there was this sweet little stone cottage with bits of carving from some old ruin set in the front.'

'I do remember!' she said. 'You went into a sort of trance and we had to drag you away. The Aces, that's what the brothers were called – and the house was half a ruin. Surely you didn't buy *that*?'

'Yes, I did, but with the understanding that the Aces would live there as long as they wanted to. Dafydd, the last brother, died earlier this year, so I'm having some basic renovation done on the cottage, and then I'm going to live there. I'm looking forward to having my own house. Pops and Jaynie have bought me a door.'

'A door? Let's hope there's still a wall left to attach it to.'

'It wasn't that bad, Mu. I took a flying visit across to arrange the renovations, and it looks much the same as I remembered it.'

'My God!'

'You know I enjoy a challenge. Oh, and have you heard Miranda's moved back to live in what was her parents' house in Bedd?'

'What, she's left Chris?' she exclaimed.

'No, he comes down at weekends. But it's strange he's agreed to let her out of his sight when he's always been jealous of her seeing even old friends like us, isn't it?'

'It is strange,' Mu agreed. 'I haven't had a letter for a while, and it must be – oh, four years, nearly, since I last saw her. She'd put on a bit of weight – all that cooking, I suppose. Have you told her you're going to be her neighbour?'

'I've written – she's bound to be delighted I'm moving to Bedd. And I'm going to have to be very careful about how I pronounce that, or people will get the wrong idea!'

Mu had begun to see the advantages. 'You'll only be an hour or so's drive from me, and near to Swansea, for the shops and the direct train line to London.'

'I hate shops.'

'Well – food? You aren't terribly domesticated, are you?'

'I'll buy a huge freezer and fill it. And I *can* cook when I want to, it's just there are usually more interesting things to do.'

'Did the cottage have a bathroom?' she asked suddenly.

'No – the Ace brothers thought indoor sanitation was a filthy modern idea, but I'm having one put in.'

'It all *sounds* OK, though I can't see you settling down anywhere for very long. Still, the Gower is quite trendy now, you know, so you could always sell it again.'

'I won't ever want to sell it, even though the Gower is running over at the gunwales with arty types, according to Lili Ford Jakes, who's bought a weekend cottage there too. But I hope it's not that bad, or if it is, that everyone will get tired of it and go away.'

'How is Lili?'

'Oh, the usual – except when she was drunk she confided in me that she's the reincarnation of a vampire. I was surprised – an interest in the occult should, like the writing of poetry, be something you get over by the age of sixteen.'

'But are vampires carnate in the first place?' said Mu, puzzled. 'Or do I mean incarnate? Can you be reincarnated as something that wasn't . . . excuse me, my brain hurts.'

I shrugged. 'She has to have some justification for leaping at men out of the darkness and biting their necks.'

Mu giggled. 'She doesn't!'

'She does. One of the Creative Breakers complained to Bob. I might have a use for Lili: she bought her cottage in Rhyss because she's in pursuit of a local man, but she'll probably have sucked him dry by the time I move in, so if Dave comes down and makes a nuisance of himself, she'd be just the one to sort him out.'

'My goodness, that's brilliant! Do you think she'd go for him?'

'Why not? Dave's everything she ever asks for in a man: tall, handsome, virile, tricky and devious.'

'Set her on to him!' Mu enthused, then, raising her glass, added, 'And here's to the Ace in her Hole.'

'Thank you, but it won't be a hole when I've finished it. Even Aunt Pops keeps referring to it as "your hovel", but you'll all have to eat your words: I'm good at fixing things.'

Mu grinned.

'What? I *am* good at fixing things – all kinds of things! I mean, only look at Bob and Vivi: if I hadn't stepped in and told him that he wasn't too old for her, and her that no one cared about dowries or that sort of stuff any more, they'd still be gazing soulfully at each other across the dining table.'

Without undue modesty, I have to say that I'm a born organizer with numerous successes to my credit. In fact the only major failure I can think of is my inability to get Ambler anywhere near a hospital for a sperm count. He has a phobia. Mu's had all the tests, but he won't.

If he had, maybe we wouldn't have had to slog our hot, weary way barefoot up a lot of concrete steps on Mount Tsambika next day, together with a miscellaneous collection of (mainly)

Greek women, one of whom was doing the climb painfully on her knees, and I don't think she'd started at the car park like we did either.

It's a pilgrimage in aid of fertility. You have to climb up the hill to the Chapel of Our Lady, where you eat a piece of lamp wick. (Yes, really, I defy even de Bono to make a lateral leap and explain that, though I suspect Freud might, poor deluded creature.)

Following this ritual, pregnancy is almost guaranteed to happen, though you have to name the resultant offspring Tsambika or Tsambikos or it snuffs it, which seems a bit unchristian.

Still, Mu had been determined to do it ever since she read about it in some travel guide, and although she really didn't expect it to work . . . she sort of *did*, too. The triumph of hope over intelligence.

We'd made an early start on the long toil upwards, but already the noise of the cicadas rubbing their thighs together, or whatever it is they get up to (and don't bother looking in my *Spiral Bound* guidebooks for that sort of detail, because you won't find it), was pretty deafening.

'This had better work,' panted Mu as we reached our goal, and I paused to slide my feet into my sandals before we went in, rather like putting on Sunday best for church. 'Now all I have to do is eat the lamp wick.'

'But only a little bit of one, I hope. It's probably cotton soaked in oil or fat or something, so it'll grease your tubes beautifully,' I suggested.

'The wrong tubes, though – and hadn't you better wait out here in case the magic works on the wrong person?'

'No, I don't think it could: if *I've* got a biological clock it's a limp, Daliesque thing like a dead Dutch cap, draped over my pelvis with the hands barely twitching. But I could give it a go, if you like, and if it works, you can have the baby?'

'You are silly,' she said severely, but I did sneak in after her and eat a bit of wick too. Why shouldn't I keep my pregnancy option open? In China, sisters used to give one of their offspring to infertile siblings, so perhaps it was remiss of me not to have offered before.

But such is the way of these sudden impulses that no sooner had I swallowed the unappetizing morsel than I began to see some major pitfalls in my reasoning.

While my stomach made valiant efforts to reject the greasy gobbet (a sure sign that it was a bum idea), it didn't quite make it, and people sticking their fingers down their throats in church is frowned on.

It was just as well I didn't really believe in these superstitions.

The atmosphere on the way down was much jollier, with everyone laughing and joking, sometimes rather bawdily, and when we got back to our hotel Mu said she was glad she'd done the pilgrimage. 'And when I get home I'll just have time to ravish Ambler to within an inch of his life before he goes off to Egypt again.'

'I don't suppose he'll struggle, though he may be too weak to paddle his canoe. You know, Mu, in the church I was thinking—'

'You were thinking if I had an ounce of gumption I'd have snuck off by now and had AI!' she interrupted.

'No, that wasn't quite what I—'

'But Ambler wouldn't hear of it, and I do love him . . . so the idea of foisting a cuckoo into his nest seems a bit underhand, to say the least.'

'It would only be a half-cuckoo,' I pointed out, diverted.

'But what I was really going to say was that perhaps I could have a baby and give it to you, and—'

'That's very, very sweet of you, Sappho,' she broke in. 'Only, being adopted, I don't have any relatives – any real family of my own. But if I had a baby myself, it would be. Do you see?'

I blew bubbles like a guppy while I digested this. I was drinking retsina in the hope it would dissolve the wick, which seemed to be coiled like a small tapeworm in the pit of my stomach.

I did see her point, and of course I was assuming that I was still able to have offspring, and Old Mortality hadn't already snatched the cup away untasted, which he might have done . . . and which would definitely make me feel resentful.

It would be like being given a present with a timer attached to it – an egg timer – and having it whipped away before you'd got around to opening it. You might not have liked what was in it, but it was *your* present.

However, that very night I dreamed I was giving birth to a table, and I had terrible trouble with the corners.

Was my subconscious trying to tell me something?

Chapter 5

And So to Bedd

'How about that one?'

Mu pointed down to the other end of the Val-U Used Cars forecourt, where an old Volvo estate in an unremarkable shade of brown squatted balefully, like the last brontosaurus daring a meteorite to get it.

'Why that one?' I enquired as we walked down to inspect it, closely trailed by Mr Val-U himself, who was a short, square man with a big mouth, like a human box.

'Oh, I don't know, it just sort of reminds me of you: it's big, the same colour as your hair, and looks like it would come off best in an argument.'

'Probably drinks petrol like a thirsty camel.'

'It's been modified,' Mr Val-U informed us in suitably hushed tones. Presumably this is some sort of vehicular castration. 'And it's very economical, considering.'

Considering what, I didn't ask, since I was rather taken with its neat, solid, rectangular aspect. This was a car that had matured rather than got older. There may be a message in there somewhere for me.

Its matching my hair was the clincher, and at least it was big enough, since the design was clearly intended for huge Swedes with arms like gorillas and legs like stilts. I've met one or two Swedes who look like that. Do *I* look like that?

I made Mr Val-U a very happy man, but not as happy as he was before I beat him down on the price by pointing out several minor defects, and twice pretending to walk away washing my hands of it. Once you've haggled in a souk it all comes naturally to you, but he seemed quite unnerved by my technique.

Driving my purchase back to Mu's I had good cause to congratulate myself on choosing an estate, for I acquired a really lovely old reclining leather chair *en route*.

OK, as Mu pointed out, it's really a dentist's chair, but it is genuine black leather and chrome, and very comfortable.

Some workmen were carrying it out to a skip, and they were more than happy to help me put it in the car instead after an exchange of filthy lucre. We had to unscrew one or two of the detachable parts first, but I dare say I won't be needing most of those anyway: Bedd might not be very exciting, but I'm unlikely ever to be spending the evenings examining my teeth in hinged mirrors.

The chair was another nice thing for my cottage, like the Portuguese door Pops and Jaynie bought me. They didn't stop at the door, either – there was a whole vanload of stuff coming over at the weekend.

My belongings from Bob and Vivi's were currently all at sea on a slow boat to Tenby, and I still had everything at Mu's to pack up.

For a free-wheeling globetrotter that was a surprising number of possessions, though most of them were highly impractical things, like pottery and carvings, and enough sarongs to curtain the white cliffs of Dover, while, as Mu practically pointed out, what I actually needed were washing-up bowls and toilet brushes.

She actually drew up a horrendous shopping list of what she called 'Essential Items', but I found a store that sold a complete home-starting basics kit in a big box and ordered one. Everything came in white, white, or white, but I'd got lots of colourful stuff to spread around already.

It's odd to realize that while I *can* quite happily live out of a rucksack, where my own home is concerned minimalism is not my style.

But I was really looking forward to making a permanent base camp now, particularly since on this visit I'd been absolutely terrorized by Mu's vast, half-wild Egyptian cat, Ankaret, though she was currently retired to some fastness to have a surprise litter of kittens.

I didn't think Ambler would be too pleased when he returned from his expedition because, from the sound of it, Ankaret terrorized him, too.

There were two letters awaiting me when we got back to Mu's house, one from Bob containing the happy news that Vivi was expecting. While we were both pleased, Mu went a bit quiet, and took herself off to prepare a special dinner on the pretext of it being my last night before I moved to Bedd, although we'd been feasting every night for the last week anyway: a prolonged wake for Mu's thirty-ninth birthday.

(Miranda's birthday was the previous week – I sent her a long plastic tube containing thirty-nine giant jelly beans. There were forty, but I ate one, which felt a bit like buying someone's wart for sixpence.)

After Mu had gone I settled down to read the other letter, which was from Aunt Pops, expecting the usual mix of dippiness and practical advice, and instead found she and

Jaynie had been worrying over some light-hearted remarks I made while staying there, about lamp wicks, and how having a baby is one of the few things I haven't tried yet.

The general gist was that I should resist any mad notion to go forth and multiply. As Pops put it:

> . . . realizing that procreation might be an option you may not have for much longer does not mean that you must immediately get pregnant while you still can! At thirty-nine you'd probably find it difficult anyway, and older mothers are subject to more complications. A baby should not be an impulse buy, darling.
>
> We considered it some years ago, and decided not to bother.
>
> Jaynie got a bit broody again when she turned forty, but then bought the Harley-Davidson, which has given her years of pleasure. You can't always say that about children.
>
> Pregnancy must totally take over your body, and you are such a control person, dearest Sappho, that I'm sure you wouldn't like it in the least. And a child takes over your life, too.
>
> There's also the small matter of a sperm donor – unless you have someone in mind that you haven't told us about? We would love you to find that one special person – Jaynie and I have been so happy . . .

And so on.

I simply couldn't understand why even people who know me well were so aghast at the mere thought of my having a last-egg-in-the-box baby and, perversely, it made the idea of playing a sort of Russian roulette with some suitable sperm seem scarily attractive.

*

After dinner, and rather a lot of wine, the conversation turned inevitably to Vivi's news.

'It isn't that I'm not really, really pleased for her,' Mu said earnestly.

'Of course not – I know that.'

'Just that I'm jealous as hell. You know,' she added, propping her pointed chin in her hands, 'all the time I was saying that I didn't expect the Tsambika pilgrimage to work, secretly I did. Isn't that sad? I must be a prize pregnancy bore.'

The pilgrimage didn't work for me either, but then, that might have had something to do with my not having had sexual congress within living memory.

'No, you're not a bore,' I assured her. (Not since I'd suddenly become personally interested in pregnancy, anyway. Before that I just automatically tuned it out, along with other boring subjects like sport.)

'I hoped it would work, too . . . except the problem is probably Ambler's, and since he won't get himself checked out, you've reached an impasse.'

'A dead end to the maze, with the clock ticking the last minutes,' Mu agreed sadly.

'I think I really might start a baby in my gap year before senility. You can share it,' I offered.

She smiled. 'You must be joking! What would you do with a baby? You can't just stick it in a rucksack and go!'

'Why not?' I asked, puzzled. 'In lots of countries they do just that.'

'Sappho, you're not serious, are you?'

'Well, you can't say it wouldn't change my life, and I wanted to find something that would give me a new direction before my fortieth birthday. But it's in the lap of the gods whether I actually get pregnant, isn't it?'

'The lap of the sperm donor, actually – unless you've already got someone in mind?'

'Not yet, but there's still time. I'm not looking for a Significant Other, just a Significant Sperm.'

'Roxana said *I* ought to consider AI.'

'What, Ambler's *mother* thinks you ought to have AI? When did she say that?'

'She popped down a couple of weeks ago when she was over from Kansas with Chuck.'

'Chuck?'

'Her fifth. He's nice – small, chubby, seriously rich. He took me to one side and told me that Roxana was "one hell of a sensitive little lady" and he meant to look after her.'

'Sweet but misplaced. She's got even more of the tiger in her tank than Lili.'

'Yes, but she isn't getting any younger, and I think she ought to hang on to this one. We had what she called a "little girls together talk" and that's when she said Ambler must be firing blanks and I should try someone else.'

'What, like the milkman?' The suggestion seemed a bit over the top, even for Roxana.

'No, of course not! She said it still needed to be a Gray-thorpe baby, and so it had better be Simon.'

'Simon? The only Simon I can think of is Ambler's baby brother.'

'That's the one: only he's now Ambler's seriously hunky, nineteen-year-old student brother. They do grow up, you know, Sappho! He also looks like Ambler, except there's more going on behind his eyes.'

I stared at her, digesting the implications slowly. 'But, Mu, won't Ambler suspect—'

'He won't know anything about it, and since I'd make sure

I seduced him just before any attempt with Simon, even *I* won't be a hundred per cent sure whose it is – if it works.'

She gave a sudden shiver: 'I do love Ambler, and I don't want to lose him, it's just I really, really want a family of my own.'

'I do understand, Mu, but what about Simon? Surely—'

I stopped dead again, beginning to see even more pitfalls.

'Roxana had already talked to Simon about it, and he doesn't mind at all. In fact,' she added primly, 'he's always had a bit of a crush on me, and was apparently disappointed when told his personal services weren't required, just the goods.'

'The *goods*? Oh – I see.'

'Well, I hope so! I've never been unfaithful to Ambler yet, and were I to start it would be with someone a little older than Simon. Not that young, lithe and muscular aren't terribly attractive attributes in a man.' She looked pensive.

'Mu!'

'It's all right, I'm not seriously tempted, and Simon's promised Roxana he wouldn't let on to Ambler or do any "wink, wink, nudge, nudge" business. She's threatened to kill him if he does – or cut off his allowance, whichever is more painful. But I don't think he would because he's very fond of his brother.'

'Yes, but isn't this carrying brotherly love too far?' I protested weakly. Honestly, that Roxana! The more I thought about it, the more unnatural it seemed for her to be offering her youngest son as stud to his brother's wife.

'Mu, what if Simon marries and has children, and the cousins meet and fall for each other, and . . .'

'Unlikely – and you, as the godparent, would just have to put a damper on it.'

'Thanks a lot.'

She shrugged. 'It probably won't work anyway, so the problem won't arise – and we're hardly talking *Flowers in the Attic* here, are we? But I might as well try. And I wondered . . . since your cottage is within easy reach of Simon's university in Bristol, whether we could meet there?'

'You want to use the cottage? Of course you can. But how – you know, if you aren't going to sleep together, how are you going to do the deed?'

Call me naïve, but it isn't something I've ever given much thought to. AI clinics just suggest rubber gloves and giant syringes, which actually turned out to be nearer the mark than I expected.

'Turkey baster,' Mu said.

'Turkey baster? Are you serious? Will you have to call the baby Bernard Matthews? Or Bernadine? Or Cherry Valley—'

'That's ducks,' she interrupted coldly. 'And I could use a teaspoon instead, but a baster would give the sperm a bit more of a start.'

'Yes, but if you used a teaspoon you could call the baby Apostle or Ratstail.'

'Shut up.'

'Or Mustard. Mustard Graythorpe.' I looked at her sideways and saw her lip twitching as she tried not to laugh. 'Or then again, you might just get tempted with young, muscular, sexy Simon.'

'I may, but I'd never be able to look him in the eye – or anywhere else – afterwards, and this way I can, because it's all one remove away. If you were serious about having one too, you could try Simon!'

'You know I don't go for blonds – I'm looking for someone tall, dark and attractive.'

'Like Dave.'

'Like Dave, but sane – someone I can shake off afterwards.'

'Sappho, you aren't *really* serious, are you? I thought you were joking.'

'Wait and see,' I told her.

Providing I found a suitable donor, that is, and Old Mortality hadn't already cancelled my option.

I still had my doubts about Mu's scheme, but I've never been one to hang back when my friends need help or advice. Miranda clearly needed me to infuse a little bit of backbone into her, too, and, fortuitously, here I was, more or less on the spot.

They needed a Good Fairy, and I was that fairy. Admittedly a bloody big fairy, but still, never look one in the mouth. Not unless you want your hand bitten off, anyway.

Titanic Titania.

Thus it was that one sunny, cold, early March day I extricated two of Mu's cats from the comfortable leather interior of the Volvo and went to Bedd.

Bedd is Welsh for 'grave', and the village takes its name from the cromlech on the crest of moorland behind my cottage. Clearly, mortality is all around me, since the Acre to Aces Acre was sold off as a burial ground in the eighteenth century, and is full of mossy angels and illegible slabs, but it makes for quiet neighbours.

I was following on the heels of the small removal van bearing my belongings, augmented by the Fantasy Flowers paraphernalia. Mu was adamant that she'd had enough of it, and I was loath to abandon a business where money oozed in by every post when I'd had one of my brilliant ideas about disposing of it . . .

It felt good to be on the road in my very own car, although

driving habits in Britain had taken a turn for the worse since I last got behind the wheel. About half of all the drivers had lost the use of their indicators, and most men seemed more willing to overtake me on a blind bend at seventy than drive behind me, until I stopped and unpeeled the 'Women are natural leaders – you're following one now' sticker that Mu had put on the bumper, when things improved slightly.

Have you ever wondered why most men drive with only one hand on the wheel, and what they're doing with the other? No? Well, my theory is that they're doing one of three things: some are illegally bleating into mobile phones, another third have a finger stuck up their nose, and the rest are pulling that funny little grimace that means they are adjusting their personal equipment.

I was so glad I'd chosen such a solid car: Personal Protection. I stuck a tape in the player and my heart was light as the Volvo ate up the miles to my home with all the ponderous grace of a Sherman tank, to the strains of old favourites like Motörhead, Dire Straits and Queen.

People can be very odd. At one traffic light, minding my own business and harmonizing with Freddie over 'Bohemian Rhapsody', I noticed the man in the next lane giving me a very funny look.

Why? Was *I* staring at *him* just because he was playing some inane jingle with a backing beat like two people beating a weasel to death with tennis rackets?

And if Mu is right about Motörhead being the Mantovani of my generation, he'd better become accustomed to this sort of thing, for in a few years he'll find little old ladies head-banging at traffic lights, me among them. (In my case, *big* old lady.)

'Bee-el-zeebub has a devil put aside for me-e-e, for ME-E!' I screeched happily as the lights changed and the car next to me stalled. After he'd done all that noisy revving up, too.

'Eat dirt, punk,' I said as he vanished in the wing mirror.

Before leaving the main roads for the narrow twisty lanes of the Gower, I stopped and studied the map, after which I found my way to Bedd with very little difficulty, despite the increasingly heavy showers of rain.

Three roads lead into Bedd and my cottage is the last house on the narrowest and steepest of them all, the one running up towards the stone cromlech.

Breasting the final crest of the lane with the rain pounding the roof like mailed fists and the windscreen wipers slowly and heroically pushing waves off the glass, I started down what looked like a river of mud. A lesser car might have floated.

A small white van was pulled into the side halfway down, with some poor soul crouched over a flat tyre, so I considerately slowed, meaning to give it a wide berth and not add to their misery by soaking them in passing.

'Meaning to' is the operative phrase, because just as I pulled out to pass, something long, gingery and weasel-like streaked across the road liked greased string, making me swerve violently, and sending a long, curling wave of liquid mud over the head of the unlucky wheel-changer.

Hello, chocolate soldier.

There was a bellow of surprise, rage, or shock – it must have been freezing – and of course I pulled in, meaning to apologize and explain.

I wound my window down and waited, since there didn't seem much point in my getting drowned just to expiate my sins, and I could see my victim approaching in the wing mirror, growing ever bigger and more glistening.

'Look, I'm terribly sorry,' I began contritely, the second he was close enough to hear me. 'I swerved because this weaselly thing ran across the road suddenly, and . . . and . . .'

I looked up.

And up.

Or maybe *I* was shrinking away to the size of a Christmas fairy doll?

Out of the mud-plastered visage of the Giant Thing from the Slime Pit two eyes burned with a colourless demonic fire, and wordless (fortunately) rumblings of incandescent rage issued from between wolfish teeth gleaming whitely against the black primeval slime.

Dragonslayer? Had my characters finally managed to escape from my head and live lives of their own?

Instinctively I threw the car into gear and took off down that road like a bat out of hell. Sometimes discretion can be the better part of valour.

A last glance in the mirror before I turned the corner showed me that he wasn't chasing me but sitting down in the road, probably unintentionally.

Shaken, I pressed the button on the memo recorder, which was hung from a leather thong around my neck for hands-free great thoughts, and, as I pulled into the yard behind Aces Acre, safely out of sight, began to intone: *'Dragonslayer rose from the slime pit, his eyes burning through the black coating of . . .'*

Home alone – almost.

The van had unloaded its strange cargo and gone, but upstairs the electrician was still wrestling with his snaky coils, and somewhere a plumber was swearing (or perhaps Welsh just sounds like that).

It was all supposed to be finished before my arrival, but

they both assured me they were nearly done. They will be, if they're lying.

There was no sign of Miranda when I arrived, other than a substantial home-made fruitcake sitting on the kitchen table, though she'd let the workmen in earlier.

The said table was a strange greenish Formica affair with glittery bits embedded in the top, which presumably the Last of the Aces didn't want when he cleared the house.

Neither did I, strangely enough, or the peculiarly slithery leatherette and horsehair sofa.

Still, the roof was finished and the walls had all been stripped of their cold porridge woodchip, and painted white. The ghastly little lean-to greenhouse thing tacked on to the front of the house, and made out of old window frames and bits and pieces, was still there.

It was supposed to have been removed by the builders, but it could stay for the moment and house the Fantasy Flowers impedimenta (though I'd make sure the builders didn't try to charge me for taking it away, when they hadn't).

My phone line was installed ready for any relayed bouquet orders from Mu. I could manage those quite easily for the time being – I'd always helped when I was staying there so I can hand-tie a posy with the best of them.

I was just thinking that with a bit of luck I wouldn't have to do it for long when, as if on cue, the kitchen darkened like an instant eclipse: something *huge* was blocking the doorway.

'I-it's m-me!' stammered a small voice.

Chapter 6

Crackers

'My God!' I exclaimed incredulously as she moved into the room and the full, eye-boggling horror burst upon me. 'Miranda?'

Her huge blue eyes overflowed, darkly splattering the vile tented thing she was wearing.

'I-I know I'm g-grotesquely fat!' she quavered.

There is a time and a place for brutal frankness and, this being it, I gave it to her straight. 'The only grotesque thing is that *dress*, Miranda. I've never seen anything so repulsive in my life! Where did you get it from? The Marquee de Sade? Tents "R" Us? I mean, even if it weren't that strange cross between khaki and decayed diarrhoea yellow, those psychedelic squiggles would still make it a definite and resounding *NO*. Have you had a taste transplant, or something?'

Her tears fell faster and I was just thinking I might have gone a *smidgeon* too far when I saw she was smiling through them.

'Oh, S-Sappho,' she quavered, and I sprang up and gave her a hug with my own eyes smarting, although that might have been the op art effect of all those dancing squiggles. 'And I thought you w-were d-disgusted about my weight!'

I held her off, slightly amazed. 'What, you thought I'd say: "Begone, elephant woman, I'll have no overweight friends?" *Really*, Miranda! Have *you* ever said to me: "I won't be friends with you any more, you're much too tall and bossy, and what's more you have size eight feet"?'

Miranda gave a familiar youthful giggle, an echo of Miranda Past.

And really, I don't know what she's bothered about, for she will always be beautiful: it's in the bones, even if some of them are buried a little deeper than they used to be. Actually, her head and neck look just the same – lovely cheekbones, upswept corn-gold hair, eyes the French blue of a 2CV . . .

In fact, it's just as if a sculptor has started carving out his Galatea from styrofoam, finished the head, but merely blocked out the rest before knocking off for tea.

But there were advantages, as I pointed out over coffee and her delicious fruitcake, while above us the plumber and electrician discussed rugby in shouts like a celestial fan club. She'd always wanted a cleavage, so why not play up her assets now she'd got them?

'There d-didn't seem much point in b-bothering once I got over a size fourteen and Chris made it clear he found me emb-barrassing. And it's not much fun shopping for clothes when most of them d-don't fit you. Most really b-big clothes are just d-designed for coverage – like summer and winter covers for sofas. Nowadays, if it fits me I b-buy it, even if it's something I wouldn't even have given the d-dog to lie on b-before.'

'Ah, yes – how is Spike?'

'He's fine. Very old for a Labrador, of course, and he's on a d-diet too. I'm kinder to him than I am to myself. I've b-been on every d-diet known to woman for the last three years, and every time I fail, my weight goes up even further than b-before.'

'Yes, I've heard that can happen. I read some women's magazines in Greece, and dieting was the only thing they talked about other than sex.'

'I'm sort of in a vicious circle, Sappho,' she confided, 'and I d-don't know how to get out. The fatter I grow, the more self-conscious I get and the more I stutter. And then Chris says even more hurtful things about my weight, so I feel even worse and eat more for comfort . . .' She stopped and looked at me helplessly. 'D-do you see?'

'Oh, yes, I see, all right, and I think you ought to divorce the bastard – the sensible option. After all, he's just some little red-haired git who's climbed to fame and fortune on the back of your cookery skills and hard work.'

Her pretty pink mouth curved into a startled smile. 'You haven't changed much, Sappho.'

'No, so people keep telling me. I don't know if that's good or bad.'

'Good! I feel b-better already. B-but you d-don't understand, Sappho – Chris and I are a partnership. TV is all about personality, and I couldn't d-do that with my stammer, could I? And Chris isn't creative – he can't d-do innovative cookery, and that's where I come in.'

'It would be a partnership if you got any credit for it, but I mean: are you mentioned on the series credits? In the spin-off cookery books? Get paid for your work?'

'Well, *no*, b-but—'

'He's a user, and he needs you more than you need him.'

'He could probably manage without me now, b-because they'd just hire a team of ghost cooks to d-do it for him.'

'But he'd have to pay them, and wasn't Stingy always his

middle name?' I pointed out. 'Tell me: do you still love him?'

She was silent for a minute, and then she said slowly and with an air of surprised discovery: 'Well, sort of. I loved how he *was* . . . only he seems to have changed and he's b-been horrible to me since I started putting all this weight on, though that's my fault, isn't it? B-but I mean, what would I d-do without him? I've never worked, the only money I've got he's given me.'

'Yes, you idiot, but that's your money, too – you've done all the hard work on the cookery, while he's just the public face. It's about time you stopped thinking of yourself as some kind of appendage, and think about what Miranda Cotter wants instead – or the Miranda Lacey you were when you wrote *The Stuffed Student*.'

'B-but I can't *d-do* anything else. I'm fat, ugly, useless and in-incoherent!'

'And brainwashed,' I added, giving her some more coffee, this time adding a small slug of dark rum (possibly my only weakness besides Daniel Day-Lewis). If that didn't shiver her timbers she was beyond saving.

'The only success I've ever had has b-been *The Stuffed Student*, and now my editor wants me to d-do a new upd-dated edition. I was excited about it, but when I told Chris, he wanted me to put his name on it too, b-because it would sell more! And call me a nasty, mean person, Sappho, b-but I d-don't want to in the least – I mean, it's *mine*.'

'Of course you don't – it's nothing to do with him.'

'No, and my editor agreed with me.'

'Good for her – you stick to your guns.'

'I have and he wasn't pleased. And, Sappho – they want me to write a new b-book after that, about party food for students on a b-budget.' She brightened: 'I thought I'd call it *Feeding the Party Animal*. What d-do you think?'

'Wonderful!' I toasted her in laced coffee. 'There you are, a jot of resolution and the start of a breakaway career. You can embrace the second oldest profession open to women, just like me.'

'Sappho!'

'Writing,' I explained patiently.

Her expression was pleased but doubtful, but that was OK, because I've got enough backbone for more than the two of us.

'I'll have to finish writing the b-book for the latest TV series first – *Chris Goes Crackers*. It's b-been advertised!'

She gestured with the biscuit barrel she'd been clutching on her lap since she arrived and which I'd assumed to be in the nature of a security blanket. 'This is for you – a house-warming present. It's full of b-biscuits – my house is full of b-biscuits.'

'Tell Chris you want your name credited equally in the book and the TV series,' I said firmly.

'He would go b-ballistic – and say it's all part of my neurosis.'

'Neurosis? What neurosis?'

'He thinks I'm having a sort of b-breakdown, what with D-Dad and Mum d-dying within a year of each other, and the weight piling on uncontrollably. He said I ought to live d-down here quietly for a b-bit until I'm b-better.'

'Better than what?'

'I *have* d-done one or two odd things lately,' she admitted. 'B-but I feel all right.'

'Odd things? What sort of odd things?'

'Oh, like the koi in the freezer,' she said.

'The coy what?'

'Koi – they're the fish D-Dad used to keep in the garden

pond. One morning they weren't there, and I found them in the freezer. Packaged, d-dated and labelled: "Eat within three months".'

I choked on my coffee. 'You think you did it?'

'Who else could it have b-been? B-but I d-don't remember doing it. Chris said he'd woken up the night b-before and heard the freezer lid slam.'

'Late last night, I heard the freezer slam . . .' I crooned thoughtfully to the tune of 'Big Yellow Taxi'.

'It's a big pond, I seem to recall. Was your nightie wet? Pools of water all over the place? Bloody knives? Muddy feet?'

'No, nothing like that – and I d-didn't even have a fishing net, though funnily enough I found one later on top of one of the garage b-beams.'

'Chris was home at the time, you said?'

'He-he'd left the morning I found them . . . B-but—' her eyes widened – 'b-but he wouldn't . . .? Why should—'

'Any other odd happenings?' I interrupted.

'Only little things, like finding the ham in the tool b-box, and the hammer in the fridge, that sort of stuff.'

'And Chris was home at the time then, too, I expect? Really, Miranda, the man's doing this to try to manipulate you back into line! He thought he had you safely stashed away down here working for him until you started showing signs of independence!'

'D-do you really think so? Then I'm not going mad? B-but surely Chris wouldn't . . .?' She stopped and sighed. 'I suppose he *might* – b-but it's nasty. I was attached to those fish!'

'Presumably, you're attached to your sanity, too?'

She sat up straighter. 'If I really thought—'

'That's that, then,' suddenly broke in the electrician, a lugubrious dark man, who had come downstairs unnoticed.

'New sockets in, rewired. Accident waiting to happen, that old wiring.'

'Good – thanks. I'll get the plasterers back in to fill all those little holes and channels you've gouged out.'

He stared at me. 'Can't make an omelette without breaking eggs,' he pointed out reasonably.

'True. Now, I'll want you back later to rewire the barn, or outhouse – whatever you call that old building at the front. I just want some light in it for the moment until I decide what to do with it.'

'Make a nice holiday cottage,' he suggested.

'I don't need a holiday cottage, I live here,' I told him. 'I could turn part of it into a garage and extend the house into the rest, but I'd need to get planning permission, I suppose.'

'Might fit you in next Wednesday.'

'That would be all right – there's no rush. Now, let me see that cut finger again before you go.'

He whipped the injured hand behind his back. 'No, it's fine – honest!'

Men can be so childish about these things.

'Let me see. We don't want it getting infected, do we?'

He began to sidle past me. 'No, really, that stuff you put on before stung like hell.'

'You can't make an omelette without breaking eggs,' I reminded him. 'If it hurts, it's working. Perhaps a little more antiseptic . . .'

He edged round me and backed towards the door. 'I'll look after it,' he said quickly, and darted out to his little van.

'Pity,' I said. 'It was a nasty cut. Still, if he gets infection in it and his finger drops off, at least I'll know I did everything *I* could.' I turned my attention back to Miranda, who was looking in a puzzled and slightly rosy way into her coffee cup.

'Is this one of those new flavoured coffees?'

'Yes, rum flavour. Now, listen, Miranda, there's something I really, really need your help with.'

She went pinker with astonishment. 'Me? You want me to help you?'

'Yes. Tell me, do you like flowers?'

'Flowers? Yes, of course – b-but I can't d-do weeding any more, I get tired and my ankles puff up, so if you want me to help with your garden—'

'I haven't got a garden, I've got a sea of weeds and rubble that merges into the moorland, and a cobbled yard buried under a sea of filth,' I pointed out. 'No, I meant, do you like flower arranging, that kind of thing?'

'Oh, yes, I love it – and there was a weekend flower arranging course at the village hall here only a couple of weeks ago. Llyn at the village stores persuaded me to go, and I was good at it.'

'That's great. Now, come into the lean-to and I'll show you something.'

She followed me out and stared, baffled, at the cartons, tea chests and bundles of foliage, ribbons, flat-packed gift boxes, and two folded pasting tables.

'This,' I said grandly, with a flourish of my hand, 'is Fantasy Flowers. Flowers That Say It for You.'

'Say what?' she asked.

'Absolutely anything.' I delved into a carton and came up with a pile of the little *Meanings of Flowers and Foliage* booklets.

'You see, Mu and I set the business up together a couple of years ago and put adverts in various magazines, and it really took off. The clients tell us what message they want their bouquet to deliver, and we make it up and send it off with a copy of the booklet, so the recipient can work it out. Mu's been doing it ever since, but she's bored now and wants to wind it up. And I haven't had time for it for a while – but you have. I mean, there's a steady trickle of orders, but you could work it up into a really good thing.'

'M-me? You want me to work for you?'

'No, I want you to work for you – take over Fantasy Flowers entirely. You could do it from here for the moment, if you wanted to, but if you expand it you'll eventually need more room, and I'd like to demolish this little architectural excrescence one day.'

Miranda was looking poleaxed.

'What's the matter?' I asked anxiously. 'If you don't like the idea, you only have to say. I know I'm bossy, but it seems to me that a business of your own would give you more independence from Chris, and that could only be a good idea. And it will take up just a small part of the mornings, so there'll be lots of time left for writing cookbooks.'

'*Like* the idea?' she repeated. 'Oh, Sappho, I've b-been such a poor friend over the years and now – now you're handing me a ready-made b-business, and I d-don't d-deserve it!'

'Well, there's no need to cry about it. Do you want to do it?'

'Of course, b-but – could I, d-do you think?'

'Of course you can. Why don't we unpack it all this afternoon, and I'll explain it to you? Mu is carrying on taking the orders for the moment, and leaving the instructions on the call minder here every morning.'

Miranda still seemed a bit stunned, but that was probably because she'd suddenly realized she wasn't on her own with her problems any more.

'This is all a lot to take in,' she said dazedly. 'Look, why d-don't you come b-back with me now to The Hacienda for lunch? You can see Spike. I d-didn't b-bring him b-because I couldn't remember if you liked d-dogs or not.'

'I do, and I'm going to get one, though it should be a cat.'

She looked at me.

'I'm a single eccentric female – I should have a cat. But bring Spike round with you any time. And I'll be glad to come for lunch, because I haven't brought much food with me, though the village shop sounds enterprising – they put a leaflet through the door. I'll follow you round when the plumber's finished, shall I?'

'Right – and thanks, Sappho.'

'What for?' I asked, surprised.

'For making me feel there is a future, something to live for.'

'There's *everything* to live for.'

'B-but I'm nearly forty, and all I've ever d-done is make a mess of things.'

'You're nearly forty, I'm nearly forty, Mu's nearly forty – it's time to rise like a phoenix from the ashes of our youth and take a Virtual Bungee Jump for the Soul.'

Miranda giggled.

'It's all right for some,' the plumber said, passing through with a length of pipe curled round his neck like a too-friendly python.

'Yes, it is,' I agreed. 'How are you doing?'

'Central heating's working, if that's what you mean. Can't you hear it?'

Now he came to mention it, there was a lot of clunking and rumbling.

'Good. The rest I can do myself in my spare time – if I ever have any, with the next *Vengeane* book to write.'

'Book?' said the plumber, helping himself uninvited to the contents of the biscuit tin.

'She's the Sappho Jones who writes fantasy b-books,' Miranda said eagerly.

'Never heard of them, but I don't get the time to read books. These biscuits are good.'

'I'm so glad you like them. Mrs Cotter here made them.'

'You're a good cook,' he told her.

Miranda flushed with pleasure. 'Thank you.' She hoisted herself to her feet. 'I'd b-better go and let Spike out. See you later, Sappho – and thanks.'

'You ain't seen nothing yet!' I said, and then firmly removed the biscuit tin from the plumber's hands.

Chapter 7

Spiked

Miranda's parents had had the happy notion of calling their ranch-style bungalow The Hacienda, which, while better, say, than Dunroamin' or Thistledome, was unsuited to the locality. (Admittedly, Pops and Jaynie call their Portuguese house Pop'n'Jays, but that is firmly tongue in cheek.)

When I offered to find Miranda some more suitable alternatives she said she'd never heard of a Thistledome but rather liked it, and I was glad to see that her impish sense of humour had not been entirely eroded away by Chris.

The only anomaly in the clean, bright and modern interior of the bungalow was the fat, smelly old chocolate Labrador, Spike, who clearly had no idea he suffered from something even his best friend wouldn't tell him about. Having the instincts of a gentleman he politely heaved himself up and wheezed his way over to greet me, head down and legs plodding determinedly like a clockwork toy, and I appreciated the thought, if not the odour.

Miranda brought in a tin containing two more entirely different varieties of home-made biscuits, just in case I should feel peckish in the ten minutes or so it would take her to make the sandwiches. She declined my offer of help, although Spike went along to give her a hand, but left me with a folder of newspaper cuttings for entertainment.

It seemed that Dorinda Ace (she of the poison pen, 'give my husband back his cottage or else' letter) vanished last October, and there had been no trace of her since. Some of the articles described her husband as 'distraught', and he was reported to have spent a lot of time helping the police with their inquiries.

Obviously they suspected that Disappeared Dorinda was also Dead Dorinda, but if she were related to Chinless Charlie Penryn, she could just be Dotty Dorinda and have wandered off, for there's a strong strain of loopiness in that family.

Not that Charlie isn't unfailingly amiable and polite, apart from a slight tendency to ask total strangers if they'd like to hang anything on his knob (like in the nude statue episode).

On her way to the kitchen Miranda had warned me not to believe what they said about Gilbert Ace, because she was at school with him and he wouldn't hurt a fly, but she was clearly biased.

After this I had a look at the bookshelves, which were full of the old cookery tomes Miranda loves, except one entirely devoted to all my *Vengeane* novels and *Spiral Bound* guidebooks. I found this touching, for she must have bought them: Chris certainly wouldn't have wasted his money on me.

Taking out a glossy new hardback copy of *Dark Hours, Dark Deeds*, I signed it 'With love to Miranda' and put it back.

On top of the cottage piano was an old photograph of Mu and Miranda, both dainty blondes, with me looming in the middle like a great dark thorn between two roses. There was also a studio portrait of Chris looking slickly handsome in a foxy kind of way, and smiling as though he'd just discovered the alchemic formula for turning food into gold (which he had, and what's more, married it).

Sitting down at the piano, I flexed my fingers and then rattled off a few bars of 'The Hokey Cokey', which is one of my limited but select repertoire of pieces. My spirited renditions of this classic have on innumerable occasions broken the ice in remote corners of the world. You'd be surprised if I told you all the strange places where the ritual performance of 'The Hokey Cokey' is now a regular event.

Since I was giving it my all, the ringing of the telephone took a few moments to gain my attention.

'"You put your left leg in, your left leg out. In-out, in-out, shake it all about,"' I sang happily, finally shimmying across and picking up the receiver.

'Who is that?' demanded a startled voice. 'Miranda?'

'No, why should it be?' Belatedly I remembered where I was. 'It's you, Chris, is it?'

'Look, is that the cleaner?' he snapped impatiently. 'Can you get Mrs Cotter for me?'

'It's Sappho, and I'm afraid Miranda's busy right now.'

'Sappho? Sappho who?'

'Really, Chris, how many do you know? It's Sappho Jones, of course.'

There was a silence.

'Are you still there?' I queried.

'What are you doing in Wales? What are you doing in *my* house?' he snapped.

'Land of my distant forefathers, and it's Miranda's house.'

'My house – Miranda's house – what does it matter? What are you doing there?' he demanded, making it sound as if I'd broken in to steal the silver, or something.

'I'm here to steal the biscuit recipes,' I said.

'*What?*'

'Not really – just my little jest. What do you want?'

'To speak to my wife!'

'She's in the kitchen getting lunch, but I'll take a message. Did you know I had a house in the village?'

'No I did not! Now, if you could get my wife—'

'Is it important?' I interrupted. 'Only I'm rather hungry, and we have a lot to do this afternoon.'

'We?'

'Miranda's helping me. Would you like her to call you back this evening?'

'No, I'll be out,' he snapped, 'but you can tell her I can't make it down this weekend, I'm going to be tied up.'

'I'm sure you are. You want to be careful, though; it's easy to go too far when engaging in that sort of prac—'

'Just tell her!' he broke in, his carefully modulated tones cracking slightly.

'OK. Well, I can't tell you how much pleasure it's given me to hear your voice again after all this time, Chris, because it isn't measurable. See you around. Bye-ee.'

As I put down the receiver, Miranda made a timely entrance bearing the sort of tray on which you could have arranged a sucking pig (or a Ken Smollett) whole. On it reposed a buffet meal for a wedding party of a hundred or so.

'Would you mind b-bringing in the coffee tray, Sappho? I'll have to keep Spike off the food. He's so greedy – aren't you, d-darling? And the vet said no more cake.'

She fed him a bit of everything else, though.

'Chris phoned,' I remembered to tell her as I crammed dainty little sandwiches whole into my mouth, two at a time. It's so difficult to sink your teeth into that sort of thing.

'Chris? B-but why d-didn't you call me?' She started to heave herself upwards like a reluctant volcano.

'Oh, do sit down, Miranda!' I snapped impatiently. 'He only wanted to tell you he isn't going to be back this weekend, which is good news because you can get on with Fantasy Flowers, while I sort the house out.'

'B-but I ought to phone him straight b-back.'

'No, you shouldn't. Haven't you been listening to what I've been saying to you? I said you might phone him back tonight, but he's going out. And so are we. We'll have a bar meal at the Pike and Gasket to celebrate your new enterprise.'

Miranda looked from the phone to me, and opened and closed her mouth silently like a starving chick. 'D-do you mean the Eagle and Stone?'

'Whatever. And bring Spike with you this afternoon, the walk will do him good.'

She brightened, but still looked uncertainly at the phone. 'Perhaps I ought just – I mean, he must have b-been so surprised when you answered, and b-be wondering . . .'

'Let him marinate for a bit.'

'I expect he'd like to know how the b-biscuit recipes are d-doing b-because the publisher wants the manuscript by the end of the month. Everything's written d-down, b-but it wants typing out, and I'm so slow at it. Violet D-Duke usually d-does it for me, b-but she and her sisters have b-been away visiting relatives in Australia.'

I sat up a bit straighter: 'Violet Duke?'

'Yes, the D-Dukes are your nearest neighbours, and there are three of them: Violet, Pansy and Lavender.'

'Poor Pansy. Dafydd Ace mentioned nosy neighbours once, but if Violet can type she's the *ideal* neighbour.'

'She was a secretary until she retired, and she d-did a

76

computer course recently so she's very up to d-date. They're all about seventy, b-but still working. Pansy is the local d-decorator – she carries everything around with her on her b-bike and trailer. Lavender is a gardener – light gardening only – b-but she paints watercolours of flowers in the afternoons at the Castle Craft Centre.'

They all sounded enterprising, but I was more interested in Violet's accomplishments. 'Do you think Violet would type my work up for me from cassette tapes and hand-written notes? I hate doing it myself and it takes for ever.'

'Of course, and she's terribly efficient. She'll d-do it on her computer and print it out.'

'Wonderful!' I sighed. 'I can see that coming here was a brilliant move. In a couple of weeks not only will I have the house straight and my regular writing routine established, I will have my very own typist.'

And maybe I will be writing *Spiral Bound: Last-Shot Pregnancy* too, I thought.

That afternoon I successfully unloaded Fantasy Flowers on to Miranda. She soon got the hang of it, and I left her perusing the order books and unpacking foliage, while I went to browbeat the plasterer into returning to fill in the various cracks and channels left by the electrician, so that I could slap on a coat of nice clean white paint.

I didn't expect to live in a plain white house for ever, but I would repaint as the inspiration took me.

By the end of the afternoon the house looked better, and I joined Miranda in the kitchen where she was sitting with Spike over a cup of coffee.

'How are you doing with the flowers?'

'Oh, fine. It couldn't b-be easier, really, could it? The

b-booklets spell out the messages, and the flowers are all labelled – everything's there ready. And I know how to put together a Victorian-style posy. It's fun! How can Mu b-bear to give it up?'

'You know Mu – low boredom threshold. And she's been commissioned to do a whole series of *Corduroy Cat* picture books, because the first was such a success.'

'I should think children love them. Isn't it odd that none of *us* has children? I was upset when I lost that one just after we were married, and for a couple of years when no more came along – b-but really, I d-don't mind at all now. It wasn't meant to b-be.'

'I never even gave a thought to having children until recently, when someone pointed out that I was leaving it very late. It's gained an insidious fascination since then, so who knows, I might just do it for my Duke of Edinburgh's Challenge Forty Award.'

Miranda looked unflatteringly aghast. 'You aren't serious, are you? What you need is a d-dog like Spike, not a b-baby! Unless – I mean, there isn't anyone special, is there?'

'No, there's no one at all, but that doesn't matter, does it? I could even go to a clinic and pick a sperm, though actually if I did decide to do it, I'd like to check out the donor first.'

Mu certainly had, but I didn't tell Miranda about the impending teenager-and-turkey-baster situation, because Mu would, if she wanted her to know.

'. . . sea-washed pebbles,' Miranda was saying.

'What?'

'Under the silt in the courtyard – there are those lovely b-big smooth pebbles, and with some tubs of flowers and the outside paintwork d-done . . . and then a vista d-down the garden . . .'

'It's a rumble in the jungle at the moment, but I can picture it. Still, I need to sort out the inside of the house first so I can settle down to write and earn some money. And at least all that grey woodchip is off – it was like being surrounded by cold cellulite,' I said with a shudder. 'I'm going to buy gallons more white paint, a basic tool kit and stuff tomorrow. It's all going to cost me a fortune.'

'This table b-belonged to the Aces, d-didn't it? D-didn't Gil want it?'

'Apparently not, and it's pretty loathsome . . . though it's sort of begun to grow on me.'

'We could go to a car b-boot sale,' she suggested. 'Llyn at the shop goes to one every Sunday and she gets great b-bargains.'

'Does she? Do you think it might be fun?'

'Well, I might find some more cookery b-books, and I've always wanted to collect old kitchenware, only Chris said it was just a d-dust magnet.'

'Forget what he thinks and get a life.'

I stretched and yawned. 'We'd better get cleaned up and go to the pub before I fall asleep – and I've got a busy day tomorrow. My furniture from Aunt Pops is arriving.'

Miranda's face lit up. 'I'd forgotten Poppy and Jaynie! Remember when they arrived outside our d-digs at midnight on a b-big noisy motorbike, and serenaded you from the lawn with a mandolin and a paper and comb?'

'Was that the time they forgot to bring any clothes, and the suitcase was full of salami, olives and Portuguese wine for me? They still come over on the Harley, you know, to stock up with Marmite and crisps, but I think they like the excuse for a long run and some English beer.'

*

79

When I got back from the pub I lay awake on my perfectly comfortable camp bed for hours despite being exhausted, thinking about things.

Just why is everyone trying to put me off having a baby? I mused. I'm very fit, everything still works (as far as I know) and I fail to see why a child should be such a tie. After all, I was very happy with Pops and Jaynie when my parents went off to do their own thing, and I have lots of people I could park mine with (park and ride) if I wanted to.

Or I could take it with me on my travels, which would probably be very good for it.

There's the problem of finding a suitable sperm donor before August and the big Four-O, of course, and since my preference runs to dark-haired men I'd probably feel more drawn to a dark-haired child. I need someone who won't try to interfere afterwards, too.

It's a pity Simon is blond, because it would have been very convenient – though on second thoughts if Mu and I both got pregnant and had matching babies it would be a bit hard to explain.

It *could* be quite tricky finding a sperm donor . . . all the decent men I know are married, and you can't simply request to borrow someone's husband, or even just their sperm.

Unless it was my friend Tom Mac, perhaps (who writes all those really erotic fantasy books), because he's so fertile his wife would probably be glad if I removed some. But however dark and attractive he is, in a Charles Stuart sort of way, he's shorter than me and that is somehow a bar. Whose genes would win out?

I'll put him on the reserve list.

Maybe before Big F Day in August I'll find someone so attractive I'll do it the traditional way, though I've never been one for sudden impulses. And nowadays you have to think about Aids and stuff, which is so unromantic: but then, so is the clap and herpes . . .

I fell asleep trying to formulate a polite phrase of enquiry into a potential donor's medical status. It was tricky.

Chapter 8

Egged On

I had intended taking a week or two off writing in order to sort out the cottage, but old habits die hard, and I found myself leaping out of bed at five ready to work next morning, despite the exhausting day before.

By fiddling with the mechanics of the dentist's chair I achieved a reclining position of maximum comfort from which to dictate the next episode of *Dark Destinies: Deathless Delights*, which seemed to be taking off in unexpected directions.

At seven I stopped for breakfast, which is when I discovered that Miranda had pushed a note through my letter box at some time during the night.

Dear Sappho,

I'm putting this through your door because I can't live with my conscience any more, especially when you've been so good to me. I just have to tell you. I'm sure Mu knows already, although she's never said anything.

It's this: remember the day Dave sprung a surprise engagement party, and you turned and left him flat the second he tried to present you with the ring? I felt sort of sorry for him, and you didn't come back, and he – well, I suppose you knew I always had a bit of a crush on him. I'm not attempting to excuse myself. What I'm trying to say is that I had a bit too much to drink and ended up in bed with him that night.

The baby I lost just after I married Chris was probably Dave's. There, I've never said anything about it to anyone before (especially Chris) and the guilt has been enormous. I'm such a worm. I'm sorry, Sappho, and I'll understand if you never want to see me again.

Miranda

Honestly, bottling that up all this time – and quite point-lessly, too. Dave's main defects were his inability to keep his trousers on or his mouth shut about his conquests. I scribbled a postcard back:

7 a.m. I already knew most of that, you dimwit, though it does explain why you married a little twerp like Chris. See you later for posy packing.

Love, Sappho

When I walked down and popped it through her letter box I could hear Spike's snores reverberating.

At least, I hoped it was Spike.

The village slept under a crystalline coating of dewdrops. Wrapping my hair around my neck twice for warmth, I carried on past The Hacienda and up on to the moors, following the track past the cromlech – a sort of a giant stone table, minus, I'm told, the burial that once gave the village its name – and back down again into the lane just beyond my house.

There was probably still time to get another couple of hours of *Vengeane* in before there was any possibility of the furniture from Portugal arriving.

The idea of giant stones and tombs had rather got me going again . . .

'Come,' said Dragonslayer, 'I have discovered the Place of Stones that I thought was but a legend, and you must lend your strength to mine before the Ancestors will speak to me.'

I was already on Planet Vengeane as I turned into my gate, which is why the voice suddenly addressing me from behind the hedge nearly sent me into orbit, but it *was* an exceptionally high, carrying voice.

'Hello, there!' A head covered in lavender-blue pin curls popped up on a neck like a stiff twist of pink rope.

I noticed for the first time that the hedge now sported a radical haircut extending to a point halfway between us: the lopsided Mohican look.

'You must be our new neighbour? Wait, and I'll come round!' she announced, and a moment later a tall, thin, elderly lady clad in pinkish tweeds and large pearls strode through the gate, hand outstretched.

'Sappho Jones? So pleased to meet you. How exciting to have a Real Author living next door! Pansy and Lavender will be so pleased. My sisters, you know. I'm Violet Duke.'

'I thought you must be – Miranda Cotter told me about you,' I said as my hand was enfolded in a wiry clasp. 'I'll feel a little less isolated now I know I have neighbours.'

'We've been away, you know, visiting our youngest sister, Lily, in Australia. Quite an adventure.'

Good grief – if they arrived back only last night and already knew my name and that I was a writer, the local grapevine must be super-efficient.

It was. 'Dear Gilbert – have you met Gilbert Ace? – kept us

up to date with what has been happening in Bedd during our absence. And last night he collected us from the airport and drove us home. Such a sweet boy – his mother was one of my oldest friends. And poor Dorinda! If only I'd been home at the time, I might have been able to prevent her disappearance in some way.'

'How do you mean?' I asked, puzzled.

'I'm not precisely sure, dear, but I got to know Dorinda very well while we were taking evening classes in computer studies together, and she's a very forceful woman. I could at least have assured the police that she would never have done anything so weak as to lose her memory and wander off.'

'Then what do you think did happen to her? An accident?'

'More than likely, for she was convinced that there was another bone cave in the Gower cliffs still to be found, one even more spectacular than that of the Red Lady of Paviland. You do know about the Red Lady, Miss Jones?'

'Yes, and didn't the bones turn out to be a man's?'

'That's right – so amusing! And Dorinda was systematically searching for another cave, but she had a secretive nature – a dislike of sharing the limelight, I'd call it – so she wouldn't even confide in poor Gil about the areas she was covering. I told her it could be dangerous, so if she did have an accident it is quite her own fault that no one knew where she was.'

She paused and looked at me triumphantly – and she wasn't even out of breath.

'But Miranda says her car was never found,' I pointed out.

'Well, I could be quite wrong,' Violet said cheerfully. 'It could be Foul Play.'

'You mean Gilbert—'

'Oh, not Gilbert! I didn't mean *Gilbert*. Absolutely out of the question! He's such a sweet-natured boy and he absolutely adored Dorinda. And it wasn't that nice potter, Nye Thomas, from the craft centre either,' she added to my surprise. 'Lavender knows him quite well, and she said he couldn't possibly. He may have argued with Dorinda over his little chalet being an eyesore, it's true, but nothing more. Besides, he looks so like an angel he couldn't possibly be bad.'

'I don't think all murderers are ugly men,' I suggested. And Lavender was quite wrong about the potter, if that was him I tried to drown in mud, because he looked a far remove from angelic.

'Perhaps not, but in this case I trust Lavender's judgement. No, if it was Foul Play one of those Strange Men must have come across Dorinda when she was alone on the cliffs.' She looked at me triumphantly. 'They're always ready to take their chance, you know.'

'I'll bear it in mind.'

'One flashed at me when I was collecting driftwood only last autumn. He was wearing a wool overcoat, which must have been terribly itchy – and serve him right. He said: "Cop a load of this!" '

I choked slightly. 'How awful! What did you do?'

'I just said: "Not today, thank you, young man," and walked on.'

'That must have depressed his pretensions.'

'I expect the cold wind already had,' she remarked drily, and then added with a sudden change of subject: 'Like gardening?'

'No.'

'No?' she repeated.

'Not at all, though I like sitting in one with a drink on a nice day.'

'Oh?' She regarded me curiously, for obviously I was some

strange breed she hadn't previously come across. 'Well, you're a writer, aren't you – don't suppose they go in for it much. My sister Lavender does most of ours, but we all give a hand and – oh, here are Lavender and Pansy now.'

Lavender was squat and puffy-necked like an amiable toad, while Pansy, the painter and decorator, was a stocky competent-looking woman with short white hair and matching overalls. She gave me a firm handshake, barked that she was pleased to meet me, but must get off to a job, and with no more ado wobbled off on a heavily loaded pushbike and trailer, holding a stepladder under one arm.

'Bye-ee!' chorused her sisters, staring fondly after her and waving until she vanished towards the village. I hoped she had good brakes, because it can't be easy cornering with a ladder under one arm.

'I've got a goitre,' confided Lavender, adjusting a wet hen kind of hat as though she might find an egg under it.

'Yes,' I agreed, for I'd been trying not to let my eyes rest on this fairly spectacular (and surely unnecessary?) affliction. 'So you have.'

'It's a gift from God,' she explained, while behind her back Violet grimaced and made unkind finger-to-temple motions.

'He moves in mysterious ways,' I said.

'Would you like me to cut your side of the hedge? I do gardening, you know, but not heavy digging. I'll give you my little information sheet – and Pansy's, too, though I expect you've already done most of your painting and decorating. And Violet—'

'Yes, I was going to ask about that.' I turned to Violet: 'You do secretarial work, don't you?'

'Typing, computers, anything!'

'It's my books – I still dictate most of them on to tape, but I

87

write some parts in longhand as well, so it's all rather scrappy. I'd love someone who could type them up for me, so I could make alterations easily.'

'I could put them on to the computer,' she said efficiently. 'Then print them out. It's so easy to change things on the computer. The old days of three carbons and lashings of Tippex are long gone.'

'I see,' I said appreciatively and, leaving Lavender clipping my side of the hedge in a dainty yet efficient manner, took Violet inside to arrange terms.

Treasure trove: graphite transmuted into gold.

Later, after Violet had left carrying the first instalments of *Dark Destinies: Deathless Delights*, and the Pickford's van had dropped off my Portuguese furnishings, so that the house now looked less as if I was merely camping out in it, I went down to investigate the village shop.

It's really quite extraordinary: an Aladdin's cave of the mundane.

There's no need to go further afield unless you mind paying slightly more than the big supermarkets, or object to being given a verbal third degree by the proprietor, Llyn.

When I emerged I was carrying a tin of white emulsion, brushes and sundry edibles to keep me going, including six free-range eggs in a thin brown paper bag, which I clutched precariously to my chest.

This necessitated my backing out of the swing doors, and when I turned round I found myself unexpectedly nose-to-T-shirt with a customer about to come in. There was an ominous scrunch and something cold and glutinous came between us.

I fell back and gawped at him, and you can understand

why: he was much taller than I – six foot six, at a guess – no Schwarzenegger, but broad in the shoulder and chest, slim-hipped and long-legged. He had a mane of white-gold curly hair, a cleft chin, and light, almost colourless eyes, like crystal. If Lucifer in *Paradise Lost* had looked half as beautiful, you would have expected all the other angels to defect to his side *en masse*: come on down, the price is right.

Yes, he was more like Dragonslayer than Dragonslayer – it was scary – but I was not about to be unnerved merely because my characters were escaping from my novels and destroying my groceries. Thank goodness I hadn't dropped the rum.

'Sorry,' I snapped brusquely, 'but you should have seen me coming. I think you've broken all my eggs.'

There was no reply, so I looked up (and up) to see him staring at me through narrowed eyes, which were turning a sort of angry leaden colour – very odd. I was beginning to wish I hadn't invented him, or had made him a little blond wimp instead.

From that grainy old photo Lili sent me I'd assumed he was just the usual blue-eyed blond. Anyone who knew him and read the book would recognize him . . . so I could only hope he didn't read fantasy.

I gave him a glance of acute dislike and he looked taken aback.

'Aren't you the woman who tried to drown me in mud yesterday, and – what's the matter?' he added, in a curious voice, and I snapped out of my appalled trance and stepped back.

'Nothing. I'm perfectly all right, which is more than I can say for my eggs. Sorry about the T-shirt, but you should look where you're going.'

The bag still dripped in a disagreeably viscous way on to my bare feet, but there might be survivors.

'I'm sorry my T-shirt presumed to cross your path,' he said sarcastically.

'Can't make an omelette without breaking eggs!' chortled the plumber cheerily, edging past our little tableau.

I eyed him with disfavour and said severely: 'I'll see *you* next Wednesday!'

His smile vanished and he scuttled into the shop.

'Perhaps you'd like to let me into the shop too? Unless you'd prefer to toss some other noxious substance over me first?' suggested Dragonslayer nastily.

No, not Dragonslayer – merely a potter, and an irate one at that. But all I'd done was splash mud and eggs over him, and a man who spends his days making mud pies shouldn't quibble at that.

For a moment I contemplated explaining the muddy road incident, but the sight of him towering over me, muscular arms crossed over his besmirched chest and frowning, just irritated the hell out of me.

'You seem to have covered yourself in clay already,' I pointed out, for he was liberally decorated in grey splashes from head to foot, including a diagonal stripe across one side of his nose.

And since his T-shirt had a Turner painting on the front that was also blown-egg coloured, you couldn't really see the stains I might have added.

But instead of saying so in my usual fashion, I found myself moving around him as though he was contagious and making off.

Towering over her weakened form Dragonslayer stared angrily down at Nala, his arms folded across his broad chest . . .

Was it too late to change him into the villain and redeem Raarg?

I needed a hero.

'Why,' I enquired of Miranda after our first Sunday car boot sale in the company of Llyn Smith, owner of the village shop, 'does Llyn have two l's and pronounce her name like a Welsh swearword, when she's a Brummie? And why on earth did she call her children Rhubarb and Aphid?'

'Astrid and Rhiannon,' murmured Miranda absently, flicking through an ancient and tattered recipe book, one of several she'd purchased earlier. Then she looked up, smiling happily. There was a smudge of mud on her forehead and her fingers were grubby.

'Llyn's b-been here five years, and she's so d-determined to fit in that she goes to extremes.'

'Like the Technicolor handwoven Welsh tweeds?'

'Worse – in high tourist season she wears full traditional costume with the red cape and b-big b-black hat. She's taking Welsh language classes, too. She might have gone a b-bit over the top b-but she means well.'

'The road to hell is paved with good intentions,' I said. 'Still, I have to hand it to her, she's got a good eye for a bargain.' Llyn's estate car, which I was following, carried a Welsh dresser strapped to its roof rack that would set an antique dealer swooning.

Car boot sales may prove to be addictive, for as well as purchasing useful things like curtain poles, I seem also to have acquired what can only be described as junk, like a peacock basket chair and a camel saddle stool slightly leaking its stuffing.

Miranda had bought lots of weird old kitchen utensils as

well as the cookbooks, and the back of the Volvo car was pretty laden, what with all that plus Spike, who was lying on a crocheted afghan disseminating odour of smelly old dog.

'It's b-been such fun today,' she sighed happily. 'And tomorrow there may b-be some flower orders to d-do, though I'm sure there would be lots more if we put one or two little adverts in the right places.'

'If *you* put one or two adverts,' I said. 'It's your business now.'

'If I got more orders I'd have to find a b-bigger workspace quickly,' she mused. 'I wonder how much renting one of the studios at the craft centre costs. Though I'd only use it in the mornings, of course.'

'Why don't we go and have a look one day?' I suggested. 'I haven't been there yet.'

'All right. D-did you know that Lili Ford Jakes is chasing one of the craftsmen from the centre in the most b-blatant way? He's the most handsome man I've ever seen, and it's odd but he reminds me of D-Dragonslayer, that d-dishy new man in your last novel—'

'I've already bumped into him,' I interrupted hastily. 'He's really nothing like him – and Dragonslayer isn't dishy.'

But if Miranda recognized the description . . .?

With a sigh, I explained the coincidence, only hoping I wouldn't one day have to do the same to an irate potter.

That afternoon I saw Miranda in the village chatting to a small bearded man who rather pointedly turned and made off long before I got there. I guessed it was Gilbert Ace before she told me.

I hoped he soon recovered from his pique over my buying the cottage, for the Gower is too small to go on avoiding people all the time.

I suspected he and Miranda of being a bit soft on each other. Gil sounded malleable and even more persuadable than Miranda, so I thought they might do each other good if I got rid of Chris, though I'd need to discover what happened to Disappearing Dorinda first.

In fact I ought to be getting on with it, because it might be the bad-tempered potter instead, and I'm quite fond of Lili – or fond enough not to wish her to vanish permanently.

For some reason I seemed to be avoiding little white vans.

I wondered what Nye is short for . . .

Chapter 9

Chris Cross

Dear 'teenage fan',

Go wash your mind out with (cold) soapy water.

And no, the photograph on the back of my books isn't recent, it was taken years ago. I am now a wizened old crone.

Sappho Jones

After only a couple of weeks in Bedd, life had begun to drift into a comfortable pattern. It's very seductive, this settling down business.

Every morning I woke early, had two hours of *Dark Destinies: Deathless Delights*, went for a walk – often along the cliffs at Rhossili – then worked on the book again.

Miranda let herself into the cottage at some point in the morning to sort out any Fantasy Flowers orders, posting the result *en route* to The Hacienda for an afternoon of recipe devising. Mu was already doing extra illustrations for the new edition of *The Stuffed Student*, which she said she'd bring with her when she came down.

My early chapters of *Dark Destinies: Deathless Delights* had already been deciphered and printed out by the amazing

Violet, who was now reading all the *Vengeane* books from the start to get a feel for my style.

Quite often I had lunch at the pub, which saved my having to cook anything later, and maybe Lili would turn up, or Miranda would come with me, although she was very critical of the cooking. The only lunch Lili seemed to eat was the olive in her dry martini, but I thought her slightly haggard appearance was due to the lack of progress she was making with her potter.

'All that wet clay is so sexy, somehow,' she confided one day soon after my second encounter with her intended prey. 'I don't know why, unless it's the slippery moistness? And why is he so resistant to my charms? I mean, with his last girlfriend turning out to be gay, you'd think he'd be grateful for someone totally heterosexual showing an interest in him.'

'What do you mean, his last girlfriend was gay?'

'It's true, Sappho. Remember I told you about when I first saw him at the craft show, arguing with his ex-girlfriend? Well, apparently they'd been together since art college, only she prefers living in London and he didn't, so it sort of dwindled down to weekends and so on. But then she moved in with a female friend and ditched Nye.'

'That doesn't make her a lesbian, though, Lili,' I said patiently.

'No, but listen: while I was in Greece she came down here and had a flaming row with Nye, and the upshot was she went straight back to London. So when I heard about it, I wondered if she was trying to get him back, so I thought I'd go and see her on the pretext of being interested in the hand knitting. I meant to tell her to stop jerking him around if she didn't really want him, so he was free for someone else. But when I found the house she was just coming out, and she and this other woman had a goodbye smooch on the doorstep.'

'You mean a real smooch sort of smooch, not just an affectionate hug and kiss between friends?'

'A real one. But the interesting thing is that although his ex-girlfriend is small, dark and skinny, she either had a healthy tapeworm, or a bun in the oven.'

'Is it Nye's, do you think? Perhaps that was what she wanted to talk to him about.'

'I asked him, and he said definitely not, but he isn't very forthcoming on the subject of the old girlfriend – Eloise, her name is. In fact, he's gone into a complete bad-tempered gloom – unless he's always like that.'

'Perhaps he still loved her, so when she dumped him, it came as a big shock?'

'I suppose so, but at least now I know why he's gloomy, so it gives me a handle on things – I'm being all friendly and supportive and applying balm to his soul and I'm willing to apply it to any other bits he wants, too. I'll sneak up on him eventually – provided the police don't arrest him.'

'They're not likely to, are they?' I asked.

'He does seem to have been the last person to see Dorinda Ace – you do know about the missing Dorinda, don't you? Nye lives in one of half a dozen decaying Victorian chalets in a field called Preece's Plot. Dorinda's a councillor, and they'd just given permission for redevelopment of the site. Nye had a real ding-dong row with her about it, and she hasn't been seen since. The police had him in for questioning, but they're more interested in Dorinda's husband, Gil, who's this quite cute but drippy little man – but so was Crippen. Reading between the lines, he was Miranda's childhood sweetheart. Isn't Miranda *huge*? Greenpeace should campaign to protect her with the other whales.'

'We don't *all* want to be lollipop women with big heads and emaciated bodies,' I retorted unkindly, when I could get a word in, though Lili is not that skinny; she does have a figure. 'Your potter seems to have a bad temper. Don't you think you ought to be careful, in case he did something to her?'

'He says she just drove off in high dudgeon after the row, though you couldn't blame anyone for doing her in, because she sounded a horribly bossy, overbearing sort of woman – a history lecturer and an authority on ancient burials on the Gower. Too dreary for words. Maybe it was the henpecked house-husband?'

'Or perhaps she just took herself off. Miranda said they never found her car,' I suggested.

Lili lost interest in Dorinda. 'It's time Nye cheered up and found himself a new girlfriend – me. It's getting very frustrating, though at least because of him I bought my cottage in the trendiest place of the moment, before prices absolutely went through the roof.'

'I've . . . bumped into your potter once or twice,' I confessed cautiously.

She grinned rather maliciously. 'I know. As soon as he described this madwoman who tried to drown him in mud and eggs, I told him you were an eccentric who wrote fantasy novels. He sort of assumed Sappho was your pen name, and you were writing gay fiction, so I didn't disillusion him, because I don't want him getting too interested in you.'

'Thank you, Lili, but he was probably only interested in me in a "where does she live so I can go and kill her" way.'

'I don't know . . .' she said thoughtfully, 'but anyway, if you've got Dave Devlyn on a string, you don't need Nye.'

'You can have *him* as well; I don't want either of them.'

'Simple, then – tell the dishy photographer you're gay, then point him in my direction.'

'Yes, Lili, but he knows very well that I'm not,' I said patiently. 'Besides, I have enough trouble with people assuming I chose the name Sappho because of that connection, and wasn't just christened with it.'

'Like Nye – and it really did the trick, though actually he seems to have been boringly faithful to his dismal hand-knitted Eloise while they were together – and all he talks about now is his work. It's unnatural.'

'Maybe he loved her and his ego's so dented his libido has sunk without trace?'

'Mine certainly will, at this rate,' she said gloomily. 'But I know I'm his type – small, dark and slim – I just have to get him to notice me.'

He'd certainly noticed me, but I didn't think that's quite what Lili had in mind.

I'd never seen a man resist a full-frontal assault by Lili before. Things could get interesting if she stepped up the campaign.

As the next Chris Cotter-infested weekend approached, Miranda became more and more distracted, and I just hoped all my good work independence-instilling and backbone-infusing wouldn't be wasted.

But it wouldn't really surprise me if she buckled right back down to slave mentality and I had to start all over again on the following Monday.

On Friday morning she came and did the flower orders so quickly I only knew she'd been by the lingering odour of Old Dog when I got back from my walk.

She'd left me a note though.

Have to rush back and start cooking food for usual party tomorrow night, but will be in early tomorrow to do any flower orders. Plastic box in fridge has pilaff for you to try – new recipe for *Feeding the Party Animal*! I thought you could have it tonight and tell me what you think? Reheating instructions on box.

Love, Miranda

So she wasn't completely buckling down, then? That was a hopeful sign.

I nearly missed her again on the Saturday morning – she'd crept around so early I was still reclining on the lounger, trying to beat Dragonslayer into submission.

Nala seemed to be a trifle nervous of Dragonslayer: I thought it disconcerted her that he was so much bigger and more powerful than herself when she wasn't used to it, but he needn't think he was going to get things all his own way.

'Dragonslayer felt the dark shadow of foreboding touch his mind and shivered: what could be coming to threaten him – or those he held dear?'

When I heard Miranda I popped my head round the conservatory door and said: 'I loved the pilaff. You should definitely use that one.'

She jumped, dropping a handful of pinks ('always lovely').

'H-hello, Sappho. I hope I d-didn't d-disturb you? I'm a b-bit early, b-but I have to get b-back to cook Chris's b-breakfast.'

'Isn't it a bit tragic that a TV chef can't cook his own breakfast?' I asked.

'He got in very late last night, Sappho – and he d-drives d-down. It's a long way. Anyway, lots of people are coming round tonight and I've got to get things ready. I hope you're going to come too? Lili usually d-does – Chris d-doesn't really like her, b-but she knows absolutely *everyone*.'

'She certainly gets about,' I agreed. 'And it's kind of you to ask me, Miranda, but I'm not much of a party animal and Chris doesn't like *me*, either!'

'I like you,' she said stoutly, 'and Chris will have to get used to your b-being here, won't he?'

Or not, as the case may be, I thought. Miranda may have weakened a bit but she was still showing faint signs of independence, which he certainly wouldn't like and would lay at my door.

'I'll see how I feel later,' I said. 'But Dragonslayer is getting awfully uppity and I may have to sort him out tonight. And it's time Raarg had a resurgence.'

Speaking of which, there was still no sign of Dave resurging into my life. Could he have finally given up? How ironic if he had, just when I'd finally settled within his reach!

In the event my visitor that afternoon was almost as unwelcome as Dave would have been: Cookie Chris turned up unannounced on my doorstep.

I let him in, but only as far as the kitchen, not wanting my inner sanctum besmirched.

Predictably, he'd come to order me to leave Miranda alone. Striking a pose by the cooker he said I was a bad influence, and had even almost convinced her that he – Chris! – had done all the odd things that had been happening, not her.

Also, she really wasn't up to running any kind of business, so that it was unfair of me to dump one into her lap and expect her to take it on . . . and more to that effect.

I just folded my arms and looked down at him while he ran his course, but when he added that he'd told Miranda not to associate with me any more, and I was not welcome in his house, I said I'd no intention of ever visiting his house, but Miranda's was another thing entirely.

Then I added kindly that he could have saved himself the trouble of visiting me, because all his little machinations were totally transparent, and he slammed out.

It's a pity I don't have one of those hidden cameras, because I could probably get good money for film of smiley old TV chef Chris Cotter throwing a wobbler.

Of course, after this I was quite tempted to turn up at the party just for the hell of it, but any unpleasantness would upset Miranda, so I decided just to carry on with the insidious influences when he'd gone back to London.

I didn't see Miranda again until Monday morning, when I deduced from the dark circles under her eyes and her hunted, anxious expression that as far as she was concerned the weekend hadn't been one long round of delirious pleasure.

'How was the party?' I asked. 'I had lunch yesterday with Lili at her cottage – a very bijou des res – and she said she persuaded her potter to go to the party with her, but when they got there and she finally made her move, he recoiled with horror. She was very put out.'

'Oh, I wish you'd come, Sappho – it was d-dire! What with Chris saying horrible things to me in a kind voice as though I were a half-witted child, and Nye trying to avoid Lili, and Lili getting plastered . . .' Miranda shuddered. 'And then Gil was d-depressed b-because the police had him in again for questioning about D-Dorinda.'

'Sorry I missed it,' I said sincerely, for it sounded more interesting than I'd expected. 'But I thought I'd better not, because Chris isn't too pleased to have me back. I mean, just think what amazing depths you've sunk to already due to my influence – running your own business, writing your own recipe books, going to car boot sales . . . It's all a positive orgy of depravity.'

'It's an orgy of d-delight,' Miranda corrected me. 'And d-do you know, I think I've b-been losing weight, too! My clothes feel sort of loose.'

'That's hardly surprising – you've been so busy rushing here and there lately that even Spike looks slimmer. So – are you going to carry on, or do what Chris wants and give up Fantasy Flowers, stop seeing me, stop writing your own cookbooks and only write his?'

She sat up straight and a slightly martial gleam came into her soft blue eyes. 'No, I'm not! He's quite wrong about me – I feel b-better than I have for years! And although he said that my even *suspecting* him of d-doing those odd things, like the koi in the freezer, showed that I was b-batty, I'm not sure . . .'

'Of course he did them,' I assured her. 'You're saner than I am.'

She seemed to accept my judgement, and we settled back into our routine perfectly happily until the following Saturday (mercifully a Chris-free zone), when she burst in upon me mid-*Deathless Delights* in a state of almost mindless panic.

'Sappho,' she cried. 'Something else happened yesterday, something really strange – and Chris couldn't have d-done it this time, and—'

'Calm down,' I said soothingly, 'and tell me all about it, but slowly. And for goodness' sake, *sit*!'

She subsided, panting, though at least not with her tongue hanging out like Spike.

'Yesterday morning, after I'd got home from here, a woman came to the d-door and said she was delivering the clothes I'd

102

ordered the day b-before – a lot of clothes – from an expensive shop in Swansea.'

'Well, that doesn't seem too scary. *Did* you order any clothes?'

'No, I d-didn't. B-but the thing is, Sappho, they were all size ten, and I haven't b-b-been a size ten for years . . . and they were lovely clothes, the sort of things I might have ordered if I was still slim.'

'A straightforward mistake, delivered to the wrong address?' I suggested. 'But I suppose that's the first thing you checked?'

'Yes, and it was clearly my name and address on the d-delivery note. The woman d-didn't know anything – she was an assistant, and she was d-delivering them as a favour, b-because they normally d-didn't d-do that.'

'What about the shop? Did you phone them?'

'Yes, I got the manageress, and she was very polite, b-but clearly thought I was mad as a hatter! She said the woman who'd b-bought them gave my name, and was small and very plump, with b-blonde hair, and she thought she must b-be b-buying the things for her d-daughter as a surprise. She paid a lot extra to have them d-delivered to my address.'

'When did she say the woman ordered the clothes?'

'Just the d-day before – the Thursday. And I always go into Swansea on Thursdays, to the supermarket.'

I tried to remember . . . 'Did you go in as usual last Thursday?'

'No, that's just it! I popped in here first thing – there was just that b-big b-bouquet to d-do, the unrequited love and jealousy one.'

I nodded. 'Yes, I remember that – it was then I realized you were much better at it than Mu and me.'

'That's kind of you, Sappho, b-but I d-don't think I am.

'B-but anyway, I d-did the order and then d-dropped it in at the post office on the way home to collect my shopping list and leave Spike. Only as soon as I opened the d-door I thought I could smell gas, so I called Spike and went and phoned the gas people up from next d-door, and they came out and there was a leak. Then it was too late to go anywhere.'

'You didn't tell me about that – but at least it proves it definitely couldn't have been you, doesn't it?'

'Yes . . . but I b-began to d-doubt . . . I mean, last night I got to thinking about it: there were the other strange things that happened, and it was my usual d-day for shopping, so I b-began to wonder if I had gone in after all and imagined the rest. And, Sappho, this one can't have b-been Chris, b-because he couldn't d-disguise himself as a b-blonde woman, could he?'

'No, but he'd have no problem sending someone down for the day. Miranda, I'm positive he's behind all this. It's a control thing now, to stop you showing any independence. Face him with it and see what he says.'

'Oh, I couldn't! And h-he wouldn't have played a trick like that, surely, b-because i-it's cruel. I-it's b-beyond a joke.'

'That's because it was never meant to be a joke. And yes, it is cruel, and it's been thought up by someone close to you, like the other things. Who else could have got the fish and put them in the freezer, for instance? Look, you're going to London on Monday to see your editor, aren't you? Why not go round to the house and have it out with Chris afterwards?'

'B-but it's d-different when he's there, Sappho. I always end up b-believing everything he says . . . until afterwards. And he won't b-be there on Monday, b-because—'

She broke off when the doorbell rang in a determined sort of way, and I had to go and answer it.

It was Lili, almost sober.

'Hi!' she said brightly, walking straight past me and into the living room, where she greeted Miranda, then pulled a bottle of gin out of her capacious shoulder bag and looked around vaguely. 'Got any glasses?'

I brought some in, and tonic water, since she was quite capable of drinking it straight from the bottle otherwise, and at least Miranda and I could dilute ours.

Lili coiled herself on one end of the slippery settee and downed a glassful with a contented sigh.

'Saw you with your admirer yesterday,' she said to Miranda, who was sitting primly on the other end of the sofa.

'Admirer? What d-do you mean?'

'Gil, the possible wife murderer. Of course, Nye might have done it, but it all adds a certain edge to their fascination, don't you find?'

'D-don't be silly,' Miranda said, going a bit pink. 'Gil is certainly no murderer, and he isn't my admirer, just a child-hood friend who's been going through a really b-bad time lately. First he thought he was going to inherit this cottage, and his wife made so much fuss about it when he d-didn't that he nearly had a nervous b-breakdown – he's terribly sensitive. Then D-Dorinda d-disappeared and he's really only just start-ing to get b-back on his feet again – she used to run his life for him. And I'm sure Nye Thomas wouldn't kill D-Dorinda just b-because she wanted to knock the chalets d-down and expand the golf course.'

'He might have done if she was wearing one of those horrible golfing outfits – the Head Girl at the Chalet School look?' I suggested flippantly. 'Or the Rupert Bear men's version. Wearing either of those should be severely punished.'

'Yes,' agreed Lili enthusiastically, 'some of those trousers are verging on the Bay City Rollers, and that's a check too far.'

'It's not funny,' Miranda said reproachfully. 'Think of poor D-Dorinda.'

'Probably got tired of Gil and ran off,' I said.

'Yes, he's not very exciting,' agreed Lili. 'But as long as she doesn't turn up in Nye's garden I don't really care.' She gulped half her drink and added, 'Did Sappho tell you all about Greece, Miranda? I don't know why I go out there every year. There are never any decent men, and Bob's gone so stuffy: said I was giving middle-aged British women a bad name. Cheek! Me – middle-aged!'

She took another long pull of gin. 'One of the Creative Breakers was this funny little fat man and he kept making passes at Sappho. Then he tried to book an extra week so he could do my course, only his wife had a dicky fit and hauled him off, thank God. And Sappho went away for a week with Mu Greythorpe to climb hills and eat candles.'

'Candles?' said Miranda blankly, and I sat bolt upright and glared.

'How did you know that?'

'Why, was it a secret? I haven't told anyone about it, don't worry,' she said.

'It wasn't candles either, but lamp wick.'

She shrugged. 'Candles, lamp wick – weird.' She turned back to Miranda: 'It's some sort of fertility rite, apparently.'

'It's supposed to be,' I agreed reluctantly, for I didn't want Mu's problems spread far and wide – especially when she and Simon might soon be coming together *à la* baster under this very roof.

Miranda stared at me. 'B-but you d-don't want to get pregnant, d-do you? Really? I assumed you were joking!'

'I hadn't thought of it at the time. I went because Mu wanted to,' I said.

'Well, if Mu can't get pregnant it must be her fault, because there's nothing wrong with that big blond hunk she married,' Lili said thoughtfully.

'Lili – you haven't—' I began furiously.

'Keep your knickers on,' she said equably. 'No, I haven't – though I would if he would!'

I thought 'keep your knickers on' was pretty good coming from Lili, who probably mostly didn't bother wearing them.

'No, I meant he just *looks* sexy. But I assumed he and Mu didn't want children – like you and Chris, Miranda.'

'M-me? Oh, no – we wanted children, b-but they d-didn't come along . . . and it must b-be my fault b-because women are so much more complicated than men, aren't they? Chris went to a clinic and had a sperm count and everything, and he was fine.'

'Did he?' Lili sounded surprised. 'He had his vasectomy reversed, then?'

'Vasectomy? He never had a vasectomy, Lili!'

Her eyes gleamed with the bright malicious pleasure of the born stirrer. 'Oh, yes, he did – didn't you know? He was in at the same time as my first husband, Kevin, years ago. A private clinic in London. Well, well!'

Miranda went so pale I thought she was going to pass out, and Lili must have thought so too, for she leaped up and rammed the gin bottle between Miranda's teeth and tilted it until she began to cough and choke.

There's nothing like having your throat cauterized with neat spirits to bring you back from the brink of gibbering hysteria.

'What a bastard, not telling you,' Lili said, regarding the

spluttering, choking Miranda with the satisfaction of a job well done. 'You should have his balls.'

'Looks like someone already has,' I pointed out, diluting Miranda's glass with lots of tonic and handing it to her.

She gulped it down, then looked piteously at me and quavered, 'How could he let me think . . .? All these years? And those tests I had too – some of them quite horrible – where they pump stuff through your tubes.'

And there was the lost baby that was probably Dave's, too, which must have made her even guiltier when no more came along.

'Get your revenge, darling,' Lili urged her bracingly. 'Go out and screw everything in sight. It's not too late for a baby, is it?'

Miranda sniffled, her eyes still watering from gin and emotion. 'N-no. I'm thirty-nine b-but I suppose I could still. B-but who would want someone this huge?'

'That's a point,' Lili conceded, and I glared at her.

'Anyway, I think I've lost the urge for b-babies now. I'd rather have d-dogs.'

'Right,' agreed Lili, and added enviously: 'And you're only thirty-nine! Wish I was: so many men, so little time! And I'm getting nowhere fast with Nye. He's OK with the loving-balm-on-his-wounds stuff, but any hint of passion and he's off. It's terribly frustrating.'

She dipped into her capacious bag again and fished out a sheet of newspaper, which she unfolded and shoved under my nose. 'Look.' She indicated some highlighted parts with one blood-red talon.

'Heart Lines?' I said dubiously. 'You haven't taken to answering ads like that, have you, Lili?'

'It's just a bit of fun to pass the time while I work my wiles on Nye. See this one?'

'"Randy tup seeks little ewe lamb for frisks"?' I said dubiously.

'No, not that one – though it's a possibility. Look there.'

The next one down read: 'Dark Lady seeks vigorous input.'

I blinked. 'Strange way of phrasing it.'

'It's me – I put that one in, and I've had nine replies already!' She pulled a handful of letters from her bag, and a photo fluttered out, coming to rest, face up, on the carpet.

She picked it up and brandished it. 'I asked for photos and this one sent me a picture of his equipment!'

Something like a flaccid pink sausage had been laid alongside a ruler, and assuming that it wasn't a trick ruler, you'd get quite a lot of money if you charged by the inch. Width-wise, if it was a hot dog I'd ask for my money back.

It was the sort of thing that made you wonder where on earth the description 'horny' came from: I mean, what's horn-like about willies? In my – admittedly limited – experience they tend to look more like malformed sticks of rhubarb.

'Lili, you aren't really going to meet any of these, are you? Especially this one – you'd only recognize him in a nudist camp. It could be dangerous. Who knows what sort of oddball answers this sort of ad? And what about your potter?'

'I'm just dying for a bit of excitement; this is only a little diversion to while away the time. I'm not serious.'

'Random sex with a stranger is a *diversion*?'

'Only if I really fancy them. Don't look so revolted, Sappho, we're not all made like nuns, you know.'

'Evidently.'

'Meet in a public place first,' suggested Miranda sensibly. 'Somewhere where you can see him b-before he sees you, and then if he's awful you can go away again.'

She'd picked up the photo and was studying it closely.

I tend to forget she had her own random sex phase at university, and has therefore had more rhubarb than I've had hot dinners.

'I d-don't think much of *that*,' she commented critically.

Chapter 10

Loosely Basted

The morning after her London trip Miranda phoned me up early to ask, in a tear-sodden voice, if I could do any flower orders again that morning, because she wasn't feeling too good.

'What's the matter?' I demanded. 'Did you ask Chris about the vasectomy when you were in town yesterday?'

'N-no, b-because I wasn't sure Lili had got it right, when I'd had time to think about it. Anyway, Chris wasn't supposed to b-be there, and – and I can't talk just now, Sappho.' There was a gulp and muffled sob. 'I'll see you tomorrow.'

She saw me sooner than that, for ten minutes later I was at The Hacienda, demanding to know what had happened.

'Oh, Sappho!' she wailed, wringing her hands. 'I promised Chris I wouldn't talk about it to anyone, b-b-but I'm so miserable – I feel I'm going to explode or something! I just don't know what to d-d-do . . .'

'I *always* know what to do,' I assured her as she crammed a large piece of chocolate fudge cake into her mouth and became incoherent. Spike whiffled round her feet, inhaling crumbs.

'I should have smelled a rat when he suggested I move

111

'd-down here,' she said bitterly when her mouth was temporarily disengaged. 'He wouldn't have let me out of his sight b-before I put all this weight on and now he's ashamed of me.'

'Yes, he was always unreasonably jealous. What's he been doing? Or should it be whom?'

'Oh, it was awful, Sappho! After I'd seen my editor I took a taxi to our London house, meaning to collect a few things: the original notebooks for *The Stuffed Student*, and my b-blini pan. I-I knew Chris would b-be away until that evening, so I took his favourite d-dinner d-down with me in a chill b-bag as a surprise when he got home, and I was just about to put it in the fridge when I heard a noise . . .'

She paused, and her eyes filled again. 'I certainly surprised him all right – naked on the B-Bokhara in front of the fireplace in the living room with that food technologist female, Susie!'

'Not a pretty sight?'

'N-no – it was sort of totally unreal, and they b-both leaped up like one of those awful farces while I simply stood there numb from shock, until Susie – who has a gorgeous figure even if her face is all angles, like b-badly folded origami – said, "Oh, look, Chris d-darling – an escaped Great White Whale." '

'The cow.'

'Well, then I completely flipped and threw the d-duck *à l'orange* and the raspberry pavlova at them, and ran out of the house.'

'Well done. There's nothing like a flying duck.'

'That raspberry will never come out of the B-Bokhara,' she wailed.

'Why worry? You'll never want to see it again anyway. So, what did you do then?'

'I came straight home, though I d-don't remember how I

got here. I d-don't remember anything until I'd collected Spike from the neighbours and wept all over him.'

'Why didn't you phone me? I'd have come round.'

'I was going to, but Chris d-drove straight d-down after me – he was there almost as soon as I was. And he was in a complete state, Sappho, he really was. He insisted it was all a mistake and said he was glad I got there b-before anything happened, b-because it had b-been an impulse of the moment with Susie making all the running. And it will never happen again, b-because he really loves me.'

'And I'm Tilly the Tooth Fairy,' I said drily.

'Really, Sappho, he d-does still love me,' she said earnestly. 'Only I'm now so grossly fat it's a real turn-off. It's all my fault for letting myself go, and not making an effort to look nice. I knew he d-didn't want to b-be seen out with me any more, and I d-didn't want anyone to see me either, even you and Mu.'

'Of course Chris's affair isn't your fault, you dumb cluck! The weight is nothing to do with it either: you don't stop loving someone just because they now come in economy size. You're still Miranda, aren't you? The gifted cook, whose perennial best-selling recipe book was written while she was still a student, and who is the real creative mind behind Chris Cotter, TV chef and well-known glove puppet?'

'I-I d-don't know . . . Chris can be so cruel, b-but really he meant to help me whenever he made d-disparaging remarks about my size, although actually they had the opposite effect, because they always made me go away and eat chocolate.'

'He's a manipulator. He's making himself feel better by putting the blame on you, but it's not your fault.'

'Sappho, he *cried* with remorse, and said it would never happen again if I forgave him. And he will try and get d-down most weekends, though to b-be honest, I d-don't see much of him then b-because it always seems to b-be open house on a Saturday night. He's so popular.'

'Anyone prepared to throw a party most weekends is popular. What did he make you promise to do in return?'

'Go on a strict d-diet and b-become the Miranda I used to b-be, the one he was proud of. He says if I really love him I'll lose the weight.'

'Mental cruelty, blackmail and manipulation. Divorce the bastard,' I advised her.

'B-but he d-doesn't mean it like that! We talked for hours . . . and I even asked him about the vasectomy, Sappho, and he said Lili was quite wrong and he'd never have d-deceived me like that.'

'He would.'

'No, I'm sure he was telling the truth . . . only after he'd gone b-back in the early hours of this morning I felt b-bereft, and miserable – and hungry. That girl is only twenty-three, Sappho, and so slim, even if she d-does have a nose so sharp she could drill holes with it and she makes squiggle quotation marks in the air with her fingers when she talks. She varnishes food to make it look pretty for the cameras, so she's always there, while I'm here d-devising fattening recipes for Chris, and feeling miserable.

'And the unhappier I feel, the more I eat, and the fatter I get. And the fatter I get the unhappier I feel, so the more I eat . . . and so on. I'm just one great b-big fat failure. I might as well eat myself to d-death. I *am* eating myself to d-death . . .'

'I absolutely forbid you to eat yourself to death,' I told her firmly. 'I'm going to put you on a diet.'

She sniffled and looked up at me, surprised.

'It's one I got from a romantic novelist called Peggy Mulvaney – she swears by it. It's called "The Gin and Bear

It Diet". You must have *two* large gin and tonics every day, but otherwise you can eat and drink anything you want. Apparently you neither lose nor gain weight, but you feel very happy about the situation.'

Miranda put the half-eaten slab of cake down as if she was surprised she was holding it, and a faint watery smile bobbed to the surface.

So did Spike: one leap and a gulp and the abandoned cake was gone.

Who'd have guessed the old dog had that much spring left in him?

*

Dear Tom,

Your problem is that your wife understands you, and so do I.

But I could meet you for lunch on the 31st if you like? I'm coming up to London then to be interviewed on a book-centred radio programme.

The snotty bastards said they'd invited two 'serious novelists' and me, so they deserve all they're going to get. The first person to say the words 'literary novel' will have their head shoved into their water glass.

Love (but strictly no physical contact),

Sappho

PS. I am also now invited to appear on a TV show – as a children's author! Do none of them ever read the books they discuss on these programmes?

*

Miranda was subdued but taking my advice about the gin, and generally carrying on with her life.

On the Wednesday after the sordid revelations we went

down to the Castle Craft Centre to make enquiries about a studio for Fantasy Flowers, but the rents were quite high, and the only vacant one was much larger than she needed.

'If that's what they charge, Lavender Duke must b-be making good money with her paintings,' Miranda commented as we emerged from the converted turret that housed the office.

The surroundings were admittedly picturesque, and the castle had clearly undergone several transformations in its life-time: the *stones* were original, but except for the outer wall, not necessarily in their original order.

In the car park was a familiar-looking little white van, but after all, the man worked here.

'And Lavender only uses her studio in the afternoon,' con-tinued Miranda. 'B-because she's gardening in the mornings.'

My attention was suddenly caught by what she was saying. 'Does she? Why don't you show me where her studio is?'

She turned back obediently. 'I thought you d-didn't want to look around the rest of the workshops today? B-but it's d-down here.'

We made our way along a stone passage lined with windows on the inner wall, so visitors could see the craftspeople at work. Some were glazed and some were open, with just a waist-high barrier separating them.

I didn't need Miranda to tell me when we got to the potter's den: the cluster of drooling women pressing their noses to the glass was a dead giveaway.

His studio was quite dark, unlike the well-lit workshops we'd already passed, and within it the potter lurked like some vast spectral creature of the Underworld.

He appeared to be entirely oblivious to his audience, for his broad back was turned away, revealing the white-gold hair curling on his neck, as he worked at something on the table before him.

It must have been hot in there, because he'd taken his shirt off and his skin glistened. Every time the muscles on his back flexed there was a sort of unilateral sigh.

He started to turn round so I hastily grabbed Miranda's arm and hurried her past, for the last thing I wanted was to be caught goggling at him like a zoo visitor.

Lavender's studio was at the furthest end of the passage, and she was in the final stages of selling a large and splashy flower painting to a Japanese couple when we arrived. They appeared to be tourists and left carrying it between them, so I wondered how they were going to transport it home.

As soon as she was free I explained to her why we were there, and without prompting she immediately exclaimed, 'But, Miranda, if you only want a workshop in the mornings and I only use it in the afternoons, we could share! There's plenty of room.'

'D-do you mean it?' Miranda's face glowed. 'Oh, Lavender, that would b-be perfect! And it all b-being flowers, they sort of go together, d-don't they?'

Lavender enthused, and they were soon deep in discussion of the finer arrangements. Lavender became quite taken with the idea of painting Bouquets with Meanings (*nice* meanings) and she was sure that Miranda would get more orders from people who'd seen her work at the studio . . .

When they left for the office to finalize things, I trailed slowly along behind, inhaling the wonderful smell of the leather shop next door, and planning the removal of the horrible little conservatory from the front of my house once Miranda had taken the flowers away. Then I could have the Portuguese door installed, instead of the ramshackle one currently in place . . .

It was only when something grey squidged between my toes

that I realized I'd come to a stop outside the potter's lair.

Fortunately he'd gone – everyone seemed to have gone, it must be getting late – but he'd left a slippery clay snail-trail behind him.

The clay felt cold and rather nice, so I squidged a bit more, until all at once I realized I wasn't alone: the spectre of the castle stood right in front of me, staring down at my bare feet. Then his gaze slowly travelled upwards until it reached my face, and suddenly I felt as if I was in one of those dreams where I'm walking naked down the main street without realizing it until too late.

Most odd: and anyway, he was the semi-nude one, for although he'd put a shirt on, it was unbuttoned. I haven't been that close to so much male chest hair for years.

I couldn't begin to describe the strange expression on his face, but bemused would be the closest. His eyes were blank grey echoes of the ancient stone walls: the lights were on but there was nobody home.

'Someone could slip on this wet clay,' I said severely, and he journeyed back from wherever he'd been and smiled.

For a man with such Fallen Angel beauty he suddenly looked alarmingly vulpine – a suggestion of sharp teeth waiting to rend, perhaps, like Dragonslayer.

But at least, I thought, he can't read minds.

I was wrong.

'Everyone's gone – there's no one here except you and me,' he said, again with that wolfish smile and I felt the heavy silence settling around me. 'The clay will be dry by morning and I'll brush it away.'

It was certainly drying on my feet like cement, so that if he didn't stop blocking my way he might have to brush *me* away in the morning, too.

Except he'd totally lost interest in me: his eyes took on that faraway expression again and this time he simply walked round me without another word into his studio and closed the door.

'Sappho!' called Miranda, from somewhere beyond the shadowed corridor. 'Sappho?'

'Coming!'

'Do not let me detain you if you have important business,' Nala said sarcastically, but she said it to the empty air: Dragonslayer was gone . . .

Mu arrived on Friday, for the morrow was turkey basting night, though if it worked we could call it Thanksgiving. In fact, we could call the *baby* Thanksgiving Graythorpe. Sounds quite Quakerish.

She wasn't supposed to be late – it didn't take me that long to drive here from Pembrokeshire – but I'd forgotten her inability to turn right at junctions, a trait that renders even the simplest journey fraught with difficulties.

By the time she made it I had to prise her fingers off the steering wheel, but once she was indoors with a drink in her hand she was fine, except for refusing to sit on the lounger.

The alternative was the hideously uncomfortable camel saddle stool, or the Gil-rejected leatherette and horsehair sofa, which has seen better days, most of them on the horse.

She brought six bottles of red wine as a house-warming present, and those might account for my unusual tardiness the next morning.

Miranda had produced three boxed floral tributes – or insults – by the time I emerged from Vengeane and Mu yawned her way downstairs.

Miranda's appearance didn't come as such a shock to Mu as it had to me: I'd discovered a mail-order company that designed perfectly wearable clothes in larger sizes and she was wearing jeans and a flowing tunic in a pretty blue that matched her eyes.

We were soon celebrating our being all together again with coffee and the huge box of home-made jam doughnuts she'd brought.

Then we settled down to update Mu with the local gossip, starting with Dorinda.

'I call a man who mislays his wife more than careless,' Mu said, biting into her second doughnut with a crunch of sugar.

A trickle of red jam ran down her chin, making her look like an extra in a cut-price Dracula film.

'Begone, foul fiend.' I made a sign to avert the Evil One.

'He d-didn't mean to,' explained Miranda earnestly. 'He's d-dreadfully upset about it.'

'And she might have been disposed of by this potter that Lili is pursuing – with no luck, so far. His girlfriend turning out to be gay after they'd been in a relationship for years seems to have turned him into a misogynist.'

'Oh, Nye isn't like that at all,' protested Miranda. 'I'm sure he was really hurt, b-but perhaps it's just that he isn't ready for another relationship yet?'

'Nye?' said Mu.

'It's a Welsh name,' explained Miranda. 'It's really Aneurin – Aneurin Thomas.'

'He must be something special if Lili's interested. She only goes for the spectacular.'

'He is very handsome,' Miranda agreed. 'Have you read Sappho's last b-book yet? B-because he looks exactly like D-Dragonslayer, and—'

'It was a coincidence,' I interrupted hastily.

Mu looked at me.

'*Mostly* a coincidence,' I qualified. 'Lili sent me a blurry black-and-white photo of him in a letter, but I'd forgotten about it. Only my subconscious must have picked up on it for Dragonslayer, and the strange thing is that Nye has all the things that I gave Dragonslayer that I couldn't have known from the photo, like his peculiar eyes, and the way his ears go pointy at the top, and his eyebrows slant upwards . . . and that silver-gilt hair.'

'Is he of this world?' Mu asked drily. 'Or an alien? And what's peculiar about his eyes? How many has he got?'

'Just the two,' Miranda said. 'Very light-coloured.'

'Entirely colourless,' I put in. 'Like raindrops.'

'The pupils have a d-dark edge, Sappho, and I wouldn't say they are always colourless—'

'No, sometimes they reflect things like a silver mirror,' I agreed. 'And when he's angry they go leaden grey.'

They both looked at me.

'What? So I've met him a couple of times by accident – and he always seems to be cross about something.'

'You d-didn't tell me,' Miranda said.

I shrugged. 'Nothing to tell. He's not very interesting – you know my opinion of handsome men. Speaking of which,' I added, changing the subject, 'there's been no word or sign of Dave since I got here – this must be the longest ever gap.'

'Maybe he's got tired of it?' suggested Miranda hopefully. 'He's a most peculiar man . . . I mean, I often used to b-bump into him in London and he b-behaved as if we b-barely knew each other, and yet he's b-been stalking you all these years.'

'He's batty,' Mu said. 'But let's hope his absence from the scene means he's had an argument with a London bus or some-thing,' she added unkindly. 'Otherwise he's bound to pop up sooner or later.'

After a while Miranda went home to design a new advertisement for Fantasy Flowers, ready for when she moved it over to the craft centre in a couple of weeks.

Luckily Chris was off whipping up a froth somewhere else that weekend, so she had the house to herself. She hadn't bothered to tell him about her plans since he was so averse to them, but at least she wasn't knuckling under and abandoning them.

I brought Mu a bit more up to date with the mysterious incidents and my neighbours, the Dukes, and then after lunch we went for a walk just to fill in the time before Simon arrived.

I don't know about Mu, but I felt nervous.

He came up from Bristol on his motorbike, not so much the god in the machine as the god *on* the machine, all glowing skin and nicely moulded black leather.

'Have you got the goods?' Mu demanded without finesse, almost as soon as he was in the door.

Now, just where did she think he could have hidden anything in that outfit? And the cold air wouldn't have done it much good if he had.

He took off his helmet, revealing an aureole of curly gold hair, and blue eyes with a touch of devilment in them.

(Blonds were proliferating in my life to such an extent lately, what with Mu, Miranda, Ambler, Dragonslayer and now Simon, that I was starting to feel as if I belonged to an entirely different species.)

'You only want me for my—' he began.

'Simon!' Mu yelled. 'You promised to be good!'

He grinned. 'I am good, and if you'd like Personal Service I could prove it – to you or anyone else?' he added, hopefully eyeing me.

'No, thank you,' I said primly, though actually feeling rather flattered. 'But it was kind and noble of you to offer.'

Simon resignedly went off upstairs alone to do his stuff, about which I firmly refused to think (except to hope he could find his way through all that leather) and I'd just come into the sitting room with a fresh pot of coffee and the rest of the box of doughnuts, when Miranda rushed in with the news that Deadly Dorinda's car had been found in the Bottomless Pool.

'They were d-draining it, and it was at the b-bottom,' she explained breathlessly.

'How can the Bottomless Pool have a bottom?' I objected.

'That's only its name. Actually, it is very d-deep in the middle, b-but it shelves at the sides, and that's where the car was. Completely empty too, and it looks like it's b-been there a long time.'

'No Drowned Dorinda?'

'No. And there's another thing – it's b-been b-broken into! There was a hole d-drilled through the lock. So joyriders probably took it and then pushed it into the pool. It's just off the road – it would run d-down quite easily.'

'Is that good news?' asked Mu, who'd been rather abstracted from the conversation, and no wonder. 'I mean, good for your friend Gil? After all, presumably there are spare car keys, so he wouldn't have had to break into it and steal the car, even if he murdered Dorinda?'

'He wouldn't murder D-Dorinda!' Miranda objected. 'B-but you're right. I expect she parked the car in a remote spot and it was stolen. Then something happened to her while she was trying to get home.'

'I suppose someone could have found her alone,' I agreed, 'though it would be two coincidences, wouldn't it? First the car stolen, then an attacker.'

'Yes, b-but coincidences d-do happen.'

'Yes, they do.' Like Dragonslayer and the potter being such an exact match, for instance . . .

A thundering on the stairs heralded Simon's reappearance, looking pleased with himself. With the air of a secret agent he passed something surreptitiously across to Mu.

Miranda broke off and stared at him.

'Oh – this is Ambler's younger brother, Simon,' I explained. 'You must have heard Mu mention Miranda, Simon?'

'Of course,' he said, smiling seraphically, and in automatic response she silently offered him all the remaining doughnuts.

Well, he was a growing boy – and that probably accounted for the way he could get one whole into his mouth, too.

'If you'll excuse me . . .?' Mu murmured, vanishing upstairs clutching her prize to her bosom, though I suppose if she'd been clutching Simon to it, it would have made for a more difficult situation.

It's just a trifle difficult sustaining some semblance of normal conversation when you know that your best friend is upstairs performing strange rites with a baster and the sperm of the man eating doughnuts like a schoolboy in front of you, but I rose above it. And at least he wasn't rising above . . .

Mmm. All this sex in the air sort of gets to you. Maybe, I thought, I'm about to have a kind of second spring . . . or an Indian summer? Perhaps my next *Spiral Bound* guide-book should be *Spiral Bound: Sex*. (Or does that sound a bit S & M?)

A journey in search of a dark-haired, attractive (but not handsome), tall, unattached, straight, medically-certified-free-from-anything-disgusting, male.

Actually, finding a unicorn might be easier. Still, at least

I'm not desperate enough to find Simon tempting, possibly partly because he looks like Ambler, whom I love dearly in a sisterly way, but without Ambler's cuddle-blanket appeal.

Miranda, who'd clearly realized there was a subplot without guessing what it was, pulled herself together and poured Simon coffee, then began to discuss his university course with him. Then somehow it came out that he was a big *Vengeane* fan, and was in fact wearing one of the *Dark Planet* T-shirts under his leathers. (I just loved that creaking noise they made when he sat down!)

'. . . *as he carried her through the forest Nala could feel his heart beating through the soft leather of his tunic and hear the soft susurration as his thighs . . .*'

'What?' said Simon, staring at me strangely.

'Nothing,' I said, hastily clicking off the memo recorder and smiling brightly.

We had an animated three-sided discussion about why Raarg doesn't ever deserve to get his hands on Nala even if he is redeemed, unless he conquers his dark side and achieves Cosmic Karma, though Dragonslayer very well might if he plays his cards right. Raarg might then fall into the hands of Sirene, the queen harpy, who is morally unfettered like Lili, only without a vestige of a conscience.

At this point Lili/Sirene also wandered into the room. On Grand Central Station I sat down and had an insemination party.

'There you all are!' she said accusingly. Lili Ford Jakes, Secret Party Police. 'I've been sitting in the pub for hours because I'm sure Nye said he was going there, but he didn't show, so here I am.'

She spotted Simon and, deciding she'd made the right

decision, bestowed a sultry smile on him that caused a slight halt in the doughnut consumption.

'Didn't you say Mu was coming this weekend?' she asked.

'She's upstairs – chipped nail varnish.'

'She doesn't still hand-paint them, does she? You can get all kinds of transfers and stick-on things now, you know,' she said, then, abandoning the topic, began to make preliminary overtures to Simon.

Poor Lili! The very first note of a – surely familiar? – powerful motorbike stopping outside had him out of the door like lightning.

I followed after him, and without too much surprise found the Harley-Davidson parked there with Jaynie, small and plump in red and white leathers like a very special ripe tomato, deep in conversation with an enthralled Simon. Pops, her long grey plait thrown around her neck like a muffler, sat in the sidecar puffing at a hand-rolled cigarette.

She unfolded herself, stepped out and gave me a kiss. 'Surprise, darling! We thought we'd just pop over and see the hovel, but don't worry, we aren't staying here. We've booked a room at the local pub for tonight – the Frog and Ratchet.'

'Toad and Blowpipe,' I corrected.

'Eagle and Stone?' suggested Miranda faintly, having followed us out, and was instantly recognized and embraced by Pops. Jaynie broke off briefly and hugged everyone indiscriminately before plunging back into an enthralling discussion with Simon in which only words like 'cc's' and 'cylinder heads' could be heard.

I speak many languages, but not Motorbike.

We left them to it and went back in, together with a couple of bottles of Portuguese wine, some salami and a lot of olives. Mu had descended, and quite a party developed before

Simon popped back in to say goodbye – with a wink at Mu, sitting demurely next to Miranda on the horsehair sofa, and a kiss blown at Lili, before leaving with that sexy leather-thighs-slithering-together sound again . . .

Oh dear.

Lili didn't leave until the last drop of booze ran out, when the rest of us repaired to the pub for dinner, halfway through which Pops demanded a large pair of scissors from the waitress and casually hacked twelve inches or so off the end of her plait, because she said it kept getting in everything and had nearly caused an Isadora Duncan by getting caught in the bike wheels on the way down.

I must have inherited my rogue Rapunzel genes from Pops' side of the family.

It was late when Mu and I finally staggered back to the cottage and slumped down wearily, trying to raise the energy to make that final mile to bed.

'There are rows and rows of Chinese characters imprinted on the inside of my eyelids,' Mu said drowsily. 'That's strange, isn't it?'

'Perhaps you were made in Hong Kong?' I suggested, just as the phone rang. 'Who on earth can that be, at this time of night?'

It was Ambler, reporting outbreaks of sneezing and runny eyes among the felines, and seeking guidance, which woke Mu up, and she ordered him instantly to drag the vet from his bed to minister to them, in case it was cat flu.

'And don't take no for an answer! No, there should only be eight cats and the kittens, Ambler. If there were eleven at tea-time you've been feeding the neighbours', too. Now, do what I said and I'll come back early tomorrow.'

Mu left at dawn. I'd already worked out the best left-handed circular route back for her, and stuck the road numbers across her dashboard in fluorescent Post-it notes.

After that I managed to do a whole chapter of *Vengeane* before I heard the sound of the Harley, and I only just remembered to dash up to the spare room and hide the turkey baster box before giving them the guided tour.

Fortunately they loved the cottage, and Jaynie promised to find some blue and white tiles for the kitchen to replace the mottled beige ones. Pops, always good at interior design, helped me rearrange the furniture and hang some drapes, and before I knew it, it all looked totally different and much more comfortable.

After this we stretched our legs over the moors at the back and went up to the cromlech to admire the distant view of the silvery sea, before Pops and Jaynie packed the sidecar and drove off, tooting the horn and taking a giant avoiding swerve around Pansy as she wobbled out on her heavily laden bicycle.

The subject of late motherhood hadn't raised its head above the parapet.

Peace slowly descended on Aces Acre.

Dear Pops and Jaynie,

I'm staying overnight in London, since I've suddenly become a media person. However, once I've done these two shows I don't suppose I'll ever be asked again.

The film rights for the *Vengeane* novels are being negotiated for, which may make the tax man very rich, but I don't suppose will do me a lot of good. And look what they did to *Dune*!

I thought you'd like this postcard of Millais' *Ophelia*, which reminded me of Miranda when she's feeling depressed. A sort of beautiful half-wittedness, just letting herself drift down the river of life with a limp bouquet and an expression of gormless resignation.

I put it down to low blood sugar. In Selfridges I discovered lovely long-stemmed flowers made out of sweets and sugared almonds, and bought some for Miranda to nibble on if she feels gloomy. I bet if Ophelia had had a bunch of those she wouldn't have been such a wet lettuce.

It was lovely to see you both, even so fleetingly: next time you must stay in the cottage.

Love,

Sappho

Chapter 11

Aces High

April came in like a badly stuffed lion and proceeded to leak, off and on, most days.

It had been another of the Chris weekends, where Miranda was briefly present on the Saturday morning, but abstracted and ready to dash off to do her master's bidding. Not a lot seemed to have changed since the small clothes incident or the infidelity, and I didn't suppose she'd told him about the craft workshop scheme either.

But then, he had had years to perfect ways of making her feel very unsure of herself, a sort of mental bullying technique.

On Sundays there were, of course, no flower orders, but I expected to see her on the Monday.

I'd done a good morning's work, and felt the need of a cliff walk, despite it being a pretty murky sort of morning. When you've got to go, you've got to go.

The car park at Rhossili was deserted, and when I got out of the car and set off along the cliff path a thick mist wrapped my head like wet, earthy sacking.

There was that familiar sense of treading along the edges

of unseen chasms, even though this morning I couldn't see them.

You might think this was a bit foolhardy, but at Rhossili I could feel the pathway beneath my feet even though, in deference to the chilly wetness of the day, I was wearing shoes. The texture of the sheep-nibbled turf on the seaward side is quite different.

The mist was delicious, like walking inside loosely knit marshmallow. Cold, damp tendrils richly scented with the sea, trodden grass and warm wet sheep invaded my lungs as I moved through the muffled dream landscape.

Twice a seagull ripped past my ear as it took last-minute avoiding action, and once a sheep leaped from under my feet and lumbered off with a strangled bleat.

I went as far as the triangulation point, and then leaned on it, transposing all these fog-invoked thoughts to *Vengeane*.

Nala moved slowly through the eerie twisting spirals of mist, feeling the way with all six senses . . . but even so, a bronze-winged beast of Megadorr sprang into the air with a cry like a screeching demon from right under her feet, rudely awakened and hungry.

Another gull screeching past my ear like a howitzer made me jump practically out of my skin: there seemed to be lots of them suddenly, circling with mad yelps just out of sight.

And what were those strange, bobbing shapes, no more than a change in the density of the fog, which seemed to hover just ahead of me on the cliff edge? The birds' yelps took on the sound of insane laughter . . .

No, not the birds – for surely that *was* insane laughter? Was I alone on the cliff top with a giggling maniac?

'*Ger-on-i-moooo!*'

Now that I *must* have invented, for who'd be standing on a cliff edge in wet mist (besides me), shouting and laughing?

The voice, distorted as it was, sounded sort of familiar . . .

It was probably in my head. It's so hard to tell the difference sometimes, isn't it? I mean, what's real, and what isn't real – and of course Vengeane *is* real to me.

Cautiously I crept forward off the path to where the sound might – if it existed – have come from, and another sheep (or something) moved off past me into the murk. Or maybe my eyes had begun inventing shapes?

Only a madman would leave the path in this weather . . .

Something soft wrapped itself around my legs and I fell forward with one hand clutching empty air and the other frantically grabbing tussocky grass. There was an interesting interlude while I slowly shifted all my body weight back on to firm ground and sat up.

My would-be assassin was an old raincoat. Kicking it away I got up and felt my way back to the path with extreme caution and the feeling that even a hardened brink-lover like myself would be better off somewhere else.

And I was getting wet. It wasn't that my hundred-per-cent waterproof wasn't working – it was – but it was shedding a hundred per cent of the rain on to my legs. It didn't mention that on the label.

My eyes were so encrusted with blown salt spray that they felt (and probably looked) like frosted grapes, and the wind was rising to a demonic shriek in my aching ears.

Enough.

I love being alone, but that morning I wanted to be some-where where I could see I was alone, though I filed all those lovely sensations of muffling, howling opacity away for future reference.

It was now later than I thought, for the National Trust shop sported a glimmer of light, and the car park held a scattering of cars and one coach – but not a human was to be seen.

Had aliens abducted them to conduct more weird sexual experiments? How many did they need to do? Why didn't they just pop out of their spaceships and buy a load of women's magazines, which would tell them more than they ever wanted to know about sex on Planet Earth?

But no, everyone was in the Seaspray Café.

The forcibly decanted tourists (it's Monday – you *will* see the cliff top at Rhossili) were well settled in with postcards, guidebooks and coffee, and a group of happy hikers occupied one corner.

They all had bright red socks on: maybe that's how the aliens recognize each other when disguised as humans?

In another corner were a pair of thwarted and sullen hang-gliders, prevented from hurling themselves Icarus-like into the void by an inability to see where they were going. But at least they were fully clothed. I've had a warped inner picture of hang-gliders ever since I saw a film on TV at Mu's about nudists going about their usual pursuits stark naked. It certainly gave whole new connotations to the words 'hang-gliding'.

I hung my anorak up and slid my feet out of my wet shoes. They looked a bit blue, but would soon thaw out.

None of the tables was free, but one was inhabited only by a morose individual reading a tabloid newspaper.

Figuring, perhaps illogically, that anyone preferring rude pictures to words would be disinclined to be chatty, I squidged across and asked if the other chairs at his table were taken.

He barely glanced at me, but his expression suggested that sharing his table with a bedraggled female of uncertain age was not high on his list of must-dos for today. Still, he didn't protest when I swept his belongings off one chair on to the next and sat down.

I was suddenly hungry: very, very hungry. And cold.

The only-here-for-the-money student waitress might avoid eye contact, but she couldn't escape my voice, which has a certain depth and resonance when in need of sustenance – and the potential for a living on the stage had I been of a more exhibitionist nature (and if leading men came in larger sizes).

'Full English breakfast,' I said, smiling at her reassuringly, for she was clearly of a nervous disposition. 'Coffee – *lots* of coffee. With milk, no pots of that Polyfilla substitute. And I'll have the coffee now, while I'm waiting for the breakfast.'

'Coffee comes *with* the breakfast.'

'Mine will come before, during, and after,' I said encouragingly, and she stared blankly at me before wandering off, scratching her head with her pencil.

Perhaps I was wrong about her being a student, for what could she be studying? Unless it's hairdressing, for that look of having stuck your head in a blender for ten minutes must surely be intentional?

Before I'd had time to do more than blink the crusting of salt off my eyelashes, she was back with a pot of coffee, a mug, and plastic containers of something that described itself as half-milk. What was the other half? Bonemeal?

'This is the Coffee with Breakfast,' she explained earnestly. 'If you want more, it's extra.'

'Fine,' I said warmly, 'well done.' And wrapping my icy hands around the mug, began to gently steam, noticing for the first time that the morose bearded one had abandoned his comic and was, frankly, staring at me.

He looked vaguely familiar, and not unhandsome, resembling a small Spanish grandee, though the way his eyebrows trudged up and down like hairy caterpillars when he slurped his tea rather spoiled the effect.

'Poor weather for a holiday,' he said with a slight Welsh accent, absorbing with evident approval the clinging of my wet jade-green T-shirt over the lower foothills of the Himalayas. Probably made him feel at home after Page Three.

'I'm not on holiday, I live locally,' I said, not prepared to elaborate further, since although I could take him with one hand tied behind my back, disclosing the name of my village seems to arouse nothing but levity.

'Strange I haven't seen you about before, then?' he said to my breasts, puzzled. 'I live in a bungalow a mile or two along the cliffs. Let me introduce myself – I am an Ace.'

'I'm sure you're an absolute Trump,' I assured him kindly (though not Donald, despite the waitress's near-Ivana hairdo).

His gaze moved at last to my face, and his expression changed to one of outrage: '*Gilbert* Ace.'

'Of course – I've seen you in the distance talking to Miranda, that's why you looked slightly familiar. Well, well – at last we're alone together.'

He bristled like an angry prawn. 'You're that Sappho Jones woman! Let me tell you that I was Dafydd and Gethyn's nearest male relative, and Aces Acre should have been mine. It's belonged to the Aces for centuries!'

'And there have always been Starkadders at Cold Comfort Farm,' I intoned pleasantly, and he glared at me.

'It's not a joke,' he said. 'Not to me, it isn't.'

'Look here, you may be a bit miffed about it, but the cottage was theirs to do with as they wished, and this way they got to live in it all their lives and could still afford to do all the things they wanted to.'

'Yes, like fritter a fortune on giant TVs and exotic cruises,' he snapped.

'They had fun, so why not? And you got the house contents

and what was left, didn't you? You've just told me you've a bungalow of your own, so I don't suppose you really need the cottage anyway. I'm sorry and all that, but there it is.'

'The solicitor said there was nothing to be done,' he conceded ungraciously.

'Then I hope you aren't going to hold it against me, because it will be awkward since we're both friends of Miranda's and keep bumping into one another.'

'I'm not one to hold a grudge,' he said stiffly and clearly untruthfully, 'and any friend of Miranda's is a friend of mine.'

There was just a tinge of the soppy about him when he said her name, which made me wonder if he still had a soft spot for his childhood sweetheart. I was pretty sure Miranda was fond of him, but I mustn't forget the missing wife. He may not look a potential Bluebeard, but I thought we needed to know exactly where Dorinda had got to.

'Good,' I said. 'I hope we can be friends, Gil, because the Gower is such a small place that birdies in their little nests must agree.'

Relays of breakfast began to arrive, and he watched with a slightly bemused expression as I methodically dealt with it. I'm a big girl and I need sustenance, especially sustenance I don't have to cook myself.

'I'm always ravenous,' I explained, lavishly loading my fork with sausage, egg and fried bread. 'But particularly today – the cliff walk was very bracing.'

'You really shouldn't go on the cliff path in this weather,' he reproved gravely. 'You might have gone over.'

'Not unless I'd strayed from the path, and that's clear enough.'

He shook his head gloomily. 'It's easily done.'

'Not by me.'

'You'd be surprised at the silly things people do on cliffs,' he told me.

'No, I wouldn't be surprised in the least. But it's strange how the mist plays tricks with your perceptions. I mean, at one point I thought I heard someone shouting near the cliff edge, and moving about, but of course it was just a sheep bobbing along on one of those tracks. And then, while I'd stepped off the path to investigate, I fell over an old raincoat that was blowing about.'

He looked startled. 'Do you actually think there might have been someone there, on the edge?'

'No, of course I don't – I mean it's not exactly Beachy Head, is it? They don't queue to jump off?'

'There have been several tragic episodes associated with these cliffs,' he assured me, and then proceeded with great relish to tell me all about the various accidents and suicides that appeared to have littered the cliffs and beach with bodies over the last century, though since he didn't look any older than me he can't have eye-witnessed all of these events. If he had, though, his conversational style might have *driven* some of them over the edge.

'I'm an expert on local matters,' he finished modestly.

'Um,' I said, through a mouthful of egg and bacon.

'I don't know if Miranda told you, but I'm a keen ornithologist. You've probably come across my latest publication: *A Guide to Unusual Bird Visitors to the Gower*?'

No, but I would probably feature in the sequel, *More Even Weirder Bird Visitors to the Gower*.

'I'll be sure to look out for it, Gilbert,' I said kindly, remembering what Miranda had told me of his near nervous breakdown, domineering wife, and police grillings. 'But I have trouble telling my kestrels from my hawks, or even, my kestrels from my knaves.'

He looked at me with serious, glossy brown eyes. 'You should start reading my weekly "Nature Notes" in the local paper, and then you'll soon know your way around the feathered world. It's fascinating, quite fascinating, I assure you. I have my binoculars trained on the cliffs at all hours of the day.'

And the night too, I shouldn't wonder. I supposed he knew I was a writer too, though it didn't seem to make him feel matey. But perhaps he didn't count Fantasy as real writing. Lots of people don't. I laugh all the way to the bank.

By now I'd lavishly loaded the last of the butter on to my toast and scrunched it up, feeling another chapter of *Vengeane* forming nebulously in my brain recesses. An idea of amazing brilliance was coming into being . . .

'Raarg must seem to die, yet be reborn as a fitting mate for Nala, warrior-queen – yet the Grisund Oracle has told her that Dragonslayer is her future mate!' I exclaimed, putting my coffee cup down with a clunk.

Through the purging fires of Meldroth the—

I got up. 'Excuse me,' I said, and leaving him open-mouthed (though maybe he was just in Page Three mode again) I made for the exit, irritably fending the waitress off with a handful of money. 'Keep the change,' I said, snatching my anorak and shoes. 'Something urgent . . .'

The rain had almost stopped but I hurdled great pools of water as I took to my heels across the car park.

And just as the windscreen wipers slowly parted the last, scattered drops, the Last of the Aces emerged from the café and gesticulated wildly.

I gave him a friendly salute and drove past, already muttering into the tape player.

In the mirror the slight figure turned and trudged off in the direction of the cliffs.

'It's going to be – a lovely day . . .' I sang, forgetting to switch the recording button off. 'Lovely day, lovely day, lovely day, love-ly day . . .'

Chapter 12

Spotted

Raarg's epiphany just seemed to ripple off my tongue and into my tape recorder as if it wanted to be written.

'*They laid the naked body of Raarg at her feet, unmarked by the fires of the Abyss except for a faint, strange bronze sheen to the skin . . .*'

Now warm and dry, I reclined comfortably on my Dentist's Delight lounger in a long, loose, embroidered black robe, letting myself dwell on all the appalling things that were about to happen to gorgeous, villainous Raarg before he was purged of evil. Or maybe not.

'*Cowering, drenched in the sweat of fear, Raarg—*'

'S-Sappho!'

'Damn!'

I clicked off the recorder and levered myself reluctantly from the warmly moulded leather. While subconsciously I'd been aware of Miranda coming in earlier to sort out the flower orders, I knew she wouldn't disturb me when I was working unless it was something important.

She was in the conservatory, hovering like a shy fish at the front of the aquarium, together with the cause of her interruption: he was substantial, and wearing a navy uniform the size of the Isle of Wight.

'C-Constable Gwynne,' she introduced, gesturing with a handful of dried henbane, as if I could have missed him, and then made off muttering something about coffee.

'Is that Gwyn as in Nell?' I enquired interestedly.

'I don't know any—' he began, then broke off and frowned portentously at me, giving me the impression I'd just thrown him off his internal script.

Anyway, Nell Gwyn had a pretty, cheeky little face, and this poor boy's was so cratered by acne it must have made a close shave difficult. Maybe his girlfriends found the tufted effect endearing? The Acne of Perfection.

He stood among the hanging foliage, an innocent strayed into a witch's coven but determined to do his duty.

'Are you Mrs Sap . . . Sap-ho Jones?' he enquired, as if owning to such an outlandish name could get me arrested under the Meaning of the Act.

'Soft p's, Constable,' I explained, 'Saffo – after the ancient Greek poetess. And I'm a Ms – I've never even technically been a Mrs.'

Clearly The Biggest Spotty Dog I Ever Did See cherished an innate feeling that women who called themselves Ms were leftish, feminist lesbians, though I hope he didn't suspect poor Miranda of being my partner. She wouldn't like it: and anyway, the only meaningful relationships she's had recently have been entirely blameless ones involving chocolate fudge cake.

'I see,' he said severely, though clearly he didn't, and scribbled into a little book not unlike the ones I use for my *Spiral Bound* jottings. 'I wonder if I might ask you one or two questions, madam, in connection with an inquiry we're at present making?'

'You'd better come into the sitting room,' I said resignedly, though I couldn't immediately recall any transgressions, even of a motoring kind, 'but it's a damned shame about Raarg – I've completely forgotten what I was going to do with him next.'

Spotty Muldoon looked pink and baffled, so I added kindly, 'Never mind, it isn't your fault, Officer.'

His Adam's apple bobbed up and down in a demented lift sort of way and throughout our conversation his eyes tended to wander towards my cleavage and jump away: but then, this happens a lot.

My bust may be disproportionately huge but at least it's gravity-defying – and long may it hold its own.

'I-I'm sorry if I've called at an inconvenient time,' he began. 'Perhaps you'd like to go and get dressed first?'

'It is inconvenient, but you're here now so we might as well get on with it. And I *am* dressed – this is a Bedouin thobe. I often write in it, it's kind of inspiring – *The Sheik* and all that, you know. Or perhaps you don't know? Never mind. Do take a seat,' I added.

He clapped eyes on the dentist's chair beyond me and made an odd choking sound: this season, policemen's faces will be crimson . . .

Does it remind him of some strange instrument from a kinky magazine, even though I've removed all the weirder attachments? What *did* he think I'd been up to? My reassuring smile didn't seem to cheer him either, and he sank slowly backwards on to the bedspread-covered sofa opposite, looking horrified.

I tied my loose hair into a bell-rope knot, then perched on the recliner. 'What did you want to ask me about, Officer?' I encouraged, seeing he'd lost the thread of his narrative and was clinging to the notebook as a drowning man clutches a lifebelt.

He cleared his throat. 'We – er – we're investigating an accident on Rhossili cliffs early this morning and believe you may be able to help us with our inquiries.'

This morning? Already it seemed *days* ago when I walked through wet mist on the cliffs.

'Yes, I did walk the cliff path first thing, battling with the elements – but the elements won. What are you inquiring into – and how did you know I was there?'

'A local resident made us aware of the matter and gave us your description.'

'What matter? I had a chat with a Mr Gilbert Ace in the Seaspray Café – would he be your snitch? And what exactly have I done?'

'Nothing, madam, we just want you to—'

'Help you with your inquiries?' I finished helpfully.

'Yes,' he agreed stolidly. 'Mr Ace, who is known to us,' as a confirmed wife murderer, and they would get him yet, his expression strongly suggested, 'reported the conversation with you because you mentioned a possible incident on the cliff top, and he stated that afterwards, feeling some disquiet, he walked to the spot you had described and made a search.'

A cold knot formed in my bowels or somewhere equally horrible. 'Oh, no, don't tell me that someone *did* jump off that cliff and all I did was go and have a nice hot breakfast in the café!'

'Possibly, but we don't know for certain, madam. Mr Ace found a raincoat near the edge, which was not wet enough to have been out for very long, but a search has revealed no further evidence.'

I stared at him, weighing it up logically. 'It's a bit thin,' I commented, relieved. 'One damp raincoat, no bodies.'

He made a note, licked a finger, and turned to a fresh page. My misplaced levity had probably earned me a place in his little black book as Gower Murderer Number Two, after Gil.

'There was no form of identification in the coat,' he conceded reluctantly, 'and the cliffs are popular with the tourists: all sorts of things get left behind.'

'But not usually raincoats early on a cold misty morning? And the only tourists I saw were in the café. But then, if it was a suicide, why would they take their raincoat off?'

'Suicides don't always think logically, madam.'

That's right, make me feel guilty again.

'But anyway, even if someone did leap off just as I got there, there wasn't anything I could have done, was there?'

'No, I expect not, madam, but in the circumstances we need a statement of the occurrence in case evidence turns up later. Perhaps you could just tell me in your own words exactly what happened?'

I tried to give him some idea of what conditions had been like that morning, but with the contrariness of April the day was now warm, mild and entirely inoffensive.

Like me.

'I couldn't see anything much, but sheep were sort of bobbing about, and the gulls were screaming – one screamed really loudly just after I heard the voice, so then I realized that that was probably what I heard, which seemed quite likely since my mind was on *Vengeane* . . .'

His pencil stopped and he stared accusingly at me. 'You heard a voice? You haven't mentioned that before!'

Miranda jingled her way in with the coffee tray as I answered patiently, 'Because I probably imagined it, along with everything else – apart from the raincoat. I must have done, mustn't I? Because no one would be standing on a wet misty cliff at the crack of dawn shouting "Geronimo!"'

Miranda started and the tray began to tilt alarmingly. I leaped up and just managed to catch it before everything fell off, then set it down on the table while she plumped limply down on the opposite end of the sofa to the surprised police-man, who suddenly rose several inches into the air, like Krakatoa, only quieter.

'S-sorry,' she muttered. 'C-clumsy.'

'It's that tray – it's warped.' I turned back to the young man.

'There, you can see how silly it all is, can't you? Who'd be standing on the cliffs shouting that? It's hardly in the "Famous Last Words" category. So I imagined the whole thing, and the raincoat probably blew there from the car park or the path.'

With a long-suffering sigh he snapped his little book shut, and his eyes lost their Rising Young Officer gleam and turned as dull as dry pebbles.

Picking up the coffee pot, shaped like an outlandish green monster poised over the cowering naked figure of Raarg, who formed the spout (a recent present from a fan), I said brightly, 'Coffee, Constable?'

You could tell he wasn't a coffee drinker from the speed with which he declined and jumped to his feet. Perhaps Earl Grey would have gone down better? But also it was clear that he thought the whole episode was a complete waste of time.

I saw him out through the rather bare white kitchen, and the ranked Fantasy foliage, though it was more of a chase than an escorted departure.

'Suspected Witches Coven' would probably feature strongly on the next page of his notebook.

He paused at the door for a last regretful glance down the front of my thobe, turned, fell over an empty tea chest, recovered, and marched away solemnly with his ears burning brightly like twin beacons: each one big enough to receive satellite TV.

Chapter 13

Dogged

When I went back indoors I found that Miranda had resumed her interrupted posy making, and was busy with henbane (imperfection), poison ivy (obvious), and Scotch thistle (retaliation).

Let's hope the recipient has a sense of humour, I thought.

Her small hands deftly twined green and purple striped ribbon around the stems and tied the little booklet to the finished bouquet.

'What's the significance of "Geronimo", Miranda?' I enquired when she had packed it in its box. 'You nearly dropped that tray when I said it.'

And now I'd come back down from Vengeane with a bump I noticed a couple of other odd things – like it being midday, whereas she usually came in to do the flowers early in the morning, and her looking . . . well, *fraught* was the only word. Her hands trembled as she labelled the box.

And come to think of it, where was Spike? 'G-Geronimo? Oh – it's just silly, really – it's one of Chris's words. He-he always shouted it at the critical moment when we were . . . well, *you* know.'

'No. What—' The penny dropped. 'Oh, *right.*'

I didn't really want to know that. And didn't someone who shouted 'Geronimo!' at the moment of orgasm merit an instant Bobbitt pinking shears job?

'Yes, and I was already thinking about him, because we had an argument last night. He says now he wants me to spend most of my time in London again, because my living down here and associating with you was changing me into a different person.'

'Yes – great, isn't it?'

'I *told* him you weren't doing anything except making me see things in perspective, and that I loved running Fantasy Flowers and hated living in London. He was really angry, and I got very upset and went to bed . . . and when I woke up early this morning he'd already left for London without a word, or a message, or anything. He starts recording the *Crackers* programme today.'

'Well, you surely don't think that Mr Chris "Cute Buns" Cotter was chucking himself off the cliffs first thing this morning in a fit of pique, with the immortal word "Geronimo!" on his lips?'

'N-no, but—'

'Phone him up if you're worried.'

'I h-have, but there's no answer – and it's not him I'm worried about: it's Spike. There was no sign of him this morning. I haven't seen him since I went to bed last night.'

'He's vanished?' I said, amazed. That a dog so elderly, obese and smelly could vanish was a trick worthy of Houdini.

She nodded, her huge blue eyes anxious. 'I think he must have got out when Chris left, but I searched and searched for hours this morning and there's no trace of him.'

'You should have told me at once, so I could help you,' I

said severely. 'Never mind those flowers – Spike is much more important. Let's go and plan a campaign.'

'There was only one order, and I've done it now. I'll drop it off at the post office on the way to pick up the posters,' she said distractedly.

'Posters?'

'Yes. When I couldn't find him I took his photo into Swansea and arranged for a hundred posters to be printed, with a reward.'

It's amazing how the power of love can stiffen the spine of even the limpest lettuce, isn't it?

'Right,' I said, battening down my astonishment. 'First, let's try phoning Chris again – what's the number?'

I dialled, and a familiar voice said dulcetly, 'Hello, this is Chris Cotter speaking.'

'Good. This is Sappho—'

'Sappho? What do *you* want? Haven't you interfered enough, with—'

'Shut up and listen,' I broke in. 'When you left here this morning did you let Spike out?'

There was a small silence. 'Spike?'

'The dog, remember? Where was he when you left this morning?'

'No idea: in his basket, presumably. Did you phone me up just to grill me about the dog? Why don't you ask Miranda?'

'You didn't see him at all this morning?'

He gave a theatrically long-suffering sigh. 'I didn't give him a moment's thought.'

'He's missing and he must have got out when you left – or something.'

'Then I hope you aren't accusing me of kidnapping the smelly old creature – and by the same token I think I would

149

have noticed if he'd tried to sneak past me. I expect Miranda forgot to let him in again last night and he's wandered off.'

Miranda, whose head was next to the phone so she could hear every word, paled and looked aghast.

'Of course she didn't.'

'She might have done, what with all these funny things she's been doing since she moved down to Bedd.'

'Oh, come off it! We know you organized those, and you're the one who's always been a bit funny, only not ha ha!' I put the phone down, not entirely convinced that he hadn't done something with Spike to get back at Miranda, but we had to eliminate the obvious first.

'Come on, Miranda,' I said bracingly. 'Of course you let Spike in last night, and my gut feeling is that Chris let him out this morning and doesn't want to say, so now he can't be found. He'll be around somewhere.'

Her lovely face crumpled and a tear slowly slid down her cheek. 'But I called and searched everywhere. You . . . don't think he's dead, do you?'

'I hope not, Miranda, but let's not jump the gun.'

'If he was hurt he always came to me, and he never ever strayed.'

Too fat, poor creature.

She got up, clutching the bouquet box to her bosom with an air of resolution. 'I'm going home to see if he's come back, then I'll go into Swansea and get the posters, then—'

'Hold it!' I said. 'Give me the name of the print shop and I'll get them delivered.'

'I don't think they'll do that – but it was Quicksilver Print.'

'They will if I cross their palm with Visa cards, and they can send them out in a taxi. Meanwhile we'll carry out a systematic search of the village. You go home and I'll join you as soon as I've changed my clothes.'

Quicksilver did indeed obligingly say they would plastic-wrap the posters and someone would drop them off within the hour, after I promised large amounts of money. Then I assumed dog-searching clothes and set out with only a small mental sigh for my almost finished chapter.

Outside, the fickle day had turned to raining cats, but unfortunately not dogs. Bedd is normally quite a pretty village, but it looked dark and dismal, as did the mentally challenged sheep hanging around Llyn's mini mart awaiting sandwich-bearing tourists.

They made a half-hearted rush for me as I went past, but then sheered off, bleating.

Miranda, not having found a repentant Spike in the porch, was showing a tendency to run round in circles like a headless chicken until I took charge.

'Right, we'll do this methodically. There are three roads out of Bedd, one of them mine, which is so steep that I think you'll agree Spike could never have got much further up it than my house. Now, how far would you say he was capable of walking?'

'About a mile?' she ventured.

Love is blind. Miranda's certainly was, or she'd never have married a scheming little git like Chris in the first place.

'A mile. Right.' I would have been astounded to discover that either of them could walk a quarter of that, though Miranda did seem to have perfected the art of moving twenty stone about effortlessly, like so much billowing cloud.

'So: we'll take a side each, and go along looking and call-ing for about a mile along both main roads, and then if there's still no sign of him, the posters will have arrived and

151

we can put some up around the village while we search that.'

'I put a reward of a hundred pounds on the poster. I thought someone might have taken him because he's such a nice dog, but if they see the reward . . . Do you think it's enough?'

'I think you'll be deluged with ancient Labradors,' I said wryly.

As to someone taking a fancy to the gross, smelly old beast: who am I to scoff? I spend my life in Fantasy land.

So we beat the boundaries as I suggested, shouting, 'Spike! Spike!' like a couple of vampire hunters, with me at least expecting to find a dead dog in a ditch at any moment. But all to no avail. I even went up my own steep lane shouting, and searched the Aces Acre graveyard.

By then the posters had arrived, and with the assistance of some local children we scoured the village itself, putting posters up as we went.

Everyone knew Spike by sight, but no one had seen him that day.

Yes, Spike had become the Invisible Dog.

Chapter 14

Shabby Tigers

The cat flu having been a false alarm, Mu decided to come back for a long weekend – but by train this time.

'But not for another go at the you-know-what,' she explained. 'I'll only find out this weekend whether it worked or not – but I'm sure it hasn't.'

'Can you find out for sure so early?'

'Pregnancy tests show you're pregnant from the first day of a missed period – only I'm not going to miss one because I feel just the same. I'll have to try again in a couple of weeks, if Simon is agreeable.'

'Simon is very agreeable. But I'm glad you're coming over this weekend.'

'Why, has that barmy git caught up with you at last?'

I had no trouble identifying Dave from this description. 'No, funnily enough there's been no sign of him. And anyway, he isn't a problem: he's all mouth and trousers. I can take care of him. No, it's just that I may have witnessed a suicide – sort of – and Spike, Miranda's dog, has disappeared. He was too old and fat to get far, and I'm worried Chris may have done something with him in a fit of pique over Miranda's rebellion. He's such a control freak, and she's really getting the bit between her teeth now.'

'I thought it was strange you'd been there a couple of months without a revolution breaking out,' she said. 'You can fill me in when we meet. I'll stay till Monday, if that's OK? I'm sure Ambler can manage to feed the cats until then, if I leave him simple written instructions.'

There was an aggrieved rumbling sound that told me Ambler had come into the room – and just as well he was out of earshot when she was going on about Simon!

'Oh, by the way, I'm bringing you a house-warming present,' she added, and giggled.

'I've already had a—' I began, but she'd rung off.

God knows what the present will be, I thought. With Mu it could be almost anything.

Mu's cropped ash-blonde head was visible in the door of the train as it pulled into the station, and by the time I'd walked down to the carriage she'd kicked two elegant tapestry cases on to the platform with thumps that would have set off an earthquake had we been in a volcanic area.

She followed them carrying a large wicker hamper, which she thrust into my arms: 'Here we are, your present – the ultimate Dave Deterrent.'

'He doesn't seem to need deterring any more—' I began, then broke off suddenly as the basket began to vibrate to the sound of unearthly yowls. 'What the hell is this? Banshee in a Box?'

'Not exactly.'

I staggered, regained my balance and turned an accusing glare on her. 'Tell me you haven't brought me a cat!'

'What else?' she said blithely and, commandeering a trolley, dumped both cases on it. I hastily added the basket, which moved about with a life of its own like a jumping bean, as the sound of rending claws began to draw nervous attention from passers-by.

It was noticeable that no one had got out of the same carriage as Mu: evidently they had had the sense to vacate it in case whatever was in the basket got out.

'She's been working on that basket on and off all the way down, the little rascal,' she said affectionately. 'Perhaps we'd better get her into the car?'

The look I gave her spoke volumes, but there was nothing for it but to lead the way.

Mu put the basket on the back seat and weighted down the lid with one of the suitcases. A wicked set of claws appeared through the little wicker portcullis and scored a direct hit on its tapestried surface.

'There, that should hold it until we get to Bedd,' she said unperturbed, then giggled. 'I'm sorry, it's that name: it brings out the schoolgirl in me.'

'It did with me too, but I've got used to it – and anyway, it just means "grave" in Welsh, which is definitely not humorous. Now, about that tiger in the back—'

She clapped her hands. 'Oh, the sea! Wonderful! Can we go round by Mumbles? I know it's a bit of a detour, but I just love it. I'd like to live in Mumbles. I found a village in Yorkshire once called Slack Top, which was tempting – and there was a Slack Bottom too, but I think that would be going a bit too far.'

'You know, you fell in love with Ambler's house in Pembrokeshire before you fell in love with him.'

'It was a close-run thing. But he did sweep me off my feet, didn't he?'

155

'Action Man personified: he saw, he fell in love, he didn't hang about. And you and that house fit together. Ambler's just the bun round the cheese: a bit of substance.'

'He's that, all right, and time hasn't staled his infinite variety, because he never had any – always boldly going where few have gone before.'

'But always coming back,' I pointed out. 'How did the Nile trip go, by the way? I never asked last time. Oh, and thanks for that picture you sent of Ambler in his canoe wearing a *Vengeane: Dark Planet* T-shirt.'

'Fine, except for a crocodile that took a very Hook-like fancy to him or his canoe and followed them for miles. His task while I'm away is to sort out his notebooks for me, so I can type it up into the usual Boy's Own Adventure yarn.'

'How is that scary cat you brought back from Egypt? Ankaret, was it? Did you ever decide which of the others fathered the kittens?'

'Oh, yes, it's definitely Coochie.'

I racked my brains. 'Coochie? Is that the big, daft hairy creature someone sent you from America? The one that hadn't . . . er . . . developed properly?'

'The Maine Coon, that's right. I think they gave up on him too soon, or he had a surge of hormones when he saw Ankaret!'

Something between guilt and amusement in her voice suddenly warned me what the much-abused basket contained.

'Mu!' I beseeched, taking my eyes off the road for one horror-struck second. 'Tell me you haven't brought me the bastard offspring of a wild Egyptian village cat and a retarded Maine Coon!'

'Of course,' she said simply. 'I saved the best for you, and you'll absolutely adore her – she has such character!'

'That's just what you said about the last man you tried to fix me up with,' I said bitterly, 'and it sounds as if she might adore me – to eat.'

'I picked her very carefully. And just think, Dave has an absolute phobia about cats – probably why I didn't fall for his charms like most other women – so he's never going to darken your door again, is he?'

'He's lost interest anyway,' I said. 'There's been no sight or sound of him. Maybe he's met a Significant Other. Or Others. Anyway, his phobia didn't stop him coming to your house that time to try to see me.'

'I think he'd just forgotten about the cats. He never came again, did he?'

'No, but that might be something to do with Ambler throwing him out.'

'You know, somehow I find it more worrying that he hasn't contacted you since you moved here than if you'd found him salivating on your doorstep. He's definitely severely warped where you're concerned.'

'I know. I was so braced to repel boarders, it was a bit of an anticlimax when there was no sign of him.'

'Perhaps he's just playing hard to get?' she suggested.

'Suits me – I don't want him.'

By now we were running down off the moors into the village, with the glint of the sea beyond, then I was pulling round the barn into the still-overgrown courtyard.

I hefted her luggage, leaving the cat basket for her, for there was already a bloody rend in my jeans and thigh. Those claws were razor sharp.

She followed, holding it at arm's length. 'You know, being right at the edge of the village you need a guard like this.'

'I intend to get a dog,' I said pointedly.

157

'Dogs have no dignity.'

'There's precious little dignity about whatever you've got in that basket!'

'You'll see,' she said, stepping through the conservatory. 'Fantasy Flowers is still here?'

'Yes, though Miranda is arranging to share a workshop at the craft centre with Lavender Duke, one of my next-door neighbours. She's a flower painter, and only uses it in the afternoon, so it will all fit together nicely. We're going to move it all down there soon, and then Miranda's going to advertise a bit more, and she's having an extra phone line put in The Hacienda, just for orders.'

'Sounds organized. You've really turned her into a revolutionary then? I can't imagine Chris giving his blessing to all of this independence.'

'He's not only *not* happy about it, he's been trying to frighten her back into line with all those pranks,' I said. 'And now Spike – I'm feeling more and more sure that he must know something about that. Come into the sitting room and I'll tell you all about it.'

Mu followed, carrying the basket. 'We'd better let the cat out first.'

'Fine, I'll get the chair and a whip, shall I?'

She gave me a withering look.

Chapter 15

Cat Flap

The half-grown kitten was big, and I mean: BIG. Also impressively stately once released from what she clearly considered sordid bondage – and the most peculiar cat I'd ever seen, resembling a big, shaggy, brindled leopard.

Mu had brought emergency cat rations, which accounted for at least some of the weight in her luggage, and proceeded to provide me, unasked, with a crash course in feline keeping for beginners.

The cat listened carefully – she looked smart enough to open her own tins – but I didn't bother, since my intention was to ensure she got back on the train with Mu when she left. It was probably the cat's intention, too, since she was giving me the impression that the accommodation wasn't quite up to the usual standards.

'You know,' I confided when we settled down later with a bottle of red, and a plate of (Miranda's) macaroons, 'I still can't quite believe the house is mine and I can afford to live here. I keep expecting my books to suddenly fall out of favour, or something.'

'Well, they aren't going to,' Mu said firmly. 'Fantasy is more popular now than it ever was, and anyway all these spin-offs – the T-shirts and the cartoon series and all that – mean that you can amass a little nest egg and sit on it even if it should somehow stop paying so well.'

'Any nest egg seems to be snatched away by the tax man. I still don't see why I have to give him so much of the money I worked hard for. Why can't my accountant haggle a bit?'

'Poor Mr Grace is tearing his hair out over your last accounts,' she replied, sticking a leather cushion behind her back and arranging herself gracefully on the sofa. 'All those carrier bags full of scribbled-on bits of old envelope and foreign receipts. I really don't think I'd suggest souk methods to him. You can't buck the tax system – Ambler pays even more than you.'

'That's because he's much richer. How is he? Doesn't he mind you popping down here again?'

'No, he thinks it's doing me good, and you know he likes you – he considers you a fountain of wisdom and good sense.'

'He isn't very bright, is he? But lovable. What about you – have you finished the next *Corduroy Cat* picture book?'

'Yes, it's done and gone. They want yet another one after that, too, so it seems to be going on and on – but they get someone else to write what story line there is, so I don't get all the proceeds. I'm doing illustrations for Miranda's *Party Animal* book, too.'

'You should write something of your own – something longer, for an older age group.'

'Me? I'm an illustrator, not a writer. What sort of book could I write?'

I thought about it seriously. 'It *would* have to be a cat book . . . about an adventurous cat . . . a bit like Ambler! A sort of

Indiana Cat, always off on expeditions to far-flung corners of the earth . . .'

Her green eyes glinted. 'It sounds wonderful . . . but I don't think it's in me to write that sort of thing.'

'Yes, it is. By the time you've finished editing Ambler's adventures they sound really gripping, even though I know his Sherpas have just carried him to the top of the peak and put him down in front of the camera!'

'Really, Sappho, he isn't that bad! The Sherpas in Nepal *insisted* on carrying him the last little bit of the way after he fell over his rucksack and bust his ankle. They liked him.'

'Whatever. Look, what if I give you a brief outline of each story and you can fill it in and do the pics? How about that? If there's one thing I have an excess of, it's stories.'

I could see I'd given her thoughts a whole new direction and when I returned from the kitchen (where I'd come under heavy scrutiny from my uninvited lodger) bearing coffee, she was scribbling away on some scrap paper she'd found next to my chair.

'Hope you don't mind me taking this,' she muttered, looking up. 'Just wanted to get the idea down while it was still there.'

'Take all you want,' I said, setting the tray down. 'Who was it who said she couldn't write her own stories?'

After a few more minutes of scribbling her eyes focused again and she commented, 'Nice coffee pot.'

'It was sent by a fan – she made it herself. I get all kinds of little gifts from fans these days, they're so kind, but this is the best so far. Just look at poor Raarg under that dragon!'

Mu studied it closely. 'Yes, but if Raarg were *really* like Dave he'd have leaped on it and rogered it to death by now.'

'I think that would be a bit over-ambitious even for Dave,

161

let alone Raarg, and my readers would be a little surprised.'

'Not half as surprised as the dragon.'

I regarded Mu with affection: she might look as snooty and remote as the snottiest of her cats, but her staunch loyalty and friendship has never wavered – and I hope I've always been there for her, too, when she needed me.

'I like your fingernails,' I said. 'Weren't they nautical scenes last time?'

Mu has been painting pictures on her nails for years, long before it became fashionable. She can do both hands, though the left is always neater than the right.

'Yes, and Ambler liked the nautical stuff, but he's not keen on my star clusters theme and says it looks like I've caught my fingers in a door. Look – I'm pleased with this one – it's the Trifid Nebula.'

'I'd never have guessed,' I said truthfully, but I thought the dark blue backgrounds and silvery-white specks very attractive. 'Ambler's just got no artistic sensibility.'

'No, but at least he's never been a jealous monster, like Chris. How's the revolution progressing?'

'Very well. It was a revolution waiting to happen. Miranda's so busy trotting round here to do the flowers, and off to the craft centre trying to organize that, and revamping *The Stuffed Student*, and trying out recipes for *Feeding the Party Animal*, that she hardly has time to eat – she must have lost a couple of stone since I got here, without trying.'

'Any sign of poor old Spike?'

'No, none, though we've been out searching every day. Miranda's put posters up everywhere with a very attractive reward, and there were a few false sightings, but no Spike. I'm suspecting more and more strongly that Chris has done something horrible to him, like stuff him in the car when he set off to London and dump him by the roadside halfway there.'

'He'd be capable of that,' Mu said, 'and where else could he be? Unless he's gone to join that missing woman – what was she called?'

'Dorinda. There's no sign of her either, but I've now met her husband, so I may be able to ask him some leading questions soon about where she's got to. There must be some hint that's been missed somewhere.'

The cat was reclining in the kitchen, having been shut out of the living room on my insistence, but as we carried the tray back in she sidled over, leaped up and twined like a fur stole around my neck.

'There, she likes you already,' Mu said, pleased. 'What are you going to call her?'

'Temporary Infliction?'

The brindled cat muffler rolled down the length of my hair and vanished under the table where she began to play with my bare toes.

Can you file cat's teeth?

'Tomorrow we'll have to get a few little things for her,' Mu said pensively.

'Like?'

'A litter tray, collar, bowls . . .'

'Is it worth it for one weekend?' I enquired pointedly, but she gave me a big smile.

'I knew you'd like her.'

The leopard gave me a centuries-steeped-in-sin look and I said nastily, 'Shouldn't she be snipped, or whatever they do to them?'

'Up to you. Ankaret was terribly fussy until Coochie came along – must have been the American accent.'

'I think I'll call her Tut, or Mut,' I said, struck by inspiration.

'Don't be silly,' Mu said severely, and the little stinker under the table took a none-too-gentle bite at my big toe.

Chapter 16

Suspicious Circumstances

I left Mu to sleep next morning and, after my *Vengeane* stint, drove to Rhossili and walked along the cliffs for the first time since the possible suicide.

It wasn't much after seven. The sky was clear enough to show me the great sweep of dark honey-coloured beach below, and there was no one else about.

It was great for thinking: thinking nasty thoughts, that is.

Standing right at the end, around where I must have fallen over the raincoat (though it's hard to tell exactly in the light of day), my suspicions coalesced into more of a certainty.

Later, when Miranda came round to the cottage to check for flower orders (one, relayed by Ambler; Miranda's new phone line is scheduled to be put in this coming week), it was clear by her blue-ringed eyes and pallor that Spike still hadn't turned up.

But then, I hadn't really expected he would have.

'And Chris phoned last night to say he's coming d-down this evening, and he's invited an old friend to stay with us – and he's *already* spread the word that we're having a really 'b-big party on Saturday night, and I d-don't feel remotely in the mood.'

'Tell him,' Mu suggested, buttering toast lazily at the kitchen table. She was wearing the oversized T-shirt she'd slept in, and her pale hair stood up in spikes, but she still looked better than most people who've only just fallen out of bed.

When I got up that morning I wasn't just having a bad hair day, but a Coco the Clown day, and it took lots of cold water and brushing to get one hank at the back to lie flat. Funny, you'd think the sheer weight of my hair would keep it down, wouldn't you?

'It was too late to tell him when he phoned me,' Miranda pointed out. 'He'd already invited lots of people and he gave me a list of everyone else he wants, as well. I only hope they all fit in. B-but I need b-both of you to come, too, for support.'

'But Chris hates us, Miranda,' I said. 'He isn't going to be very pleased if we turn up.'

'I'm not very pleased about the party, b-but it's *my* house and if I want to invite my friends I will.'

'That's the spirit,' applauded Mu. 'Do you want any of this toast?'

'Oh, no, thanks,' she said. 'I've got to go to the craft centre. I'm moving everything d-down today.'

'We'll help you – it will all fit in the two cars – and then we can leave you to sort it all out while we go and get some essentials for this creature.' I gave the Feline Fiend a dirty look and it stopped edging nearer the milk jug and sauntered off as if it had never even thought of such a thing.

'Oh, is she staying? I thought Mu had just b-brought her for company.'

'She's a house-warming present,' Mu explained.

'A rejected house-warming present,' I said firmly.

'You've lost weight, Miranda,' Mu observed, swiftly changing the subject.

'D-do you know, I hadn't weighed myself for ages, and then this morning I d-did and I was on the scale again!'

'On the scale?' echoed Mu.

'It only goes up to twenty stone and last time I was more than that. Now, I'm only a teeny bit over seventeen stone! I d-don't know how that happened. And I keep noticing things, like it's easier to b-bend d-down and I can walk to Llyn's shop without pausing halfway for a b-breather.'

'It's all this running about, what with the flowers and books and everything,' I said.

'I seem to have lost my appetite, too, since Spike vanished. It's strange, I usually eat when I'm sad, and eat when I'm happy, and eat – well, all the time.'

'You look good,' Mu said. 'And I love all these floaty tunics you wear, too.'

'They're out of a catalogue, b-but if I lost a b-bit more I'd fit into a size twenty and then I could buy clothes from ordinary shops like Marks and Spencer.'

Well, I can't say it's *my* idea of bliss, but it obviously gave Miranda something to aim for.

'And suddenly I feel that I want to b-be thinner so I can d-do all kinds of things,' she added.

'If it's bungee jumping I'd lose a bit more first,' Mu advised.

Miranda smiled. 'Not that sort of thing! B-but I've never b-been further abroad than Europe, and that was with Chris, so I only saw hotels really, and they all look the same whichever country you're in. I've always envied you and Sappho being able to go to all those exciting places and visit the sights.'

'But I kept inviting you to come abroad with me,' I pointed out.

'Yes, well, Chris always managed to stop me somehow, and later I was afraid I wouldn't fit in a plane seat, and they'd charge me for excess b-baggage, or something.'

She sighed. 'You will b-both come to the party, won't you? I feel Chris has only organized this to get b-back at me for standing up to him before he went to London, and he d-doesn't care about poor old Spike in the least – he just told me to go and get another dog!'

Her eyes filled. 'I know he must be d-dead, b-but if only I knew for certain what happened . . . that he d-didn't suffer.'

The nasty thoughts I'd had on the cliffs at Rhossili, which had been fermenting gently in the recesses of my mind like primeval slime, oozed back up into my consciousness. What if Chris didn't care because he *knew*?

There was only one way to find out so, after helping Miranda to transport Fantasy Flowers to her new workshop (with no sign of the mad potter in his bat cave, this time), I told Mu we were off to Rhossili for a bracing cliff walk.

'You went there this morning, and I'm not one for bracing walks. Besides, I want to look at the craftspeople here, and the shop.'

'We can do that another time: today I want you to see the spot where the suicide was supposed to have jumped off. I've got a nasty idea, and I very much want to have it proved wrong.'

It was still quite a bright day and lots of people were about, so it didn't look remotely sinister, the way it had in the mist. I showed Mu the spot marked X, and then we walked right along the huge beach below, but found nothing except fresh air, tourists and the soft-bellied underparts of (clothed) hang-gliders.

It was quite a hike back up from the beach, so I rewarded

Mu with a second huge all-day breakfast in the Seaspray Café.

It was the same Hair Attack waitress, who, surprisingly, remembered me and brought coffee straight away without being asked.

I've maligned the girl: she will go to the top of her profession (whatever it is) with a memory like that.

We'd almost finished, and I was studying my coastline map, when Supergrass came in and sat down at the other end of the room. He gave his order, then sat fiddling with his binoculars as if the instructions were written on the inside in Japanese, which perhaps they were, until he suddenly looked up and spotted us.

He shot over eagerly, bringing his tea with him: a bad sign.

'Ah – Miss Jones! Or may I call you Sappho?' he exclaimed with dreadful mateyness. Clearly our *entente* is unfortunately now *cordiale*. 'May I join you? What an unexpected pleasure to see you again so soon. I only hope the police didn't come round annoying you in the midst of a tricky chapter? I'm sorry I had to tell them about you, but I felt it was my duty . . . though they have been very unpleasant to me, *very*!'

He looked pointedly at Mu.

'My friend, Mu Graythorpe,' I said. 'Mu, this is Gilbert Ace.'

Mu had been slowly submerging white sugar cubes into her coffee, but she looked up with her black-ringed green eyes, and said, 'Hi!'

A gleam of eager interest lit his simian eyes. 'Not – surely not – *the* Mu Graythorpe, who illustrated Ambler Graythorpe's *Travels with My Yak in Tashkent* and—'

'Yes,' sighed Mu.

'And you illustrated that best-selling children's book – what was it? *Calico Cat* . . .'

'*Corduroy*.'

'How wonderful to meet you!' He began to lower his bottom on to the nearest seat without taking his eyes off her.

'Do join us,' I said heartily, beating his behind to touch-down by a millisecond. But irony was wasted on him – his antennae were too busy twitching.

'I'm an author too, you know,' he said modestly. 'I write books on ornithology.'

'Oh, yes?' she said politely. I removed the almost empty sugar bowl from within reach. When I was a little girl, Aunt Pops always told me eating too much sugar would give me worms, though she never specified what kind.

'Gil is the man I met here after that possible cliff suicide – the one who snitched on me to the police,' I explained.

'Oh, not snitched, dear Sappho – it's just that it was my duty and I'm sure they weren't suspicious that you'd done anything, though it was such an insalubrious morning for a cliff-top walk.'

'Yes, wasn't it? And you'd walked even further along it than I had, too, since you live on the other side.'

'My constitutional – I walk along the cliffs regularly in all weathers!'

'A creature of habit,' I observed.

'Habits are usually either dirty or boring,' Mu murmured languidly, having recaptured the sugar bowl and emptied it.

Gil went pink. 'Not at all, my dear Mrs Graythorpe, not at all. Nature's infinite variety never renders the walk the same twice. There's always something new to observe.'

'In a thick sea-mist?' I enquired.

'I found *you*, did I not?' he said gallantly.

'Only in the café – and actually, I found *you*, since there was no other table with space free.'

He laughed as if I'd said something funny and fondled his

brown beard. 'Miranda says she hopes you'll both be at the party tomorrow. I can't tell you how excited our little literary and artistic community will be to meet you – quite ecstatic.'

'Oh, really? They must be hard up for thrills – and I don't like ecstatic parties,' I said. 'I'm past the age for that sort of thing.'

'Oh, I don't know,' Mu said, striking a pose. 'Naked adoration never really palls on one, don't you find, Sappho?'

'Oh, one tires of everything eventually, Mu,' I replied in world-weary tones.

A worried expression crept into the glossy brown eyes: do people without a sense of humour realize they haven't got one?

Of course Mu and I aren't *that* well known – we're certainly not on the lips of the general public, and though I occasionally get recognized in the street, especially after that TV appearance (though I suspect that's notoriety rather than fame), it's only because I'm so tall and have very, very long hair: it makes me a bit easy to spot.

That chat show was a mistake – the host obviously had never read a book in her life, so my sarcastic ripostes to her insulting questions fell on deaf ears. And I looked strange, since I wouldn't let the make-up girl near me in case I was allergic to whatever she wanted to daub me with. Everyone else looked like a walking Pollock on set, but I'm told the effect appears natural on screen, while I looked as if I'd been dead for a week.

Gilbert had regrouped while my mind wandered. 'And have you – may I call you Mu? – come to visit and admire our wonderful scenery?'

'I came to see Sappho, so the scenery's a bonus,' Mu replied demurely, even though she was probably having the same mental vision of teenagers and turkey basters as I was.

'I thought I'd show Mu the site of the mysterious raincoat, and then we walked along the beach in search of the missing owner, though I suppose the police have already done all that.'

Gil preened a little. 'If only you'd asked my advice first, or the police had! From my years of observation I could have told them that anything going off the cliff at that exact point would not wash up down there' – he indicated the great curved beach – 'but in a spot on the other side of the headland, if at all.'

He sat back complacently, awaiting our admiration.

'Take us there,' I said.

Chapter 17

Doggone

'It's quite a scramble down,' Gil warned.

'That's fine, we were only just saying that we longed for a good scramble, weren't we, Mu?'

Since she'd already spent an hour or more promenading down a windswept beach, followed by the long, steep climb back up, her agreement was resigned rather than enthusiastic.

Gil was certainly right about the scramble: we were soon following in his wake down a vertiginous sheep track to a lonely cove, on the far side of the headland to the putative jumping-off site.

Gil chatted all the way down, without seeming to need any reply, which was fortunate, since Mu and I were both fully occupied in clinging to the cliff face.

Did I realize, he enquired, that I was named after a famous Greek poetess who died falling off a cliff? I'd better be careful not to follow suit, heh, heh!

Mu and I made eyes-crossed, tongue-out gargoyle faces at each other behind his oblivious back. And he was certainly spry, for he went down there like a mountain goat, confessing sheepishly over his shoulder that he was a twitcher, which I'd previously thought to be some strange religious sect like Holy Rolling, but which turned out only to mean that he spotted rare birds like other men spot trains, and pursued the sightings all over the place.

We arrived somewhat dishevelled and out of breath at the cliff base, glad to feel the sand beneath our feet.

The sun was shining, the sea was going 'shush! shush!' and the gulls were kicking up a hell of a racket. Gil was still maundering on.

'On this very spot last year I saw a very rare visitor indeed. A—'

'What are those gulls over there making such a racket about?' Mu broke in without ceremony. 'By the rocks?'

She began picking her way delicately through the snares of seaweed to where a small humped shape, beset by flying scavengers, was being gently nudged by the sea's advancing lip.

I followed, despite Gil's plaintive bleat of, 'Better let me go first, ladies – it may be something unpleasant!'

Ignoring him, we shooed off the gulls and stared sadly down at what had once been a gross, smelly, beloved old dog; a dog who had never known a moment's fear in his life – I hoped. I *hoped* it had been that way right to the end.

'It's – oh, it's only a dog,' Gil said, sounding relieved, though looking a bit white behind the navy-lark beard. 'Come away – it's a bit grisly, but the gulls will clean it up. It's Nature's way, you know—'

He broke off and exclaimed with horror, 'What on earth are you doing?'

With reverent revulsion I was unbuckling the pulpy remains of a gay tartan collar from around the old, sodden throat that would never now whinge for another chocolate biscuit.

'There's no way anyone could tell how he died now,' observed Mu. 'Something other than the gulls has been at him – there's not really much left at all. Maybe there are piranhas off the Gower?'

'I suppose you mean to return the collar to the owner,' twittered Gil, 'which is a kind thought, perhaps, but then again, it might upset—'

'It's Spike,' I interrupted. 'I'd know that collar anywhere. Miranda's Spike.'

Gil blanched even further and his mouth caught a few passing sandflies. 'But that can't possibly be Spike! We're miles away from Bedd – what on earth would he be doing here?'

To do him credit he looked genuinely shocked and upset when I showed him the name disc on the collar. 'Poor Miranda! I suppose the senile old thing just wandered away and tumbled over the cliffs . . . but I never dreamed he could get this far.'

'Spike was incapable of wandering much further than the back garden, and unless he'd learned to drive a car or fly since I last saw him, he certainly didn't get here under his own steam,' I snapped, and Gil recoiled a little, looking hurt.

'Perhaps boys larking about? A visitor who took a fancy to him?'

'Perhaps anything,' I said shortly. 'But what shall we do with the remains? There's not much left, and the tide's about to take it away again.'

'Do? You can't mean . . .?' Gil gibbered.

'It wouldn't stand being moved up the beach, Sappho,' Mu pointed out, 'certainly not back up that cliff path. Besides, there doesn't seem much point. Miranda shouldn't see him like this. Gil was right – let Nature take its course. Its second course, from the look of it, if not its third. The tide's about to turn – let's send old Spike out with it like a Viking.'

So we did, with the help of a largish piece of wooden pallet, some tinder-dry flotsam, and Gil's lighter, though I didn't think Spike himself would burn, since he was too wet.

Gil seemed reluctant to take the lighter back from my hand afterwards, and also disgusted by our wading about floating a smelly dead dog off the rocks in our bare flippers, but I can assure you now that whatever diseases of the feet dead dogs give you, we didn't catch it.

Escorted by a mourning phalanx of thwarted gulls the sad carcass was borne away on a plume of smoke, while Mu, shading her eyes, intoned the immortal words: 'I am going out and I may be some time.'

'And will the clock strike half past three, and Gourmet Dinner for my tea?' I contributed.

'Farewell, beloved old companion,' contributed Gil more prosaically, but it was a nice thought.

Gil continued to distance himself from us, even after we'd bathed our legs in a nice clean rock pool. Having seemed oblivious previously to anything other than boobs and birds, he suddenly seemed to notice Mu's appearance: the fingernails, the Gothic Vampire draperies and the big black boots (when she put them back on), and for the rest of the Annual Outing of Dog Launchers treated her as if she were in the final throes of something very, very unmentionable and catching, that even Authorship wasn't enough to redeem her from.

Fortunately I had a plastic bag in my pocket for collecting shells, which I stuffed the collar into. 'I'd be grateful, Gil, if you keep our find to yourself until I've broken the news to Miranda.'

This was not a task I relished, for while it might be a relief to her to know for certain that Spike was dead and there had been no visible signs of violence, the truth of how he died and got to Rhossili might prove even more upsetting.

Still, she was an adult with the right to the facts, unadorned by my interpretations. When she got her hands on the person who flung poor old Spike off the cliff, dead or alive, I'd like to be there.

Gil, strangely eager now to leave us, made off in the direction of home. I think any faint erotic attraction I might have held for him had forever been overlaid with defunct Spike.

'Do you know what I'm going to do now?' I asked Mu as we wearily hauled ourselves back up on to the cliff path.

'Go straight home and have a hot bath, with lots of scented stuff in it?' she said hopefully.

I shook my head, though the thought had its attractions.

Duty first.

'Have a look at the raincoat Gil found on the cliff top?' she hazarded.

'Got it in one.'

'Two,' she corrected.

We tried the nearest (tiny) police station and discovered the mac in a box marked 'Lost Property'. In the absence of a body, interest had obviously waned.

It was a man's medium-sized beige trenchcoat – but I know women who wear those – and fairly new, with nothing in the pockets, and no helpful name tag.

The officer had lost interest and was wrinkling his nose over the strange odour that had invaded his office, and his brow over a crossword puzzle.

'In a pig's eye?' he muttered.

Mu and I spread the mac open. Inside was a coating of chocolate-brown dog hair and a warm, familiar, fusty old-dog smell.

The coat turned into a shroud before our very eyes.

'Four letters . . .' mused the officer.

'Stye,' I choked, blinking rapidly.

'Oh, thank you, madam. Stye it is.' He wrote it in and then looked up. 'Now, does either of you ladies recognize the raincoat?'

'I'm afraid we've never seen it before,' I said with perfect truth, and handed it back.

Chapter 18

Bolted

For some reason when we got home, the cat didn't want anything to do with us, but retired into the conservatory looking disgusted.

I bagged a quick first shower, though you can't wash the smell of dead dog out of your head, then left Mu to soak in the bath while I went round to break the bad news to Miranda.

From past experience, I've found that the best way is to give it to them straight without trying to wrap things up, so that's what I did, telling her everything we'd done, but without drawing any conclusions.

Then I tactfully went to make a drink while she cried over the once-bright tartan collar.

When she'd got over the first shock I explained that we hadn't been able to bring his body home and had instead given him a Viking funeral, which she approved of. Then I described to her exactly *where* we'd found Spike and how we'd gone to look at the raincoat at the police station.

'B-but he could never have got d-down there on his own, could he?' she said, puzzled. 'How d-did he – who could have . . .? And the raincoat – you think someone wrapped him in it?'

Her eyes brimmed over again. 'I've b-been getting all these phone calls since I put Spike's poster up . . . and I suppose I'll go on getting them for weeks!'

'We'll take them down again for you – all the ones we can find. Weren't there a hundred?'

'Yes, and I put them *everywhere*.' She'd sunk down into her chair and clearly wasn't going to be up to much for a while. 'B-but I can't remember where!'

The phone rang and I answered it: it was someone else reporting seeing a dog like Spike. There were three more calls until I took the phone off the hook. Miranda had fetched two boxes of chocolate flakes out of the kitchen by then, the mini ones for cake decorating, and was tearing the cellophane off with her teeth.

'I'm going to get Mu and go on a poster hunt now,' I told her, not without an inward sigh for poor, neglected, interestingly new-minted Raarg. 'Leave the phone off the hook for a couple of hours. And tonight we'll go to the pub to drown our sorrows.'

Suddenly conscious of my unfortunate turn of phrase I added quickly, 'Be ready at eight, and we'll call for you on the way.'

'I-I d-don't want to go out to the pub or anywhere else. I couldn't possibly—' The words came out accompanied by a shower of chocolate shards, since she was now cramming flakes in by the handful. 'And Chris d-doesn't think the pub is very salubrious.'

'Bugger Chris. Not only is it salubrious to the point of being staid, it's a damn sight better than sitting here alone. Anyway, Spike deserves a wake and you can tell us all about his happy times, which is what a wake's for.'

*

Poor Mu and I got to know the ins and outs of the Gower extremely well that afternoon.

I drove, and she poster-spotted, leaping out to tear each one down. It didn't do the nail paint much good, but it was her own fault: if she'd mastered the art of turning right, she could have driven.

The cat had elected to come with us and, short of a bloody battle, declined to be removed. But despite my misgivings she behaved impeccably, perched bolt upright on the back seat like a dowager.

'Eighty-eight,' Mu said wearily as we reached the outskirts of Swansea on one of our wider sweeps. 'I'm knackered and I need food.'

We settled for iced Italian coffee and cake at the Marina, where we could park and leave the cat to guard the car, with all the windows cranked open an inch – though there aren't many antique Volvo thieves about.

On the way out of Swansea again we stopped to purchase an expensive but tasteful cat collar and other items Mu assured me I would need, despite my resistance.

Then she chose a cat flap, even though I told her I wasn't having chunks taken out of my beautiful Portuguese door.

'It can go in the conservatory door, then,' she said.

'The conservatory is about to be demolished.'

'Then you could have a lovely new one, instead.'

'We could buy a lovely big new basket, so you can take her home again with you,' I suggested, but she just smiled and said she was sure I was joking, but if I really didn't take to the cat she would always have her back (though I suspect by then we'd need one of those travelling cages circuses have).

The cat seemed quite taken by the collar, which had

cunning little elastic inserts, so it didn't get hung up on things, and a bell. I have no wish to receive small dead offerings of inoffensive birds and mice, however well meant.

It all cost me a fortune, but we found a Spike poster pinned up in the shop as a bonus.

Eighty-nine.

By returning homewards with all the frilled convolutions of an intestine we managed to clock up ninety-two, which seemed to me to be a near miracle. It was a testament to Miranda's love that she'd had the stamina to put them all up in the first place.

We were shattered by our traumatic day, and somewhat surprised to find Simon pottering around the courtyard awaiting our return.

'You didn't order a Second Coming, did you?' I said to Mu.

'Not yet – I won't find out whether the first one worked until Sunday.'

'Then you're going to have to take him away and explain the facts of life and times of the month and stuff to him.'

But it transpired that he was only on his way up the Valleys to a friend's party and, having learned from Ambler that Mu was here, thought he'd drop by, in case he was needed.

Mu provisionally booked him for a fortnight hence, we plied him with food and drink, and then he went off to his party without a care in the world.

Ah, youth . . .

I was sitting at the green-metallic-flecked Formica table (which I'm ashamed to say I'd fallen in love with by then and intended to keep), when Mu came back from seeing him off.

I'd fed the cat gourmet chunks in a new china bowl and she'd retired replete to the top of the radiator, where she lay in an improbably furry oblong parcel like a cheap rolled rya rug.

'Sphinx!' I exclaimed, as Mu wearily sank on to a chair and held a cup out for tea. 'That's what I'll call her.'

Mu began to spread her nail-repairing kit out around the tea things. 'Well, it's not bad. I'll Sphinx about it, and let you know.'

I groaned.

By the time we went to collect Miranda we were both stiffening up from all the cliff scrambling – Throbbing Thigh Syndrome. I'm not as fit as I was before I came here; I'll have to do more hills.

To my surprise Miranda was ready to go out, though very quiet and with reddened eyelids, but also with the resolute expression of a woman who has been doing some hard thinking and come up with unpalatable answers. She isn't stupid even if she's spent all her married life being told she is, and once she'd thought about the combination of 'Geronimo!' and men's raincoats she was bound to draw the same conclusions we had.

The Spoon and Lizard had once been a small pub, but had expanded in a reasonably picturesque way to meet the demands of hungry tourists. It was busy even this early in the year, but we found a corner and ordered hearty food, for there's a time and a place for cholesterol, calories and alcohol, and this was it.

Miranda grew up in Bedd, but strangely enough I seemed to be acquainted with a lot more people than she, though perhaps eating at the pub a lot had introduced me to a wider circle.

After a bit I spotted Lili installed in one of the little mock horse-box affairs around the far side of the room. She saw us at the same time and smiled and waved, but then made 'keep away' signals. The man she'd boxed in there was a darker shape in the shadows beyond, but there was a gleam of pale hair: the potter.

Well, 'potter and clay endure', as Browning once said, and she was safe from interruption from us tonight.

She must have had to leave him to his own devices at some point, though, for later, while we were drinking Irish coffee, she came across and sat down with us, looking disconsolate.

'Bolted, the bastard!' she said. 'You know, I'm starting to lose faith in myself. I've never had to admit defeat yet but – tell me truthfully all of you, have I lost my charms?'

'No, they all seem to be still there,' I said. 'Perhaps you're just not his type?'

'I'm *exactly* his type – small, slim, ravishing and dark, like his ex.'

'Then maybe he doesn't want to be reminded of his ex?'

'Let's have another Irish coffee,' Mu suggested brightly. 'Will you join us, Lili? And just look who's—'

'Miranda, *there* you are!' Chris's voice broke in, stiff with anger.

Chapter 19

Icing Over

If Chris was expecting the usual crumbly fondant Miranda he was in for a shock, for she snapped back in rock-hard royal icing mode, 'D-didn't you see my note?'

What with everything else, I'd totally forgotten that he was supposed to be coming back this weekend, but evidently she hadn't.

He looked gobsmacked. 'Yes – yes I did, but I expect you to be there when I get home, not carousing in the pub!'

'And in such bad company,' chimed in Mu helpfully. 'I didn't think anyone used that sort of line any more, Chris.'

Apart from a disgusted look, he ignored her, but clearly he was becoming conscious of the stares of the curious for he plastered an unconvincing smile on his face and moderated his voice. 'Is it too much to ask that when I bring a friend down for the weekend, you're there to greet him? What will he think?'

'Perhaps that you should have given me some warning of what time you were arriving?' Miranda suggested coldly.

His jaw dropped despite the interested audience, and he looked more Mr Weasel than jolly TV cook.

'We're just about to have another drink,' I said. 'Hadn't you better get back to your guest?'

Pop goes the weasel: for an interesting moment I thought he might try to commit violence against my person, a definite mistake since I'm bigger than he is. All his enticing little freckles ran together into one red blur of fury, but after an internal struggle he managed to regain control of everything except the twitching muscle in his cheek.

'Certainly,' he said, straightening up and unclenching his hands and teeth (and probably his buttocks). 'But naturally I was worried about Miranda when she wasn't home – she doesn't usually go out at night, and in her present mental state—'

'Apart from natural grief over Spike, I'd say her mental state was more normal than yours,' Mu said.

This time he actually looked at her, smiling more confidently. 'Ah, yes, but you don't know all the funny little things she gets up to, does she, darling?'

'Yes, she does. We *all* know you've been doing those,' I said contemptuously.

'Yes,' added Miranda, who had whitened but not dissolved (like coffee creamer), 'and speaking of funny things, Spike has been found washed up on a b-beach near Rhossili. Now, how on earth d-do you think that happened?'

'I – er – I've no idea. Rhossili? Extraordinary!' He'd gone pale and the façade was definitely cracking.

'It's raining tonight,' Miranda added with seeming inconsequence. 'Where's your raincoat?'

'My-my raincoat? I left it in L-London,' he stammered, backing off. 'Look, Miranda, I'd better go back to the house and see how – I'll see to things.' And he practically ran out of the pub leaving us all staring after him, Miranda with a very unloving expression.

'D-did you see his face? I'm not living with a murderer!' she declared.

Mu and I exchanged looks. 'There isn't any hard evidence that he had anything to do with Spike's disappearance,' I said. 'It's all circumstantial.'

'You saw his expression – he d-did it. I expect he was so angry when he left for London, just b-because I'd stood up to him for once, that he took it out on my poor old d-dog like Mr B-Barrett would have done to Flush if Elizabeth hadn't taken him off to Italy with her.'

'Elizabeth who?' demanded Mu, who had lost the thread. 'Flush?'

'B-Barrett – when she eloped with Robert B-Browning. She insisted she take her spaniel, Flush, with them b-because she thought her father would d-do something horrible to it when he found out about the elopement.'

'Right. But somehow I can't see Chris actually *murdering* poor Spike – he's so *mimsy*,' Mu said. 'It's more likely he just found Spike dead when he went down that morning, and decided to dispose of the body.'

I could see that Miranda wanted to believe in Spike's natural demise, but was not totally convinced (and neither was I, actually), and when we'd had another round of cream-topped Irish coffees, she said she was going to get the truth out of Chris, but whatever happened he would be moving into the spare bedroom tonight and then, after the weekend, out of her life, too.

It might be the drink talking, but I'd never seen her quite like that.

We didn't leave until throwing-out time, and parted on the village green from where we could see Miranda's house. She set off like a juggernaut in search of something to squash – or someone.

But I expected her sense of propriety would keep the lid on things until their guest had departed, though Mu thought she'd simply buckle down again from sheer force of habit. Still, if Chris hadn't come up with an explanation to put his actions in the best possible light by now, he was not the sneaky, devious little weasel I thought him.

We'd see the next evening, for Miranda insisted we both go to the party to support her. We anticipated it would be interesting in a Chinese curse 'may you live in interesting times' sort of way.

We walked companionably up the narrow winding lane into the darkness beyond the Dukes, who always left a small mock lamppost lit up outside. Then I felt the back of my neck prickle.

'Someone's watching us, Mu.'

She scanned the darkness dubiously. 'I can't see anyone.'

'It's just a feeling . . . but it's going, so perhaps I imagined it.'

'Or maybe Dave's found you again?'

'He'd have walked straight into the pub as if he expected me to be pleased to see him. He doesn't try any of that stalking business since that time I thought he was a mugger and half-killed him.'

'Probably just your neighbours looking out, then,' she said. 'After all, you've been here for weeks, within easy reach of Dave – he could have found you if he wanted to. Perhaps he simply got bored with it all. We're none of us spring chickens any more.'

'Speak for yourself: I intend springing for as long as I can.'

I switched on my torch as we went round the dark barn into the even blacker depths of the courtyard. I vowed to remember to leave a light on in the kitchen if I went out in the evening.

'You need a new gate, the fence mending, an outside light or two . . .' Mu said, thinking along the same lines. 'Smoke alarm, burglar catches on the window. Burglar alarm.'

'Razor wire, shotgun, guard dog?' I put in.

'That's going a bit too far, and now you've got the cat you don't need a dog.'

When we went in, the guard-cat blinked at us in the sudden light and made noises that I hoped indicated welcome, before resuming her game of batting a piece of paper round the floor.

To her vociferous disgust, I captured her toy and smoothed it out: none of the paper in my house is blue.

The only legible bit said 'pho'. My name? 'I will phone'? 'Speak phonetically'? The bit of handwriting was too badly defaced for me to be sure – or for it to be recognizable.

Maybe it *was* Dave lurking out there after all?

If it was, I hoped the cat ate him next time. By then she would probably be big enough to play with him first.

Chapter 20

Breaking Up Is Hard to Do

Fortunately I never suffer from hangovers (I may sometimes drink a lot, but I always know when to stop), so my early morning writing session went just as well as usual.

Raarg, having seemingly been transformed, was now showing signs of slipping back into his evil ways, although Nala hadn't found out yet. Dragonslayer was getting up her nose, but she was also attracted to him.

I hadn't got the faintest idea what was going to happen. They'd just have to fight it out among themselves – like Miranda and Chris, if she didn't bottle out of a confrontation at the last minute. Mu and I would find out that evening.

Since Mu was also up and about bright and early we made an impulse decision to have a day out to Laugharne on the Dylan Thomas tourist trail, leaving an indignant cat alone with the new litter tray.

Laugharne is a magical, peaceful place, surprisingly unspoiled by its claim to fame. The boathouse where they lived is a museum now, and tiny, so what with the warring Thomases, the children, and the dog, it's no wonder Dylan went off to his little wooden hut to write.

We had lunch at a pub, and then spent much longer walking around than we'd intended, making us quite late back home. The phone was ringing as we got in and Mu answered it while I fed the cat and did vile things with litter trays, which is definitely not a fun part of cat keeping.

'Either you learn to use the toilet, or you go,' I advised her as she watched me clean up the mess. 'And another thing – stay off my kitchen work surfaces, or else!'

I could tell how impressed she was by the quality of her yawns.

'That was Ambler,' Mu told me, coming back in. 'He wanted to know how many cats he was supposed to be feeding this time, because there are six more than on his list.'

'He's being taken for a ride by the local moggies again, then?'

'He certainly is. They must put the word out as soon as they see me leave with luggage. If I don't get back soon we'll be bankrupt and all the local cats will have died of obesity.'

'It's a pity we've got to go to the party tonight.' I propped a print of the Laugharne boathouse in front of me. 'My feet are tired – yesterday was pretty hectic.'

'Miranda's counting on us, and if she's had things out with Chris she'll need our support even more,' said Mu. 'But we could always arrive late and leave early.'

'It's getting late now and we're not even ready,' I pointed out.

'You've got nine messages on your answering machine. Aren't you going to listen to them?'

'No, there isn't time and they won't be anything interesting. I'll run through them later. Look, here's a spare door key in case you want to slope off from the party earlier or later than me.'

'Thanks: I might at that, since I'm not going to know anyone much, am I? Except Gil, if finding a dead dog in someone's company counts as acquaintance.'

'Lili will probably be there.'

'Will she bring that dishy blond man we saw in the pub? I wouldn't mind a closer look at him.'

'I don't know, and I wouldn't call him dishy. He's bad-tempered, too.'

I sighed. 'I've never really seen the point of parties. I usually spend them trying to escape some small man who's measuring me up like Everest for future ascent.'

'You always manage to shake them off. And think positive, you might enjoy it. I'm going to change.'

I suppose I might just spot my Dark Donor at the party, but then again, pigs might fly.

When Mu came down she was wearing a jade-green silk shift dress that reflected her eyes, set off her ash-blonde hair and roused my envy, for it's not the sort of dress that suits me at all. And it was a change from her usual black outfits.

My dress was a vaguely Victorian garment of amber lace over satin, which I'd recently discovered in an antique shop. Most vintage clothes are midget-sized: whoever owned this one must have been a giantess among her peers, maybe even an ancestress of mine.

My hair had been quietly growing away as usual (it has a secret plan to take over the world), and had once more reached hazard lengths, besides being a constant temptation to the cat. Mu cut a foot off the end with the kitchen scissors and offered to do it in a French plait, but there wasn't time so I just let it hang.

We left lights on and the radio on low to keep the cat company, then stepped out into the rain under a big umbrella.

It wasn't far enough to justify taking the car, but I was wearing silly sandals, for once, with slithery soles and high heels, so my part was more of a soft-shoe shuffle when we did our 'Singin' in the Rain' impersonation.

We deduced from Chris's expression that he'd seen us dance up the drive, but at least he didn't slam the door in our faces, which would not have surprised me.

On Mu he bestowed a look of acute dislike and said how nice it was to see her, and was she still married to Ambler? To which she replied that unless you could get a divorce in two hours she supposed she was, and passed in smiling blandly.

It sounded like feeding time at the zoo in there.

Chris was regarding me like the cat who had not only got the canary, but was having it for tea later, lightly warmed up on toast. He said he was so glad I'd come because he had an old friend of mine staying with him whom I would just love to see again.

I was certain who it was then, but I resisted my first impulse to turn round and go away, although when Chris took my arm and attempted to propel me into the room I shook him off.

I removed my rain cape and gave him custody of that instead, then followed Mu down the hall and into the living room, which was solid with bodies and noise.

As we paused on the threshold Chris called shrilly from behind me, 'Here she is!'

A man, taller than the rest, turned to look at me, raising mobile eyebrows in a dark, handsome face. A very Byronic, masculine face, brown eyes glistening under long lashes and crisp black hair that was trying to curl at the ends.

It was, of course, Dave Devlyn – and better to meet him here and get it done with. Since he hadn't contacted me for months, I even wondered if perhaps this was a coincidence and he wasn't interested any more.

But no, he began to forge towards me, shedding adoring women as he came.

Miranda bobbed up beside me, covered in glistening ice-blue fabric like a small iceberg and with an expression in her eyes to match. 'I phoned you earlier – d-didn't you get my messages?' she hissed. 'I d-didn't realize who it was until I got b-back from the craft centre at lunch time – he'd gone to b-bed when I got home yesterday.'

'We've been out, but it doesn't matter, I might as well get it over with. Why are we whispering?' I added.

'I d-don't know.'

'Have you had things out with Chris?' I asked.

'Yes – I'll tell you all about it later and D-Dave's staying on the Gower, b-by the way. He's going to photograph everyone for a b-book.'

'*Everyone?*'

'Everyone arty,' she qualified. 'It's all this New Cornwall stuff again.'

'Oh shit!' I said. Then: 'Look, Mu's intercepting Dave!'

Mu is five foot three and Dave might have gone straight over her like a juggernaut had she not said something that clearly stopped him in his tracks. His eyes never left me as he bent his dark head and replied.

Whatever he said, she didn't like it. There was a yelp, and Dave resumed his progress, limping.

Like me, Mu was wearing high heels, for a change: it doesn't do to become a creature of habit.

She gave me a grin and headed off towards the dining room while Dave loomed up and attempted to sweep me into his arms. He smelled rather delicious, and there was nothing wrong with his muscles, because it was quite a tussle holding him off. I had to use my elbows for leverage.

'Sapphie darling – here you are at last! Aren't you going to kiss me?'

'Hello, Dave,' I said unenthusiastically. 'Still crazy after all these years?'

'Crazy for you,' he said, smiling disturbingly down at me. 'You look like a barbaric queen in that dress, with your hair loose and all that chunky amber – that's the way I'm going to photograph you for the book. There's no one like you.'

'There doesn't seem to be anyone else like you either, thank God,' I rejoined, trying to ease back a bit before his body heat singed anything. When I haven't actually seen him for a while I tend to forget just what he's like – sexy, attractive, successful, devious . . . fixated. It's that certain mildly insane glint in the eye whenever he looks at me that gives it away every time. It was still there.

'You know you've always loved me,' he said confidently. 'So now you've finally got the wanderlust out of your system—'

'What do you mean, I love you?' I demanded. 'I *don't* love you – I don't even *like* you!'

'You don't mean it: the attraction's still there, I can feel it. Why try to deny it?'

'Oh, yes, and I suppose you've devoted yourself to a life of celibacy for my sake?'

'No, but *you* seem to have for mine, darling.'

'Don't flatter yourself: the whole experience with you was such a disappointment I decided not to bother any more.'

He was unruffled. 'I know you're not the frigid spinster you like to pretend.'

'Lukewarm, these days, and not even tepid where you're concerned. Face it, Dave: I'm just not interested.'

He frowned and moved closer (if possible). 'Sapphie, don't jerk me around – it's time we got back together. When Chris told me you'd settled here I knew it. I'm going to be down here for quite a while, so you'd better get used to the idea fast.'

'Dave, I'm *not* jerking you around: I really am not interested in exchanging anything with you except a wave and a hello in passing.' If I didn't see him coming first.

'I'm going to be staying at the village pub from tomorrow – unless you will have me, Sapphie. *Will* you have me?' he said throatily.

'No I won't!' I exclaimed impatiently. 'Why don't you listen to what I'm saying?'

'I walked round and put a note through your door last night,' he said obliviously. 'Didn't you get it?'

'No, the cat ate it.'

'Cat?' A frown marred his brow. 'Oh – Mu's staying with you, isn't she? Has she brought one of her damned cats with her?'

'No, it's mine: a big, beautiful, half-wild cat,' I added with relish.

'You know I can't stand cats! Get rid of it.'

'Why the hell should I? The only thing I want to get rid of is you! If you don't come to the house it won't bother you, will it? So just leave me alone, Dave. I won't even say "let's be friends" because we were never that, just lovers. Stay away.'

I pushed past him, intent just on getting away, though I could feel his eyes boring holes in my shoulder blades until I moved into the dining room.

I didn't think it would be too long before he followed me and made a scene, and the thought of escaping back to the cottage and my guardian kitten was very tempting.

I looked round for Mu, who'd managed to insinuate herself

on to a sofa next to Lili's potter, while Lili herself hung off a little, scowling and outmanoeuvred.

Nye Thomas's white-gold hair was bent near to Mu's ash-blonde bob like a pair of conversing angels, and the muted light shadowed the dark hollows beneath his high cheekbones, and the small cleft in his chin. He had the sort of lips that made you want to touch them.

Repulsive: I'd had enough of vain, handsome men.

Turning away in disgust I helped myself to a full glass of red wine and some of Miranda's delicious nibbles: then, more slowly, another glass of wine, and finally I began to relax a bit.

After all, there really was no need to get rattled, just because Dave was a tiny bit unbalanced. Once he saw I was blatantly uninterested he'd probably come to his senses.

Passing behind the disconsolate Lili, I murmured, 'Dave Devlyn – in the other room.'

'What? Really? Why didn't someone say?' she exclaimed, perking up, and made off like a heat-seeking missile.

I moved on to the helpfully labelled non-alcoholic fruit punch, and Gil hove up beside me towing a small red-faced Scot, whom he introduced as Rory McCrory, a thriller writer so Scottish he sounded bogus. Why do I attract this type of small man?

It's not as if he didn't have a certain charm either, but by then it was all fairly awash. Gil had taken my arm while introducing me and was still holding it in a vaguely proprietorial way, his fingers tightening as Rory issued a series of invitations to me, ranging rapidly downwards from dinner to five minutes in the garden, none of which I took seriously.

A few moments later I heard him repeating the same offers to Mu, who had been ousted from her love seat by other admirers, and I'd have joined them if Gil hadn't still been doing limpet impersonations.

'Can Mrs Graythorpe's name really be Mu, I wonder?' he said, smiling. 'Perhaps – Muriel?'

'She's always called Mu,' I assured him enigmatically, having been sworn to secrecy years ago on the subject of Mu's name. 'Something to do with her mania for cats.'

'My wife likes cats,' he said pensively, and sighed.

'Does she?' A human touch. I wondered if Dorinda had just run off or had gone through that great Cat Flap in the Sky – and if so, whether Gil helped her there. Or the potty potter.

'Yes, her cat – poor Muff – she misses her so much. She would never have left her.'

'Muff? What an original name!'

'She was – is – a very original woman. We were very close. Whatever happened, she had no intention of leaving . . . it must be amnesia.'

For one horrible minute I thought his brimming eyes were going to overflow, and I patted his hand consolingly as he fought back the tears with a manly snivel.

'I know she'll return one day, and she'll find everything just as she left it. I dust her computer daily,' he added inconsequentially. 'When she comes home you must meet – I'm sure she'll get to like you, and all that business with the cottage will be forgotten.'

'Why, thank you, Gil.'

'Yes, she doesn't like modern manners, of course, but I'm sure once she knew you she'd overlook all that.'

All what? I wondered. I wasn't sure whether to be insulted or not.

'Perhaps,' he added, 'you'd like to come to tea tomorrow and meet Muff?'

'Well, that's very tempting, Gil, but—'

I broke off, for suddenly I felt, rather than saw, a dark brooding gaze fixed on me. I'd almost managed to forget my problem for a few minutes there, but if Dave had seen me fending off Rory, and chatting so confidentially with Gil . . .?

Poor harmless Gil didn't deserve the jealous anger he was likely to be on the receiving end of. I smiled quickly at him and said, 'That would be lovely – but in a day or two when Mu's gone back? Can I give you a ring? Excuse me.'

I seized the moment and sidled off behind the nearest knot of people into the hall, ready to escape, only to find my exit blocked: Chris was standing in front of the door with his back to me talking with someone.

I did a quick reverse through the door behind me, which turned out to be the kitchen, but no sooner was I in than I remembered there was no back door out of it.

But I could at least keep watch and pop out when the coast was clear, snatch my cape and go home.

I'd had enough, and as Jane Austen once said, the sooner every party breaks up the better.

Chapter 21

Punch Drunk

Shutting the door behind me I leaned against it and closed my eyes, feeling like a hunted creature. Something big: an elk, perhaps?

But as I patted the top of my head to check for antlers it crossed my mind that maybe I'd had a *smidgeon* too much to drink on an almost empty stomach. Though actually, I carry my drink well and I had only two glasses of wine before I changed to non-alcoholic punch.

'Tired . . . but I'll be fine, absolutely fine . . .' I murmured – and that was all right, because elks don't talk.

Opening my suddenly heavy eyelids I found myself looking down into a pair of strangely pale, horribly familiar eyes. 'Silver pennies,' I muttered. 'Who pays the ferryman?'

The potter, who was sitting at the table, regarded me with the wariness of the hunted.

'Why worry?' I asked him. 'I'm the elk.'

'What?'

Detaching myself from the door I pulled up a chair, and sat down opposite him. 'What're you doing?' I said, picking up the scraps of paper spread in front of him. They had names on – women's names, and phone numbers.

He leaned over and took them out of my hands. 'Emptying my pockets – I don't notice half of these going in. Women sometimes just push them into my hand, or my pocket – or under my studio door when I'm working. I—'

'Like to sit about gloating over them?' I suggested.

'No, I don't!'

'It used to happen to my ex-boyfriend too, and he loved it – kept them all. He's out there now.' I nodded at the door. 'Why don't you go and compare notes?'

There were some open bottles of wine on the table and fresh glasses, so I poured myself out a large glass of red.

Dragonslayer's face glowered across at me, just the way I'd imagined it: high cheekbones, narrow, long-lashed eyes with a suspicion of a slant and the colour-changing abilities of a chameleon, a quirky mouth and the platinum hair. The pale irises of his strange eyes had smudgy dark edges, and the lashes were interestingly darker at the roots, like badger hair . . .

'Bright Lucifer,' I toasted him.

The glower turned to a look of resignation. 'Have you had too much to drink?'

'I know who I am,' I said with some satisfaction. 'I know who you are too.'

He removed the bottle and filled his own glass. 'I suppose you followed me in here?'

'Listen, Narcissus, I had no idea you were in here, and even if I were looking for a man, which I'm not, I don't like blonds, especially pretty ones.'

He curled his lip. 'I suppose you prefer women.'

I stared at him. 'For goodness' sake! Can't a woman simply not find you attractive without that old "she doesn't fancy me so she must be a lesbian" line? What's your problem? I only came in here to get away from an old boyfriend!'

He looked down, shuffling his bits of paper and crushing them into a ball. 'Sorry – you must think I'm totally conceited,' he muttered.

'That's right – I do.'

He shot me a leaden, brooding glance from those changeable eyes and I shrugged. 'Well, it's your problem.'

The door burst open and a small, beaming drunken man galloped in like an inebriated whirlwind. 'Sappho, my bonny lassie!'

I relaxed with a sigh. 'Oh, it's only you, Rory.'

The arm he draped across my shoulders was as much to steady himself as anything more amorous. He stared belligerently at Nye. 'And is yon long streak of nothing what's keeping ye from the friends that love ye?'

He struck his breast, reeled back coughing, and cast his red eyes up in anguish.

'That gesture could only be really effective when you're wearing a kilt, Rory,' I advised kindly.

'Lassie, ye're breaking my heart.'

'Liquid doesn't break, it just runs somewhere else.'

He gloomed soulfully at me. 'From the moment I set eyes on ye, I knew ye were the one, ye big Amazon beauty!'

'Now look here, Rory!' Nye half rose to his feet as Rory made an inept attempt to embrace me, which I fielded without any trouble.

Rory reeled back, a look of comprehension on his face. 'It's like that, is it? I can see when I'm not wanted!' And out he staggered again, collecting a full bottle of wine in passing.

I sighed, drained my glass, and then refilled it. 'Why do I always attract small drunken men?'

'Who can tell the source of our mystical allure?' Nye said sarkily, and I relaxed and smiled at him.

'My turn to sound conceited?'

When I got up my legs seemed to belong to some other person – or possibly two people going in different directions – but it didn't matter because my head was quite, quite clear. I opened the kitchen door a crack and peered out.

Dave was in sight, with Lili trying to train herself up his side like ivy, so I quietly closed it again, jammed a chair under the handle, and looked around for an alternative exit. A scene seemed imminent, and I'd definitely had enough for one night.

The window over the kitchen sink was one of those modern ones that opens like a door if you twist the handle the right way and say 'Open sesame'.

I took off my sandals and tossed them out first before hitching up my cherished amber lace and getting one knee on the sink.

Goldilocks enquired mildly, 'Don't think me nosy, but what are you doing?'

'Climbing out of the window. What did you think I was doing, taking a sponge bath in the sink?'

'There's no need to be sarcastic, it's just a bit unusual for a guest to leave by the window halfway through a party. More of my old-fashioned prejudices, I suppose. Do you make a habit of it, or is that a stupid question, too?'

'I discovered a long time ago that a sudden departure from the nearest window is worth a thousand explanations,' I said, not really paying him much attention, being more concerned with wishing Miranda had installed one of those trendy Belfast sinks, strong enough for me to stand in.

He set a kitchen chair down next to me and patted the

seat enticingly. 'Wouldn't it be easier if you stood on this?'

'Thank you, but I'm quite capable of getting out of a window on my own,' I snapped ungraciously, but since the chair was there anyway I climbed on to it and stepped across on to the sill.

'Are you avoiding someone?'

'No.' I clung to the window frame and added, over my shoulder: 'Well, not in the sense of being afraid to go out of the door, more in the sense of having had enough of conceited, loopy men for one night.'

The kitchen door gave a sudden rattle and the chair I'd jammed under the handle moved a fraction, startling me so that I sat back on the mixer taps. This is not something I'd recommend for fun.

'Nye?' cooed Lili's voice seductively. 'The door seems to have stuck.'

Damn! She must have failed with Dave, too. Perhaps she really is losing her charms.

'I'm coming with you,' Nye announced suddenly.

I looked at him, eyebrows raised, and he added: 'In the sense of being scared shitless to go out of the door.'

'Please yourself.' Who knew, if we both vanished, Lili and Dave might get it together out of sheer frustration.

Out I jumped, landing up to the ankles in a cool, moist, freshly dug border, and had time to spot one sandal in the light from the window before the blond bombshell launched himself out of it.

He landed gracefully on something that scrunched, and promptly fell over. 'Oh bugger,' he said, 'I landed on a—'

'Sandal,' I said bitterly, snatching the crushed remains from under him, limp as a boned herring.

I tossed it away again without bothering to look for the

other and set off barefoot. It had stopped raining, fortunately for my amber lace, and everything had that dark, rich, fruit-cake smell.

It was a night for walking. I could walk for miles and miles, just inhaling that lovely cool, dark aroma . . . preferably without a spectral follower.

'I'm sorry about the sandal,' he offered tentatively from just behind me.

'It doesn't matter,' I said tersely, but actually it did: when your feet are size eight it's not easy finding something fragile and glitzy for those over-the-top occasions. I loved those sandals. I may have to go back and give them a ritual burial the next day.

Still, it was good to be out here. I inhaled the night air with satisfaction and strode out briskly through the village. 'Why *do* I go to parties?' I said rhetorically.

'I don't know, why do you go to parties?' Nye said, falling into step with me, uninvited.

'Aren't you going to ask me why I went out of the window?'

'To avoid someone, you told me. And not Rory, whom you dealt with effectively, or poor old Gil, who I noticed trying to corner you earlier. Now, Gil might bore you to death but otherwise he's harmless enough.'

'Allegedly. What about the Mystery of the Vanishing Wife? Could it be Dead Dorinda?'

I mean, I do sincerely hope not, since I had it in mind to pair Gil and Miranda off together for mutual support if their respective spouses could be disposed of tidily.

'Come to that, weren't you Murder Suspect Number Two? Do you murder anything other than expensive sandals? Should I be walking in dark lanes with a murder suspect?

In fact, why am I walking down dark lanes with you? Why don't you *go away*?'

'If I killed every irritating woman who crossed my path I'd be a mass murderer by now,' he said evenly. 'And I'm seeing you home.'

'I'm not going home. Do you think Gil might—'

'I've only known him a couple of years, but I think he's genuinely lost without his wife, however bossy she was. And what do you mean, you're not going home?'

'You're Welsh, aren't you?' I asked, diverted by the faintest lilt in his voice.

'My father was, hence the Nye – Aneurin – but I was brought up in Manchester. I went to college in Wales, though, where I seem to have acquired a touch of the accent.'

'It adds to your considerable personal charm,' I said bitchily.

'How would you like a dip in a cold muddy ditch?'

'Huh, you and who else?' I retorted inelegantly, and he laughed. 'And haven't you got a home to go to?'

'I told you – I'm seeing you home first.'

'And I told *you* – I'm not going home, I'm going for a walk.'

He stopped dead, pulling me to a stop with him. 'You mean, we're *not* heading for wherever you live?'

'No, I just said: I'm going for a walk.' I firmly removed his hand from my arm. 'Goodnight, Nye.'

'Goodnight nothing!' he said as I turned away. 'You're heading out of the village, and I'm not letting you wander alone around the moors at night.'

'I'm a big girl now, and I often walk around here at night if I've been working all day. Up the lane to the cromlech, then across the track to the road down to my cottage.'

'In bare feet?'

'Frequently. Why not?'

There was a small, irritated silence. My bare feet were silent on the pavement, but he was amazingly quiet for such a big man.

'Shouldn't you go home and throw pots or something?'

'In the middle of the night?'

'Perhaps not. What do you make, Nye? Plates and stuff?'

'Didn't you go round the craft centre when you were helping Miranda set up her flower business in Lavender's workshop?'

'No,' I said shortly. I wasn't going to linger somewhere where I might have to talk to one of my characters, especially when he'd already lost his temper before. He'd have thought I was one of his drooling admirers.

'You should come and look round.'

'The last time I bumped into someone unpleasant.'

'I didn't mean to be unpleasant . . . I was just thinking about the piece I was working on. I have strong feelings about my work,' he muttered. 'That's what Eloise said – I could only get passionate about my work.'

That struck a chord. 'Me too,' I said sympathetically. 'Eloise is this ex-girlfriend Lili's been going on about?'

'I suppose she's told everybody!' he snapped. 'Do you know what it feels like when your girlfriend of half a bloody lifetime ditches you for a *woman*?'

'Obviously not, though I would have thought it was the ditching bit that mattered.'

'I'm not anti-gay, if that's what you mean, it was just that I'd had no idea until the moment she said she was leaving me and why,' he said. 'I must have been blind, because she told me she'd always had affairs with other women and she didn't count it as infidelity – and then she'd fallen in love.'

'But Lili said she tried to come back?' I stopped and looked at him in the moonlight, all silvered and a bit spooky.

'She came here one weekend and pretended she wanted us to get back together, but it was in the hope of getting pregnant because she and Lou – her partner – wanted a baby.'

'How do you know?'

'Because when I wasn't *that* glad to see her, she lost her temper and told me.'

'Oh?' I turned and plodded on, thinking about it. Wasn't that a little the way *I'd* been planning to use some hapless male without telling him? Mind you, most men don't seem to care about ethics so much as getting their end away.

'I'd have liked children, but it was never the right time for her,' he said moodily. 'She wouldn't marry me, either.'

'Probably that bad temper.'

'I haven't got a bad temper!'

'No, and it never snows in Iceland,' I said. 'Try asking Lili: she'll marry you in a flash.'

'I'm staying single from now on, and even if I weren't, Lili is a man-eater – in more ways than one. She jumped out at me and tried to bite my neck the other day!'

'She always spits the bits out afterwards, though,' I said helpfully.

'So who was this old boyfriend you were running from?' he asked.

'I was not running, merely avoiding.'

'Who were you avoiding, then?'

'Did you meet Dave Devlyn? He's here to photograph the Gower's artistic riff-raff for a book. Tall, dark and handsome?'

'A maiden's dream?'

'Nightmare. We had an affair years ago when we were still

students, but then I got cold feet and sheered off, and he's never quite managed to forgive and forget. He has this fixation that I'm playing some long-running game of hard to get.'

'And are you?'

'No – single eccentric female, that's me. S.E.F. I've even got a cat.'

'Oh?' he said thoughtfully. 'Does that make me an S.E.M.? I haven't got a cat,' he added.

'No, it makes you a W.O.B.: Weird Old Bachelor.'

'Thanks. And maybe I am mad, at that, standing here in the rain discussing abbreviations when we could get into this bus shelter until it goes off and we can go home.'

I hadn't realized we'd stopped moving, or that it had started raining again. 'You can go home any time you like,' I assured him, but I did let him pull me into the dark, sheep-smelling hut while the rain pattered down outside like footsteps . . .

There *were* footsteps.

Chapter 22

Stoned

Without further ceremony I dragged Nye into the darkest corner and he came unresisting: women probably do that sort of thing all the time.

When I shivered he put his arm around me and drew me into him, in a friendly sort of way. I was starting to feel as if I'd known him a long time, like Mu.

Well, almost. And it was nice to lean on something warm and bigger than myself, because it was a bit chilly and my legs still felt sort of detached from me . . .

'It must have been the non-alcoholic punch,' I muttered. 'Did you have the punch?'

'No.'

'There you are then – I don't get drunk, because I have great self-control,' I assured him. 'So someone spiked the punch. Probably one of those pure alcohols that make you go blind.'

'Wha—' he began.

But I slapped my hand over his mouth and hissed: 'Shh!'

Footsteps approached, paused, then faded back towards the village centre, and I slowly removed my hand from Nye's mouth, but not before he'd kissed the palm of it.

He pulled me to him and pleaded huskily, 'One last kiss before the bus parts us for ever, Blodwen!'

'You're an idiot,' I told him, grinning, and then he did kiss me in a light and friendly way that took a sudden turn of direction and went on a bit.

A *lot*, actually: this was a man who could kiss for England. When our lips finally and reluctantly parted I didn't move, just stared at what I could see of him: one big, shadowy shape – and I thought: it's true what they say, all cats are the same in the dark.

His being blond, handsome, short-tempered and possibly a murderer sort of paled into insignificance after that kiss. I've never felt so little, weak and light-headed – though maybe that was the punch?

'Let's try that again,' he said softly, suiting the action to the words.

'*Resistance is useless!*' bleated a Dalek voice in my head. 'Resistance is useless,' I agreed during a later pause for breath, but some of my brain cells had woken from their coma and had begun to send messages: *Sappho, you're in a bus shelter snogging a strange – very strange – man, who's both bigger and stronger than you.*

And another thing – it had suddenly gone very, very dark.

I pushed myself away (about a quarter of an inch) and said urgently: 'I've gone blind. Have you gone blind too?'

'Blind? No, of course not.' He relaxed his arms a bit, and I could feel my lungs going in and out like a pair of relieved bellows. 'Why should I be blind?'

'There was something in that punch.'

'I didn't drink it, and you're not blind, it's just dark in here. Look at the doorway, where the streetlight shines in.'

I had to open my eyes to do that, which is when I finally

acknowledged that I was absolutely ratted. Let's face it, anyone who doesn't realize she's got her eyes shut is drunk in charge of her legs, and her brain is operating on Impulse Drive only.

What she needs to clear her head is fresh air and a brisk night walk over a deserted stretch of moorland to an ancient hilltop grave. She needs the willpower to overcome her baser instincts, which are telling her she's got a two-handed grip on something mind-blowingly attractive, and set out.

Self-control.

'Excuse me,' I said politely, pushing off from an expanse of chest like a muscular spring board and aiming at the door.

I must have taken him by surprise, because I was off the road and halfway up the track to the cromlech before he caught up with me, and when I turned and ordered him to go away he just stood there looking stubborn with his arms crossed, and the moonlight making his eyes and hair glimmer in an unsettling way.

No wonder Dragonslayer set poor Nala on end, following her through the dark forests!

But now I knew he only *looked* spectral – he was solid and warm enough to the touch: hot and hard, even. And stubborn. So I gave it up and continued following the broad grassy path up to the tomb, which has the rare distinction of not being anything to do with King Arthur. Going by the number of Arthur's Stones he must have been shredded and scattered to the four winds.

My head had cleared, and so had the rain, leaving a half-moon and twinkling stars. I felt good. Hitching my skirts up, I climbed on to the huge flat stone.

'*Nala stood at the Place of Stones, and defied the Forces of Darkness to touch her in her invincibility . . .!*' I exclaimed, feeling inspired and wishing I had my little recorder with me.

Twirling quickly to drink in the stars made my head suddenly swim and my knees buckle, and as something huge and dark came up to meet me I thought: this is it! I'm on the brink . . . falling . . . falling . . .

Then Nye's strong arms swept me up and deposited me without ceremony on to the damp slab of stone, though I clung to him when he would have let me go, because otherwise I would have carried on falling, through the rock, and the bones and the soil and the worms and the . . .

'*Now* will you go home?' he said, sounding so exasperated that I tried to explain why he had to hold me, and not let me fall into the Abyss, like Raarg, but he obviously didn't grasp the idea until I kissed him. Maybe kissing was his first language?

I forgot where and when and why after that, and it was just us, cocooned in a warm private world of our own. Everything else ceased to exist, and we ended up lying entwined on the stone, though I'm not sure who was the sacrifice.

Probably Nye, because I think he would have drawn back at one point except I wouldn't let him. Never mind true unions of the soul: half a loaf is a lot better than none.

That was one hot rock. It was also an uncomfortable rock after a while, even if Nye by then was cushioning most of it for me, and a chill wind was taking advantage of my extremities.

'So you're not a pansy potter?' I said into his ear.

'So Lili lied, and you're not gay?' he returned.

'No,' I agreed. 'But I *am* celibate.'

'Yes, I can see that.'

'Was,' I qualified. 'Will be,' I added, after another minute's thought. 'This is just a small aberration caused by spiked alcohol. I don't like blond men – especially bad-tempered ones.'

He propped himself up and glared at me. 'So you said earlier – and not only am I not bad-tempered, I refuse to be a small aberration! And – it was all right, Sappho, wasn't it? I did ask you before I—'

'It was fine,' I interrupted hastily. Typical male, worrying about his performance! Did he want a score card? 'And I don't know what you're so cross about – you probably sleep with a different woman every night of the week . . . except poor Lili.'

'I'll have you know I haven't been with a woman since Eloise left me – probably why I was so desperate I let you seduce me tonight on this damned uncomfortable rock!'

'*I* seduced you—' I began indignantly, and then stopped because it was all too true. 'Well, I'll have *you* know that *I* haven't been with anyone for *years*, and that punch mustn't have been spiked but *poisoned* to make me want to get anywhere near such a bossy, opinionated, conceited – oh, words fail me!'

He smiled unnervingly: 'Then one good thing at least is that if neither of us has been putting it about then we won't have exchanged any interesting diseases.'

I stiffened. It had been so long, and the Fall so sudden, that the practical aspects had escaped me entirely, along with my much-vaunted self-control.

'You may think I'm conceited,' he added coldly, 'but I don't walk around with a pocketful of condoms, even if you'd given me time to use one. But I did ask you if it was all right.'

'Yes, and – oh!' The penny dropped: I'd just had unprotected sex with a stranger . . . and while that might have been what I'd been vaguely contemplating at some point, not *this* stranger. 'And you aren't even what I'm looking for!' I told him bitterly.

'What *are* you looking for, Sappho?'

'Someone tall, dark, attractive and not living on my doorstep.'

'But you just ran from someone tall, dark and attractive,' he pointed out.

'I didn't run away; it was a strategic withdrawal. And he's tall, dark, attractive and insanely jealous. But you're right about tonight – if neither of us has been around there's no harm done, is there? Now, if you'd just like to get off me, I'm going home.'

And write and write before I forgot all this . . . if it's possible to forget, although some aspects were already pretty hazy to me, like how we actually ended up lying on the rock together in the first place. What happened next is permanently engraved on my back like a sort of lewd Rosetta Stone, though I'd need a mirror to read it.

Nye shifted his weight a little. 'You'll have to let go of me first,' he pointed out mildly, which was when I realized I was still clasping his broad, muscular, warm back with both hands.

Our lips were about two centimetres apart and closing fast when a faint, wind-borne voice exclaimed in foreign-accented delight: 'See how right to be visitink the stone in the moonlight! How fascinatink to see these old fertility rituals.'

'*Ja,*' chimed in a second person. 'As the moon rises, so is he risink and—'

We froze.

'Oh my God!' Nye hissed. 'It's Ceri's "Mystic Celtic Midnight Tour" – and they're coming this way!'

As one we rolled off the rock, hastily adjusted our somewhat damp and dishevelled clothing, and set off down the hill away from the voices.

Fortunately this was towards Aces Acre, since I didn't fancy parading through the village in my present state, even in the dead of night, though I'm not sure Nye felt the same way. He was laughing so much I would have left him behind had he not taken a firm grip of my hand.

I'm sure Dragonslayer wouldn't have laughed at this point: he has too much dignity.

Sobriety set in, and horror at my sudden lapse from well-ordered self-control: I'd taken not just a jump but a *leap* in the dark, and the sooner I got home and exorcised it on to paper the better.

'Hey,' Nye said, 'slow down. It might have been worse – they could have been a few minutes earlier and spoiled something very special.'

'Huh!' I said inelegantly, wresting my hand away and making for the gap in the wall that led down into my lane.

Mind you, just imagine if they *had* been a bit earlier – or later – or if Dave had caught us up there. It didn't bear thinking about.

'It's all right, you don't have to pretend it meant anything to you, Nye. It was good, it's over. My house is just here, so thank you and goodnight.'

'Sappho,' he said, the laughter gone out of his voice. 'Sappho, come back!'

But I made off down the lane, the slick mud under my bare feet reminding me of the day I'd first seen Nye in his incarnation as the Giant Thing from the Slime Pit.

Then I skidded to a halt and listened, for there was a terrible scream, a banshee of despair that brought the hairs up on the back of my neck – and it was coming from the direction of home.

'What the hell was that?' cried Nye, keeping pace with me

as I ran round the corner of the barn and stopped dead in my tracks.

In the courtyard before the open door Sphinx lay as still as her namesake, in a pool of spreading dark blood, while Mu lamented and wrung her hands.

What a Lady Macbeth she would have made.

Chapter 23

Well Read

For a moment we stayed still, absolutely transfixed. Then Mu ran forward to kneel on the rain-soaked cobbles in her green silk shift.

I was so glad she'd stopped screaming.

'Something hit her . . .' she muttered as I knelt beside her, and examined the fragile skull with sensitive fingers. 'She sneaked out when I got back, and I'd just picked up the torch to go and look for her when I heard a noise and saw her lying here.'

'Do you think anything's broken?'

'No, but there's a deep cut . . . all this blood!'

'She's breathing all right,' I said anxiously. Nearby a rock glistened with more than just rain, quite a heavy rock to hit a little cat. 'We need something to stop the blood and a vet—'

'I know a good vet who'll come out,' Nye broke in, startling Mu, who hadn't realized he was there. 'He's a friend. Where's your phone?'

Mu took him off, and came back with a clean towel, which she used to staunch the bleeding. 'It must have been Dave, Sappho – he's mad enough, and he hates cats. He and Lili were

218

getting on like a house on fire at the party until they found out you and Nye had vanished. I told them it was ridiculous to think you'd gone off together, but . . .'

She stopped and stared at me over Sphinx: 'But actually you *did*, didn't you? I thought you'd simply had enough of the evening's entertainment, and left.'

'I did. Nye followed me.'

'Oh? Well, anyway, Dave dropped Lili like a hot potato and went rampaging off to look for you, and Lili said she'd had enough and she was going to walk home – she borrowed your rain cape. After that I decided to come back to the cottage, expecting to find you here, and Sphinx got out – which I'm terribly sorry about. I should have been more careful.'

Sphinx made a little restless movement as Nye returned. 'He'll be here in a few minutes, and he says not to move her.'

'Good.'

'So, who do you think tried to brain your cat?' he asked conversationally. 'How insanely jealous is this old boy-friend?'

'Jealous enough,' Mu assured him. 'I was just telling Sappho I thought it was him.'

'But why? I mean, I know he doesn't like cats, but why should he lob rocks at one?'

'Why not, if he came here looking for you and found Sphinx instead?' she said.

'But it's hardly likely to endear him to me, is it?'

'No one ever said he was thinking clearly where you're concerned. I expect he forgot all about me and the kitten and just convinced himself you were here alone with Nye.'

I rubbed my forehead wearily where a headache was beginning to form, though not a patch on the one poor old Sphinx would have. 'Come to think of it, he did say he'd put a note through my door last night, so he knows where I live, but it could just as easily have been some local lout's idea of fun.'

A torch flickered round the corner of the barn and came to rest on our upturned faces. 'Can this be the vet already?' Mu said.

'No, we'd have heard the car,' Nye answered. 'It's Chris.'

It was, too. He halted and said intelligently, 'Hello, has something happened?' then spotted Nye and looked knowing. 'So this is where you got to, Nye?'

'Someone's thrown a rock at Sappho's cat and knocked it out,' Nye said, ignoring the wealth of innuendo. 'I don't suppose you passed anyone on the way here?'

'No – not a soul. People have been appearing and vanishing all evening, and now Miranda's gone missing too. I thought I'd see if she was here.'

'Why would she come here in the middle of the party?' Mu said reasonably. 'She probably just went into the garden for a bit of fresh air.' Her tone suggested she saw through his excuse for nosiness.

He turned back to Nye. 'She's been a bit absent-minded and unpredictable lately, and the shock of her dog going missing seems to have played on her mind, and—' he broke off theatrically and exclaimed, 'Good God! What if it was Miranda who came here tonight and—'

'Threw a rock at my cat?' I finished scornfully. 'Come off it, she loves animals, and there's nothing wrong with her except being married to you. I'm going to phone The Hacienda now and I bet she's been there all the time, which is more than can be said for you.'

'And here's the vet,' Nye said. 'You go in, Sappho, and we'll sort Sphinx out.'

With a backward glance at my poor, battered cat I went

to phone, and after some delay got Miranda herself. It still sounded exceedingly lively at the party.

'It's me – Sappho. Chris is here, and he says he's looking for you.'

'For me? I've b-been looking for him – there's no wine left and everyone's hanging about, so I've had to get another case out of the garage myself.'

'I'll send him back now. Thanks for the party – but I must dash. The cat's had an accident and the vet's here. Oh, and Miranda,' I added as an afterthought, 'watch the punch – I think someone's spiked it.'

'I know, I found three b-bottles of very strong vodka under the table and everyone who d-drank it is *legless*. That's why everyone's still here – they can't d-drive home and the taxi's d-doing relays.'

When I went back outside Sphinx had been carefully stowed in the back of the vet's white estate car, and he was reassuring.

'Just concussion, cuts and bruises, I think, but I'll take an X-ray, and keep her overnight, at least. Ring tomorrow afternoon to see how she is.'

'That's going to cost you a packet, calling the vet out at this time of night,' Chris said as the tail lights vanished into the lane.

'It's worth it,' I said shortly, wondering suddenly if he might have lobbed the rock, since I'm certainly not his favourite person and it *would* be a way of getting back at me. 'You'd better get back to The Hacienda. Miranda's been looking for you, because the wine ran out, and someone spiked the punch, so most of your guests are incapable of driving home. The local taxi's doing shifts but you could be up for quite a while.'

'Then perhaps I could persuade Nye to come back with me?' he suggested. 'Night's still young, Nye?'

'The night may be, but I'm not,' Nye said. 'No, thanks.'

Chris shrugged, said, 'Goodnight, then,' and walked off, but Nye showed no sign of following suit. Instead he trailed us back into the cottage.

'Well, so much for my favourite dress,' Mu said as the light fell on to the bloodstained green silk. 'And what have you been doing to yours? It's got even more stains than mine, and . . .'

She petered out as she got her first full sight of Nye under the kitchen light: he was even more dishevelled than I was. His hair was all over the place, and we were wearing His and Hers matching streaks of mossy green.

'It's a nasty night for a walk,' I said lamely. 'And I owe you a new dress – it's my cat.'

'Yes, but *I* foisted her on to you; you didn't want her really. I'll go and put this dress in cold water and see what happens.'

'It will shrink, but the stains won't. Let's face it: it's had it, and so has mine.'

'It's worth a try. Go and take yours off, and I'll put them in together.'

'Does anyone want me to take my clothes off too, or shall I go home?' Nye asked hopefully.

'I've no objections,' Mu said, grinning. 'But you've been great, getting the vet and everything – why don't you stay and have a hot drink before you go? We'll be down as soon as we've changed.'

Nye looked at me, but I avoided his eyes. I was so tired things had started taking on a surreal air, especially the brightly lit kitchen. It was still white, and the glittery green Formica table was mind-boggling. A Magritte steam train chugging out of the fireplace would have added a homely touch.

'Sorry about the decor,' I said wearily. 'Go through to the living room – it's more comfortable.'

'I'll put the kettle on first – you two go and change.'

When I came back down, clean and wearing my thobe, Mu had already put the dresses into a bucket of cold water, and made hot cocoa.

I felt better without the green slime, and the sheep droppings wedged between my toes.

The living room was cosy with the fire turned on, especially once I added a good slug of dark rum to my cocoa.

Mu had bagged the lounger and lay stretched out like a guest at a Roman orgy, leaving me the choice of the camel stool, the basket chair, or one end of the sofa.

The sofa was the best option, even with Nye occupying the other end. He looked as immediately at home as the cat, and in a different way just as unsettling.

'Did you really go out of the kitchen window?' Mu asked sleepily. 'Lili said you'd abducted Nye. That was after Dave lost interest in her and started rampaging about looking for you.'

'She did,' Nye said.

I opened my eyes. 'I did not – you insisted on following me because you were scared of Lili, and then you wouldn't go away.'

'I couldn't just leave you walking off across the moors in the dark.'

'She does it all the time,' Mu said.

'And it wasn't any of your business,' I added. 'I'm big enough to take care of myself!'

'You're big – I'm bigger,' he said, smiling enigmatically.

'I could take you with one hand tied behind my back!' I said incautiously.

'I thought you already had?'

Mu sat up a bit and looked at him with some interest, and

admittedly he is worth looking at if you like that sort of thing, but he also has the kind of pale skin that looks bruised under the eyes when he's tired.

'I didn't touch him,' I said hastily as she turned an accusing gaze on me.

I'll qualify that: I didn't hit him, though if he didn't stop smiling like that I still might.

'Did you tell him why you went out of the window?' she asked. 'To escape your mad ex-boyfriend, who stalks you?'

'Mmm – though I still don't think he's dotty enough to stone Sphinx.'

'He's capable of more than you think when he's in one of his jealous rages.'

'Sappho didn't tell me much, anyway,' Nye said. 'We were . . . sidetracked.'

'Let me give you a brief scenario,' Mu offered.

'He doesn't need one – it's nothing to do with him,' I objected.

She ignored me and with admirable conciseness (she can't have touched the punch) gave him a potted version of my situation with Dave, what Chris had been doing to unbalance Miranda, and what we thought had happened to Spike.

Then she added, 'But at least now we know that *you* didn't have anything to do with Gil's wife vanishing.'

I'd almost nodded off, but I jerked awake at this. '*Do* we?'

'Of course we do.' She smiled at Nye. Another conquest. 'And now I've met Gil, I don't think he did it, either, so . . .'

But by now I was half-dozing to the gentle rise and fall of the conversation, and when I drifted back to the surface she was saying: '. . . put butter on her paws.'

'What?' I'd slumped against Nye's shoulder, and his arm was around me. 'Has Nye got a cat?'

224

'Not yet, but he's thinking about it.' Mu was grinning, for some reason – perhaps I'd been snoring. 'I thought you'd gone to sleep.'

I sat up straight. How did I finish up on this end of the sofa? And I'd never put my head on a man's shoulder before without getting a crick in my neck: Nye had novelty value, if nothing else.

'What were we talking about?'

'How you came to live here – Dave – the books – Miranda – everything,' he said casually, and I gave Mu an aggrieved look, which she returned innocently.

'Just putting him in the picture. After all, if Dave is going to be around for a few weeks you might need some help when I've gone.'

'Why should I need help? I can cope – I always have.'

'It's a bit isolated here.'

'Not after some of the places I've lived in.'

Mu swung her legs off the lounger and stood up muzzily.

'I've had it – I'm going to bed. Goodnight, Nye – maybe I'll see you again before I go home on Monday?'

She wouldn't blink an eyelid if he were here at breakfast, but he wasn't going to be.

'I'll be off, too,' he said, seeming to read my mind, 'unless you'd like me to stay and protect you?'

Too late, the wolf has been in the sheep fold already.

'No, I don't. I don't need you,' I snapped ungraciously.

'Don't you, Sappho?' he said softly, then added with total inconsequence: 'Your eyes are sherry-coloured, like your hair.'

'Just boring old brown,' I stammered, going all hot – probably a pre-menopausal symptom common to thirty-nine-year-olds.

He got up rather stiffly, stretched (which was quite pleasant to look at), and put his somewhat mired leather jacket on.

Something – I think it was compunction – made me say, 'Nye, watch out for Dave, won't you? He can get irrationally jealous, and if he thinks . . . Well, just watch out, that's all.'

'Don't worry about me,' he said. 'Look, Sappho, tomorrow I'll be working at the studio, so why don't you come down? Bring Mu, if you want to, but come?'

'I always work in the mornings,' I said stiffly. Well, it's true, isn't it?

'Then come in the afternoon, and tell me what's happening on Planet Vengeane.'

I started. 'How did you know that?'

'From Miranda – I asked her about you.' He patted the zipped inside pocket of his jacket. 'She loaned me your last novel.'

Traitor! And no wonder I seemed to be coming out in bruises in strange places . . .

'You won't like it,' I assured him. 'Anyway, if you do read them you ought to read the first one,' I babbled. 'Give me that one, and I'll lend you the first book and—'

'No, I think I'll read this one and work back.'

'It won't make sense.'

I was fighting in the last ditch, did he but know it, but he just smiled and turned to go. 'Lock up carefully, and I'll see you tomorrow.'

I didn't deign a reply to this, and he added, 'Bedd was never this interesting without you, Sappho Jones!'

He has a very beguiling smile when he pleases.

It didn't please: I pushed him out and locked the door after him. After a moment I heard his footsteps going away across the cobbles.

Chapter 24

Impulses

I woke up at my usual time next morning, but lying on the reclining chair rather than in bed, with an aching head and a throbbing body.

But at least the throbbing body was my own, that was something to be thankful for.

How could I, even under the influence of alcohol, have been so abandoned with Nye Thomas the previous night? Even when I was younger and had over-indulged in drink, it didn't lead me to have wild sex on ancient tombs with disturbing strangers.

So perhaps it was just my fate – like Nala? Except Dragonslayer seemed pretty smitten with her, whereas I was sure Nye wouldn't give me another thought. Indeed, since I was finding the whole episode highly embarrassing in the light of day, I sincerely *hoped* he never gave me another thought.

And I was not going to worry about pregnancy, either: a one-night stand at my age couldn't be much of a risk. I mean, look at Mu – all these years of trying, and nothing, even with Sexy Simon . . .

'Sappho!' hissed Mu at that exact moment, sidling into

the room bearing a pregnancy test at arm's length before her, as though it might explode in her face. 'Sappho, it's *positive*: look!'

Sitting up with more haste than care, I managed to tilt the whole chair mechanism, precipitating me into a neat backwards somersault that fetched me up against the sofa, to Mu's astonishment.

'It's all right, it's not something I make a habit of,' I told her, picking myself up and going to take a look at the test, but without any great hopes. Mu had had a pregnancy testing kit in her luggage ever since her wedding day, and we'd had one or two false alarms before. But there were no two ways about this one – it was positive.

'I sort of began to wonder because I'm usually like clockwork, and should have started yesterday . . . only I didn't. And then I decided to get up early and do the test today and there it was! Oh, Sappho!'

We stared at each other, and then it was hug and tears time until our brains started to tick, and she said what we were both thinking.

'It must be Simon's, mustn't it? First time lucky?' (There goes another theory.) 'Only I have to convince myself that it's Ambler's.'

'It still *could* be, there's no way of telling, and goodness knows, it's going to look like him, isn't it?'

I looked at the test again and swallowed hard, thinking of little alien-eyed cuckoos in nests . . . But of course *I* wouldn't get pregnant first time. Coincidences like that don't happen.

I could even go and have the morning after pill thing just in case – or just leave it to the gods and wait and see? What if I was pregnant and got rid of it because Nye wasn't the right father, and then I never got pregnant again?

Wasn't this more or less what I wanted – except with a well-vetted, dark-haired man, not some other-worldly near Schwarzenegger with a wicked grin, who just happened to be handy during the ten-minute window of opportunity when my body broke a lifetime's habit of saying, 'Not today, thanks,' and instead screamed: 'Yes, now!'

It was a hormonal Last Chance Saloon, and not only were my hormones driving me, they had road rage.

Can't stop. Won't stop.

I didn't even check for rocks when I jumped off: my flight was premature, I was slightly singed around the edges, but at least my wax hadn't melted yet. I'd wing it.

'You look sort of – strange,' Mu said.

Demented, I should think.

I went and put my arms round her and gave her another hug. 'Sorry, it's a shock – I'm going to be Auntie Sappho at last! And it is, and always will be, Ambler's baby.'

'Yes,' Mu agreed, bursting into tears. 'And I'm so happy!'

'You've waited so long for this moment and I never used to understand why you wanted it so much, but I do now – just when it may be too late for me.' I shivered suddenly. 'Or maybe not.'

Mu sniffled back a happy tear and gave me a sharp look. 'Sappho, you didn't whisk Nye away last night in order to use him to try to get pregnant, did you? I mean, it was perfectly clear what you'd been up to, but *tell* me you took precautions. He's not even your type!'

'Of course he isn't my type – it was just the spiked punch.'

'But it's so unlike you.'

'I know, but he was an impulse buy while under the influence.' I shrugged. 'It was a leap in the dark. Well, a jump in the dark, actually.'

'*Sappho!*'

'I'm prepared to take the consequences of my actions, though statistically, there are extremely unlikely to be any.'

'You're an unknown quantity, not a statistic, Sappho. Once might be enough. You'd better think now what you're doing before it's too late.'

'No, I'm in free fall. Nala and I are going to await our fate.'

She looked at me doubtfully.

'Cheer up, you should be ecstatic.'

'I feel happy but sort of anti-climactic.'

'We'll go out later and celebrate; have an afternoon out.'

'But aren't you going to see Nye today?'

I stared at her. 'No, why should I?'

She stared back. 'Didn't he ask you out?'

'We've been out,' (and in and out) 'and that's it – ships that pass in the night.'

And suggesting I go down to the castle is not the same as asking me out. Not that I'd have gone anyway. And what's he going to think if he reads that book? If I was a coward I'd be buying a ticket to Portugal to stay with Pops and Jaynie.

The vet rang just then, saying that Sphinx was a lively little cat with a headache, and could be collected at ten, which was good news.

Mu commandeered the phone after that, to arrange an early train back next day so she could tell Ambler the good news face to face. Then she spoke to Simon, and finally rang the unsuspecting Ambler, to tell him the time of her return.

She popped her head back in to report that Simon seemed so pleased at his prowess that he was thinking of offering himself as a sperm donor, but by then I'd gone back to Raarg and the annoying Dragonslayer, whose physical attributes seemed

230

to be occupying Nala rather a lot, so Mu went away again.

Raarg only seemed like a reformed character, so however attractive he is, Nala couldn't have him, and she was afraid of being overpowered by Dragonslayer and losing her powers, in more ways than one.

The poor girl was between a rock and a hard place and no mistake, and I thought it was time both Raarg and Dragonslayer suffered a bit.

I disposed myself more comfortably on the black recliner, adjusted hair and robe, and clicked on the tape recorder.

It emitted a soothing Pooh Bear hum and I felt the beginning of some horrible experience for Raarg sneaking up, and a bit of a comeuppance for Dragonslayer: so big, so powerful, so damn sure of himself.

But some disturbing element in the room kept calling me back from Vengeane. Some distillation of Nye's presence still remained: clean linen, freshly mown grass, and a shot of ozone would be about the nearest description I could manage. The air around where he sat last night still twanged.

Damn.

I pulled myself together and dealt with Raarg first: if Dave was responsible for last night's stoning he deserved all Raarg was going to get . . .

'*Raarg felt the prickling of fear along his spine, and shivered uncontrollably – for something, some evil, was approaching . . . a retribution for his abusing of the Oracle's gift . . .*'

One chapter later the door opened enough for a ruffled-looking Sphinx to stalk through and look up at me, mouthing silent insults. If gurning was an Olympic sport, this cat would be in with a gold-medal chance.

For a minute I thought she was a ghost, then I bounced upright. 'Oh God! Ten – and I forgot—'

'Relax,' Mu said, following the cat in. 'I borrowed your car and collected her. Doesn't she look sweet with that shaved bit over one eye?'

'No, I don't think I'd ever call her sweet, but she has a certain raffish charm. Thanks for fetching her – you should have called me.'

'You may not thank me when you see the bill. Never mind. And guess what: I put both our party dresses in the washing machine on the very-delicate-you-shouldn't-really-be-trying-to-wash-this-garment-are-you-mad cycle, and they've both come out unstained, unshrunk and uncreased.'

'It's a miracle,' I said. 'In fact, it's a day of miracles. Do you think Sphinx would be OK alone if we went out somewhere?'

'I'm sure she would – she needs to sleep it off. Where shall we go? How about the Castle Craft Centre, after all? Nye will probably still be there,' she said slyly.

'No, thanks.'

'You can't fool me into thinking you aren't attracted to each other. The air crackled between you last night.'

'Let it crackle. It'll wear off. It was only a temporary lust-type thing; he's so not my type. And I'm an old dog set in my ways.'

'Bitch.'

'What?'

'Old bitch set in her ways.'

'Oh. What shall we do for lunch? How about Oxwich Bay, where we can eat at the hotel and then have a good blow along the beach? I feel I need my cobwebs removing.'

'I should think your corners have already been well cleaned out,' she said vulgarly.

I gave her a look and went to get ready. One cannot walk

along a windy beach in a thobe. It gets wrapped around your legs and trips you up.

The weather looked changeable, too, and it was a pity Lili still had my cape.

'We could stop at Lili's on the way home and get my cape back,' I suggested. 'You can protect me if she gets violent, and I'll assure her that I haven't got designs on her potter, so perhaps she'll forgive me.'

He was evidently not really interested in me. After all, a casual invitation to look at his mugs and jugs was not a romantic assignation. I remembered his eyes the previous night, sending me messages I didn't want to hear. Or might not have translated properly? Perhaps I should check my back again for the code?

We walked along the beach at Oxwich after lunch in companionable silence, and called at Lili's cottage around tea and gin time, but there was no reply when I knocked.

Perhaps she struck lucky at the party and hadn't come home, alone or otherwise? Or maybe she'd made an assignation with Dave, only he had to stop and stone a cat first?

I was going to try phoning later, but when we got back Miranda was waiting for us in a froth of impatience.

'Oh, Sappho, at last! They've found poor Lili unconscious on the moors with a head wound. She must have b-been out there all night.'

'Stoned?' I asked.

Chapter 25

Exposure

We calmed Miranda down with my universal panacea of rum-spiked coffee, and she told us what she knew.

'The postman spotted her this morning, just b-by the ruined cottage on the edge of the village – the Rhyss road, so she was going home. Something red was flapping about, so he went to have a look and it was your rain cape, Sappho! And there poor Lili was, unconscious, though the police said it was just mild concussion and exposure, only if she hadn't b-been wrapped in the cape it could have been worse.'

'Oiled silk is quite warm and waterproof,' I agreed, when she stopped for breath. 'And how was she concussed? I mean, I suppose Chris told you that my cat was stoned last night, so maybe there's a connection?'

'They aren't sure whether it was just an accident and she caught her head on the stones around the d-doorway, b-but low down, so she must have b-been falling when she d-did it. B-but they think she might have gone in there for shelter when that sudden shower started – and then perhaps she slipped as she was coming out. B-but they aren't certain, and when they came to see us this morning, Chris told them about your cat,

234

and they want to speak to you. I've b-been trying to phone you, only there was no answer.'

'We've been out this afternoon – celebrating: Mu's pregnant,' I told her.

'Oh, Mu!' Miranda squealed, hugging her. 'Oh, Mu, I'm so happy for you.'

'Thank you – but it's a secret between us until I tell Ambler – and it's early days yet; anything could happen.'

'You'll b-be fine, d-don't worry.'

I'd been thinking: 'If Lili was wearing my very distinctive red cape . . .'

'A very unique cross between smuggler's moll and Big Red Riding Hood,' added Mu.

'She b-borrowed it b-because she was a b-bit miffed when you and Nye vanished more or less at the same time, though she'd b-been getting on like a house on fire with D-Dave until then. It was quite funny when they surfaced and realized you and Nye were b-both gone.'

'Didn't we leave a chair jammed under the kitchen door?'

'Yes, someone had to climb in and remove it. Then Lili got very d-drunk when they couldn't find you. It was awful – almost everyone got d-drunk b-because of the spiked punch. Lili insisted on walking home rather than wait her turn for the taxi.'

'Where was Dave?'

'I d-didn't see him for ages after that, b-but much later he came d-downstairs with this awful woman from Port Talbot – supposed to be a painter. I d-didn't invite her, she came with someone, and she said D-Dave had b-been there for hours, so I d-don't know.'

I looked at Mu and raised one eyebrow. 'Perhaps he was

there all the time, or maybe he was here stoning the cat, but why would he attack Lili?'

'Because she was wearing your cape and lurking invitingly about in dark, ruined cottage doorways?' Mu suggested.

'She's about three feet shorter than me,' I objected.

'It was dark – and raining.'

'And why would I be on the other side of the village heading away?'

She shrugged. 'Why not? You walk for miles at any time of the day or night that takes your fancy.'

'You really shouldn't d-do that, it could be d-dangerous at night alone, Sappho.'

'A woman must do what a woman must do,' I said.

'And you weren't alone last night,' Mu pointed out helpfully.

Miranda looked at me, round-eyed. 'Chris said when he came b-back from here that you and Nye had b-been together and—' She stopped abruptly and blushed.

Was 'I had sex with Nye Thomas' indelibly stamped on my forehead I wondered.

Flustered, she hurried on. 'D-Dave had come d-down so he heard that . . . and he d-didn't look too pleased.'

'*I'm* not too pleased, if Chris is announcing details of my supposed sex life to rooms full of strangers,' I snapped.

'The only people still there waiting for the taxi were too d-drunk to take it in.'

'Except Dave. Strange how he managed to avoid the punch, wasn't it? Almost as if he knew,' I said.

'He d-did know – he b-brought the super-strength vodka with him and put it in. I asked him, and he seemed to think it was funny. And then I told him I wanted him to leave my house,' she added. 'Fortunately, I was too b-busy to have d-drunk much myself, b-but even then I felt fairly woozy. People have b-been coming back to fetch their cars all d-day, and the ones I've seen looked horribly hungover. D-Dave's moved to the Eagle and Stone now.'

'Well done,' applauded Mu. 'Did he seem worried at all about Lili?'

'Not really. He said he was sorry she was hurt, b-but at least she'd b-been found in time and was alive.'

'Warm and caring as always,' I commented. 'What about Chris?'

'I just left him to it in the early hours of the morning and went to b-bed – and I locked the b-bedroom d-door again. Then after D-Dave moved out I told him I knew he'd thrown Spike over the cliff and he admitted it. Only he said Spike was d-dead first.' Her eyes filled. 'He'd run into him while reversing the car out to go b-back to London and he thought I'd b-be less hurt if Spike just d-disappeared.'

Even as we comforted her, I wondered if it had really been that way – or if so, whether he had killed him accidentally. He's a nasty bit of work.

Miranda seemed to agree. 'He tried to make it seem as though he'd d-done it to spare me, b-but I think it was just b-because he d-didn't want to face me with what he'd d-done, and it made it so much worse! Anyway, I said that was the final straw and I was now convinced he'd played all those tricks on me too, and I'd had enough, what with mental cruelty and infidelity, and I wanted a d-divorce.'

The worm turns with a vengeance. 'Well done! What did he say?'

'He's stormed off, presumably b-back to London and he said I could phone him when I've come to my senses.'

'Nice line,' Mu commented critically.

'That's it, we're finished,' Miranda said, and sniffled a bit. 'It's all horrible and sad, b-but at least now I've got Fantasy Flowers to distract my mind. Gil stayed late last night, helping. He's a teetotaller and he d-doesn't like mixed drinks, so he d-didn't even have the punch. So what with my b-business and my cookbooks and my friends, I'm sure I'll survive.'

It was disquieting that Dave was staying on in the village, but no more than that – he'd never frightened me . . . though I suppose he might if he'd really flipped and taken to braining cats and people with rocks. I couldn't really see it, though.

Still, I'd sorted him out before, I could do it again.

'Have you phoned the hospital about poor Lili?' I asked Miranda.

'Yes, and she's come round, b-but she's still a b-bit confused. I'm going to go and see her this evening.'

'I could come with you,' I offered.

'Perhaps b-better not. I d-don't know how much she remembers, and you d-did go off with Nye.'

'Yes, but not in the sense of going off, more in the sense of happening to leave at the same time. And she can have him, I don't want him.'

'Nye might have something to say about that,' suggested Mu. 'You can't play pass the parcel with him, or if you do, someone's got to keep him when the music stops. The last one to unwrap him,' she added rather vulgarly.

I don't remember any music. The stars may have been playing celestial symphonies, but if so, I was too occupied to notice.

Chapter 26

Rocky Horrors

Miranda went home to change before setting off to visit Lili in hospital. She said she might pop in on the way back, but then she must go home for an early night so she could get up in time to do the flower orders next morning, which would be the first day that the advert with her own Fantasy Flowers telephone number appeared.

I'd miss her coming in and out to do the flowers, but at least I could now demolish the conservatory, except it was sort of handy for the cat. I wasn't cutting cat flaps in my Portuguese door, which was still leaning decoratively against the kitchen wall, since I was thinking of setting it into the front wall of the barn.

I'd already had someone round to draw up plans for the barn, and he pointed out that there had originally been a door there, with a passage leading to another blocked-up door into my kitchen. So I could have a hallway and front door on to the lane, though I'd have to wait for planning permission for the rest of the barn.

After Miranda's artless confidences about how helpful dear Gil had been the previous night, I thought I'd better get on and find out whether he really did do in his wife, so I rang him and reminded him of his invitation to tea, and we fixed it up for Tuesday, at two. Then he told me Violet Duke had been there earlier, because it had occurred to her that there might be vital information on Dorinda's computer that could give them a clue to her current whereabouts.

Of course, Gil is useless where computers are concerned, and so am I, or one of us might have thought of it earlier. At some point, I'd really have to embrace the new technology.

'*Did* you find anything useful?' I asked.

'Not yet, because Dorinda protected her computer with a password and it took us all afternoon to guess it – "Paviland".'

'After the cave where the bones of the Red Lady were found?'

'Yes. *I* thought of that one,' he said proudly. 'Once we were in, Violet had a quick look at the files, but she couldn't see anything that sounded helpful without opening them all, so she's coming back when she's got more time.'

By this stage I didn't think a delay in finding Dorinda was going to matter one way or the other, but I didn't say so.

Mu and I had both begun to flag by this time and were just rooting in the freezer, trying to choose between the stacked and labelled cartons of Miranda's ready meals, when two policemen came to see us.

How popular we were!

It was Constable Gwynne again, and an older man with beady eyes, a moth-eaten moustache and yellow fingers: very specific jaundice or a nasty cigarette problem?

They were still doing the rounds of local partygoers *re* Lili's stoning – or being stoned – so I took them into the living room while Mu went off to make coffee.

I sat down on the lounger and the two men took the sofa opposite. Inspector Crabtree, as Spot had introduced him, took out a cigarette packet.

'You don't mind . . .?' he began.

'Actually, I do,' I said, and he gave me an unfriendly look and put the packet away again.

Sphinx walked in and sat down right in front of poor PC Gwynne, staring, so maybe she'd never seen spots on that scale either.

'We're trying to trace Mrs Jakes's last movements,' the inspector said. 'And also we were told there was a stone-throwing incident here last night, too.'

'*Ford* Jakes. Ms.'

'Is it hyphenated?'

'No.'

He gave me a look.

'Someone threw a stone at my cat late last night and knocked her out. I've got the rock – I put a tea chest over it to keep the rain off, in case there were fingerprints, though I don't suppose it's easy getting them from a rough surface like that.'

'Almost impossible, miss.'

'Ms.'

He gave me another dirty look, and poor PC Gwynne scribbled away.

'Miranda Cotter's told us all about the Lili incident, and I'm amazed the postman ever spotted Lili from the road if she was lying in the doorway of that ruin,' I said.

'He – er – stopped for an urgent call of nature.'

At least he didn't use the nearest telephone box. What is it with men and their compulsion to pee in small enclosed places? Territory marking?

Mu came in just then with the tray, and was introduced

and brought up to date with the conversation, if it could be termed as such.

She sat in the cushioned basket chair smiling winsomely.

Inspector Crabtree was chewing the ratty yellow moustache, which should supply him with enough nicotine to stop withdrawal symptoms for several hours.

When I pulled the little table closer and began to pour out coffee from the Raarg pot, the two policemen exchanged glances for some reason. Perhaps they didn't like coffee, but were too polite to say so.

Then we ran through our recollections of who was at the party, which they must already have been given, but I wasn't much help because of course I'd left early, and neither was Mu, who hadn't stayed much longer.

'Did either of you speak to Mrs – Ms Ford Jakes last night?'

I shook my head, because I considered whispering 'Dave Devlyn' in her ear in passing didn't count.

Mu said, 'I had a chat with her, but it wasn't relevant. I mean, she didn't say: "I'm going to meet a man in that ruined cottage on the Rhyss road later, and he might lob a rock at me," or anything.'

They gave her a look and she added, unabashed, 'She was just as usual.'

'I see.' Inspector Crabtree turned back to me while Constable Gwynne finished scribbling hastily and turned over a fresh page.

'Now, I'm told that you left by a slightly unusual route?'

'I went out of the kitchen window,' I agreed.

'Any particular reason?'

'I wished to leave and there was a man I didn't want to talk to in the hallway.'

'And you left with a Mr Aneurin Thomas?'

'He followed me out. We didn't leave together.'

'He states that he was trying to avoid the attentions of Ms Jakes. Perhaps you would care to tell me what you did next?'

His tone suggested he could make a pretty good guess.

What *had* Nye been telling him?

'We went for a walk up on to the moors, and then came back here.'

'Indeed? But you'd left your rain cape at the Cotters, hadn't you? Didn't you get very wet during that sudden downpour?'

'No, we sheltered till it went off. Was that the crucial time? Well, why didn't you come straight out with it?' I demanded. 'Nye and I were together until long after that, because he came back here with me. So neither of us could have had anything to do with it, if it *wasn't* an accident – though it seems to me it might well have been, and my poor cat was the only real victim last night.'

'And what time did you discover that your cat had been hurt?' he said in the voice of one humouring an imbecile.

'It was about one-ish,' Mu said. 'She got out when I returned from the party, and I heard a noise and found her. I got the impression of someone running away.'

'But you didn't actually see them?'

'No, but it was probably Dave Devlyn, the man Sappho was trying to avoid at the party.'

'You can't accuse him without any proof!' I protested.

'Is there any reason why he should do such a thing?' the inspector said patiently.

'He's madly jealous of Sappho – they used to be an item years ago – and he's prone to doing spiteful things to get her attention.'

'We've already spoken to Mr Devlyn, and I believe he was

otherwise occupied at the time, although both he and Mr Ace went out at some point for a breath of air.'

After a few more seemingly random questions he said that would be all, and added that although Lili was now conscious and making a good recovery, she hadn't been able to recall anything about what happened yet.

When they left I insisted they took the rock that struck Sphinx with them, which they would have forgotten if I hadn't reminded them. Sherlock Holmes and Dr Watson they ain't.

They seemed keen to get away, colliding with Nye as they went around the barn.

He was wearing clay-bespattered cords and a scowl. I'd learned by then that his strange eyes are a barometer for his feelings: leaden grey means trouble.

I had an instant flashback to the night before, which I could have done without, and which probably helped to make me sound flippant, when I said, 'Hello, Nye! This is a surprise.'

'Is it?' he said coldly, continuing to glower down at me.

And loom. I wasn't used to it.

'Your cat gets stoned, Lili may or may not have been attacked last night while wearing your cloak by the same person who did it, and you're surprised I've come to see if you're all right?'

'Oh, we're absolutely fine – and so is Sphinx, as you can see,' I said airily.

'I think it's really thoughtful of you, Nye,' Mu said. 'Why don't you come in? I'll make some fresh coffee – or tea?'

Traitor.

'Coffee would be wonderful,' he said, tiredly pushing tumbled white-gold hair off his forehead and leaving a greyish streak in its place, which strangely did nothing to mar his looks.

'I've been working all day – the policemen interrupted me – but apart from that . . .'

I didn't let him get further than the kitchen. Not only was he covered in clay, but I didn't want to encourage him to stay; the room seemed very full of him, his long legs occupying half the floor space under the table.

'When you didn't show up at the studio I assumed you were otherwise occupied, with the cat and the police,' he said to me. 'But evidently not.'

Mu gave me a thoughtful look. 'We went out this afternoon to Oxwich Bay, Nye. I didn't know you'd definitely agreed to meet at the castle.'

I gave stirring the coffee the careful attention it deserved. 'We didn't. I might have said I'd call in sometime.'

'And we passed by it, too!' Mu said regretfully. 'I'd love to see your work, Nye, but perhaps Sappho could come tomorrow and then tell me about it, because I'm going home first thing. Will you be there tomorrow?'

'I'm always there.'

'You aren't now,' I pointed out, rather snappily.

'I left early – I wanted to make sure you were all right.' He frowned. 'Too many odd things seem to be happening lately, what with Dorinda Ace vanishing, and your cat being hurt, and then Lili. But Lili might be an accident, and the cat your loopy boyfriend's doing.'

'Ex. Long-past ex.'

Miranda walked in through the open door. 'Sappho? Oh, there you are – and Mu. I've b-been to see Lili, and she's going to be fine – they might let her out on Tuesday. Only she says she can't remember anything. She asked me to d-drop a note off for D-Dave D-Devlyn, which is odd, isn't it? Except they d-did seem friendly, so perhaps—'

245

She stopped dead, having spotted Nye, and blushed.

'Hello, Miranda.'

'Never mind him,' I said dismissively. 'Sit down – have some coffee while it's still hot.'

Nye cast me one of his unfathomable looks, though how you can be so very fair and yet look so darkly brooding is beyond me. At least the leaden aspect had departed, leaving just a hint of gunpowder smoke in its place.

He smiled enchantingly at Miranda, though. 'I know all about Dave,' he said helpfully. 'I think I know all about everything,' he added after a minute's thought. 'Mu filled me in last night.'

I gave her a look – how long *was* I asleep on that sofa? Long enough for my entire life history?

'I'm sure Lili must have just slipped and caught her head,' Miranda said. 'And the cat – well, D-Dave seems likely, he's so jealous of you and he hates cats . . . and he d-did leave the party for a while. B-but he says he was gone only a few minutes, and then he went upstairs with this girl.'

'Chris came here,' I said. 'But that was just pure nosiness.'

'And Gil went out for a few minutes too, the police said,' Mu added.

'Oh, it wasn't Gil – he *likes* cats. Anyway, he just wouldn't,' Miranda declared confidently. 'I hope the police aren't going to start b-bothering him again. He certainly wasn't gone long enough to get up to the cottage where they found Lili and b-back.'

'Maybe it was later,' I suggested, 'and Lili'd arranged to meet someone there – like Nye.'

'Leaving aside the fact that the police say she was struck before the heavy rain, when you may recall we were otherwise engaged, why would I want to do that?' he asked.

'She had a hold on you?' I suggested.

'Blameless past,' he said, unimpressed.

'You were secretly married and—'

'No I wasn't!'

'You were having an affair and—'

'You must know I wasn't interested in her. Why are you trying to prove it was me?'

Our eyes met and I said, surprised, 'I'm not – just tossing out various scenarios.'

'It's not very fair to poor Nye, though,' objected Mu. 'We know he didn't do it. This isn't a novel.'

'Ah, yes – the novels,' Nye said, and stared at me broodingly again. 'I started *Vengeane*: *Dark Hours, Dark Deeds* last night when I got home.'

'Weren't you too tired?' I blurted out, and then blushed.

'Yes, but I feel it may hold the key to everything. Some of the characters seem strangely familiar.'

Oh God! I may have to leave the country sooner than I'd thought . . .

Miranda sighed. 'I'm so tired, I'm going to go home. Sorry for b-bursting in like that b-but I got to thinking and . . .'

'It's all right,' I said.

'I only hope D-Dave d-doesn't d-do something in a jealous rage b-because you left with Nye last night,' she added. 'B-but then, if he and Lili got friendly . . .?'

I yawned. 'He won't be around for long – he'll take his photos and go away, and anyway, I'm not afraid of him.'

'You could force the issue,' Nye suggested. 'Meet me at this pub he's staying in for a drink tomorrow night, and see if he's jealous or indifferent. At least I'll be there to protect you if he turns nasty. And perhaps seeing you friendly with someone else is all it needs to make him see he's holding out false hopes.'

247

'I'm not friendly with anyone else,' I said coldly.

'You can pretend.'

'That might be a good idea,' Mu said. 'I'm worried about leaving you here alone tomorrow.'

'With the cat – unless you'd like to take her back with you?'

'You need her, even if she isn't stone proof.'

'I'm fine on my own,' I insisted.

'Of course, if you're too frightened to try it – or too scared of me—' Nye began.

'I certainly am not! I'll come with you tomorrow, but don't blame me if it gets rough.'

'He's old enough and certainly big enough to take care of himself,' Mu said. 'She accepts your offer, Nye.'

'Thank you,' Nye said. 'And what have I got to lose? If he's still hung up on Sappho, isn't he going to have it in for me already? I might as well get some pleasure out of the situation.'

'What sort of pleasure did you have in mind?' I asked suspiciously.

'The pleasure of your company, what else? Don't go out after dark,' he added, like I'm going to take any notice of him.

Chapter 27

Sweet and Sour

Did the usual chunk of novel the following morning. Nala was vacillating in a most unusual and annoying way.

She hadn't quite accepted that Raarg, however handsome, was not the man for her, or that it would be better to rule and live alone than be overwhelmed mentally and physically by Dragonslayer.

I wasn't sure my readers were ready to accept that, either.

When I'd finished it was time to drive Mu to catch her train, but unfortunately minus the cat.

She was high as a kite with nerves and excitement – but also full of enthusiastic plans for her Indiana Cat-type book, which was taking shape. It was strange how everything was sort of bursting into bloom at once.

'Now you can go home and spend the rest of the day making yourself beautiful for Nye's benefit,' she informed me, standing in the carriage doorway.

'It would be more likely to put Dave off me if I looked an absolute dog – and I don't know why I said I'd go to the pub with Nye. It's a stupid idea. If Dave is there, he'll just make a scene.'

'Yes, but he thinks you've saved yourself for him all these years, so if he sees you involved with another man it might just disillusion him: shock him back to his senses, even.'

'I'm not sure he's got any, other than touch and taste. And what if it was he who attacked Sphinx, and even Lili? If he did, then he's just a bit over the edge, don't you think? And seeing me with a rival might push him into doing something even worse.'

'I thought you didn't believe he did those things? Haven't you been telling me all these years that he's just harmlessly malicious?' she said.

I shivered suddenly. 'Yes, but there was something in his eyes at the party that – well, it didn't frighten me exactly, but it made me think he was just a little demented on the subject of yours truly. I can't imagine why.'

Mu gave me a hug. 'I'd better get in before the train leaves me behind. And don't worry – Nye will look after you!'

I think he's already done that, and once was enough.

But on the whole I had a feeling that if I tried to wriggle out of tonight he'd come and get me. I didn't know why he wanted to get involved in my affairs, but I supposed, as he said, he was big enough to look after himself.

Mu pushed the door window down. 'Don't cut off your nose to spite your face: I'd go anywhere Nye asked me, Ambler or no Ambler!' she called.

'No you wouldn't – you're all talk and no action,' I said rudely as the train began to pull out.

As soon as I got home the Three Graces waylaid me, although two of them departed to jobs after greeting me, leaving Violet in charge of the interrogation.

Could they be a family-sized coven?

'Heard about that Lili Ford Jakes woman,' she informed me. 'Lavender and Poppy think she was just drunk and fell while trying to shelter from the rain. Shame, though. Still, Miranda says she's going to be out of hospital tomorrow, though she can't remember anything about it.'

'Perhaps it'll come back to her?'

'Perhaps it will, and then we'll know the answer to "Did she fall or was she crushed?"' she chortled. 'Wearing your cape too, wasn't she? Makes you wonder – especially after your cat got struck by a stone the same night. Quite a coincidence.'

'Isn't it? Lili borrowed my rain cape since I'd left it behind at Miranda's party.'

'Was that when you borrowed the man she had her eye on?'

Good grief! Does she know *everything*? This isn't bush telegraph, it's bush telepathy!

She chuckled. 'Adonis! Nice man, though.'

'You know Nye, don't you?'

'Know all the people in the Castle Craft place – have tea in the café there twice a week with my friends, for a gossip.'

She peered over the hedge as if someone might be hiding behind it and added, *sotto voce*: 'There was a man hanging round outside your barn earlier – dark, handsome, bit-of-a-devil type.'

Dave to a T. I suppose he didn't dare come nearer because of the cat. There was no sign of him now, but I was starting to think having my front door on this side of the house, so people couldn't lurk unseen, would definitely be a good move.

'The ex-boyfriend, I presume?' Violet said interrogatively. 'Had the look of it: thwarted Heathcliff. I hear he's staying at the village pub.'

251

She *must* be a witch – but at least she couldn't know about Nye and me on the rock . . . could she?

To my relief she changed tack. 'That friend of yours, Muriel, was out in the garden with a cat yesterday.'

'Mu,' I corrected. 'Her name isn't Muriel.'

'I don't see what else it can be short for,' she said, but I just smiled enigmatically.

'What did you think of the cat?'

It turned out that she's dying for a weird kitten just like mine if Coochie and Ankaret will oblige again.

The Gower will be overrun with enormous and peculiar moggies.

Miranda delivered a rush-order bouquet before lunch – to me.

It was a Victorian-style Declaration of Love posy – I didn't need to read the booklet. Lemon geranium – the meeting; red roses – declaration of love; stocks – lasting beauty; phlox – unanimity; and heliotrope – love and devotion.

There was no card – I suppose the flowers said it all, as they were meant to – but it was from Dave. He'd discovered Miranda was running Fantasy Flowers and assumed she'd been the one who had set it up originally, and she hadn't disillusioned him.

Miranda said he'd been Mr Charming when he ordered the posy, apologizing for spiking the punch and telling her he loved me just as much as ever. He seemed to think I'd just taken Nye for a walk (like a dog) on the night of the party, in order to make him jealous.

Miranda said her heart was a *little* touched, he seemed so sincere, and I said in that case she was touched in more ways than one.

*

252

Nye picked me up at seven and for once he was not streaked with clay, so maybe he wasn't on the warpath this time. But I did think he must have had second thoughts about the scheme, because his mind was so clearly elsewhere.

I asked him if he wanted to call it off, and he came back from wherever it was for long enough to say, with some surprise, that he didn't and he was hungry, so hurry up.

Friendly but detached, like the cat. Just what I wanted, wasn't it?

I'd sort of assumed we'd eat at the Newt and Rocket in the village, but instead we drove into Swansea in his little white van (which was a trifle basic as to comfort, and reeked of wet clay and damp sacking), and went to a Chinese restaurant.

I wield a mean pair of chopsticks.

All through the meal Nye kept scribbling things on bright Post-it notes, but after a bit he seemed to come back to Planet Earth and put them away in his pocket.

'*Dragonslayer was abstracted – something was occupying his mind to the exclusion of all else, including her presence . . .*'

'Sorry, did you say something?' he asked.

'No,' I said hastily, pressing the Off button. Perhaps a memo device on a cord was a little bulky for personal jewellery, but if I leave it behind I always regret it.

'I'm ignoring you,' he said kindly, 'but I was just working something out, and you know how it is when your mind's on your work?'

I nodded. I did understand, though I couldn't imagine what was vital about the design of a mug or plate. Still, he was obviously a dedicated craftsman, which is something all writers ought to be too, and often aren't. Sloppy workmanship.

Now he'd fully resurfaced he was again the man of the

night of the party – the one before we jumped off the Point of No Return.

It was like putting a familiar coat on: something in cut velvet, with a five-figure price tag attached. I knew I couldn't afford it, but I enjoyed wrapping it around me just for a while.

He has a deepish voice, which is just as well: you don't want a man that size who squeaks (assuming you want a man).

He said all the chalet dwellers in Preece's Plot had been served notice to fold their tents and steal away, because the demolition was due to take place in the autumn.

'But surely they're Victorian, aren't they? Shouldn't they be preserved for posterity, or something?'

'I don't think posterity wants them. They're decayed to the point of no return. We've all bodged them up as best we can, because the landlord's been letting them fall about our ears in an attempt to get us out. I love it down there, but there's no mains sanitation, the water's from standpipes, and there's a bit of a rat problem.'

'*Rats?*'

'Mostly outside the houses,' he said nonchalantly, 'but these being wooden chalets the rats sometimes chew their way in. And mice, of course, but they're not so much of a problem.'

Or merely not such a *big* problem?

'So, how long do you have before you move out? And where will you go?'

'Until September. A few people wanted to try to barricade themselves in to stop the development, but really it's on its last legs anyway. So some of them are going to go and live in the yurt village up in North Wales, and a couple of the families will probably be rehomed by the council, and then the rest of us will just have to find somewhere else.'

'Do you know where yet?'

'No. But I haven't really thought about it. I might find a cottage to rent, but now the Gower's so trendy I could be priced out of the market and end up in a caravan.'

'You don't strike me as a happy camper.'

He grinned. 'I don't really care where I live as long as I've got the workshop, though somewhere with a studio so I could work at home would be perfect. Maybe one day . . .'

'But you need the craft centre as an outlet to sell, don't you?'

'Not really. I sell almost everything I make through commission, or London galleries.'

'Oh?' Really, I ought to go down and see what it was he actually produced. He must be good at it . . . as well as other things.

'I'll come down to the castle tomorrow and look round.'

'I've heard that before. I'm just surprised you didn't chicken out of tonight.'

'I am not, and never have been, a coward!' I stated.

'Is that why you drove off the first time we met, after drenching me in icy mud?'

'I pulled in, didn't I? If you hadn't lost your appalling temper and looked as if you were going to murder me, I would have stayed.'

'I haven't got an appalling temper and I wouldn't have hurt you, I was just going to ask you if you had a wheel brace.'

'A likely story. And I don't know why you insist you don't have a bad temper when you seem to lose it so easily.'

He stared at me in seething silence for a moment, but his eyes were only hint-of-a-tint, so I knew he wasn't really mad.

You know, I thought, his eyelashes are *really* interesting – darker at the roots and shading off towards gold at the end – and the more I look at him, the more readily I could believe he's from another planet.

The more I looked at him, the wider his grin got.

I looked away hastily, and laid my chopsticks down. 'Well, that was a very nice meal,' I said, declining the dessert menu. 'And I've enjoyed this evening – there's no reason why we can't be friends, after all.'

'After all what?'

I ignored that. 'But I've thought about this scheme you and Mu have hatched up to scare Dave off, and really I've come to the conclusion it'll only make him worse if he sees us together, and also put you at risk of his jealous temper. If I just keep rebuffing him, he'll probably finish his work here in a week or two and go off back to London.'

'And then again, he might go off in a complete huff if he sees us together in a *very* friendly way, and that will end it once and for all,' Nye suggested. 'Which is what you want, isn't it? Or is it? You haven't still got a soft spot for him, have you?'

'No I haven't!' I said strongly.

'Then if I'm willing to take the risk, why not? And if, as you say, we're going to be friends, he's going to see me around with you a lot, isn't he?'

There's friends and friends. Maybe we could be pen pals for a year or two?

'And I intend to be around as long as Dragonslayer is,' he added. 'How did you pick on me for your hero?'

'Dragonslayer is *not* the hero! He's just a peripheral character who's got too big for his boots – and he *isn't* you, either! He just – coincidentally – happens to look a bit like you.'

'A bit as in "mirror image"?'

'Coincidences happen,' I defended myself hotly. 'Actually, Lili showed me a really bad photograph of you *months* before

I ever met you, and that must be where I got your description from, but the details that weren't in the photo really *are* just coincidence.'

He looked at me quizzically.

'It's true!'

'Right. I can't wait for the next book. When's that due out?'

'I'm still writing it,' I said stiffly, putting the cash for exactly half the bill down on the table with a thump.

'Time to beard the lion in his den? Or shall I just take you safely home and go and poke him with a sharp stick, to see what his bite's like?' he said.

Just you wait, Dragonslayer!

Chapter 28

Testing Times

It was latish when we pulled up outside the Rat and Casket, and bright lights and loud voices spilled out of the open door, though actually it sounded fuller than it was.

There was no sign of our quarry, so after collecting a couple of drinks we went and sat in one of the alcove seats – the one Lili sometimes cornered Nye in.

'He probably isn't coming – or he's been and gone. We could just have this drink and go home,' I suggested.

'Give him time: he'll probably feel the magnetic pull of your presence.'

I gave Nye a frosty look and he edged me into the corner and draped his arm around me affectionately.

'What are you doing?' I demanded.

'Window dressing: I think we ought to look friendly.'

'There's friendly and friendly, and I've never been one for canoodling in public.'

Or anywhere else much, come to that, which I probably told him when I was punch drunk.

'Canoodling is a lovely word. If you can have kissing cousins, why not canoodling friends?' He raised his glass and smiled down into my eyes. 'Here's to us.'

'This is all the us there is going to be, so I suppose I can drink to that.'

'That's not the impression you gave me up at the cromlech,' he said reproachfully.

'I was drunk, as you know. A gentleman wouldn't mention it again.'

'Do you know any?'

'No,' I said shortly.

'And I wasn't drunk, just rash enough to let you drag me up there and have your way with me.'

'I didn't drag you up there, you insisted on coming!'

'It's all right, I wasn't complaining: love is more than just who does what to whom.'

'What?' I stared at him, wide-eyed (and probably open-mouthed), and he leaned his head conspiratorially close until his lips grazed my ear.

'He's here!' he whispered softly. It tickled.

'Who?'

'The lion – and he's seen us. Just carry on looking at me adoringly the way you were.'

A blistering retort sprang to my lips, but before I could say anything Dave was upon us.

'I'm not interrupting anything, am I?' he said with an undertone of menace and sat down opposite, uninvited.

Nye smiled politely. 'Not at all. Didn't we meet at the Cotters? You're Dave—'

'Devlyn,' he responded automatically, fixing burning dark eyes on me. 'I've been looking for you, Sapphie.'

'Have you? I thought you'd be busy with your photos.'

'I only booked into this dive because it was near you, so we can spend some time together – and then you vanish. I sent you a bouquet to tell you how I feel. Didn't you get it?'

'Yes, but I've had a busy couple of days – I've got a novel to write, you know. Anyway, I don't want to see any more of you than I have, and I don't actually care how you feel.'

'I suppose you've found out about that girl at the party, but she didn't mean anything. She was just there when I couldn't find you.'

Complimentary.

'Sappho and I were a bit bored by the party, so we went for a walk together and discovered we had such a lot in common, didn't we, darling?' Nye chipped in helpfully.

'Uh? Er . . . yes, we did, didn't we?' I squeezed his hand and beamed adoringly at him and he blinked.

Dave abruptly sprang to his feet, upsetting the table and sending the contents of the glasses into my lap. I wished I'd gone for a short drink.

'Don't think you can play those little games on me, Sappho, and get away with it!' he snarled, like a *West Side Story* version of Heathcliff. 'What's he got that I haven't?'

'Sanity?' I suggested, then saw something so unbalanced in his eyes that I did an out-of-character Shrinking Violet into the shelter of Nye's arm, which made matters worse.

'As for you, Golden Boy,' Dave continued, 'Sappho's mine, always has been, always will be: and if you think you can change that you're wrong. Now get out! I'll see her home!'

He reached downward with the intention, I think, of grabbing the front of Nye's shirt and pulling him out, only it didn't quite work that way: Nye rose like a coiled spring and struck him neatly just under the chin.

Dave's mouth closed with a snap like a castanet and he sat down with more haste than speed on the floor, looking dazed.

'My hero!' I said to Nye, who seemed rather pleased with himself. 'Quick, let's go before he starts again.'

'I'm not running away—' he protested, resisting as I dragged him through the circle of mildly interested faces. 'We ought to settle this once and for all.'

'To the death? I'm not having a fight over me in a pub as if I was a raffle prize. We're not living in a soap. Come on, you've stirred things up enough for one night.'

He halted outside the pub in the cold night air and said accusingly, '*I've* stirred things up? What did you ever do to get the man in such a state in the first place?'

'Fell in love with him – then fell out of love with him again – but, my God, it was *years* ago!' I said bitterly. 'You don't think I've been secretly encouraging him ever since, do you? That I *like* this sort of scene?'

'No, I don't, so stop glaring – and get in the van if you're determined to leave it like this.'

He started the engine just as Dave staggered outside, one hand to his jaw. Sighting us, he lurched over and tried to catch hold of the passenger door as we pulled out.

'I know all about you, you bloody pansy potter with a dyke for a girlfriend!' he yelled very rudely (and not entirely accurately). 'Sappho—'

'If I'm a pansy you've nothing to worry about, have you?' Nye said coolly through the half-open window, moving away just as Dave tried to open the door.

We left him gesticulating and mouthing after us: not a pretty sight, had I cared, but I was choking back inopportune giggles.

Since my house was so near I thought Dave might follow us at a run – or a lurching stumble – but there was no sound of pursuit when we got out of the van. All was still.

'What are you laughing about?' Nye stopped and stared down at me, and his look of outrage set me off again.

'The . . . the pansy potter bit,' I gasped. 'The irresistible allure of alliteration – first me and then—'

A pair of strong arms yanked me practically off the ground into a crushing embrace, which might have started out temper-driven, but soon softened into something more demoralizing . . .

That Dalek voice was bleating again: *'Resistance is useless!'* It was no use, there isn't a jot of romance in me.

'Resistance is useless,' I agreed when I came up for air.

'What?' Nye sounded shaken out of his cool.

'You don't have to demonstrate to me you're not a pansy potter – I already know.'

'Well, I admit to being a potter.'

I fended him off when his arms tightened again, even though my knees were trying to fold. 'It's all right, I don't need a repeat demonstration.'

'Sappho . . .' his voice softened and his grip relaxed, 'I didn't mean to go all caveman. Did I hurt you?'

'Only the three crushed ribs, and they'll soon mend,' I replied, breathing cautiously. My knees were now Poorly but Stable so I removed myself to a safer distance.

'Well, thanks for an interesting evening,' I said politely.

'The pleasure was all mine,' he rejoined gravely. 'Or then again, maybe not?'

'I don't think Dave felt much pleasure tonight. In fact we might have made things worse.'

'He does seem a little beyond reason about you,' he agreed, 'but having started we can't stop now.'

He might be right.

'What did you have in mind?'

'Casual stuff – you coming down to the workshop tomorrow, like you said you would. I'll meet you in the café there for lunch, and we can hold hands, gaze into each other's eyes . . .'

'It would put me off my food – and anyway, there's a flaw in the plan: Dave wouldn't be there to see it.'

'Word will get about,' he said vaguely.

'Yes, and if it reaches Lili she'll probably lynch me. And what about my work?'

'Don't you usually do most of it early in the day?'

'Yes, but it depends.' I sighed and gave in. 'Oh, all right, I'll come, but only because I want to see round the craft centre.'

'Right. Sure you wouldn't like to try that kiss again before I go? I have a theory about time standing still I'd like to test.'

'No.'

'And you don't want me to stay the night and guard you, in case Dave comes round?'

'He won't – the cat, don't forget.'

'Right, might as well go home then.'

As I unlocked the door I looked back and found him still watching me, though I couldn't see his expression in the shadows. I hoped Dave wasn't lying in wait for him somewhere, in Mad Assassin Mode.

'Be careful on your way home,' I warned him.

'Don't worry about me,' he said, sounding surprised. 'No, on second thoughts, do worry about me. At least it means you'll be thinking of me.'

'Don't be silly,' I said severely, and fell over the cat.

My gestures often turn out to be large, but seldom grand.

Chapter 29

Gingered

Next morning I thought about maiming Dragonslayer just a little bit, *à la* Mr Rochester, but somehow could not bring myself to do it, which is not like me.

Still, I reflected, if any maiming were to be done Nala would probably do it herself.

The neat little café was quite busy, but Nye had bagged a table overlooking a small garden.

A party of young female tourists were attempting to take over both of them, but drifted off regretfully when Nye exclaimed: 'Darling!' as soon as he saw me, leaped to his feet and enthusiastically kissed my parted lips – parted in surprise, I hasten to add.

I didn't think we were going for this level of public affection.

I sank down on the nearest chair and draped my hair over one shoulder, so it didn't get trampled on. It was in one long plait tied at the end with a length of beaded rawhide that I'd picked up somewhere or other, and my feet were bare: I wasn't going to change my ways just because I was having lunch with an alien being.

The waitress was dressed in a sort of pseudo-Welsh costume like Llyn's. It didn't bode well for the quality of the craftwork, and I only hoped I would be able to find something nice to say about Nye's pottery.

What if it were all runny glaze and red dragons?

I was just about to demand large amounts of coffee, as usual, when I realized that I didn't want it in the least, *or* tea: the thought revolted. 'Have you got ginger beer?' I enquired.

'Yes, I think so.'

'Real ginger beer, with actual ginger in it?'

'It's in cans,' she said, as if that clinched the matter. Still, when it came, together with the fresh ham salad rolls, it was the real fiery stuff.

Salad is usually something I eat because it gets between me and my sandwich filling, but that lunchtime I really enjoyed it. My tastes must be changing . . .

'Lili phoned me earlier,' Nye said.

I felt a pang of – something, I'm not sure what, but said casually, 'Oh, did she? From the hospital?'

'Yes, but she was getting ready to go home because they're letting her out later.'

'Not on her own, surely? Or did she want you to pick her up?'

'No,' he said, 'she already had a lift arranged – with Dave Devlyn.'

I stared at him. 'How did she manage that? You know, I think there may be a whole subplot here that I'm missing.'

'She's offered to put him up while he's staying down here.'

'I bet she has! I wonder . . .' I chewed the last bit of roll thoughtfully. 'Was she trying to make you jealous, do you think? Is that why she phoned you up?'

Something seemed to be amusing him. 'No, that wasn't

what she had in mind. She wants me to keep you occupied, so she has a clear run at Dave. She said the sudden blow to the head had clarified things.'

'I thought it was supposed to have had the opposite effect? And what does she mean, *occupy* me?'

'Search me,' he said innocently.

Well, it was a tempting possibility, but I managed to resist.

He lowered his voice to a deep, intimate level, gazed pensively into my eyes and said, 'Couldn't I tempt you . . . to a piece of chocolate cake?'

'If you ham it up like this no one will be taken in for a minute, even someone as jealous as Dave,' I said severely. 'And no, I don't want cake.'

But when it came, I did absent-mindedly demolish half the substantial slice, because I was pondering Lili's doings, though Nye ate the rest.

If Lili decided to pursue him, it would be one way of getting Dave off my back, but would it work? Perhaps someone should hit Dave on the head, too?

'We can come back later and have more cake,' Nye suggested. 'I'm glad you came. I wasn't sure you'd turn up. I didn't like leaving you alone last night either, now I've seen Dave's reaction for myself. I thought you and Mu were exaggerating a bit, but he's definitely obsessed with you. So am I,' he added, picking up my hand and stroking the back with his thumb, which was interestingly pleasurable.

I let it lie: it didn't seem worth making a fuss about.

'Actually, he may have been skulking about last night, because I woke up and thought I saw someone in the courtyard . . . but I was half asleep and when I looked again there was no one there. And the cat didn't make a noise, so I assume nobody tried to get in.'

Nye looked embarrassed. 'Sorry – that was me! I came back around midnight and sort of scouted round, but the pub and the village were all quiet so after a while I went home.'

'That was thoughtful of you, Nye, but really there wasn't any danger. Dave might have hung around, but he wouldn't try to get in with the cat there.'

'I felt like a walk anyway.'

'Three miles in the dark?'

'Why not? You do the same, don't you? Though I hope you won't while Dave is running loose – unless I'm with you.'

He got up. 'Come on, Rapunzel, I'll show you around.'

I gestured at the shop as we passed. 'Don't you have anything in there?'

'Not usually, no. It's not impulse-buy stuff,' he said mysteriously, leading the way at a brisk stride across the courtyard and into the dark tunnels between the workshops.

'Do you want the complete guided tour?'

'No, I want to see yours first, then I'll walk round the rest on my own.'

Most of the workshops seemed to have closed for lunch anyway, so there were few people about other than in the shop and café.

He opened his door and switched on the light, and I walked past him into the studio. The walls were lined with shelves, and there was a huge pinboard covered in all kinds of things. But what dominated the room, and stopped me dead in my tracks, staring, was the ceramic sculpture sitting on the worktable.

Then, stunned, I walked all around it, studying it from every angle. It looked finished to me, though I'm no expert – the smooth, polished sides flowed and rippled under a mass of muted line drawings over washes of colour that curved out, and round, and up, and in . . .

I suppose if you had to, you could describe it as a pot, like you could call Michelangelo's *David* a model of a man. 'Do you like it?' Nye's voice sounded strangely unsure.

I managed to drag my eyes away from it for long enough to notice other, smaller pieces on some of the shelves. 'Like it? How can you ask me if I *like* it? It's wonderful! And I thought you were making tea sets and punch bowls!'

'There'd be nothing wrong with that, you artistic snob – the people I share my kiln with make brilliant table pottery. It's just that this is what I do.'

'Where's the kiln? It must be massive to fire this.'

'Not all my work is fired in one piece, but it is a big kiln: it's in the cellar under the west turret. I've got something firing in it now – first firing.'

'You surely can't sell *any* of these to tourists?'

'I don't try, though I do sometimes get commissions. Mostly I sell through the Crafts Council in London, exhibitions, word of mouth . . . that kind of thing,' he said vaguely. 'I don't work fast, and they take a long time, so I charge a lot.'

'They're worth any price you put on them,' I assured him, gingerly stroking the cool, fluid shape. 'This is finished, isn't it?'

'Yes, it's ready for packing. Actually,' he added with wry self-consciousness, 'it was ready on Sunday, but I wanted you to see it first.'

'And I didn't show up? Oh, Nye, I'm sorry. If I'd known about this nothing would have stopped me!'

'I can see I'd have made faster progress with you by showing you pictures of my work,' he commented drily.

How much faster did he want to go?

'What kind of progress?' I asked.

He ignored that and pointed to the copy of *Dark Hours,*

268

Dark Deeds. 'I've finished your last book, and now I'm going to read the rest in the right order. Maybe by then you'll have finished the new one? I suppose you wouldn't like to give me a hint about what happens to me, would you?'

'Dragonslayer isn't you, I keep telling you.'

'And Raarg isn't Dave and Nala isn't you, I know. It's all coincidence.'

'Nala's nothing like me, except for having long hair!'

'And being bossy.'

'I'm not bossy.'

'And *I* haven't got a bad temper.'

We stared at each other. 'I warn you,' he said with emphasis, 'if Nala goes off with Raarg at the end of this book, Dragonslayer is going to cut his nuts off and use them for marbles.'

'He can't,' I said quickly, 'he has to do what I tell him to do. Nala will only marry her equal and not someone who can best her in any way. I think Dragonslayer is a bit too sure of himself, just because they had a little fling while she was under the influence of the evil Laag drink. Dragonslayer needs taking down a peg or two.'

'I think she ought to consider what he's going through a bit more. When he came from his own country he was trapped in hers, and drawn to her even though he didn't want to be. Then he protects and rescues her as much as he can, and what does he get? Thanks, but no thanks? Wham, bam, thank you, Dragonslayer? Can't they agree to be *different* but equal?'

'Are we arguing about women's lib here, or the *Vengeane* situation?'

Or something totally different?

'I'd just like to know where you're going with it.'

'I don't know yet: it just comes in its own time. I think there'll be one more *Vengeane* book after this one, and then I'm on to something different.'

'Couldn't I read the manuscript of this one, so I know the pitfalls to avoid?' he asked.

'No you can't. My borrowing your handsome face doesn't entitle you to an advance preview.'

'Would you prefer me if I had a crew cut and grew a silly moustache?'

'No!'

'You mean, "No, I adore you just as you are", or "No, it wouldn't make any difference"?'

I turned away and fingered the tools laid out along the table edge. 'No – I mean, you're fine as you are.'

'Am I?' he said softly, reaching out a gentle hand to tilt my face up to his.

'Nye, don't—' I began, twisting away as I noticed a rapt audience reassembled behind the glass window.

I'll never go to the zoo again – and wasn't that tall, dark shape at the back . . .

'It's Dave – he tailed us from the courtyard,' Nye said, following the direction of my gaze. 'But he's gone now.'

'Oh, I see! So that was why you—'

'It wasn't,' he said, advancing with a light in his eyes. 'Come round here and I'll show you!'

I backed towards the door. 'Haven't you any shame?'

'I don't think so. Are you going to meet me later?'

'No, I'm having tea with Gil and after that I'm going to go home and do something dreadful to Dragonslayer!' I snapped, and he laughed.

'Watch out for Dave. Come back if he's still out there.'

I nodded – let him take it as he pleased – and sidled out of the door rather pink-cheeked and half-expecting a round of applause.

Of Dave there was no sign, so we might have been mistaken; this isn't his type of place at all.

Still feeling generally ruffled I walked around the rest of the studios, lingering over the leather worker's, inhaling deeply. There was an interesting furniture workshop too, which would repay a visit at a later time.

Of course, there were oodles of love-spoons and Welsh dragons, but the spoons were beautifully carved, and the dragons desirable hand-made glass ones.

They reminded me of the carving over my door – soon to be revealed again when the conservatory was removed – and I was considering buying one when I felt that old familiar feeling. The one that laser-burns a line down your conscious (and your spine).

Dave trailed me outside into the sunlit organic garden, where I tired of the me-and-my-shadow game and sat down on a bench.

'Why don't you come out from behind that bush, Dave?' I suggested, sighing.

Glowering becomingly, he emerged and sat down next to me. 'How did you know I was there?'

'Elementary, my dear Watson: you aren't a vampire, so you cast a shadow. I wish you wouldn't follow me about.'

'I don't want to. I'd rather come to your house, if you'd let me. Why are you playing hard to get?' He looked puzzled.

'I'm not playing hard to get: I'm not even playing. I'm simply not interested in you in that way any more. But I do wish you well – with someone else.'

'While you amuse yourself with this Nye Thomas? I don't

think so, Sapphie: I think you ought to tell him to leave you alone.'

There was that unnerving hint of malevolence about his voice when he added, 'Everything would have been all right if it hadn't been for him.'

'Now, look here,' I said angrily. 'I've only known him a short while, and it's none of your business, anyway. There's nothing you could do or say that would make me even want to see you again, much less live with you.'

'You love me,' he said. 'You're a stubborn, independent woman, but you've come back at last – to me. He's just a diversion, to pay me back for the other girls I've been with, even though none of them meant to me a fraction of what you do.'

Words failed me.

'I suppose you've heard I'm staying with Lili, but I'm just putting up there. She needed someone around for a day or two, and it was convenient.'

'You're *not* around, though, are you? You're here, bothering me.'

He smiled that slow, sexy smile, and said softly, 'Am I bothering you, Sapphie?'

I closed my eyes: give me strength! When I opened them again he was closer, emitting enough charm to floor a buffalo. 'Sapphie . . .' he tried to take my hands, 'why don't we start again: we've got off on the wrong foot, that's all. You and me? I could—'

'Am I interrupting anything?'

Nye stood over us, hands thrust in pockets, silvery hair ruffled and eyes like clouded silver. My heart did a bit of gymnastic wriggling as if warming up for something, but it was probably just from tension.

Dave sprang up to face him, dark and angry: they looked like positive and negative images, very odd.

'You *are* interrupting. We don't want you butting in, do we, Sapphie? Clear out and leave her alone.'

Nye's strangely beautiful eyes met mine as if seeking something – could it be reassurance? Surely he didn't think I still felt anything for Dave?

I got up and faced Dave. 'You didn't interrupt anything important, Nye. I've said everything I want to.'

Dave's eyes narrowed. 'It's like that then, is it? It's him and—'

'No it isn't, it's me. Nye isn't important, because I wouldn't have ever come back to you anyway.'

'You heard what she said,' Nye said evenly. 'Give it up – there's nothing here for you.'

He might as well have saved his breath.

'Sapphie, let's talk about this again later, alone. If you shut that damned cat away I could come round and—'

Nye was suddenly so near that I could feel the muscles bunching under the skin of his arm.

'There's nothing more to talk about, and I don't want to see you again. How many times do I have to say it?' I repeated wearily.

'Leave her alone – leave *us* alone,' Nye added, and I thought that intimate 'us' might just make Dave lose what little control he had, but the sudden advent of a crowd of schoolchildren into the garden halted his hasty movement.

'You'll both regret this!' he threatened, turned abruptly on his heel and walked away with long, angry strides.

I let out a long breath, and Nye suddenly caught me in a hard bear hug, which squeezed out any air remaining in my lungs. 'You looked so deep in conversation . . . so close,' he muttered, kissing the top of my head.

Most men would need a stepladder for that.

I disengaged myself, wheezing slightly. 'Well, hopefully, that's that. Now Lili can go to work on him, and once she's got her hooks into him we can have a monumental argument and not have to see each other again.'

'I don't mind arguing with you, and I hope Lili eats Dave alive like a spider, but I draw the line at not seeing you again. I intend spending as much time as possible with you, and when I'm not there, Dragonslayer can take over.'

Dragonslayer? Little did he know the plot complication I'd just that second thought up for him!

Something about my smile seemed to worry him. 'You won't go out tonight, will you? Just in case this isn't the end of it.'

'I've no intention of going out tonight – but not from any fear of Dave. Miranda's coming for dinner.'

How did he manage to look hungry and dejected simultaneously? Why did I weaken?

Who is the potter, pray, and who the pot?

'How do you feel about fish fingers?' I asked.

Chapter 30

High Tea

Mu phoned soon after I got back. She was feeling well and not chewing coal, or road tar, or whatever it is pregnant women are supposed to crave. I was glad Ambler was so delighted – and so unsuspecting.

I don't have any cravings, other than my usual ones for dark rum and chocolate with almonds in it, which is not surprising, since with those eyes Nye just has to be an alien and we're therefore genetically incompatible.

After jotting down my *Vengeane* ideas before I forgot them, I went to tea with Gil. He lived in a tiny, neat bungalow like a dolls' house, overlooking the sea near Rhossili, and his garden contained more bird boxes and bird baths per square foot than you would think possible.

Inside it was very chintzy, in a full-blown way, and crammed with knick-knacks. I hadn't felt so big and clumsy since I visited Japan.

Gil brought out a very *high* high tea: I was quite touched – no one had gone to so much trouble since one of my editors took me to tea at the Ritz a couple of years ago.

There was tea with milk or lemon along with little sandwiches and cakes on flowery china, laid out on the table on a matching flowery cloth with – you've guessed – flowery paper napkins.

Even the carpet was covered in overblown roses – you've never seen such a blooming room in your life. A flower fairy would have been perfectly at home there, but they don't come six foot tall with imposing bosoms and a deficiency in the wing department.

And a flower fairy would have disliked the most peculiar and off-putting aroma hovering about even more than I did.

'If you don't mind me asking, Gil,' I said, as he came back from the kitchen with a bowl of that pretty, lumpy brown sugar that looks as if it ought to be set into silver jewellery, 'what's that smell? Are your drains off?'

He put down the bowl and set out cups and saucers, placing a little paper coaster under each one. 'Oh, no, it's not the drains: my freezer's broken and the bodies are rotting. I hoped to have my new one delivered before they went off, but it hasn't arrived yet.'

I thought, great, I'm alone in a remote bungalow with a man whose wife is missing, and he's confessing to a freezer full of rotting bodies.

'I'll have to throw them out, and I've got some great specimens in there. All picked up or given to me after natural or accidental death,' he added hastily, misreading my expression. 'I wouldn't kill any birds or animals just to study them, believe me.'

'No, I'm sure you wouldn't.'

'I was really sorry about your cat being hurt, but I hope she made a complete recovery?'

'Fine. It was very odd, wasn't it?'

'Yes, very.' He looked nervously down into his cup, as if

something might be lurking in there, and then suddenly called out in a sickly falsetto, 'Muff, Muff, Muffkins! Where are you? Cream!'

The unfortunately named Muff was a white swansdown powder puff on legs. Her smug face was flat, which probably accounted for the messy way she spattered bits of cream and smoked salmon sandwich over the carpet.

Gil was very hospitable and continually pressed dainty morsels upon me, which I sincerely hoped hadn't come out of the defunct freezer.

We had quite a pleasant little chat over the teacups. He seemed very fond of Miranda – he mentioned her about six times in half an hour. And as well as birds he was very up to date on all the local gossip, but I expect it's a two-way street with the Dukes. I got the impression that his desperation to find Dorinda was partly guilt, because he's so much happier now he's got used to doing his own thing again.

He told me Violet Duke had returned yesterday to help him search Dorinda's computer and they'd discovered lots of hidden files, but unfortunately they needed yet another password to get in and they couldn't guess what it was.

Still, even if they did, she was unlikely to have left a message saying: 'Today I parked my car in a remote spot where it will be a target for car thieves and hid in a hole,' or anything helpful of that kind.

'We tried everything we could think of, but with no luck,' he said, so once we'd finished tea I suggested he put the computer back on and have another try, but to no avail. Pity, I'd had high hopes for 'Muff'.

The cat went over and tried to sit on the keyboard and Gil very gently removed her. 'Naughty little Muffkins, doesn't she want to know where her mummy's got to?'

'Try Muffkins,' I said, suddenly inspired.

'What?'

'As the password. Go on, try it.'

It didn't work – but Muffkin did.

We couldn't believe we'd actually cracked it, but our euphoria was short-lived because all the files were written in gibberish: it had to be some sort of code.

Yes, Dorinda was the Enigma of South Wales. Surely you have to be anally retentive to put your journal and notes in code, under a secret password?

Gil went all reserved after this find. He said it was so like his Dear Dorinda, and he hated trying to read what she'd obviously meant to keep secret, but he had to see it if it helped to find her. He also claimed to be brilliant at codes, so I said I'd leave him to it.

'I'll let you know if I find anything useful,' he promised. 'And thank you for finding the password.'

'Perhaps you ought to tell the police?' I suggested.

'I will if there's anything helpful to them.' He looked terrified – all that grilling, I expect. 'Otherwise I don't want them reading Dorinda's diaries.'

The new freezer was being trundled up the path from a van as I left, and it's too small to get a body in. I have a nasty, suspicious mind.

It had been a tiring day, but once I got home I settled right down to sorting out my neglected novel and promptly forgot everything else until the phone jerked me rudely out of my fantasy.

Phinny (as I'd begun to call her, Sphinx being a bit sibilant), who had been reclining at my feet like a rather odd heraldic beast, leaped off the lounger and raced round the room, tail in the air.

'Oh God!' I said as my eye fell on the clock – five thirty already, and Miranda and Nye coming for dinner!

It was Gil who'd phoned, rather distraught, since he'd cracked the code to Dorinda's diary, which was full of detailed information about her methodical cliff searches, but then the thunder and lightning had started (I must have missed that!) and the computer suddenly went off on its own.

He'd switched it off at the mains, too, but now he was afraid to switch it back on until the storm stopped.

'And I just can't settle, so I wondered if you'd like to go out for an early dinner with me?'

'I'm so sorry, Gil, but I've got guests coming.'

'*Oh*,' he said, managing to invest such pathos and desolation into the one word that before I knew what I was doing I'd invited him to come round tonight, too. (Yes, it's Singles Night.)

'It's only Miranda, and Nye Thomas – you know Nye, don't you?'

'Oh, yes – but I'm sure you don't want another guest at such short notice and—'

'No, *really* – it would be lovely if you could come, though I'm sure you'd much rather—'

But he'd enthusiastically accepted and rung off before I'd finished the sentence, leaving me wandering round the kitchen looking for something to cook. My freezer was full of delicious single-portion ready meals, most of them readied by Miranda, so they were out.

In the end I trotted down to the village stores and bought peas and prawns for risotto, and a tray of that Greek shredded-wheat type dessert, glistening with honey and nuts, which was the unlikeliest thing to find in a Welsh minimart. I wasn't surprised when Llyn said Miranda had made it, and it sold very well, but – here she tapped the side of her nose – 'Mum's the word, or they'll be sending Food and Hygiene people round to search her kitchen.'

For dangerous implements? Anyway, you could eat off any surface in Miranda's kitchen, including the floor.

Still, what with the dessert, some cheese and wine, and spicy snacks and nuts for nibbles, it promised to be a memorably filling and indigestible repast.

As I draped the glitzy Formica table with a length of sari material and set out my white crockery and white-handled cutlery, I wistfully thought of the reclaimed timber table I'd glimpsed at the craft centre. I couldn't part with my Formica table now, but I could move it into another room.

Phinny watched with interest, occasionally surreptitiously scratching at the healing gash on her long skull.

She followed me while I perfunctorily tidied up the house, and lit the fake log-effect fire in the living room, which made it look surprisingly cosy once I'd switched off the central light, which didn't yet have a shade on it.

Funny how you stop noticing things like that after a bit, but I wrote 'light shade' down on a piece of paper before I forgot it. Then I put snacks out in mismatching Chinese and Japanese bowls on the coffee table and went back to the kitchen, firmly closing the door to keep the cat off the nibbles.

Everything was ready, except me. I was still wearing my thobe, which although comfortable and beautiful was also a bit shabby from years of use. And already there was someone at the door: Nye, bearing a bottle of wine and a little round disc of goat's cheese.

He wore a fine, fleecy, faded blue sweatshirt and jeans that were for once unbesmirched by clay, and with them a winning smile.

'Nye – come in. I'm not quite ready yet, but—'

'I'm early. Is there something I can do to help?'

'No, it's all organized, thanks.' I remembered my unbrushed hair and grubby feet. 'But perhaps you'd like to open the wine while I go and change?'

'Why bother? You look beautiful in that robe thing,' he said, putting down his burdens and coming a step or two closer with a disturbing glint in his eyes.

'This? It's just something I work in,' I said, hastily backing towards the door. 'Excuse me – won't be a minute. But if you could just let the others in if they come before I'm down?'

'Others?' His voice followed me plaintively up the stairs. 'I thought it was just Miranda?'

'And Gil.'

In ten minutes I was washed, brushed, braided, dressed in loose top and velvet trousers, and in my right mind, just in time to greet Miranda and Gil, who arrived together.

Gil, predictably, presented me with a box of after-dinner mints, but Miranda brought nothing with her except an air of abstraction, which was unlike her. Bringing nothing, I mean, not the air of abstraction; anyone married to Chris would be wearing one of those.

They all watched me put the risotto on to simmer, then we carried our drinks through into the living room, where Gil eyed the furnishings with a slightly startled expression. I wasn't surprised – there isn't a floral pattern in the whole house.

Nye dished out wine and passed bowls as though he lived here, and since he seemed to be as insidious as the cat, he may soon just move in without me ever having made a conscious decision on the matter, and I'd be putting his feeding dish down with Phinny's.

He looked up, caught my eye and grinned as if he'd read my

mind, handed me my glass, and disposed himself gracefully next to me on the lounger.

'Miranda has lost her husband,' he informed me.

'What do you mean: hasn't he gone back to London? And anyway, Miranda, I thought you *wanted* to lose him?'

'I d-didn't want to live with him any more, b-but I assumed he'd gone straight b-back to London on Sunday, and now he seems to have vanished!'

'But he stayed with me last night, didn't you know?' Gil said, pausing from mechanically stuffing handfuls of Bombay mix into his mouth. 'On the sofa, because I haven't got a spare room. He'd gone very early this morning – just left a note.'

'No!' said Miranda. 'D-did he say where he'd b-been?'

'Holed up in some hotel on a bender, from the look of him,' Gil said. 'He wasn't the most welcome visitor, I can tell you, but I didn't feel I could turn him away in that state . . . and actually, once he'd had something to eat he was quite good company. I told him about trying to trace Dorinda's movements through her computer journal and he offered to help . . . In fact, when I went to bed he was still trying different passwords and he said he'd wake me up if he found it. But he didn't.'

'He's good with computers and he's always got his laptop with him,' Miranda said, 'b-but I suppose passwords are quite d-difficult things to crack, if you d-don't know the person who put them in.'

'He's very interested in ancient burial sites, too, isn't he?' Gil said, and we all stared at him, surprised.

'While I'm prepared to believe that Chris has the right kind of twisty little mind for solving computer puzzles,' I said, 'I simply can't imagine him showing an avid interest in Gower bone caves.'

'Oh, yes,' Gil mumbled through a mouthful of Bombay mix,

'he was particularly fascinated when I told him that finding a new bone cave would be as important to Welsh archaeology as the discovery of Tutankhamen's tomb had been to Egypt – a positive treasure trove.'

I thought that might be just a slight exaggeration, but it explained things for Miranda anyway. 'That's it then, Gil. He knows nothing about archaeology or history, b-but when you said treasure he probably pictured caves full of golden artefacts.'

'I don't think even Chris could be that stupid, could he?' I asked. 'But anyway, we're digressing from the main issue: if he didn't go straight down to London, where is he now?'

'He d-didn't turn up at the studios, b-because they rang to ask where he was,' Miranda said. 'So then I phoned the house and got the cleaner, and she said there'd b-been no sign of him since last Friday, when he came down here.'

'Perhaps he went on another bender?' I suggested.

'B-but he'd never miss filming a show. No, something must have happened to him – an accident? Or perhaps he was so upset . . .'

'. . . that after a night on Gil's sofa he crept out at dawn to throw himself remorsefully off the cliff?' I said. 'No way. The Chrises of this world don't kill themselves.'

'I suppose you're right,' admitted Miranda. 'And strangely, I find I d-don't much care except in a curious sort of way: not now I know he d-doesn't love the real me. Nowadays he can't see b-beyond the fat.'

'I thought you'd just had a little tiff,' Gil said, open-mouthed. 'And I'm sure he doesn't mind if you've put a bit of weight on – you're still as pretty as when we were at school together,' he said staunchly, and Miranda went pink.

There was no denying that she did look pretty – especially

since she'd started wearing real clothes, as opposed to sofa covers.

Gil followed me into the kitchen, ostensibly to help, but really to pour out his initial delvings into Dorinda's Diary: An Everyday Tale of Country Folk.

I made sympathetic noises while stirring and seasoning the risotto and removing warm plates from the oven.

'. . . the code was actually very, very simple – it just takes time to translate – and it had just got interesting when the power went off, Sappho, that's the frustrating thing! There's a list of cliff locations, showing the areas she's searched and when. But it doesn't feel right, reading her private journal when she clearly didn't want me to, only . . . I *do* need to find out what happened to her: she may have had an accident. Do you think she's dead?'

'I don't really know, but after all this time you have to consider the possibility, Gil. Now, would you call the others in for me? And try not to think about it any more tonight.'

Chapter 31

Automatic Writing

'That wasn't fish fingers,' Nye remarked later.

'Sorry to disappoint you, but I never said you were going to *get* fish fingers, I only asked if you liked them.'

'Delicious!' Gil said, like the sleepy Dormouse.

'But easy: I didn't even know what we were going to eat at five.'

'There's risotto and risotto,' Miranda said. 'Yours was perfect.'

'So was the dessert and *you* made that. I didn't know you had a sneaky little sideline in cakes for Llyn's shop.'

'It's not a regular thing, just if ever I've got a b-big b-batch of something then I take them d-down, and I wanted to try these Greek things. They're nice, aren't they? I'd love to go to Greece and collect recipes, and see people cooking authentic food.'

'There's no reason you shouldn't,' I said, surprised. 'You could come with me to Bob and Vivi's later this year – I'm teaching only two weeks this time, and they'd love to have you. Lefkada is a very nice island.'

Phinny enlivened the proceedings at this point by sicking

up Bombay Mix, which I hadn't even noticed her eating, but there wasn't much and Nye dealt with it in a practical manner. He had his uses.

We lolled about, pleasantly replete and drinking coffee, until at last Miranda said she'd better go: 'In case there's any word ab-bout what's happened to Chris.'

'I wouldn't worry. He's probably holed up at a hotel some-where in a sulk,' I said, because it would be just like him to do that, thinking it would frighten Miranda into taking him back with open arms.

'I'll give you a lift home,' offered Gil, and Miranda didn't decline: they always seemed quite comfortable together, though I couldn't tell if that was mutual attraction or just having known each other since toddler group.

Still, both having mislaid their spouses (and long may they remain so) should make a bond.

'What about you, Nye? Do you want a lift?' asked Gil.

'No, thanks, I'll walk back again. I feel like stretching my legs. But I'll just give Sappho a hand to clear up the coffee things, first.'

When I came back from seeing Gil and Miranda off, the coffee cups had vanished, but Nye hadn't. He was stretched comfortably full length on the recliner, arms behind his head, watching me from under long, gold-tipped eyelashes.

'You can't have washed up already,' I said coldly.

'I haven't, I left them in the sink; that was just a cunning ruse to stay for a few minutes. I wanted to be sure you were safe if Dave decided to come round for one last try . . . unless you'd like me to stay tonight in case?'

In case of *what*, I wondered? That I have another mad bout of Hormones Behaving Badly and jump on him?

'No, thanks,' I said primly. 'I'll be fine.'

'In that case, unless you'd care to join me on this surprisingly comfortable contraption, I'll take myself off.'

I gave him a chilly look and he smiled again with annoying equanimity and unfolded his long frame.

'Lock up behind me, and I've stuck my number up above the phone. Ring me any time you want to.'

I nearly said, 'Want to what?' but self-control, as usual, came to my aid. 'I'm going to have an outside light fitted,' I said, 'so you don't need to worry. Mu's talked me into it.'

'I'm glad someone can persuade you into doing things.' Something seemed to amuse him for his mobile mouth tilted again into that beguiling grin. 'I like Mu.'

'Well, so do I but—'

'And you can tell her next time you speak to her that I'm taking her advice – but only up to a point.'

'What advice?' I demanded suspiciously.

'It's a secret between me, Mu and the cat.'

He put on his jacket while I eyed him in some frustration. 'I don't believe she gave you any advice. About what, anyway?'

'Instinct versus strategy,' he said, stepping out into the clear, star-spangled night. 'But she might not have got it all right.'

And with that he planted a warm kiss on my lips and strode off into the night.

I slammed the door with unnecessary violence and shot home the bolts as his long, light tread went away beyond the barn.

After that I felt keyed up and full of energy. Ideas suddenly filled my mind to the brim and spilled over, and I knew I had to get them down now, this minute, before I forgot them.

Quickly I cleared away the last traces of the party, poured a slug of dark rum, and settled down in my old robe for what proved to be an epic session of *Vengeane*.

Tonight the story just told itself, like automatic writing . . . or automatic dictating. The characters jostled and bickered inside my head for their turn to talk.

Stopping only to change tapes or snatch a drink, I let the story unfold itself, though some time before dawn, in passing, I took the phone off the hook: no one was interrupting the flow, no matter how long it took me.

Even after I brought it to a surprising – to me anyway – conclusion, and the tape whirred emptily on and on, I was still thinking how the next and final book would develop . . .

So I put my notes for that on tape too, and then suddenly somehow it was the next evening, and I was stiff, tired, light-headed and elated . . . and someone was hammering on the door so hard they were liable to knock it flat and walk over the remains like a drawbridge.

In a sudden trance of weariness I trudged through the kitchen past a baleful, unfed cat and unlocked the door, but it was wrenched from my hands before I could turn the handle. Nye pounced, growling, and shook me. I went limp.

'You're all right! You're all right, Sappho!' he cried with relief.

'I'm more than all right, I'm blissfully happy, but very tired. Stop shaking me – what's the matter with you?'

'What's the *matter*? Do you know what time it is? I've been trying to ring you all day, and when I couldn't, and Miranda hadn't seen you either, I got really worried.'

'I took the phone off the hook so I wouldn't be disturbed.'

'But you must have realized I'd think something had happened to you?'

'No – why should you? I'm perfectly safe and I just had to finish the book while I was in the mood – and I *have*!'

Glorious, glorious thought!

I yawned suddenly and hugely. 'Sorry – I'm not used to people being concerned about me. What time is it?'

'Seven in the evening. I'd have been here hours ago if I hadn't had an appointment with someone coming from London. How long have you been working?'

'Since you left last night. I'm starving, and so is poor Phinny.'

'All night?'

The front door was still open, and at this point something pale and rectangular on the doorstep caught my eye . . . something vaguely coffin-shaped.

'What's that?' I said. 'Did you bring it?'

'What? No, it was there when I got here – some kind of box.'

I bent and picked it up. 'Looks like another offering from Dave.'

He stared at it. 'Not in a bloody coffin!'

'He did once or twice before he started using Fantasy Flowers, but the shock value wore off after the first.'

'Give it to me, I'll open it,' he demanded.

I was too weak to grapple for it, and anyway I wasn't very interested in another ghastly surprise, so I watched as he cautiously lifted the lid. A skittish breeze caught it and sent it flying, together with a layer of tissue paper.

Nye went rigid, for inside the box lay the pathetic remains of a skinned animal – a headless, cat-sized animal . . .

I whirled, but Phinny was still giving me a disgusted stare from the door.

'It's all right, Sappho, it's not a cat, I think; it looks more like a rabbit.'

I forced myself to look again, more closely. 'You're right, and a bloodless, ready-to-cook rabbit, at that. Could you tip it in the bin? There's a bag in there already.'

Somehow, I didn't think Bunny in a Box would be the next new Fantasy Flowers line . . .

Nye did as I asked, and then tied up the bag before putting the lid on again.

I led the way back in and closed the door. 'Do you think that was a threat to the cat, or a threat to me?' Suddenly my knees went shaky and my head seemed to be bobbing lightly away up there on its own, like a balloon.

Nye guided me into a chair. 'For goodness' sake sit down. You're shocked, exhausted and hungry. I'll make you something to eat.'

'Feed Phinny first. She must be starving, though I see she's eaten the remains of the risotto out of the pan.'

So he did, and then whipped me up an omelette. He looked terribly domestic doing it: if I'd seen him in a catalogue I'd have ordered one in Extra Large.

He has broad, square shoulders and long, long legs, though his platinum hair looked as if he'd rubbed clay through it in a fit of temper or something, which he probably had.

Generally you couldn't say he *has* a hairstyle – his hair just naturally covers his head in the most perfect way: easy. But that night he looked like a punk platinum hedgehog with badger streaks put in for effect.

The way he couldn't give a damn about how he looks is oddly endearing, and of course he'd still look sexy in a clay-sack toga and woad, though the effect would be unintentional.

Unlike Dave, who is more Armani than Accidental.

'You know,' I said, when I'd eaten the perfect omelette, 'tonight's Box of Delights is more Dave's type of thing than stoning a cat: a nasty but bloodless gesture. I really don't think you need to worry about him. He's never actually done any harm, that I know.'

'He phoned me up earlier today, and his threats were a bit on the lurid side: that's why I was so worried about you,' Nye said. 'As soon as I'd finished my business I rushed over here.'

'Oh, Nye, I hope I haven't lost you a sale,' I said guiltily.

'No.' He gave a sudden grin. 'I grabbed the money before I ran, showed him the packing cases and left him to it. I expect he thinks I'm either a raging eccentric or an alcoholic desperate for the next drink.'

I creaked wearily to my feet. 'I'm going to have a bath and then I'm going to bed. I really don't care about anything else at the moment.'

'I won't ask whether I can come and scrub your back, because you're too tired to know what you're saying,' he said.

I left him there, smiling, and almost fell asleep in rose-scented bliss.

When I went back down briefly he'd washed up, and was quite at home in the living room reading *Spiral Bound: Japan.*

'Did I hear the phone?' I asked.

'Miranda. They've found Chris's car not far from here, in a car park. His case was in it, but there was no sign of him.'

'What is he up to? I assumed he was just trying to frighten Miranda.'

'He doesn't seem the type who'd miss recording his series,' Nye said.

'No, but it's not going to keep me awake,' I yawned. 'Nothing could. I'm going to bed.'

'I'm staying here tonight, however harmless you think Dave is – unless you come back to my place?'

'No, but you do what you like,' I said groggily. 'I'm too tired to care.'

'Thanks a lot. Is that the kitchen key? I'll go home for some stuff, but I'll be back within twenty minutes and let myself in.'

'Feed the cat.'

'I already did – you were sitting there watching me.'

'Oh, did you?' I managed to focus on his face, like a vision of the Angel Gabriel with stubble, and in a bad mood. 'Sorry, Nye, I can't seem to think straight. It would be nice if you stayed. The spare room is all made up.'

I trudged off up the almost unclimbably steep set of stairs and went out like a light the moment my head touched the pillow.

Chapter 32

Dead End

I was having a blissful dream, and Nye, in the guise of Dragonslayer, figured so prominently in it that when I was awoken by a soft, warm kiss I responded with an enthusiasm that may have taken Nye by surprise.

If so, he certainly managed to rise to the occasion, and by the time I was fully aware of what I was doing I was enveloped in the sort of muscular silken warmth you don't get even from the best duvets.

We were soon well beyond the 'resistance is useless' stage, and bridges were burning behind us – and frankly, my dear, I didn't give a damn. I just never wanted it to end. I'd abandoned celibacy and converted to fornication. I was in serious danger of becoming a Single Eccentric Sex-Mad Female.

Afterwards, held snugly in a warm embrace as though I were some small, precious, breakable object (although if I were I'd have been in bits by now, instead of just singed round the edges), he said tenderly: 'This is something special, Sappho. What are we going to do about it?'

'Nothing, you're not my type,' I said rather crossly. Who wrote Nye into *my* Life Plan?

His eyes were clear and silvery and alight with feeling, but whether with love, hate or the desire to strangle me, I wasn't sure. 'You tell me that Dragonslayer doesn't get the girl in the end, and I'll believe I'm not your type.'

I looked away. 'It's a secret. Anyway, there's another book to go after that, so anything could happen.'

'I think it already has: I told you – I love you.'

'You weren't serious.'

'I was – I am! I want to be with you: "Come live with me and be my love" and all that.'

Not in a decaying Victorian chalet, I'm not!

'I'm constitutionally unable to share my day-to-day existence with anyone else,' I told him.

'I love the way you put things,' he said, kissing the end of my nose. 'I think you're really cute.'

'Cute?' I gasped, outraged. 'I most definitely am not!' Six foot of stroppy cuteness?

'I think I knew from the minute I saw you sitting in that car looking scared,' he said thoughtfully.

'I was not in the least scared!'

'You looked petrified, and I couldn't stop thinking about you, even though I didn't want to . . . not after what had just happened with Eloise. I didn't intend getting seriously involved with someone else ever again.'

'But we're not serious. Are we serious?' I stared at him. 'I don't know what's happening!'

He held me closer (if possible). 'We're serious.'

'But you were a mistake. I was thinking of starting a baby for my fortieth birthday, *not* a relationship, and I was going to pick someone out – someone dark-haired and suitable . . .'

'We could have a baby,' he said softly.

'Yes, we could,' I agreed, because – whoops! – I'd done it

again. 'I'm not on the pill or anything and that's the second time we've—'

He held me off slightly and stared at me: 'But I asked you the first time if it was all right, and you said yes!'

'Well, it was – more than all right. I wasn't thinking too straight at the time – or this time, come to that. You seem to have an unfortunate effect on my brain.'

He looked a bit taken aback. There was a line of endearingly human stubble along his jaw, so I ran my finger across it and then, overcome by a sudden impulse, kissed him.

I tell you, the cup of coffee that he'd originally woken me for was stone-cold and scummy by the time we emerged.

What was I going to do? I couldn't live with him . . . but I was beginning to wonder if I could live without him.

After a bit – more than a bit – Nye noticed that Phinny had come silently into the room and was sitting watching us with what appeared to be approval. It was definitely disconcerting.

'That cat makes me feel shy,' Nye observed. 'I'm getting up. Can you see a bath towel on the floor on your side? I was wearing it when I came in.'

He managed to put it on without disclosing any of his anatomy to the cat, but it involved contortions that made me giggle.

I lay back, smiling, with a feeling of complete mental and physical well-being: 'I finished the book!' I sighed happily.

He halted in the doorway, looking startled. 'Was I just a celebration?'

'Well, I didn't have a bottle of champagne handy, and you were the nearest available thing—'

'How long do I have to wait before you finish the next one?' he asked with interest, and I threw a pillow at him.

It hit Phinny instead, who was Not Amused.

*

Miranda turned up while we were eating toast and adjusting our caffeine levels in companionable silence.

'There you are, Sappho,' she said, walking in through the open kitchen door. 'I came round earlier, b-but you seemed to b-be having a lie-in, which is not like you!'

'I finished the book yesterday evening, and I was shattered.'

I was even more shattered now, in all kinds of interesting ways. You know that feeling of boundless energy you have when you're young and the sap is rising? As if you wanted to ricochet off the walls? Well, I hadn't got that, but this was better.

'Hello, Miranda,' Nye said, full of the joys of spring, or something like that, and she started.

I suppose it *is* darkish in the kitchen without the horrible fluorescent light on.

'Do you want some toast?' he offered.

'Er – hello, Nye. I d-didn't see you there. I d-didn't mean to interrupt, and I must get d-down to the castle and – and—'

'Have some coffee first, it's still early,' I said. 'Nye is just off.'

'Nye should have been off an hour ago,' he pointed out unfairly.

Did I lock the door? 'So what's keeping you?' I asked him.

'Why don't you come down to the studio later?'

'I might, but I've got lots of work to do, sorting out the book ready for Violet to type up.'

'You need a break first – with me. Aren't you going to hand me my bowler and briefcase?'

'I feel like a gooseberry,' Miranda said when he'd gone. 'Sorry for walking in on you like that.'

'It doesn't matter – you hardly caught us *in flagrante*.'

'Actually, I'm really pleased you and Nye have taken to each other.'

That's one way of putting it.

'B-but I'm surprised b-because I d-didn't think he was your type.'

'He isn't. I keep telling him that, but he doesn't take any notice.'

'And I must have walked past his van outside without seeing it, which shows just how thick the fog is.'

'I hadn't even realized it was foggy.' And I'd let Phinny out that morning!

'Yes, it's quite b-bad, b-but it'll lift later in the morning. Gil phoned me yesterday, Sappho – he's b-been d-deciphering the computer d-diary and he said he was finally getting somewhere, and that Chris's d-disappearance was just like when D-Dorinda went, except they found Chris's car.'

'He'll turn up.'

'I can't say I really care d-deeply, I'd just like to know what he's up to. B-besides, I want a d-divorce, and it could make it d-difficult if he d-d-doesn't turn up again.'

She finished her coffee and left. It was a pea-souper out there. 'Be careful,' I said.

'D-don't worry, I know these roads like the b-back of my hand.'

After she'd gone I'd just started to collect the disembodied parts of *Dark Destinies: Deathless Delights* when Gil rang me.

'Sappho, there you are,' he said, as though it were a surprise – but perhaps *he'd* been trying to get hold of me yesterday, too. 'I've decoded all the diary now and I know exactly which cliff area Dorinda was checking on the day she disappeared. Funnily enough, it's quite near you as the crow flies, only the nearest car park is about a mile away and the access is by path only.'

'That's great! Have you told the police so they can search the area?'

'No, because I want to go and look myself first, only I'd like to have someone with me, just in case. I tried Nye's number but there was no answer, and I couldn't ask it of Miranda, of course – she's so delicate and sensitive – so I thought of you.'

'You want *me* to come with you?' I looked, dismayed, at the mess of a book spread around me on scribbled sheets of paper and scattered cassette tapes.

'If you wouldn't mind. I could pick you up in the Land Rover. I'll be able to drive almost there on tracks your car wouldn't manage.'

'No – that's all right,' I said slowly. 'I've been shut in for nearly two days working, so I need the air and exercise. I'll drive down to that car park and walk along the cliffs till I meet you.'

'It's very foggy,' he said doubtfully.

'Miranda said so too, but you can't get lost in these lanes, there aren't enough of them, and she says it's going to clear.'

'It probably already is down at the cliffs,' he agreed, and described exactly where we were to meet. 'All right, I'll see you down there. And thanks.'

I dressed practically for scrambling around cliffs, in jeans, anorak and boots, put some cat food down for Phinny and then, as an afterthought, phoned the craft centre and left a message telling Nye where I was going and that I probably wouldn't turn up for lunch. Then I locked the door and went out into what was indeed a heavy fog, thick and stifling as wool.

I might as well not have neighbours, for all the sight or sound of life there was. But evidently someone had been prowling about, for when I walked round the barn I discovered my poor old car squatting balefully on four flat, slashed tyres.

Nye's van had been parked overnight next to mine and I was sure he would have noticed, so it must have been done since he left . . . and it was going to cost me a fortune to replace four Volvo tyres.

I felt really, really angry. 'Is there anyone there?' I demanded of the unresponsive fog, but answer came there none.

Dave? He could have been round and, seeing Nye's van was there this morning, put two and two together. He'd have been angry enough to do something that malicious.

But I didn't think he'd have hung around afterwards: slash and run was more his style.

I went back in the house to phone Gil and ask him to pick me up after all, but there was no answer. He must have already left, and since I didn't want to let him down, I had a look at my Ordnance Survey map and thought I could find my way over the moors. It was downhill the whole way, after all.

I shoved the map in my pocket and set off up the road to where the track I wanted turned off towards the distant sea, feeling nervous and angry together.

Dave might just still be out there, and although I wished to get my hands on him I didn't like the thought that he could be lurking unseen just within reach, though of course I was confident I could sort him out if he tried anything.

I found the track and strode down it, frightening sheep as I went, and looking out for the first cross track where I had to turn. It was eerie – to the point where I thought I could hear feet thudding on the turf just behind me, though there was never anyone there when I turned round.

'Sappho!' a voice whispered suddenly. It seemed to be all about me.

'Dave? Where are you, you stupid man? Come out and show yourself!' I demanded, but there was no reply – no sound at all, in fact, and since I didn't have any real option I carried on, a bit more briskly and frequently looking over my shoulder.

I was walking faster and faster, and when I finally came out into the wider path that would lead me straight down to the cliffs, I took to my heels and ran.

The fog was thinning, which was fortunate, since I met Gil's Land Rover slowly bumping into the track from a side turn, and we were suddenly nose to nose across the bonnet. I don't know which of us was more surprised.

Wrenching open the passenger door I jumped in. 'Go on – drive!' I ordered, and he obediently jolted off down the rutted track. In the wing mirror I saw Dave emerge from the fog and stand gazing after us.

When I told Gil about the slashed tyres and Dave stalking me he practically ran off the track, and kept checking his rear-view mirror, even though I told him I didn't think he'd follow us any more, and I could handle him if he did now I could see him.

He was right about the fog, too, because we soon emerged into bright, warm sunshine. Gil parked by a large rock near the cliff path, which detoured here away from the edge, since it was dangerously crumbling limestone.

He leaned on the car bonnet and consulted his notes and map. 'She'd done up to this side of the big rock, and she meant to survey the cliffs to the right on the day she vanished. She wouldn't drive the Land Rover, so she must have walked here from the car park. It's pretty remote so it's quite possible some-one stole her car if it was there for hours.'

'Joyriders,' I agreed.

Gil was carrying rope and other climbing gear as though he was going to do a Tarzan at some point (but if so, he could count me out), and we began carefully walking the crumbling cliff edge, looking as best we could, without plummeting, for signs of Dorinda.

I found it first – fell over it, in fact – and then something cold slithered under my cheek . . .

An adder? There *were* adders – I'd seen them – only this one was made of rope: good, thick, strong rope, well secured, running down over the cliff edge.

'Oh, well done!' Gil said, flinging himself down beside me and peering over the edge. 'This must be hers. Look, the rope's knotted – she always did that to help her climb back up. I'm going down.'

'The rope's wet and slippery,' I pointed out.

'It's not too bad. I'll see what's down there.' He vanished, giving me a running commentary as I stared down at the top of his glossy brown head.

'It goes over this bulge . . . then there's nothing except a small ledge blocked by a rock at the far end and it's very unstable . . .' Sounds of scuffling and a rattling of stones followed. 'Oh, I see – there's a gap behind the rock – you can just squeeze behind it—'

Voice and man vanished. 'Gil?'

'There's a cave!' he called very faintly. 'I'm going in.'

Sooner him than me – who knew what was down there?

There was certainly something up *here*, for when I glanced over my shoulder there was Dave, hot on the scent, by the Land Rover.

Persistent to the last – but he couldn't spot me lying here.

'Sappho, Sappho!' he called.

It's amazing how spontaneously such a sensible person as myself can act sometimes: I was slithering down that rope like Houdini before you could say 'slashed tyres'.

I was so glad to be on a ledge, however crumbling, that I stood with my nose pressed to the rock face for five whole minutes before Gil's head popped out from the other end of it and said: 'Hello – you've come down, have you? Take my hand and come in carefully.'

I let him guide me behind the rock, and a tight squeeze it was, too, and into the entrance to the cave. The rock face was sort of folded so that it would have been difficult to spot from the sea and impossible from the cliff top, and you had to step across a small chasm dropping straight down to the curve of deep water below.

'Have you found anything?' I asked, ducking down and slithering more or less on my bottom to the cave floor.

He shone his torch on to a heap of bones.

'Oh God – it's not Dorinda, is it?'

'Of course not – it's *much* older,' he said reverently. 'It's another Red Lady, like at Paviland. Dorinda *has* been here, though. There's her rucksack and flask. I can't see any other exit, but I haven't really explored, because I heard you coming down.'

He began to flash his torch around the walls of crumbling rock. 'It's really dangerous, you can see where it's come down here and there, and – ah! – a hole.'

He vanished, like the White Rabbit.

'Gil?' I ducked down and stuck my head into the hole. 'Gil?'

'Don't – don't come in . . .' he quavered.

'Is she there?'

And is she Dead Dorinda?

'Yes . . . she's here. There – there must have been a rockfall and she couldn't get out. The way she's lying under the rock – it's just like she's reaching out for help. God, it's ghastly! Poor Dorinda.'

She should have told somebody where she was going – it was entirely her own fault – though this was not the time to point that out to Gil. Horrible way to go.

He backed out, looking ill met by torchlight, and dislodging small stones.

'Look out!' I warned, as more began to move and we hastily retreated towards the bones.

'What are you two doing down here?' Dave's voice said suspiciously from behind us, and there he was, framed in the opening like a Neolithic Dorian Gray.

Chapter 33

On the Rocks

We stared blankly at him, for he'd appeared as suddenly as the genie in a pantomime, albeit without a puff of smoke and not half so welcome.

Hardly ruffled by his descent, he pushed back his tumbled black hair and smiled in that disconcertingly loopy way he keeps just for me.

'Was it you who slashed my tyres?' I demanded, recovering. 'And why were you skulking about in the fog?'

'You're a complete whore, aren't you, Sapphie?' he said conversationally, ignoring my questions. 'Last night with Nye Thomas, and now here you are with someone else.'

'Sappho is helping me look for my wife,' Gil said, white to the lips with the shock of what we'd just found, 'and . . . we've found her. But she's dead – there must have been a rockfall. She's back there . . .'

He gestured, shuddering, and Dave looked taken aback.

'What was your wife doing here?'

'Looking for a bone cave, but she didn't tell anyone where she was going, so when she had an accident we didn't know where she was. Poor Dorinda . . .' He looked up and said with sad dignity, 'Now, perhaps you'd like to go back up the cliff, so that we can get out and send for the police.'

But Dave had abruptly lost interest in him and was staring thoughtfully at me.

'Slashing my tyres was hardly going to endear you to me,' I said, going on the attack. 'Why did you do it? Just general temper?'

He shrugged. 'Why not? And it was even better than I expected, because you came out into the open.'

'I suppose you *know* you're demented?' I said tartly. 'I suppose it was you who threw the rock at my poor cat, too?'

Behind me Gil gave a nervous cough and said, to my complete surprise: 'Er, no – I'm afraid that was me, actually.'

He flushed guiltily under my astonished eyes. 'I only meant to frighten it – it'd caught a vole, you see, and I'm fond of voles. But you know I wouldn't hurt any living creature on purpose. And then, it was so embarrassing – I mean, being there in the first place – so when your friend came out and I heard you and Nye coming, I ran off down the garden and away over the moors.'

I decided not to ask why he was skulking about outside my house – general nosiness, I imagine. 'What about Lili?'

'Oh, now that *was* me,' Dave confessed insouciantly. 'An accident, though. She was wearing your cloak, and I saw her going out of the village. But when I tried to catch up with her she'd vanished – until she jumped out at me from that ruined cottage.'

She was probably trying to bite him.

'Then you hit her?' I asked.

'No, she just startled me, that's all, and I lashed out automatically. She fell and hit her head on the doorway. I thought she was dead, so I went back to the party and rigged up an alibi.'

'Does Lili *know* it was you?'

His brow darkened. 'It's just come back to her, unfortunately. She's . . . being difficult.'

'Oh, *good*,' I said enthusiastically. 'You mean, difficult as in "do what I want or I'll finger you to the police"?'

'How do you know? Have you been talking to her about it?'

'No, I just know Lili.'

'Lili has her attractions. But do you think I'd leave you to another man if I can't have you? No, you're staying down here – you'll both have to stay down here.'

I don't think Gil had quite taken everything in until that moment – the shock of finding Dead Dorinda had been too much – but now he gasped: 'You can't mean to leave us here?'

'Why not?' Dave said casually. 'The ledge out here is half-rotten anyway – once I've got the rope, one kick and there it goes, and no way back. I'll take the rope away, too, of course.'

He began to turn, reaching out for a handhold, and at that precise second Gil hit him in a quite impressive sort of flying tackle: all that Welsh rugby tradition, I suppose.

His impetus carried them both out, and there was a sickening thud as one or both of them ricocheted off the rock. Then they were gone.

I didn't think that was quite what Gil had intended.

When I crawled to the edge and peered down, I could see two heads bobbing about way below, where the water swirled into a small bay like someone had taken a hasty bite from the rock.

Then I remembered that Dave couldn't swim, and watched with detached interest as he floated limply face down in the water, until Gil, swimming like an otter, grabbed him, flipped him over, and began towing him towards some rocks.

What a hero! That man had unforeseen depths. He may even be worthy of Miranda, in the end.

'Is this a private ceremony or can anyone jump?' Nye enquired politely from my left, and I think I'd probably have gone in too then, if he hadn't grabbed my arm at the last moment.

'If you back in, is there room for me, too? Only this ledge is about to go, and I think I'd like to join you,' he said conversationally, and as I hastily shifted, jumped for it and scrambled in beside me.

'How did you get here?' I demanded, after a timely bit of mouth-to-mouth resuscitation.

'I got your message and I didn't like the idea of you and Gil messing about on the cliffs alone, so I thought I'd come too. Then when I was walking along the cliff path from the car park I could see you and Gil vanishing over the edge and Dave following, so I started running.'

'How much of all that did you hear?'

'Most of it. I was just about to go back up and wait for Dave to emerge so I could sock him one and rescue you, in true hero mode, when he and Gil did their stunt-man thing. Dave seemed to slam into the rock pretty hard on the way out.'

'Shame,' I said callously. 'I – what's that?'

There was a faint cry, which seemed to come from further along the cliff. 'Heeelp!' it wailed, weakly.

'I was going to mention that: Chris is stuck on a ledge a bit further back. He must have been here all the time. But the tourist boat is out there, see, and I'm sure they've spotted him because they've come in as far as they can. They'll have radioed for the coastguards.'

'Chris has been stuck here all this time? What's he doing here?'

307

'At a guess, searching for the cave. It's my bet he was so fired up with the idea of treasure that he messed about with the computer that night he stayed at Gil's house and found the password.'

'Well, it was just the pet name for the cat – Gil used it all the time,' I agreed.

'Then he cracked the code and thought he'd discovered where the bone cave was. Only he didn't quite get it right, and not only that but he must have gone down one of those sheep tracks that peter out and leave you stranded.'

'Serve him right,' I said. 'But at least the coastguards can rescue Gil and Dave too – see them on the rock there? I think they'll need a helicopter to get them.'

'They look safe enough. The tide's in as far as it will go; it'll be on the turn soon. Now it's time to get us out of here, and it's not going to be easy. There wasn't enough rope to bring it with me, and there's very little ledge left to get back across, but—'

There was an ominous rumble from deep in the bowels of the cave, like a monster awakening, and the ground seemed to tremble. We scrambled to our feet and looked at each other, then turned as one and stared down, way down, into the dark curve of water.

A couple that jump together, stay together – and we were helpfully blasted out on a cloud of dust and rock particles. Out and down, hand in hand, and it was an absolutely amazing feeling until we hit the freezing cold sea, though at least it wasn't freezing cold rocks.

I trod water, fighting the powerful undertow and searching frantically for Nye, but he popped up beside me and we were swept together past Gil's goggling face and outstretched hand, and out to sea.

Being rescued by a boatful of tourists is better than not being rescued at all, but it does mean that, being dragged aboard like some giant squid to flop aimlessly on the decking, you'll feature in about forty assorted snapshots and home movies.

My teeth were chattering so much at first I didn't notice the clicking of the shutters until a carrying, horribly familiar voice said in a lilting accent: 'How like the legends of old, isnk it? The tall, handsome merman, gold-haired, clasping his human lover to him as they are swept by the waves . . . It is interestink that . . .'

I groaned, rolled over, and was hauled to my feet by the merman as, with a great clatter, a helicopter roared overhead.

To the rescue!

'I don't suppose you've got any rum on board?' I asked hopefully of the small man tucking a coat rather overenthusiastically around my wet T-shirt.

It's unfortunate that my favourite jeans are washing about off the Gower coast, but at least *I* was not. And how did Nye, who doesn't have any hips to speak of, manage to retain *his* trousers, while mine were dragged away to be pebble-washed by the Neptune laundry?

Still, it was worth it, and I'd recommend anyone requiring catharsis to jump off a cliff. I'm certain it's done us all a world of good . . . except possibly Chris. His rescue generated a lot of publicity I'm sure he'd rather not have had, and much speculation about what he was actually doing there.

Some of my favourite headlines were: 'TV Chef in Tight Jam', 'TV Chef Gets Frozen Desserts after Cliff Exposure', and especially: 'Too Much Exposure for TV Chef?'

He was so hysterical they had to winch him back up the cliff tied to a stretcher, but it was all his own fault for nosying about in other people's computers. Besides, if he followed a sheep path down, he should have been able to get back up it again – sheep do, after all.

Miranda said he got his just desserts after what he did to Spike, and I got the impression she wouldn't have minded if he'd dropped off entirely. She'd engaged a solicitor to handle her divorce, being by then way beyond 'Disillusioned' and well into 'Militant'.

Chapter 34

Out for the Count

Dear Sappho,

Lili has written telling us how you stole her lover, which is very good, I think! I hope he is a nice man and will make you a good husband. Lili says he is a potter, like me. Perhaps you will bring him when you come to Lefkada in September? He is very welcome.

Lili tells me she has taken your old lover in return, but he did something bad so you threw him off a cliff, and now she has to nurse him back to health. She did not say what the bad thing was, and I am very curious!

That horrible Ken Smollett has already tried to book for your course and one of Lili's, though I am not counting on her making it this year, because Bob says he will not have that Dave in the house.

Do write and tell me all about your man, and how you won him from Lili! We are both well, and looking forward to the baby. Life is very exciting lately, isn't it?

Love,
Vivi

I didn't think I could live *with* Nye, but while waiting for him to surface after our cliff jump it was borne in on me that I couldn't live *without* him. It's a moot point anyway now, because in the last couple of weeks he's just quietly insinuated himself into the house and my heart in the same way as Phinny.

So I've now altered the plans for the barn conversion to provide a studio as well as living space, with connecting doors to both floors of the cottage. We are both creative people, prone to go off alone to work when the fancy takes us, and doors can be open or shut . . .

Besides, it will be useful having him around when the baby arrives (and who would have thought it? Alien Genes Take over the World!), even if he is already fussing about my eating properly and not drinking alcohol.

Personally, I can't see a lot wrong with a diet of Mars bars, ginger beer and rum, but then I haven't read the books (and nor am I going to).

He and Mu have been conferring by telephone about Correct Nutrition, though it hasn't done her a lot of good: she's throwing more of it up than she's keeping down.

What's all the fuss about? I'm not ill, and I'm going to carry on just as usual until the very last minute, and if anyone gives me any hassle I'll go and give birth at Bob and Vivi's house on Lefkada, where they will leave me to get on with it in peace.

While I was checking the builders were making a good job of installing the Portuguese door into the front of the barn, Mu's car unexpectedly pulled in and came to a rather haphazard full stop.

She leaped out and threw up behind the holly bush, and by

the time she reappeared, pale and wan, I'd turned her ignition off and applied the handbrake. The workmen were trying to pretend they hadn't noticed anything, which was tactful: if they manage to hang the door the right way up I'd give them biscuits with their elevenses.

'Oh God!' she said weakly. 'Morning sickness? Why not call it morning, noon and night sickness?'

'Come into the house and I'll get you a nice bucket,' I promised, leading the way. 'Then you can tell me what's brought you rushing down here.'

'Sappho, I'm so upset that I've been turning *right*! Across the traffic!'

'Well done: you'll probably never look back, now. And just think how much quicker it'll be to drive anywhere!' I said encouragingly as she sank down on to the sofa. I put the white plastic bucket on the floor next to her, just in case.

'I simply *had* to get here; you're the only person I can tell. And I didn't want to phone in case Ambler heard. Thank goodness he was out last night when Simon rang me!'

'Simon? He isn't making trouble, is he? I wouldn't have thought it, but if he is I'll go down to Bristol and—'

'No, no, he's not making trouble. It's . . . more the opposite. *Good* news, in fact . . . for me. You know he decided to become a sperm donor?'

'He told me. I think a lot of them are students, and at least he'd had practice.'

'They tested his sperm first, to make sure it was all right – and, Sappho, there wasn't any!'

'What, none?'

'Oh, there is *some*, apparently, but so few they fell asleep from boredom while waiting for the next one to swim past the microscope.'

'Poor Simon! What a blow!' I'd have to phone the poor boy up later and offer (non-physical) support.

'There's something they can do to help him, I think, but to be honest I didn't take that bit in, because that's when it dawned on me that the baby was Ambler's after all!'

'That's wonderful,' I agreed, though it did occur to me that *both* Ambler and Simon might not be producing at full capacity, which would mean that the ball could be in either court, as it were.

'I'm so happy!' She burst into tears, something she's been prone to lately, but I expect I would too if I was throwing up all the time.

'Let's have some ginger beer to celebrate. It should be alcohol, but Nye's hidden it.'

'I'm not surprised: you can't drink alcohol when you're pregnant.' She sniffled, and a look of surprise passed across her face: 'Do you know, I think I *would* like some ginger beer – how odd!'

'It's a bit Enid Blyton,' I agreed, 'but I just have a fancy for it at the moment and apparently ginger is very good for the digestion.'

She ended up eating biscuits too. Ginger beer: the miracle beverage.

Reviving, she began to notice things again. 'You look great!' she said slightly resentfully.

'I've never felt better, mentally or physically. Jumping off that cliff made everything just fall into place – everyone should try it.'

'Yes, but not when they're pregnant!'

'I didn't know at the time,' I pointed out. 'It wouldn't have stopped me, though: I mean, it's this microdot in a padded cell – buffered. Why shouldn't it be all right?'

She stared at me. 'Sappho, do you never feel fear?'

'Of course I do. But you can't let a thing like that stop you, can you? As they say, "feel the fear and do it anyway". What's the point of worrying first?'

'I suppose you're right, only it isn't easy. Still, there's one thing I can stop worrying about: the baby is Ambler's. My cat novel's nearly finished, too, and the *Corduroy Cat* publisher is interested, so that's going well. I must complete the illustrations for Miranda's *Feeding the Party Animal* before I do anything else.'

'Yes, she's really got the bit between her teeth on that one, but this time she's working hard for herself, not Chris. I thought I'd incited a bit of rebellion, when really it was a revolution! Next week she's off to Holland to learn a radical new technique for reducing stammering, and then there'll be no holding her.'

'But what about Chris?'

'He's conceded defeat. She threatened to give the Spike story to the newspapers, and I think he feels he's had more coverage than he wants lately.'

'What's going to happen to Fantasy Flowers? Is she going to wind it up?'

'No, Gil and Lavender are going to mind it while she's away. Lavender's finding her gardening a bit much now, so I think she's going to become a sort of partner in the business.'

'How is Gil? I suppose I'll have to forgive him for stoning poor Sphinx.'

'He didn't mean to hit her, and he was very brave attacking Dave like that, and then saving him from drowning, so he's expiated his crime. He had a bit of a guilt trip about not having found out from the computer where Dorinda was much earlier, but now I've got him sorted out he should be all right.'

'Have they removed Dorinda from the cave yet?'

'No, it's going to take quite a bit of doing, shoring the tunnel up first, though the ancient bones survived intact. Gil wants them to name the new cave in honour of Dorinda.'

'Well, why not?'

'His first suggested name was "Dorinda's Hole", until I persuaded him that "Aces Hole" sounded *much* better.'

'He has such an innocent mind, that man, it's alarming,' agreed Mu.

'I suggested he put "Fight the good fight" on her gravestone, and he thought that was a good idea, too.'

'He seems to be putty in your hands.'

'And Miranda's – but although she's fond of him, I think she's going to be jumping right off the rails just as I'm jumping back on to them. She's off with me to Lefkada in September, to research a book about Greek cooking: *Greek Stuff*.'

'But you aren't still going to teach writing this autumn, are you?'

'Why not? I'm only doing two weeks, and Nye's coming over too – it'll be fun.'

'You'll be about six months pregnant by then, Sappho, and you might not feel like it.'

'I don't see why not.'

'No, I don't think you do,' she agreed resignedly. 'And I expect you're quite right.'

'I don't think Lili will be coming out this year, because she daren't leave Dave at this stage, and Bob's flatly refused to have him in the house after the way he's behaved towards me,' I told her.

'How's Dave doing? I mean, not that I really care, but you can't say leaping off a cliff did *him* much good!'

'He didn't leap – he was pushed by Gil, and apart from two

broken arms, a ding on the head, and an internal saline rinse, he's doing fine. It's cured him of me, if nothing else. You know, one of the highlights of the whole incident was watching Lili claim him from the hospital casualty department, broken, battered, helpless and traumatized, and wheel him off to her cottage. With a bit of luck he may never emerge – and if he does he'll be a shadow of his former self.'

'It's like a Stephen King novel – only I don't suppose she'll maim him any more now she's got him where she wants him,' said Mu.

'I don't think she'd stop at anything if the urge took her. He did try to resist – said he would pay for nursing at his London flat – but Lili did this wonderfully ham act pretending the memory of who stoned her was coming back – and he caved right in.'

'Have you seen her since? I mean, they're not both still incarcerated in her cottage, are they?'

'Oh, no, she often pops in. She's not one to hold a grudge, and she fell for Dave the minute she set eyes on him. He's just her kind: tall, dark and tricky. She said she had a brief moment of indecision between the two – and anger when they both only seemed interested in me – but she finds Nye boring other than to look at because he's only interested in his work.'

I looked at Mu. 'Odd, isn't it? That's the best thing about him – it's what we've got in common. How can she say he's boring?'

'Poor taste, clearly.'

'Must be – she's absolutely besotted with Dave. And forget her vampire phase, she's now into Regression . . . or was it Transgression? Some crank comes out to visit her from Cardiff and hypnotizes her into a past life. She was an Egyptian princess, and Dave was her lover, or something. She's starting to dress accordingly in see-through muslin, like an ancient Egyptian Liz Hurley.'

'Perhaps she's having Dave hypnotized too,' Mu suggested. 'And that's why he's so malleable? Though lots of nurses marry their patients, don't they? Propinquity and dependence or something.'

'Yes, he won't get away now,' I said happily. 'And once the nuptial noose is around his throat he's had it. He'll be too exhausted to be anything other than monogamous, even when he has full use of his arms and faculties, but if he tries anything she'll rebreak them for him.'

Mu looked a different woman from the one who'd arrived so precipitately that morning, relaxed and comfortable, and with a bit of colour in her face.

'I must go soon, or Ambler will be wondering where I've got to – and why. Say hello to Nye for me. I take it he's at the workshop, potting?'

'Potting sounds an awfully mundane word for the sculptures he produces, but yes. I think he was here last night . . . in fact, I'm pretty sure he was, only I'm well into the writing now, and you know how it is. And he just steals in and out like that damned cat.'

'You mean the damned cat sitting on your knee with its head under your chin, purring?'

I looked down. 'There you are. I don't notice she's there half the time, and the same with Nye.'

'How can you possibly not notice Nye?'

'He doesn't notice me, either, when he's been struck by a brilliant idea – but it's OK. Good, in fact – we understand each other.'

And when we do notice each other, well, that's pretty good, too!

'When the barn conversion's finished there will be lots of room for both of us.'

'You love him, don't you?'

'When I made my leap, I seem to have committed myself without knowing it. I do love him, and we're fated to be a double act – or a triple act, as it turns out, what with the little silver-eyed cuckoo in the nest.'

'I don't think you should call your baby a cuckoo!'

'No, I'm going to call it Cromlech if it's a boy, or Rosetta if it's a girl.'

'You are joking, aren't you?' she asked anxiously.

'No. What about Mustard Spoon Graythorpe?'

'I'll have to call mine Tsambika or Tsambikos,' she said. 'I think the results of the pilgrimage were just slightly delayed.'

'Poor little thing,' I said.

'Tsam?'

'That's quite nice, actually. Maybe it *will* survive school.'

'How's the new book coming along?' she asked, changing the subject, and absently reaching for another biscuit: one of the curly chocolate-coated wafer ones, which I think are among Miranda's best.

'*Dark Dreams, Deadly Desires*? Very well, I think: the whole plot simply fell into my mind as I finished the last one.'

'And it's *really* the last of the *Vengeane* series?'

'Absolutely. I can't write about someone who looks like the man I'm living with, but isn't him, any more. Well, I can – I am – but he isn't going to like it.'

The biscuit was suspended halfway to Mu's lips. 'Sappho, you aren't going to do anything nasty to Dragonslayer, are you?'

'See what I mean? Just because he looks like Nye, and Nala looks a bit like me, it doesn't mean we're living parallel lives!

Nye seems to have got the idea that that's how the last book will turn out, but' – I grinned at her – 'it ain't necessarily so!'

'You can't!'

'I can, and I will: it's necessary to the story, this last twist in the tale, and it's open to interpretation. I must be true to my art!'

'Bollocks,' said Mu, but she knew I meant it.

Chapter 35

Date Expired

Nye and I are sitting on the cliffs of Lefkada watching the sun go down.

We are near the spot where I stood on my thirty-ninth birthday, feeling so panic-stricken: as though the sands of my life were starting to run out too quickly.

Well, I wanted to do something meaningful in the last year before the big Four-O, and you certainly can't say I haven't!

'It's beautiful,' Nye says softly, putting his arm around me.

'Yes, it is,' I agree, 'but the funny thing is that for the first time ever I feel homesick! I'm missing Bedd, and the cottage and even the cat. It's not that I don't want to travel again, just that I'm now always going to have that sense of being ready to go home at the end of it.'

'Home, with just you and me,' Nye says.

'And the cat. And the baby, eventually. It'll be good to get back just so I can finish the final *Vengeane* novel, too: the end of one era and the beginning of another.'

'Another fantasy series?'

'There are new worlds out there to invent and explore,' I reply.

'But first the *Vengeane* happy ending: you and me, Dragonslayer and Nala – Raarg and Sirene?'

I open my mouth to speak and then shut it again: why spoil a magic moment, after all?

Life – and the unfolding storylines of my books – are just one constant surprise to me.

And that's the way I like it.

Recipes

These are the sorts of things that Miranda is always baking, and are perfect for when you have friends coming round for tea or coffee.

Double chocolate biscotti

This recipe makes around 20 biscotti: crisp, crunchy Italian biscuits that are delicious with a hot drink or on the side of a creamy pudding. The recipe really isn't as complicated as it looks and the results are well worth it!

Ingredients:
100g butter
125g caster sugar
4 tablespoons good quality cocoa powder
2 teaspoons baking powder
2 eggs
½ teaspoon vanilla essence
200g plain flour
125g milk or dark chocolate, chopped (or you could use chocolate chips)
100g white chocolate, chopped

Method:

Preheat the oven to 190°C (170°C fan) and line a large baking sheet with greaseproof paper. Whisk the butter and sugar until pale and fluffy, then add the cocoa powder and baking powder and beat for another couple of minutes. Add the eggs one at a time, then the vanilla essence, and whisk again to combine. Stir in the flour and all the chocolate chips by hand. Cover the dough and chill in the fridge for 10 minutes.

Divide the dough into two, and roll each part into a sausage about 25cm long. Transfer them to the baking tray about 10cm apart, and flatten to a thickness of 3cm.

Bake for 20–25 minutes or until a skewer in the centre comes out clean. Remove from the oven and reduce the temperature to 160°C. Cool on the tray for 5 minutes then transfer to a chopping board.

Cut into 2cm wide slices then place the slices on the baking tray, cut sides up, and bake for 10 minutes. Turn the biscuits, and bake on the other side for another 5–7 minutes. Cool completely on a wire rack.

The biscotti will keep in an airtight container for three weeks.

Ginger thins

As Sappho says, ginger is excellent for digestion. It's great for morning sickness too. So you could almost say these biscuits are medicinal and it's therefore *essential* that you eat them . . .

This recipe makes around 40 biscuits.

Ingredients:
170g plain flour
1 teaspoon bicarbonate of soda
A pinch of salt
80g unsalted butter
4 tablespoons ground ginger
2 teaspoons ground cinnamon
½ teaspoon ground cloves
¼ teaspoon pepper

A pinch of cayenne pepper
100g dark brown soft sugar
40g black treacle
1 large egg

Method:

Mix the flour, bicarbonate of soda and salt together in a bowl. Heat the butter in a pan over a medium heat until melted, then lower to a medium-low heat and continue to cook, swirling the pan often, until the butter just begins to brown and the foaming has subsided a little. Turn off the heat.

Add the spices, the brown sugar and the treacle to the butter and mix until the sugar has melted. Whisk in the egg: you should have a dark, smooth and shiny mixture.

Pour into your bowl of flour and combine with a spatula until you have a dough – be careful not to overwork it. Cover the bowl and chill in the fridge for an hour.

Preheat the oven to 150°C (130°C fan). Line two baking trays with greaseproof paper. Put a portion of the dough on to a lightly floured surface and roll it out with a rolling pin as thin as you can make it – 1mm if possible – as they do rise a little in the oven. Use a small cutter to cut out your shapes. I like circles or stars at Christmas. Carefully lift each biscuit and place on your baking trays, leaving a slight gap between them. Repeat until all your dough is used up.

While one tray is baking, you can roll out and fill up your next tray. Bake the biscuits for around 15–20 minutes or until they are hard to the touch and a deep golden brown. Cool on a wire rack.

The ginger thins will keep in an airtight container for three weeks.

Apple fruit cake

The addition of the apples makes this a lovely moist fruit cake, and it doesn't take too long to bake.

Ingredients:
200g self-raising flour
200g dark muscovado sugar
200g butter
3 eggs, beaten
1 tablespoon black treacle
1 teaspoon baking powder
2 teaspoons mixed spice
200g eating apples, grated (about 2 medium-sized apples)
300g mixed sultanas and raisins

Method:

Preheat the oven to 200°C (180°C fan). Grease and line a deep, round 20cm cake tin. Beat all of the ingredients except the fruit in a large bowl until the mixture is thick and pale. Then fold in the apples, sultanas and raisins until all the fruit is combined and well distributed in the batter.

Pour the batter into the cake tin and bake for 50 minutes to 1 hour, or until the cake is deeply golden and a skewer in the centre comes out clean.

Turn out on to a wire rack and cool completely. The cake will keep in an airtight container for up to a week.

If you wanted to decorate it, you could top with royal icing, or an apricot glaze: simply warm 75g apricot jam with 1 or 2 tablespoons of water and brush over the cake. You could top with some chopped pecan nuts or walnuts and brush over a little more glaze.

Turn the page for a sneak peak
of the first pages of
Trisha Ashley's new novel

THE LITTLE TEASHOP OF
LOST AND FOUND

coming in Spring 2017

Prologue

West Yorkshire

Liz
March 2nd, 1978

There had been no signs to warn me of the imminent catastrophe about to overtake me – or if there were, I'd been oblivious to them. When everything kicked off that night, I felt as if I'd been catapulted straight into a horror movie and a gross one, at that – or the nightmare from hell.

Fear and confusion were quickly followed by realization, panic, shock and revulsion – for who'd have thought a birth involved so much goriness? Certainly not me, even though, ironically enough, my sights had re-focused on gaining an Oxford place to read medicine the very moment my brief first love affair had come to an end the previous summer.

But then, that wasn't because I felt any kind of vocation to heal the sick, the halt and the lame, it was simply part of my plan to mould myself so much in Father's image that he forgot I wasn't actually his biological child at all.

As these thoughts jostled chaotically together in my normally clear, cool and analytical mind, my eyes met Mum's over the small, misshapen, skinned-rabbit of a thing that lay weakly mewling on the bed between us and I expect the expression on her ashen, stunned face mirrored my own.

Her mouth moved silently once or twice, as if it had forgotten how to shape words. Then finally she whispered, 'Liz, your father must never find out!'

She was always entirely mistress of the bleeding obvious.

1

Once Upon a Fairytale

Alice
Autumn 1995

I grew up knowing I was adopted, so it was never a shocking revelation, merely one of the things that defined me, like having curly copper-bright hair, distinctive dark eyebrows, a fine silvery scar above my upper lip and pale green eyes. (Like boiled gooseberries, according to Mum, though Dad said they were mermaid's eyes, the colour of sea-washed green glass.)

As a little girl I'd sit for hours painting with Dad in his garden studio, while his deep, gentle voice wrapped me in a soft-spun fairytale, in which my desperate young birth mother had been forced to abandon her poorly, premature little baby, hoping that someone like Mum and Dad would come along and adopt her.

Or like *Dad*, at any rate, since eventually I came to see that Nessa (she'd insisted I call her that rather than Mummy, practically the moment I could string a sentence together), had had no maternal yearnings, she'd just been paying lip-service to his longing for a family, smug in the knowledge that she couldn't physically carry a child even had she wanted to.

'A bad fairy had put a spell on baby Alice, but when the nice doctors had made her lip all better, everyone agreed she was the prettiest princess in the whole of Yorkshire,' he'd finish his story, smiling at me over his canvas.

'And they put the wicked fairy in a metal cage and everyone threw rotten tomatoes at her,' I'd suggest – or even worse punishments, for some old fairytale books given to me by my paternal grandmother, including one strangely but wonderfully illustrated by Arthur Rackham, had had a great influence on my imagination. We lived near Granny Rose in Knaresborough until moving to a village just outside Shrewsbury when I was eight and I can still remember her reading to me the long, long poem by Edith Sitwell about Sleeping Beauty, once she'd tucked me up in bed. I'd slowly drift off on a sea of musical, beautiful words about malevolent fairies and enchantments.

Other favourites of Granny's included *The Water Babies* and *Alice in Wonderland* – the latter a favourite of mine, too, since the heroine had the same name. I begged for her lovely old copies after she died and Dad made sure I got them, even though Nessa was hell bent on having a clearance firm empty the whole house. She was a minimalist sort of person . . . except when it came to her own clothes, jewellery and shoes.

Our house was a tale of two parts, with most of the creatively chaotic clutter in dad's studio, which might have been stables once upon a time – until he married a wicked witch disguised as a flamboyantly beautiful ex-opera singer and she banished him there.

Anyway, you can see why I have a tendency to turn everything that happens in my life into a dark-edged fairytale – I can't help it!

'They threw stinky rotten eggs at the wicked fairy, too,' I'd once added firmly to the familiar story.

'Well, perhaps, but only until she said she was sorry and then they let her out,' Dad had amended, kind-hearted as always.

Over the years we embroidered the story with increasingly ridiculous flourishes at every retelling, but it had served its purpose, for I grew up knowing that I'd been abandoned in the village of Haworth in Yorkshire and adopted, and the reason for the filament-fine silvery scar that was all that remained to show I'd been born with a harelip.

Of course, later I realized Dad had no way of knowing whether my birth mother was young or not and also, once I became quite obsessed with the Brontë family and Haworth, I knew that it was extremely unlikely that she'd tiptoed up to the steps of the Parsonage in the middle of the night and laid me there, in the expectation that he and Nessa would shortly swing by and scoop me up. I mean, it was a museum by then, so it would have been closed and also, adoption didn't quite work like that. (I'm still surprised they let Nessa on to the register – I can only think that her opera training kicked in and she hadn't been able to resist throwing herself into the role of eager prospective mother.)

But while Nessa might only make extravagant expressions of affection towards me when her London friends were visiting (one of whom once cattily let fall the information that she hadn't had *that* brilliant a voice even before the operation on her vocal cords that ended her career), I'd known *real* love from Granny and Dad.

And I also had Lola, my best friend and her lovely parents, who owned a nearby smallholding. There we helped look after the hens and goats, ran wild in the fields and learned to bake in the long, cool, quarry-tiled kitchen. All my life, baking – even the scent of cinnamon and dried fruit – would have the power to immediately transport me back to those happy days and transfuse me with warmth and comfort.

So it was an idyllic childhood on the whole, though once the rebellious teenage hormones kicked in I began to clash more and more with Nessa.

Still, the finer details of my distant past didn't seem to matter . . . until Dad suddenly died from a massive heart attack when I was nearly eighteen and my safe, secure world collapsed around me like a house of cards.

In any ordinary family, his loss might have pulled Nessa and me together, but she was not so much grief-stricken as filled with a volcanic rage, mainly directed at me. And she became so obsessed with money that immediately after the funeral she sold the entire contents of Dad's studio (he was quite a well-known artist) to an American collector without a word to me beforehand, locking the door so I couldn't even go in there to find solace among the comforting, familiar smells of oil paint and turpentine.

That was bad enough. But then, with even more indecent haste, she moved a new man into the house – and a horrible one, at that, who was scarily over-friendly in an old-letch kind of way whenever she was out of earshot – and I came to realize that now I was just an encumbrance and she couldn't wait for me to go off to university the following year.

The pain of Dad's loss was still raw and I couldn't bear to see another man in his place, so I had the row to end all rows with Nessa, culminating in my saying that I hated her and I was going to go and find my *real* mother.

'She has to be an improvement on you!' I finished.

'You're a foundling, darling, so there's no way you can find her,' she snapped cuttingly. 'And bearing in mind that she dumped you out on the moors on a freezing cold night, she'd be unlikely to welcome you with open arms even if you did.'

Stunned into silence, I stared at her while I took in the implications of what she'd just told me. 'She . . . didn't leave me in Haworth village, but up on the moors, where she didn't think I'd be found?' I asked eventually.

Nessa looked at me, the fury dying down slightly into a sort of malicious, slightly shame-faced pleasure that shook me: I knew she'd never *really* loved me, but until recently I'd thought she was as fond of me as her self-absorbed nature would allow.

'Your father never wanted me to tell you the truth, but I think that was a mistake. And maybe she was batty and thought someone *would* come across you,' she suggested, possibly divining from my expression that she'd gone too far.

'No, if she left me at night out on the moors, then clearly she hoped I'd die and never be found,' I said numbly, for the spell of Dad's fairytale was now well and truly shattered and there was no way it could be glued together again. I felt empty, alone and lost . . . and unwanted, totally unwanted by anyone.

'I hate you!' I cried with sudden violence as hot tears rushed to my eyes. 'I wish *you'd* died instead of Dad – though you couldn't have had a heart attack, because you haven't got one. You've never loved me, like Lola's mum loves her.'

She shrugged. 'I expect Dolly actually *wanted* children, which I never did, even if I could have had them. Your father finally wore me down into agreeing to adoption and he was over the moon when we were offered a baby. But you'd only just had the surgery on your face and what with that and the carroty hair, you weren't exactly prepossessing, darling.'

Now the floodgates of frankness were open, there seemed to be no stopping the hurtful revelations, so I added one of my own: I told her that the day before, when she was out, her creepy new lover had tried to kiss me and made suggestive remarks.

'You lying snake in the bosom!' she hissed furiously, clutching those generous appendages as though she'd just been bitten there by an asp.

And though of course she didn't believe me (which was why I hadn't already told her), there was no going back after that.

Dawn found me on a coach heading to Cornwall, with the loan of Lola's birthday money in my bag, to tide me over. I only took one case with me, leaving with her for safe-keeping my most precious possessions, including Granny's books and a small portrait of me in oils, painted by Dad.

Of course Lola had wanted to tell her mum what had happened, but I'd sworn her to secrecy until I'd found a job and somewhere to live.

'I'll stay in a bed and breakfast at first and there are lots of hotels and cafes there where I can get some casual work until I find my feet,' I assured her.

Inspired by some of Dad's old stories of the Newlyn artists and our holidays in Cornwall, I had romantic ideas about joining an artists' colony, where my aspirations to become a writer and painter could be nurtured, though later I realized this was not only unrealistic, but several decades too late.

The stark reality was that my arrival, late in the evening and off-season, when many places were shut up for the winter and no one was hiring, left me without any option other than spending the first night huddled in a shelter on the seafront . . . And all too soon my overactive imagination was peopling the darkest corners with evil muttering goblins and foully hellish Hieronymus Bosch creatures.

When the cold breeze blew a discarded cardboard cup across the prom I thought it was the clatter of running footsteps and even the soft, constant susurration of the sea sounded like an unkind conversation about me.

I'd begun to write my own contemporary mash-ups of fairytales, fables and folklore, spiced with an edge of horror, but when it came to the crunch, *this* princess was no kick-ass kind of girl able to rescue herself, but a frightened waif in urgent need of a handsome prince . . . or even a kind, ugly one.

Hell, I'd have settled for a reasonably friendly frog.

Tears trickled down my face and I shivered as the cold wind picked up and wound its way around my legs.

Then, all at once, I heard the staccato tap of high heels and the excited yapping of a small dog. Before I could attempt to shrink even further into my dark corner, it dashed in and discovered me.

A torch snapped on and I screwed up my eyes against the dazzling beam, though not before I'd glimpsed the small and unthreatening shape behind it, so that my heart rate steadied.

'Well, what have we here, Ginny?' said a surprised female voice with the hint of a highland lilt. 'A wee lassie?'

Available in hardback and ebook from Spring 2017